When the Eternal Day dawns,
the Time of the Dragon Above draws nigh.
Showers of light fall upon the City of the Dead,
and after twice thirteen years the Storm Dragon
emerges.

From the land of desolation under the dark
of the great moon,
the Eye of Siberys will lift the Sky Caves of Thieren Kor.
The Storm Dragon will tread the paths
of the first of sixteen
And all of Eberron will tremble at his day's dawning.

"... Wyatt effectively mixes political intrigue with action.
This high-stakes adventure, full of violence, magic and suspense,
should entertain gamers and epic fantasy fans.
—*Publisher's Weekly*

"There's plenty going on here and, once again, it's not just
'another D&D quest shoehorned into novel form'. There are
magic items that have to be found but there are also political
machinations and evidence of a world that is slowly beginning
to embrace some forms of technology. This makes for a world
that comes across as well rounded and engaging ... There's also
a real sense of purpose about the writing that I found refreshing.
Wyatt doesn't hang around or take you off down blind alleys, he
starts you off at point A and you just know that things will end
where they're meant to."
—*Graeme's Fantasy Book Review*

JAMES **WYATT**

EBERRON

STORM
DRAGON

DRACONIC
PROPHECIES

BOOK ONE

STORM DRAGON

The Draconic Prophecies· Book 1

©2007 Wizards of the Coast, Inc.

Cover art by Raymond Swanland
Map by Robert Lazzaretti
Original Hardcover Edition First Printing: August 2007
First Paperback Printing: May 2008

9 8 7 6 5 4 3 2 1

ISBN: 978-0-7869-4854-3
620-21722740-001-EN

U.S., CANADA,
ASIA, PACIFIC, & LATIN AMERICA
Wizards of the Coast, Inc.
P.O. Box 707
Renton, WA 98057-0707
+1-800-324-6496

EUROPEAN HEADQUARTERS
Hasbro UK Ltd
Caswell Way
Newport, Gwent NP9 0YH
GREAT BRITAIN
Save this address for your records.

Visit our web site at www.wizards.com

Dedicated to the memory of my father,
David K. Wyatt and to my son,
Carter Wyatt.

PART I

When the Eternal Day draws near,
when its moon shines full in the night,
and the day is at its brightest,
the Time of the Dragon Above begins.

Showers of light fall
upon the City of the Dead,
and the Storm Dragon emerges
after twice thirteen years.

Tumult and tribulation swirl in his wake:
The Blasphemer rises, the Pretender falls,
and armies march once more across the land.

CHAPTER
1

A distant rumble of thunder.

Thunder is his harbinger and lightning his spear.

Gaven stared up into the darkness of his cell, trying to clear his mind. Trying not to sleep.

He remembered perching on a cliff face, watching a storm blowing over the sea, brooding on those words. No. That had not been him. That was the other.

Wind is his steed and rain his cloak.

The words whispered in his mind in a voice that was not his. They filled him with foreboding. Echoes of a coming doom. His skin prickled. Another peal of thunder, more distant. Sleep closed in around him.

"No no no—no sleep," he murmured. He forced his eyes open.

The Storm Dragon rises.

"Make it stop make it stop make it stop." The prayer that had been his constant companion for twenty-seven years.

He remembered standing in the stone courtyard, head thrown back, arms spread to the sky, and singing to the storm. Exultation. Lightning danced along the high tower walls, and thunder beat a cadence for his song. Until the dwarf guards tackled him, wrestled him to the ground, and beat him into unconsciousness.

. . . the endless dark . . .

The darkness swallowed him, drawing him into nightmare.

He lay entombed in the depths of Khyber. Creeping things crawled and slithered over his body. The legs of a centipede undulated across his face, his lips. He tried to lift his head, to raise a hand, to scream. He couldn't move, couldn't draw breath.

A spear of blinding light shot up from the ground, impaling him before it broke through the ageless stone above him, soaring up and up until it reached the sky, stabbing through a storm cloud to touch the heights of Siberys.

Khyber and Siberys. The Dragon Below and the Dragon Above. A bridge of light joined heaven and earth.

. . . a ray of Khyber's sun erupts to form a bridge to the sky . . .

On every side, creatures began to move—writhing, snaking, quivering. Eyes stared at him from the darkness, dimly reflecting the light. Eyes that formed no intelligible faces, leering from quivering masses of amorphous flesh or glowering alone in bestial skulls. Mouths gaped at him, toothy maws biting, serrated sucking parts trying to bore into his flesh. Tentacles grabbed at him, coiling around his limbs and probing his head.

The Storm Dragon descends into the endless dark . . .

A tentacle worked its way into his mouth, smothering his scream.

* * * * *

The waves of the Lhazaar Sea crashed against the rocks at the base of the walls of the fortress. The walls rose hundreds of feet, unbroken by windows or balconies. Four towers stood at the corners of the fortress, and a watchtower at the center pierced the night sky. This was Dreadhold: the greatest prison of the Five Nations, kept by the dwarves of House Kundarak to hold the world's most dangerous criminals—the most bloodthirsty, sadistic, and evil villains to plague civilization. Its impregnable walls also contained those who posed a significant threat to the fragile peace—or to the interests of the dragonmarked houses—but who could not be executed.

Gaven slept fitfully in his cell, the roar of the breaking waves far below nothing more than a faint whisper through the stone. His eyes shot open, and he sat up with a gasp, staring around at the utter blackness of the tiny room. He threw off his threadbare wool blanket, oblivious to the chill, and groaned. Though he couldn't see them, he felt the walls closing him in, and the moist air stifled him. He staggered off his bunk and fell into the cell's iron door, fumbling around with his hands until he found a shutter at the level of his chest. He slid it open, and a few beams of light, gray and cold, spilled into the room, shining on the sheen of sweat that covered his face. With the light came the merest breath of fresher air, and he gulped it like a drowning man.

Gaven slumped backward against the door and sank to the floor. His thin shirt did little to shield him from the cold, but the iron felt good against his back. Amid the silence of the prison night, the door at his back and the stone floor beneath him reminded him where he was, which actually reassured him. His eyes darted around as if he were still in the throes of the nightmare that had awakened him. Everywhere his gaze fell, writing covered the walls and floor.

"Gaven!" A hoarse whisper came across the hall. "What did you see?"

"The hordes of the Soul Reaver," Gaven rambled, making no effort to lower his voice. "Wild. Gibbering. Swarming out of the earth." He pressed his palms to his eyes. "Brilliant light, spilling up from the depths—a ray of Khyber's sun, a bridge to the sky."

"What else, Gaven? Tell me what else you saw!"

The lingering memories of his nightmare started to fade, replaced by a memory of the old man's mouth pressed against the shutter in his own cell across the hall. Gaven had seen him—out in the yard, in the library, always under the watchful eyes of the dwarf guards—but the image of his mouth was fixed in Gaven's mind. Pale, cracked lips surrounded by white hair, a tongue occasionally darting out to moisten them. That image merged in Gaven's mind with the vision of the Soul Reaver's hordes—tentacles, eyes, gaping mouths—and sent a wave of nausea through him.

"Tell me what else," the old man rasped.

But the vision had faded. In its place came words, something he had read once—or had he? Gaven could no longer tell which memories were his.

"When the Eternal Day draws near," he recited, "when its moon shines full in the night, and the day is at its brightest, the Time of the Dragon Above begins. Showers of light fall upon the City of the Dead, and the Storm Dragon emerges after twice thirteen years."

"The Storm Dragon will come for us, Gaven."

Gaven's laugh was utterly without humor. He stumbled to his feet, bracing himself against the doorframe. Black hair fell over his face, but he didn't bother pushing it back. He reached into a pocket in his thin breeches and found the tiny steel stylus the guards had allowed him, then stood shakily on his bunk. He stretched as high as he could toward the ceiling, and scratched what words he could remember into the stone, describing the gibbering hordes, the brilliant bridge from earth to sky. The Time of the Dragon Above and the Time of the Dragon Below. Showers of light falling to earth, and brilliant beams of light rising from the earth.

He was still writing when the room shook, throwing him from his bunk and sending him sprawling to the floor. In the dim light spilling through the shutter in his door, he saw a crack form in the ceiling and begin to spread. The shaking resolved into a rhythmic pounding—something large smashing against the tower.

"Gaven!" the old man across the hall yelled, in a hoarse voice Gaven had never heard before. "They're coming! They're here for us!"

Gaven curled up on the floor of his cell and shielded his head with his arms as shards of masonry fell from the ceiling. After one more thundering crash, the tower shuddered, and the ceiling collapsed. Gaven rolled to his right, and a great stone slab just missed him. He looked up in terror and awe, and for the first time in twenty-six years, he saw the Ring of Siberys stretching across the sky.

* * * * *

Darraun stood and surveyed his handiwork. It had taken every ounce of power he had in him, but he'd managed to weaken the magic reinforcing the walls of the tower enough for Vaskar to break a great hole in the tower's ceiling. One great crack stretched down the wall of Gaven's cell and into the cell across the hallway. Haldren's. The way into Haldren's cell was probably too small for Cart, the war-forged, but Senya was already making her way down into it. The lithe elf avoided heavy armor for exactly this reason—she liked being able to slip into tight spaces. She preferred tight-fitting clothes beneath her leather coat for a different reason. She and Haldren had been lovers before he ended up in Dreadhold, so it was fitting that her short, black curls and painted face should be his first glimpse of freedom.

Cart jumped into Gaven's cell and shifted the rubble around the cowering prisoner. The warforged moved the heavy stones with ease, metal cords and leather sinews shifting and pulsing beneath his armor plates as he worked.

Above Darraun, Vaskar circled through the sky, making short work of the manticore guardians as they swooped and dived around the dragon. Some fell victim to great blasts of lightning from his mouth, others he tore with his teeth and claws. One he slammed with his tail so hard that the beast crashed into the side of the watchtower. The three wyverns perched on the roof around Vaskar's hole watched the aerial battle with interest, as if they longed to join in, but they were well trained and wouldn't abandon their riders. They shifted their weight restlessly on their two clawed feet, flexed their leathery wings, and slowly pulsed the stingers on their tails, arched up over their backs like scorpions.

Everything seemed to be going according to plan.

Darraun jumped down into Gaven's cell. Huddled on the floor, Gaven looked up at the warforged, his eyes wide. Darraun remembered that the first warforged had been created only thirty-four years ago, and Gaven had been in Dreadhold for the last twenty-six. Had Gaven seen warforged during his imprisonment? Darraun somehow doubted that many warforged ended up in Dreadhold. So many people considered them less than human. It was hard to imagine that anyone would think a warforged criminal of any kind was too important to execute.

Darraun moved to the door and rested a hand on the cold iron. He closed his eyes in concentration, sensing and visualizing the magic that flowed through it, keeping it securely locked. He slid his hand slowly up, then down, looking for just the right place.

"Don't you want to be rescued?" Cart rumbled behind him, extending a three-fingered hand down to Gaven. "We're friends. We want to take you out of here."

Darraun smiled at the way the warforged mimicked the voice of a child coaxing a nervous or reluctant pet. Cart had made a serious study of human behavior, considering that he had spent most of his short existence as a soldier.

Darraun found what he was looking for—a knot of magic that would respond to the properly enchanted key. It was a simple matter to tangle that knot further, break some connections, cross some lines. It would take time to sort that out and get the door open, and by that time Gaven would be long gone.

Haldren's head appeared in the crack above him—Senya had

evidently succeeded in getting him out. He was an old man, Darraun saw, his hair almost completely white, only a few streaks of coppery red suggesting what he'd looked like in his younger days. His skin had the pallor of prison, his hair was wild and his beard unruly, and his lips were cracked and dry. He still had his presence, though. As soon as he extracted himself from his cell he took command of the operation.

"Darraun," he barked, "help the warforged get our prophet out of there. We don't have much time."

We have time, Darraun thought, but he followed his orders.

Gaven had taken Cart's hand, but he still stared warily at the warforged. He seemed vaguely pathetic. He was a half-elf, so he didn't look old despite his sixty-odd years. His long hair was wild but still black as night, and he had no beard. He was still well muscled, his chest and arms displaying the strength that had been nearly legendary in his time. His dragonmark stretched across the skin of his neck and upper chest before disappearing beneath his threadbare shirt.

"Gaven," Darraun said, moving to stand beside him, "the guards will be here any moment. We have wyverns on the roof, ready to carry you away. You'll be safe with us."

Mumbling incoherently, Gaven tore his gaze from the warforged and shuffled forward. Too slow—Darraun could hear the guards shouting in the hall beyond the heavy iron door. He met Cart's eyes and nodded. The warforged stooped over, put one arm around Gaven's legs, and lifted the prisoner to his shoulder. Gaven went limp, without a sound of protest or a struggle. Perching on the fallen stone slab, Cart clambered out of the cell and onto the roof.

Above him, Darraun heard Haldren's voice. "You see, Gaven," he said, "I told you he would come for us. Behold the Storm Dragon!"

If Gaven made any response, Darraun couldn't hear it. He looked around the shambles of the cell. Writing was scratched into almost every possible surface. He picked up a shard of stone at random from the wreckage strewn across the floor and turned it over in his hands, straining to read the faint, tiny scratches on what had been part of Gaven's cell wall.

. . . recapitulates the serpents' sacrifice, binding the servant anew so the master cannot break free.

Darraun raised one thin eyebrow and shoved the masonry shard into a pocket of his leather coat.

"Darraun!" Haldren roared above him. "We fly!"

As he scrambled back up onto the roof, Darraun heard shouts through the door. The guards had come and found their own door locked to them. He smiled, but he also slid a wand from his coat pocket as he vaulted into the saddle of his wyvern, eyeing the crack leading into Haldren's cell. Vaskar had already taken to the air with Haldren on his back, and Senya's wyvern lifted off behind it. Cart had put Gaven on his own mount, and the man's arms were wrapped around the thick chest of the warforged.

As Cart's wyvern lifted into the air, Darraun heard Gaven mutter, ". . . its moon shines full in the night." Then Darraun followed.

* * * * *

Gaven looked down in front of the wyvern's strong wings, and a thrill went down his spine. Below them, the Lhazaar Sea churned violently as dark clouds and gusting winds rolled in across the eastern ocean. Gaven clung tighter to the adamantine-plated body of the warforged, who had introduced himself as Cart, back in the cell. He forced his attention off the ocean below and onto Cart. He had seen warforged before, but only from a distance. The plates looked like heavy armor. Subtle engraving decorated the edges, but Gaven could tell from the way the plates moved along with the slightest shift in Cart's body that they were attached, somehow, to the body underneath, which seemed to be made of wood, fibrous bundles, perhaps some stone, and other kinds of metal. The strangest thing, to Gaven's mind, was that Cart was undeniably alive, not like some automaton made for the battlefield. He saw cords and bundles pulsing between the plates, and the warforged moved constantly just like a living person—the smallest shifts of posture, turns of his head, fidgets. Gaven had the clear sense that a sword cut would make Cart bleed, and a blow to just the right place could stop that ceaseless motion forever.

He turned his head to get a better look at the dragon. The Storm Dragon, Haldren had said. "The Storm Dragon emerges after twice thirteen years," Gaven whispered. "Where did you come from, Storm Dragon? You plan to walk in the paths? It's a long road ahead of you."

The warforged turned his head, trying to see Gaven over his

shoulder or perhaps hear his mutterings better. Gaven closed his eyes, pretending to sleep. He felt the warforged shift, turning back to watch where he was flying.

Falling—

Gaven started awake, still safe in the saddle though his arms had slipped from the warforged's chest. He blinked, trying to clear his mind from his nightmare—a strange light spilling up out of the earth, gleaming on bronze scales.

CHAPTER
2

The Lord Warden scowled, his rage written plain across his face. Of course, Bordan thought—so brazen an attack on Dreadhold was unheard of, even during the chaos of the Last War. The fact that the dragon had been able to penetrate the tower walls was astonishing. Two prisoners escaping before the guards could respond . . . well, that was simply embarrassing.

Bordan settled back in his chair and stroked his neat beard, watching the other two people in the briefing. One was a Sentinel Marshal, who had introduced himself as Evlan d'Deneith. He was frowning, which Bordan could tell had become a habitual expression for him. Evlan wore his age and his station well. The gray at his temples made him look distinguished, and he had the body of a much younger man beneath his mithral mail and black surcoat. Above the collar of his mail on his neck, the Mark of Sentinel was just visible, an abstract tracing of color on his skin that resembled the head of a dragon with long spines trailing behind the neck. Like Bordan's own dragonmark, Evlan's was an intricate weaving of blue—more a part of his skin than a tattoo, and far more elaborate than any birthmark. The skin that bore the mark was slightly raised, and Bordan knew that the 'mark gave Evlan powers similar to those of a wizard. The bodyguards of House Deneith used the powers of the Mark of Sentinel to protect their charges from harm, and the Sentinel Marshals used the same powers to protect themselves as they pursued dangerous criminals across Khorvaire.

Seated beside Evlan was another dwarf of House Kundarak, much calmer than the blustering warden. The warden had introduced her as Ossa d'Kundarak. She had not yet spoken a word. A scarlet shirt of fine silk stood out against her black skin. She sat with her hands folded on her lap, studying Bordan as carefully as

Bordan examined her. Bordan had heard that House Kundarak maintained a small force of soldier-assassins called the Manticore's Tail—or *Ghorad'din* in the Dwarven language—and he suspected Ossa represented that organization. Ossa's dragonmark wasn't visible, but her surname indicated that she carried the Mark of Warding, which the heirs of House Kundarak used to protect banks and vaults in every city of Khorvaire, as well as the prison of Dreadhold.

The Lord Warden, Zaxon d'Kundarak, wore his red-brown beard long, with braids hanging down on either side of his mouth. He was clearly struggling to keep his emotions under control, and that spoke volumes. For a dwarf nicknamed "the Old Rock," any trace of emotion that leaked onto his face demonstrated the true extent of his fury. The clearest sign of his emotional state was an angry flush of red on his bald pate, and he compulsively ran his hands across the top of his head as if trying to hide it. Each time he did, Evlan could see the tracery of the Mark of Warding across the back of his left hand, resembling rays of light emanating from a shape that some thought resembled an eye and others identified as a coiled dragon.

"Where's the damned elf?" the Lord Warden said, starting to pace again. "I have no intention of giving this briefing twice."

"That won't be necessary, Lord Warden." The elf slipped through the door, his movements making no sound, his black garb seeming to meld with the shadows. "I am sorry to have kept you waiting," he said. "I am Phaine d'Thuranni." He sat in the empty chair and did not move again, except to let his gaze rest on each of the others in the room. His dragonmark, the angular Mark of Shadow, started on his cheek and ran down his neck. Deception and illusion were the powers of the Mark of Shadow, as well as espionage.

"Glad you could join us, Thuranni," the Lord Warden said. He swept his gaze across the four dragonmark heirs. "I am grateful to your houses for offering your services to help us handle this . . . situation."

The Lord Warden's eyes lingered on Ossa as he said this; the honor of House Kundarak would recover more quickly from this blow if a Kundarak managed to retrieve the fugitives. Dreadhold was operated by House Kundarak, whose Mark of Warding and expertise with security made it well suited to keeping prisoners confined and the prison secure. But all the dragonmarked houses had an interest in the great prison, since it held many of their most dangerous secrets.

"The first prisoner is Haldren ir'Brassek, a noble of Aundair." Speaking seemed to help the Lord Warden bring his emotions back under control, and his face slowly set into a stony mask. "He was a general during the war—a hero in some circles and a villain in others. He recaptured the city of Cragwar twice, but he was also responsible for the massacres of civilians at Twilight Creek and Telthun. He led troop movements in violation of the Treaty of Thronehold before he was finally captured and brought to trial for his war crimes. He was sentenced to Dreadhold rather than face execution because many officers in Aundair's military remain loyal to him, and Aundair feared what would happen if Haldren were martyred almost as much as they feared his escape. I have already received communication from Queen Aurala to the effect that Aundair will be most distressed if ir'Brassek returns to his homeland." A thick hand ran over his bald head again, and the Lord Warden took a deep breath, staring at the floor.

"I am not familiar with the ir'Brassek family," Evlan said.

"It was once a prominent line in Aundair," the Lord Warden said, "but it has diminished. The fugitive has a few cousins, I believe, who maintain the appearance of luxury despite the loss of their ancestral holdings. The general sense in Aundair's military was that ir'Brassek wanted to restore his family name to prominence. He had some success in that regard, but obviously took it too far. I think it unlikely that he will make contact with the cousins."

"And the other prisoner?" Bordan asked.

"Gaven, formerly of House Lyrandar. A strange case. He worked for his house during the war, prospecting for Khyber dragonshards for use in their galleons. All that time crawling around the depths of Khyber must've driven him mad." The Lord Warden glanced at Phaine. "House Phiarlan claims he was involved in the Paelion affair."

Bordan nodded. The Paelion family had been a part of House Phiarlan, an elf house that bore the Mark of Shadow. Phaine's house, Thuranni, had also been one of the Phiarlan families. Some thirty years ago, the leader of the Thurannis had led his family in a brutal slaughter of the Paelions, claiming to have evidence that the Paelions plotted against the rest of the dragonmarked houses. If Gaven had been involved, then he was part of the reason that House Thuranni was no longer a part of House Phiarlan.

"During his trial," the Lord Warden continued, "Gaven swung between incoherent muttering and murderous rage. He's a strong man, and it was difficult to keep him restrained long enough to pass judgment. There was a suggestion that he was possessed, but an exorcist examined him and found no evidence of that. He was convicted, and House Lyrandar declared him excoriate."

That explains the "formerly," Bordan thought. Gaven wouldn't be recognized as a Lyrandar any more, and other members of the family would be forbidden to give him aid. That would make him easier to find.

"Why Dreadhold?" Bordan asked. "Why not execute him?"

"Two reasons," Zaxon said. "His betrothed made a rather impassioned plea for his life, asking that he be imprisoned in case some day he recovered his senses. Also, his house expressed an interest in the content of his lunatic ravings and requested that he be kept alive. When they learned that he was writing in his cell, they requested a report of what he wrote. I don't know whether they considered it useful or not."

"What did he rave about?"

"They say he always had an interest in the Prophecy of the dragons, and it's all he's talked about for the last twenty-six years. Half his speech is prophetic mutterings—perhaps it makes sense to him, but to everyone else it's nonsense. Just about every inch of wall and floor in his cell was covered with bits and pieces of the Prophecy." Bordan saw Phaine shift slightly—the first disruption of his unnatural stillness.

"How did he write them?" Evlan asked.

"We gave him a small metal stylus so he could scratch his writings on the walls." The Lord Warden's eyebrows bristled as he glared at Evlan. "Before that, he demonstrated that he would resort to writing in blood given no other means. In twenty-six years, he never used the stylus for anything but scrawling on his walls, and we're quite confident that it had nothing to do with his escape."

"I assume that you kept a copy of all information sent to House Lyrandar," Bordan said. "I would like to see it."

The Lord Warden nodded. "I think you're wasting your time. It's nonsense, and there's a great deal of it. But I'll let you sort it out."

"Is he marked?" Evlan asked.

"Ah," Zaxon said, and the hand went over the bald head again. Bordan's eyes narrowed. "He failed the Test of Siberys in his youth, and he did not carry a dragonmark before his imprisonment. However, he manifested a Siberys mark five years ago."

Bordan saw the surprise register on the other three faces in the small room. The Siberys Mark of Storm meant that Gaven had significant power—power that House Lyrandar would much rather have under its control than loose in the world. Bordan smiled behind his folded hands. That might make the chase more interesting.

Ossa changed the subject, speaking for the first time. "He was to be married." Her voice was gruff, and she tugged at one of her thick braids as she spoke.

"Yes," the Lord Warden said. "Rienne ir'Alastra was his betrothed. She was actually the first to suggest that he was possessed, and she helped the Sentinel Marshals find him and bring him into custody." He nodded at Evlan, acknowledging his order's role in Gaven's arrest.

"Did she marry someone else?" Bordan asked.

Zaxon was starting to look exasperated. "I have no further information about her, as she is not and never has been a prisoner of House Kundarak. Now, our guards have reported communication between ir'Brassek and Gaven—their cells were across the hall from each other. As far as we know, these conversations were typical for Gaven: he'd report his dreams or recite bits of the Prophecy, but ir'Brassek seemed eager to hear all that."

"Is it possible they used a code to plan the escape?" Evlan said.

"Anything is possible," the Lord Warden said, "but I believe it highly unlikely. The conversations always occurred in the middle of the night and seemed to be precipitated by Gaven starting from sleep, awakened by a dream. After telling ir'Brassek about the dream, Gaven would write it down. It's all recorded on the walls of his cell."

"They weren't confined to their cells at all times, were they?" Bordan asked.

"Of course not. Gaven occasionally had to be confined for long stretches, when he'd go into a violent phase. But ir'Brassek wasn't considered particularly dangerous or an escape risk. They both worked in the mines. They walked the courtyard when Gaven was able. And they had access to the library."

Evlan leaned forward in his chair. "Did they speak together at those times?"

"Gaven rarely spoke at all outside his cell, except to rant. Ir'Brassek approached him a few times, but Gaven either ignored him or flew into a rage, and he gave up after a while. Gaven never read, barely walked, and worked only because we forced him to."

"He was here a long time," Bordan said.

"Twenty-six years, yes."

"Was he any different before his mark appeared?"

"Not at all."

"Was there any change in him after Haldren arrived?"

The Lord Warden shook his head. "None. He gives the sense that he's not quite present, like his mind's off in the Realm of Madness while his body's trapped here."

"What are we up against, Lord Warden?" Evlan asked. "Besides the Siberys mark, what can we expect of these two?"

"Haldren ir'Brassek is a sorcerer, hence his lodging in the Spellward Tower. He likes fire, burning things down. He could, of course, be anywhere by now." A trace of Zaxon's seething rage returned to his face.

"And the Lyrandar?" Phaine said.

"Gaven no longer has the privilege of carrying the name of his house. He is . . . accomplished. He had a reputation for great physical strength, perhaps a result of clambering around in the caves of Khyber for years. He favors a greatsword in combat, taking advantage of that strength. And he also has some facility with magic beyond what his dragonmark grants him. Although the full extent of the power of his dragonmark has never been seen."

"Was there any manifestation when the mark first appeared?" Bordan asked.

"Yes," Zaxon admitted. "We had to move all prisoners and guards underground for an hour to wait out the storm."

Bordan enjoyed watching the others' eyebrows rise. He got to his feet.

"Lord Warden, House Tharashk thanks you for your confidence in us and the detailed information you have provided. On the honor of my house, I swear that I will not rest until these two prisoners are safely returned to your custody."

The others scrambled to their feet as well. "Lord Warden," Evlan d'Deneith blurted, "House Deneith promises a tireless effort to recover these fugitives. I will personally select a team of the finest Sentinel Marshals to assist me in bringing them to justice." He gave a small bow.

Phaine d'Thuranni was the next to speak, in his whispery voice. "The finest of House Thuranni are also at your service, Lord Warden."

"For the honor of House Kundarak," Ossa d'Kundarak said, "the Ghorad'din will hunt them to the depths of Khyber."

The Lord Warden stared at them. Bordan hid a smirk behind his hand as the Old Rock searched for a response to all these oaths and boasts. Finally, his eyebrows bristling again, he blurted, "Well, what are you waiting for? They're probably in the Demon Wastes by now!"

Bordan was the first out the door.

* * * * *

Bordan paced the courtyard of Dreadhold, ignoring the drizzle of rain that heralded a larger storm. Stark stone walls loomed over him, windowless and forbidding. Stout dwarf guards watched him from ledges on all sides, crossbows in their hands and axes at their belts. One archway led back into the prison interior, blocked by a heavy portcullis backed by iron-banded doors. When he was ready to leave, he could signal to the guards, and the gate would open. He tried to imagine being a prisoner—to spend all his days surrounded by those walls, those watchful guards, iron and stone on every side. Even the sky was granite.

Shaking his head to dispel those thoughts, he replayed the Lord Warden's briefing in his mind, sifting his memory for details that might be important in his coming search. He had a pretty good idea of what the others would do. Evlan would assemble a troop of Sentinel Marshals that would march across Khorvaire like overblown city guards. They'd probably question Gaven's family, find the Aundairian officers loyal to Haldren, follow up on people mentioned in the briefing. Phaine would pull together a small team of Thuranni elves more suited to assassination than investigation. They would probably pick up the trail first, and it might just be a question of whether the fugitives stayed alive until their hunters could return them to Dreadhold. Bordan wasn't sure about the other dwarf, Ossa. He didn't know much about the Ghorad'din, but he thought it was more of a covert military force than a group of trained inquisitives. It was possible that they were brought in just to make sure House Kundarak had a hand in retrieving the prisoners that had been in its care, but Bordan had no real reason to doubt their effectiveness. He just wished he had a better idea how they would go about the task.

For his part, he would start with the documents Zaxon had promised—copies of the reports sent to House Lyrandar describing Gaven's ravings.

CHAPTER
3

Gaven stared at the emerald orbs of the dragon's eyes, overwhelmed at the size and majesty of the great bronze beast. Behind those eyes, bony ridges swept back to form a crest around the back of his head, crowned with a pair of curving horns. Smaller horns jutted out along the edge of the crest, at the lower joint of his jaw, and on the chin of his beaked snout. Thick scales overlapped to form an armored plating over the front of his neck and his belly, while smaller interlaced scales covered the rest of his body. Above the muscles of his shoulders, a pair of membranous wings stretched upward and fanned the sea air. Spiked frills adorned the back of his neck down to his wings, stretched between his forelimbs and his flanks, and extended up from his long, heavy tail. Vaskar was larger than any creature Gaven had ever seen. Gaven focused on the emerald eyes and tried to listen to the words coming from the dragon's mouth.

"Listen to me, Gaven." The dragon's voice was surprisingly soft, coming from such a large creature, and it was as clear and low as the ringing of a huge bronze gong. "The Prophecy is finding its fulfillment. The Storm Dragon is ready to claim what has been set aside for him. But you have a part to play. You must—"

Haldren cut the dragon off. "We need your help, Gaven."

Vaskar drew his head back on his long neck, lifting it high. Clearly, the dragon would not lower himself to asking for help, but Haldren had no such qualms.

"You know the Prophecy better than any dragon or mortal alive." Haldren leaned forward, letting the light of the campfire dance on his face. "I've been listening to you for three years, and it's clear I haven't heard a tenth of what you know about the Prophecy. Vaskar has been studying it in Argonnessen for six human lifetimes, and there are gaps in his understanding—gaps only you can fill. Please, Gaven—please help us."

Vaskar snorted, and a bright yellow spark flared at his nostrils. Gaven started, staring up at the dragon. The Storm Dragon, he thought. He wants the Prophecy, so he can be the Storm Dragon.

Gaven looked around their little camp. They had flown through the night, and the first glow of dawn was beginning to spread across the edge of the sea to the east. The rocky cliffs of Cape Far loomed dark in the west, blocking his view of the Ring of Siberys. Cart had built a small campfire on the rocky beach between the cliffs and the sea, and Darraun was cooking some fish that he and the warforged had caught. Gaven had not been starving in Dreadhold, but the fish smelled better than anything he'd tasted in over twenty years.

He was free! The thought struck him for the first time. The dawn sky, the dancing flames, the cooking fish—he had not seen and smelled and felt these things in years. He could walk where he pleased, and no one would herd him back to his cell when the sun set. He could—he looked up at the slowly brightening sky—he could bask in a storm, and no one would wrestle him to the ground and shove him back into confinement. A gust of wind brought a salt smell off the sea, and Gaven had a sudden longing to sail again.

"Gaven?"

He turned his gaze back to Haldren. The elf woman had washed and cut the old man's hair and beard, and he'd put on a new set of clothes—tall boots, warm breeches, a shirt with just a hint of a frill at the collar, a short jacket, and a heavy traveling cloak. He looked twenty years younger. His pale blue eyes were striking, almost hypnotic. Compelling. Gaven found himself nodding.

"What . . . what do you need to know?"

Haldren sat up and flashed a triumphant smile at Vaskar.

The dragon lowered his head to speak to Gaven again. "The Time of the Dragon Above, Gaven," he said. "It is beginning. The sun is approaching the center, spring is dawning, and I saw the moon of the Eternal Day waxing in the sky. Irian draws near, and the Storm Dragon is rising. Tell me what you know about the Time of the Dragon Above."

Gaven recited the words he had spoken to Haldren earlier that night, back in Dreadhold. "When the Eternal Day draws near, when its moon shines full in the night, and the day is at its brightest, the Time of the Dragon Above begins. Showers of light fall upon the City of the Dead, and the Storm Dragon emerges after twice thirteen years."

"Yes," Vaskar hissed, "for two cycles of thirteen years I have been withdrawn from the world, and now I have emerged."

The blond man, Darraun, approached with a wooden plate loaded with fish and some dry bread. He handed it to Gaven. Gaven took a piece of fish in his fingers and put it in his mouth. It tasted even better than it smelled, and he ate with relish.

"What else, Gaven?" Haldren asked. "What is to happen during the Time of the Dragon Above?"

Gaven closed his eyes again and lost himself in a sea of memories—words mingled with images that had haunted his dreams. What is to happen? he thought. So very much. Vaskar wanted to be the Storm Dragon.

One memory surfaced in his mind: his hand traced twisting Draconic letters carved into stone. Was it his hand? Had he been there, or was it the other? Or was this a dream, a figment, and not a memory at all? He opened his eyes and stared at the crackling fire. This is what's real, he thought. This is what's now.

Still staring into the flames, he read the words from the carving in his memory, if the memory was his: "In the Time of the Dragon Above, Siberys turns night into day. Showers of light fall from the sky. The Eye of Siberys falls near the City of the Dead."

Vaskar glanced up at the Ring of Siberys, shining brightly in the night sky. "The City of the Dead," he murmured. "In Aerenal."

Haldren looked at Vaskar, then back at Gaven. "The Eye of Siberys, Gaven," Haldren said, leaning toward him again. "What else can you tell us of the Eye of Siberys?"

New words sprang to his mind almost unbidden. These he had read by firelight—torchlight—and he thought he remembered Rienne at his side as he read them. He couldn't see her, but he could feel her beside him, and it made his heart ache even as rage surged in it. He spat the words out of his mouth—they tasted bitter. "The Eye of Siberys lifts the Sky Caves of Thieren Kor from the land of desolation under the dark of the great moon, and the Storm Dragon walks the paths of the first of sixteen."

"The Sky Caves of Thieren Kor!" Haldren said, the excitement in his voice undisguised. "They are in the 'land of desolation,' Gaven? The Mournland, do you think?"

A nightmare. Gaven remembered waking up in Dreadhold, stumbling to the door, and whispering to Haldren how he had staggered across a land where nothing lived. And then he'd found words to anchor the vision, words with their cold solidity, only hinting at the terror of his dream. He repeated the words, savoring them as a shield from the nightmare. "Desolation spreads over that land like a wildfire, like a plague, and Eberron bears the scar of it for thirteen cycles of the Battleground."

Haldren furrowed his brow and looked to Vaskar.

"Shavarath, the Battleground, draws near to us every thirty-six years—that is its cycle," the dragon explained. "So thirteen cycles of the Battleground would be four hundred and sixty-eight years." He did not pause to perform the calculation.

"Four hundred and sixty-eight years?" Haldren repeated, ignoring the food that Darraun had set before him. "That is how long the Mournland will persist?"

The dragon snorted softly. "*If* those words refer to the Mournland."

"It seems the most likely candidate," Haldren said.

"One can never be certain," Vaskar responded. "Your century of war is not the only desolation this world has known. You humans are too quick to assume everything in the Prophecy applies to your works. Some dragons would argue that the Prophecy doesn't even acknowledge your existence, though of course I think they are mistaken. Nevertheless, we will seek the Sky Caves in the Mournland."

Gaven watched as Haldren and Vaskar dissected the Prophecy, ignoring him now. He was glad for the respite from questions. He stared at the dawn as it reddened the sky.

"But first we need the Eye of Siberys," Vaskar rumbled. He looked at Gaven again. "The City of the Dead in Aerenal, when Siberys turns night into day." He turned his beaked snout toward the sky.

Another image flashed in Gaven's memory, another dream—yellow crystal pulsing with veins of golden light, carved to a point and bound to a blackened branch, plunging into a body that was shadow given twisting form. He shuddered.

"What is it, Gaven?" Haldren had seen the shudder. "What did you see?"

"The Eye of Siberys," Gaven said. "A dragonshard, a huge one, the size of my hand. Formed into a weapon, a spearhead." He shook his head, trying to dispel the image from his mind.

Haldren looked up at Vaskar, who lowered his head close to Gaven again.

"A weapon?" the dragon said. "To be used against what foe?"

The endless dark, Gaven thought, where *he* waits. "The Soul Reaver."

A look of triumph flashed onto Haldren's face, and Gaven suddenly understood what was happening. The dragon knew a great deal about the Prophecy already, and he wasn't sure Gaven was worth the trouble. Haldren had probably used Gaven as a bargaining chip in negotiating his own rescue. And Gaven had just proven his worth, providing their first glimpse of a real hope of victory. Probably they knew the Storm Dragon would have to face the Soul Reaver, but this was the first they had heard of a way to win that fight.

The part of his mind that had kept him alive in Dreadhold reminded him to dole out such valuable insights slowly, to keep himself useful as long as possible.

"So the Eye of Siberys will raise the Sky Caves of Thieren Kor under the dark of the great moon," Vaskar said. "And it will serve as a weapon against the Soul Reaver." His eyes narrowed. "Is there anything else?"

Gaven didn't want to remember any more. He wanted to taste the smoke in the air, savor the fish Darraun had cooked, smell the sea and its freedom, watch the sunrise. Those things were real and present, not vague memories that might not even belong to him. He shook his head.

"That's enough for now, Gaven," Haldren said. "You've already helped us a great deal."

Gaven stared at the line of blood spreading across the horizon, trying to see nothing more than a beautiful sunrise.

* * * * *

"What is he?" Senya asked, staring at Gaven. She picked at her fish with her fingers, gingerly placing a small piece in her mouth and sucking the oils off her fingertips.

Darraun watched her with amusement, not sure how to answer her question. "Just a man," he said.

"How does he know so much about the Prophecy?"

I wish I knew, Darraun thought. But Senya didn't need to know the extent of his curiosity. "Vaskar thinks he learned it from another dragon."

"But why would a dragon teach him?" She tried to take a bite of the hard bread, but couldn't find a way to do it delicately. She balanced the plate on her knees and used both hands to break the bread into smaller pieces.

Why, indeed? Darraun shrugged, wanting to drop the conversation. To his relief, the warforged lumbered over to stand beside them. "Hello, Cart."

"Darraun, Senya," Cart said. "How's the fish?"

"Delicious," Senya said, looking back at Darraun as she said it. "Best I've ever had on the road."

"Thank you," Darraun said with a small bow of his head. "I take pride in my cooking."

"I hope your wands and scrolls will be as useful when we start fighting," she said, her face clearly indicating that she doubted they would be.

Cart rubbed his chin, a mannerism he'd certainly learned from a human sergeant during the war. "Are we spending the night here, do you know?" he said. "The general didn't tell me to set up the tents, but if we're camping I want to do it before it gets any darker."

Darraun looked back over at Gaven, Haldren, and the dragon. "I suspect we'll be moving on tonight," he said. "Forty miles is still too close to Dreadhold for anyone's taste, I expect."

Senya grimaced, looking over her shoulder at the wyverns. "I don't think I can begin to say how much I dislike those things. I feel like the stinger could stick down into my back at any second."

"It certainly could," Darraun said. "I hate the way they bounce with every flap of their wings. But I have a feeling we won't be flying anymore tonight."

"What?" Senya said. "You just said—"

"I said we'd be moving on. Not flying."

* * * * *

Gaven enjoyed a respite from questions as Haldren ate and conferred quietly with Vaskar. He took that opportunity to look around this strange group, his new companions. He'd had plenty of time to examine Cart as they rode their wyvern to this shore, and he knew Haldren's appearance well from Dreadhold, though the cleaned-up, well-dressed version beside the dragon bore little resemblance to the disheveled character he remembered from their neighboring cells.

Darraun was the blond man who had helped Cart get him out of his cell. Gaven had seen the man work some magic with his cell door, which probably meant he was an artificer, skilled with the magic of items and constructs. Scrolls and wands protruded from the pouch at the man's belt, confirming that impression. His fair hair was short and fine, and he had a day's growth of beard. His skin was tan from travel, and his cloak carried the dust of many roads. He wore a hardened leather cuirass and carried a large metal mace with a flanged head. Still, something about the way Darraun carried himself made Gaven suspect that he would not be in the forefront of any battles.

The elf woman—he'd heard Haldren call her Senya—was about as different from Rienne as Gaven could imagine a woman being. Her black hair was curly and cut short, in contrast to the way Rienne's flowed like silk. Senya's skin was pale despite all her travels outdoors, where Rienne's was a rich mahogany. The lids of Senya's eyes were heavy and tinted with a bluish black powder, and her full lips were painted red. She wore a leather coat that hugged her chest before flaring out around her legs. It was cut to reveal more of her throat and breastbone than was probably safe. He noted an amulet at her throat, shaped like a shield and studded with adamantine, that probably more than made up in magic for what her coat lacked in protective value. She wore soft leather leggings and boots that rose to her knees. The heels of her boots made them better suited to a social function in Fairhaven than walking on the rocky shore of the Lhazaar Sea.

Finished with his meal, Haldren got to his feet and lifted a hand to the others. They rose at his summons and walked quickly over to where Gaven sat studying them.

"My dear friends," Haldren said, taking Senya's slender hand and including the warforged with a smile, "and more recent acquaintances," he added with a gracious nod to Darraun and then Gaven, "this day you have done a great service to Aundair and, indeed, to the world. And, of course, you have done a great favor to me, in liberating me from Dreadhold, the prison they said was impregnable."

Haldren laughed, and Senya laughed with him. Gaven glanced at the others, but kept his attention on Haldren.

Vaskar wants to be the Storm Dragon, Gaven thought. Vaskar thinks that's a service to the world. He noticed that Darraun was staring at him. The artificer had barely smiled at Haldren's humor. Gaven decided to ignore the stare and continue watching Haldren.

"Vaskar and I have discussed the Prophecy with Gaven," Haldren continued. "We have learned much that is useful, and confirmed much that we already knew. We believe that Vaskar was correct, that the Time of the Dragon Above has begun, and the Eye of Siberys will soon fall from the sky."

He paused for dramatic effect, clearly enjoying the attention of his companions. This was a man used to addressing crowds, Gaven realized, and used to having his pronouncements greeted with cheers.

"And so we are going to Aerenal," Haldren announced.

"Aerenal?" the elf blurted. "That'll take weeks!"

"We will not be riding, Senya," Haldren said. "My magic will transport us now. We'll rest this morning at an inn in Whitecliff, in Q'barra, do some business in the city, and tomorrow head on to Aerenal."

"How soon do we depart, Lord General?" Cart asked.

"Immediately," Haldren said. "Grab your pack and we will be on our way."

"Should I clean up the campsite, remove our trail?" the warforged said.

"No. Let them find it. They'll assume we're still on the wing and look for us tomorrow within fifty miles of this site." Haldren grinned. "And we will be over a thousand miles away."

Senya left the cluster and retrieved her pack. Cart followed her example, while Darraun quickly rinsed an iron cooking pan in the surf. In a moment's time, they returned and stood around Haldren, ready for him to work his magic.

Before he did, he addressed the group again. "I neglected to mention, my friends, that Vaskar will not be accompanying us to Aerenal. The elves hold an ancient grudge against dragonkind, and Vaskar would draw too much attention to our mission there. He will rejoin us later. Vaskar," he said to the dragon, "thank you for your part in freeing me—and Gaven. Without you we would still be in Dreadhold."

The dragon nodded almost imperceptibly, then glided over to the wyverns, which shifted nervously at his approach.

"Please join hands," Haldren said, seizing Gaven's left hand in his right and pulling him to his feet. Darraun took Gaven's right hand and Cart's left, and Senya connected Cart back to Haldren. With a smile around the little circle, Haldren began a brief incantation.

The last thing Gaven saw was Vaskar closing his jaws on the neck of a wyvern and tearing out its throat.

CHAPTER
4

An instant of blackness laced with silver, then green, then they stood in a lush forest alive with the droning of insects, the songs of birds, and the screeches of monkeys greeting the dawn. In sharp contrast to the windswept coast they'd just left, the air was warm and heavy with humidity. The ground rose sharply in one direction, and peering through the broad leaves of the forest, Gaven caught a glimpse of white-capped mountains in the distance.

Haldren looked quickly around the little circle, then dropped Gaven's hand.

"Welcome to Q'barra," he said with a broad smile. "Whitecliff should be a short walk." He glanced around to get his bearings, then waved his hand at a thinner patch of forest. "Downhill."

"What are the chances someone will be looking for us there?" Senya asked. "Looking for you, I mean."

"It's almost inconceivable," Haldren said. "They'll be expecting us much closer to Dreadhold."

"They know you're a sorcerer," Darraun said.

"True, but they can't search a thousand-mile radius."

"How many major settlements are there within a thousand miles of Dreadhold?" Senya said. "It seems likely they could narrow that search quite a bit."

"Most of eastern Karrnath would have been in my reach. They don't know our destination, so they have little reason to look in Q'barra."

"Except that it's been a haven for refugees and fugitives for seventy years," Darraun said, frowning.

"True enough," Haldren said. Gaven could see that he didn't like having his pronouncements questioned, but he remained gracious. "We will exercise caution as we approach the town. They know what Gaven and I look like, of course, but they don't know any of you. They'll be looking for a dragon and people on wyverns. We have no dragon and no wyverns, so I do not anticipate any difficulty."

The memory of Vaskar killing one of the wyverns flashed in Gaven's mind.

Haldren started walking, ending the discussion by turning his back on Darraun—rather pointedly, Gaven thought. Senya followed without a moment's hesitation, and Darraun trailed after. Cart lingered by Gaven.

"So you're my faithful hound," Gaven said to the warforged.

"Hound?"

"It's your job to keep an eye on me, make sure I stay with the group?"

"It's my job to keep an eye on everyone," Cart said with a shrug. Gaven was struck at how human the warforged managed to seem, despite a face that was essentially a featureless plate of metal with a hinged jaw. Gaven nodded, and they walked shoulder to shoulder behind Darraun.

* * * * *

For all the concerns Senya and Darraun had expressed, the group walked out of the jungle and into Whitecliff with little difficulty. Apparently this frontier town was accustomed to people appearing out of the forest and strolling into town. Had they been lizardfolk of the sort that infested the jungle, Gaven was sure they would have been given a very different reception. A wall of white stone surrounded the town, presumably quarried from the cliffs of the Endworld Mountains just to the north and west that gave the town its name. The guards at the gate wore coats of metal scales and bristled with weapons. Each one carried a halberd and wore a sword, a dagger, and a crossbow. The sentries asked a few questions about their business and the length of their stay, but Haldren handled them with ease.

After a quarter-century in Dreadhold, Gaven felt overwhelmed by this first taste of civilization. The morning streets, lined with buildings made of the same chalky stone as the town's walls, were crowded with people—thronging the marketplace, visiting the temples, opening shops for the day's business. Considering the town's location near the eastern edge of nowhere, it seemed awfully crowded to Gaven. Any one of these hundreds of faces could have been someone looking for them—a Sentinel Marshal or a Tharashk inquisitive. The dwarves made Gaven most nervous, reminding him of his jailers and making him wonder how many had ties to House Kundarak. The freedom he had tasted and savored at the campfire began to sour in his mouth. Looking constantly over his shoulder hardly seemed like freedom at all.

Haldren led them through the streets, leading Gaven to wonder how the Aundairian knew the place so well. That thought made Gaven realize he had no idea of the crime that had brought Haldren to Dreadhold. Had he spent time as a fugitive, hiding in the frontier of Q'barra before he was captured and imprisoned? What had he done that made them hunt him to the farthest reaches of Khorvaire? And to what lengths would they go to recapture him?

Probably the same lengths they'll go for me, he thought, quickly surveying the faces in the crowd around him.

They reached a section of town where the stone buildings were dingy gray, and Haldren stepped through the doorway of a small hostel. A faded sign above the door showed only a unicorn that might once have been gold, but now looked dull brown. The door had been painted green a long time ago, but knives, fists, and armored shoulders had chipped away much of the color. The wooden floor inside was adorned with a frayed rug that displayed another yellow-brown unicorn marred with stains that made up a rainbow of unpleasant colors.

This was the sort of place that catered to people who would rather not present themselves at a hostel run by House Ghallanda, where they'd be required to show identification papers. A glimmer of recognition flitted across the face of the desk clerk when the man saw Haldren, but he bowed his head to hide it, taking the money Senya held out and handing over two room keys without a word. Haldren took one key and handed the other to Darraun, and they climbed a narrow flight of stairs.

"Senya and I will be here," he said as they reached the room whose number matched his key. "Darraun, you and Gaven have the one across the hall. This is not the safest hostel in Whitecliff. We've had a long night, so get some rest. Cart, stay nearby. We'll eat in a few hours, gather some supplies we'll need for the trip, and get a good night's sleep tonight."

He opened the door to his room and pulled Senya inside. Darraun rolled his eyes and turned to the door across the hall, unlocking it with the key Haldren had given him. He pushed it open and stood back for Gaven.

The room was tiny, and the furniture worn, but it was mostly clean. Gaven walked in and sat gingerly on one of the two narrow beds. It felt a bit like his cell in Dreadhold, but he wasn't sure that was a bad thing.

Darraun was still standing outside the open door, urging Cart to join them inside. "I know you don't need rest," he said, "but doesn't it feel good to get off your feet once in a while?"

"No," said Cart, and shuffled into the room. With the great bulk of the warforged, the room seemed much smaller. Darraun came in, pulled the door closed behind him, and threw himself down on the bed with a contented sigh.

"That was a long night," he said. "Are you tired, Gaven?"

Gaven shrugged. Fatigue pulled at his limbs, but he didn't want to sleep. Not really. Sleep for him was torment as often as rest. He lay back on the bed and stared at the ceiling.

"Well, get some rest," Darraun said, closing his eyes. "We've got a grand adventure ahead of us."

Despite his best efforts, Gaven's eyes would not stay open. Listening to Darraun's steady breathing, Gaven was soon asleep, and the dreams came.

* * * * *

The rope bit into his waist, under his arms and between his legs. Uncomfortable, but not agonizing. He swung in blackness, the light of his glowstone too feeble to reach any surface on any side of him. He had no idea if his rope was long enough to reach any kind of floor beneath him, or how far it might be to another wall he could use to aid his descent. He lowered himself as slowly as he could, straining his eyes to see anything—anything at all.

Rienne's voice called to him from above, where his rope slowly coiled out through a series of pulleys. Her words were swallowed in the open expanse around him.

Then the light of his glowstone fell on a roiling cloud of

darkness, and the cloud engulfed him—a cloud of silent black wings. He lost his hold on his rope, and he fell. He called out to Rienne, but the rope kept spinning out, never slowing his fall.

He was flying, broad wings outstretched in a darkness that was somehow not so dark. A churning river flowed beneath him, and he followed its course farther and farther into Khyber's depths. He came to a cascade and swooped over the edge, then alighted on the bank of a pool at the bottom. He watched a series of images dance across the swirling water of the pool, and he saw a face—a great reptilian snout topped with a massive horn. A dragon's face. His face. Then he turned, his snaky tail splashing in the water, and he saw the nightshard. Almost perfectly clear, the enormous crystal held a vein of pure purple-black color, pulsing with dim light in its heart.

He groaned, every inch of his body aching, the hard stone beneath him pressing against his wounds. He had a vague sense that he had been unconscious for a long time, and he wondered vaguely why he wasn't dead. The nightshard, though, was pulsing with violet light. He stretched out a hand, bruised and bloody, and touched it.

His mind exploded with thoughts and memories—his own and the other's. He fell back to the rock floor, his eyes glued to the nightshard, and could no longer determine who he was or how he'd arrived there. A distant voice echoed in the vast cavern above him, but it no longer sounded like anyone he knew.

* * * * *

"Gaven?"

For a moment the hand that was gently shaking him belonged to Rienne. Her head was on his shoulder, her silky black hair spilling across the bed, and they were twenty-five again. Then he woke, and there was Cart, leaning over him like a mother. When the warforged saw Gaven's eyes open, he straightened up.

"Time to eat."

Gaven shook his head to clear the dream from his memory, and sat up on the bed. The door stood open, and Darraun was not in the room. Gaven thought he heard voices from across the hall.

"Were you here the whole time I slept?" he asked.

"I was. Your faithful hound," the warforged said. There was a smile in his voice, though his face wouldn't allow it.

"Did I say anything while I was sleeping?" Gaven tried to make the question sound casual.

"Who's Mara?"

"What?"

"I'm joking," Cart said. "During the war, I knew a man who talked in his sleep. Usually about whatever woman had most recently claimed his heart. We used to give him a hard time."

Gaven tried hard to imagine the warforged as just one of the men and women in a squad of soldiers. For a moment he saw Cart in battle, an axe raised over his head, strange, cold light glinting on his adamantine plating.

"No, you didn't say anything," Cart said, gently hitting Gaven's shoulder with the back of his hand. "You snore when you sleep on your back, though."

"Sorry," Gaven said. Dreadhold had taught him to avoid confrontation, back down, apologize.

"Doesn't bother me. And Darraun snores louder. Come with me. Haldren's waiting." Cart stepped aside and waited for Gaven to get to his feet, then followed him out the door.

Darraun stood in the doorway to Haldren's room, speaking quietly to the old sorcerer. Gaven could see Senya behind Haldren, buckling her sword belt at her hip. Haldren saw Gaven emerge from the room, and cut Darraun off.

"Ah, Gaven!" he said. "I hope you are well rested. Shall we eat?"

Without waiting for an answer, Haldren swept out of the room and down the stairs. Cart followed Gaven at the rear of their little procession.

Haldren was willing to settle for substandard accommodations for the sake of privacy, but he had extravagant taste in food. He led the way to Whitecliff's finest restaurant and ordered for everyone.

"It has been almost two years since I have enjoyed a fine meal," he said, "with all due respect for our friend Darraun's expertise at the campfire. Gaven, I can barely imagine how starved you must be for such a repast."

Starved was the wrong word—Gaven couldn't remember what a fine meal tasted or smelled like. He remembered the smell of the fish on the campfire, though, and his mouth began to water.

When the food came, it was overwhelming. Half a dozen

aromatic smells blended together to form something exquisite. He attacked his plate.

"I am pleased to see you enjoying your meal so much, Gaven," Haldren said. "It is far better than the offerings at our last lodgings, is it not?"

Gaven nodded and took another bite of pheasant.

"Pheasant can be both dry and dull in the wrong hands," Haldren said, addressing the table at large. "But when prepared by my good friend Marras, it is never either." He gestured toward the kitchen. "So, Gaven, how was your sleep?"

Haldren clearly hoped that the good food would help to draw him out. Gaven chewed slowly, considering how to respond, then swallowed and said, "Not so different than Dreadhold."

"Ah, yes," the sorcerer said, his voice hushed. "Probably best not to mention our last lodgings by name, don't you think? Wouldn't want to attract any undue attention."

Gaven looked around. His eyes met those of a dwarf who quickly looked away. The pheasant suddenly did not taste so exquisite.

"Did you have pleasant dreams?" Haldren leaned forward as he asked it.

"No." For an instant, Gaven remembered his dream about Rienne, but then darker images flashed into his mind.

"What did you see, Gaven?"

Gaven's eyes fixed on the old man's mouth, just as he had seen it through the shutters in their doors in Dreadhold. A dribble of pear-cider sauce stained Haldren's white beard.

"I don't really remember."

Haldren exploded. "Damn you, Gaven, don't get coy now!" His voice was a rasping whisper, barely able to contain his fury. "I brought you out of that place because of the information locked away in that twisted little brain of yours. If you suddenly get clever and decide to start withholding information, I'll send you back there—or off to Dolurrh. Don't think for a second that I won't kill you if you stop being useful."

Gaven glanced around the table. Senya studied her plate while Cart peered around them to see if Haldren's outburst had attracted the attention of nearby patrons. Darraun watched the two of them with unconcealed fascination.

Gaven took a bite of his squash.

Clearly convinced that he was dealing with an idiot or a madman, Haldren brought his anger under control—to Senya's visible relief—and tried a different approach. He made his voice light, conversational, and he lowered his eyes to his plate as he spoke.

"Did you see the hordes of the Soul Reaver again, Gaven?"

Writhing tentacles in the darkness, a blinding beam of light stretching up to the sky. Gaven tried to remember his dream about Rienne and found that he couldn't. Her hair became a mass of writhing snakes, reaching for him.

"No," he said.

Haldren saw his unease and pounced. "What is it, Gaven? You remember something else?"

"The Soul Reaver itself," Gaven said, as if in a trance. Haldren leaned forward in his chair. "Falling or flying down from a great height, sinking into a chasm as deep as the bones of Khyber. Endless dark beneath the bridge of light. There the Soul Reaver waits."

Besides Haldren, who wore a look of smug satisfaction, the other three stared at Gaven with varying degrees of surprise. Senya might have been awed—her mouth was partly open, and her eyes wide. Darraun smiled, but there was something else in his expression that Gaven couldn't read. And Cart's face, of course, was a mask, but he rubbed his chin in a way that looked thoughtful.

Well enough, Gaven thought, let Haldren think he won this one.

Better that than to reveal what he had really dreamed.

CHAPTER
5

The meal finished, Darraun took charge of Gaven and Cart. "The three of us need to stock up on supplies for our little jaunt to Aerenal and wherever else Haldren's magic takes us," he explained to Gaven as they left the restaurant. "Haldren and Senya are going to try to make contact with some people in Aundair who will be helping us later."

"Helping us do what?" Gaven said.

Darraun arched an eyebrow at Gaven. That was the first time he'd heard the half-elf ask a question, and he was eager to see more of the workings of the mind behind Gaven's recitations of the draconic Prophecy.

"Ah, I'm sure Haldren will explain it all to you later," he said.

"I'm sure he won't," Gaven said. "He won't let me in on his plans any more than is absolutely necessary to get information out of me."

"What do you think Haldren wants from you?"

"He knows some of the Prophecy, and Vaskar knows more. But two years in a cell across the hall from mine made him think I know more than the two of them combined."

"Wild nightmares and vague visions?" Darraun said. "He could get that from a raving madman on any street corner in Fairhaven. There has to be more to you than that."

Gaven stopped walking and waited until Darraun turned to face him. "That makes two of us, then. I'm not the only one here concealing his true face."

"Three of us, actually," Cart interjected. "I'm really quite complex." He turned his head to look at both of them. "Many-layered."

Darraun gaped at the warforged then burst into laughter.

Gaven's eyes were still fixed on him, though, so he resumed a casual stroll in the general direction of the city's mercantile district.

"Very well, Gaven," he said. "Clearly you are more alert and perceptive than Haldren gives you credit for. Haldren is one of those people who believes he is more intelligent than he actually is. But what he lacks in reasoning, he more than makes up for in cunning and charisma. You will find that his most dangerous quality is his ability to inspire fierce loyalty in others." He glanced at Cart and hoped that Gaven was perceptive enough to catch his meaning.

Gaven watched him for a long moment as they walked, then evidently decided against prying any deeper into his secrets, just as Darraun had hoped he would. He figured Gaven would renew the subject if he ever managed to catch him alone, so Darraun resolved to avoid being alone with Gaven. He decided to try what he hoped was a more innocuous approach.

"I understand you were quite an explorer, years ago," he said.

"Of sorts," Gaven said. "More of a prospector. I lowered myself into caves and fought monsters, looking for Khyber dragonshards for my house. The elemental galleons of House Lyrandar . . ." He trailed off, a scowl falling over his face. "My former house," he muttered.

Darraun tried to shift Gaven's thoughts away from the family that had disowned him. "Lyrandar galleons and airships require nightshards to bind the elementals that power them, correct?"

"Airships?" Gaven's eyebrows shot up at the mention of them. "They were made to work? They were a dream of my house for a long time, but I never knew . . ."

This approach wasn't working either. Darraun cursed himself. He was dredging up too many painful memories.

"House Lyrandar put airships into service about nine or ten years ago," Cart said. "Just about every nation used them in the last years of the war, and now House Lyrandar operates passenger lines."

Darraun saw Gaven's eyes light up and decided that if Gaven ever ran off, the airship lines would be the first place to check. This, he thought, is a man that wants to fly.

"So the Khyber dragonshards bind the elementals to the

vessels?" Darraun asked again, trying to bring the subject back around to nightshards.

"That's right," Gaven said. "They have a peculiar property of binding. With the right magic, they can hold just about anything—even a human soul."

"Almost like some sort of possession?" Darraun asked.

"Sort of, yes." Gaven's face darkened again, and he didn't elaborate further.

"So all your expeditions into the depths of Khyber—is that how you learned so much about the Prophecy?"

Gaven stared blankly ahead, showing no indication that he'd heard the question. A cloud passed over the hot noonday sun, and Darraun glanced at the sky. "We'd better get our supplies and get ready to go," he said. "I understand it can rain pretty hard here in the jungle, though it usually comes in short spurts."

He quickened their pace, and they found shelter in a provisioner's shop. Heavy drops of rain started falling a moment later.

The shopkeeper was attentive to their every need, which meant Darraun was unable to keep up his line of questions. He stayed busy ordering the things they'd need for their journey, but at one point when the merchant had vanished into a back storeroom for a moment he found himself staring at Gaven's dragonmark. The intricate pattern almost seemed painted on Gaven's skin, fine tracings of blue beginning just at the ridge of his jaw, on his left side, covering the whole front of his neck, and extending down under his shirt. It probably covered his whole chest, and Darraun could see part of it extending out his short sleeve to reach his left elbow. The skin beneath the mark was redder than the rest of Gaven's pale flesh, giving the whole 'mark a purplish tinge. There was something vaguely draconic about the part that covered his neck, which must have been how the dragonmarks had earned their names.

The Mark of Storm. Darraun glanced at a window spattered with rain and wondered if Gaven's mark had anything to do with the weather outside. The rain was coming down hard now, so hard that Darraun could hear the drops splattering on the cobblestones outside and driving against the shutters of the shop. He sighed, glancing down at the fine clothes that would soon be pasted to his skin. Natural storms were one thing, but a storm caused by magic was a more unpleasant prospect. Would Gaven make it rain for the length of their time together?

All the more reason to get this over with quickly, Darraun told himself.

* * * * *

"Cart, what do you think of this?" Gaven held up a leather belt studded with wooden beads and decorative stones, supposedly made by one of the nearby lizardfolk tribes. He was aware of Darraun's gaze lingering on him, but he chose to ignore it. Darraun had been asking a lot of questions, and Gaven wanted to get him away from Cart and ask some of his own before he submitted to any more interrogation.

"Interesting," Cart said, taking the belt in his three-fingered hands. He looked down at the battered belt that held his battle-axe at his waist. "I could certainly use a new one, but I don't know about this."

"It would be a different look for you," Gaven said. The shopkeeper had returned and engaged Darraun in further discussion. Darraun deftly avoided any question of their destination, planned activities, anything that might help pursuers track them down. "What's your connection to this group, Cart?" Gaven asked. "How do you know Haldren?"

"He was my commanding officer," Cart said.

"He was a sergeant?" Gaven was stunned. "I got the sense he ranked higher than that."

"And you assume I was just a private," Cart said. "Lord General Haldren ir'Brassek commanded the Third Brigade of Aundair, Gaven. I might have made colonel and commanded a regiment myself, but Aundair's armed forces value a skill in magic that I completely lack. I was part of the general's staff."

"I'm sorry, Cart," Gaven said. "I . . ."

"I know. You were thrown in Dreadhold before the warforged proved their worth on the battlefield, almost a decade before Chase received his commission, I believe."

Cart's voice was a little too loud, and Gaven thought he saw the shopkeeper's eyes dart in the warforged's direction at the mention of Dreadhold. Damn, Gaven thought. All of Darraun's careful work undone by one slip.

"Chase?" he said, keeping an eye on the shopkeeper.

"The first warforged to hold a command over human soldiers. He served in Aundair and proved himself far more competent than the Lord Major in command of the company. In 981 his general promoted him and relieved the Lord Major of his command, but the Lord Major complained to the Queen."

Gaven watched the shopkeeper excuse himself and head into the back of the shop again.

"Sorry to interrupt you, Cart, but we need to get out of here."

"What?"

"Fast. Darraun!"

The man whirled around. "What is it?"

Gaven nodded in the direction the shopkeeper had gone. "He's going to get the authorities. We need to go." Grabbing Cart's arm, he hustled to the door. Darraun stared for a moment at the provisions spread over the countertop, then ran after them.

They hurried up the street away from the provisioner's, the rain drenching them. Only when they were about to turn a corner did Gaven risk a look back at the shop—just in time to see a trio of soldiers arrive and peer through the shop door.

"What in the Ten Seas happened back there?" Darraun said as they turned the corner.

"My fault," Gaven said. "I got Cart a little riled up, and he let a mention of Dreadhold slip out. The shopkeeper heard it and took the first opportunity to get out and summon help."

"The fault was mine, then," Cart said. "I'm sorry, Darraun. I don't even remember mentioning it."

Darraun sighed. "We were about to finish the deal, too," he said. "Now what do we do? We should find Haldren and get out of town, but we don't have supplies."

"We find Haldren first," Gaven said. "Tell him what happened, and figure something out from there."

"The general is not a forgiving man," Cart said. Gaven could hear the trepidation in his voice.

"Put the blame on me. Tell him I blurted something about Dreadhold. He can get as angry at me as he wants to, but he has to answer to Vaskar about my fate, and something tells me he wouldn't want to have to tell the dragon he killed me."

The warforged strode along in silence, making Gaven wish for the hundredth time that he could read Cart's unmoving face.

"Back to the hostel, then," Darraun said, turning a corner and leading them back to break the news to Haldren.

* * * * *

"I wonder what he's telling them," Cart said. He stood by the door of their little room, occasionally pacing as much as the tiny space allowed.

Gaven sat on the bed, staring out the window to the street below, watching for any sign that guards were coming after them. Darraun had insisted on breaking the bad news to Haldren himself, and neither he nor Cart was clear on which version of the story Darraun would tell. So far Gaven had not heard any shouting, but Haldren did not strike him as the yelling kind. For that matter, he couldn't be sure Darraun was still alive.

"Do you hear anything in there?" he asked the warforged.

"I can hear them speaking," Cart said. "I can't make out what they're saying. You can tell when the general is really angry, because he whispers. It's frightening."

The general, Gaven thought. He began to understand what Darraun meant about Haldren's ability to inspire loyalty. Haldren hadn't been a general in at least three years, but he would always be "the general" in Cart's mind.

The door flew open, banging hard against Cart's shoulder. The warforged stepped out of the way, and Haldren came barreling into the room. "We are leaving now," he said, very quietly.

Gaven looked around as if he had a pack to load, then got to his feet. Darraun slipped into the room behind Haldren, eyes lowered.

"Circle up," Haldren commanded. Senya entered, fumbling with the last buckle on her pack, and quickly joined the others in a circle, taking Haldren's right hand. Darraun stooped to lift his own pack to his shoulders, then took Gaven's hand, still avoiding his eyes. Haldren glared at each of them in turn, not even sparing Senya his withering stare, then began another incantation.

Gaven blinked, and he was in another forest, sweltering hot and buzzing with insects. Haldren freed his hands and stormed away from the circle.

CHAPTER
6

"A re you Arnoth d'Lyrandar?"

Evlan watched the old man carefully. Every reaction was important. Any twitch or shift of the eyes could reveal whether Gaven's father was aware of his son's escape or had any idea of his whereabouts.

"I am," the man said. He was hoarse and short of breath, but he stood as tall as Evlan despite his age. The hair was gone from the top of his head, but what remained still bore traces of black amid the gray and white. His dark eyebrows bristled. "What is this about, Sentinel Marshal?"

"My name is Evlan d'Deneith. I'm here to talk to you about your son."

Arnoth turned to the stairs behind him. "Thordren?" he said, and the young man who had kept a respectful distance on the stairway came to stand beside him. Thordren strongly resembled what his father must have looked like in his youth—fine, black hair cut above his shoulders and combed away from his face, high cheekbones, and proud brown eyes.

"I'm sorry," said Evlan, "I meant your other son."

"My other . . . Gaven?" The old man's skin went ashen, and he slowly sank down onto a bench. Then he seemed to recollect himself, and he looked away. "I have no other son, Sentinel Marshal. He was excoriated a long time ago."

"All the same, it's Gaven I need to talk to you about." He shot a pointed glance at the other man, but Thordren sat down on the bench next to his father, his eyes glued to Evlan.

"Is he dead?" Arnoth's eyes told Evlan almost everything he needed to know. Excoriate or not, Arnoth loved his son, and as far as he knew, Gaven was still locked away in Dreadhold.

"No. At least, not as far as I know. He has escaped."

"Escaped? From Dreadhold?" Arnoth got to his feet again, Thordren fluttering after him, trying to get him back to the bench.

"Yes," said Evlan. "According to House Kundarak, there was a dragon involved."

The old man's eyes went wide. "Where is he?"

"That's why I'm here," Evlan said. "I take it you have not received any communication from him?"

"Not in twenty-six years, no."

"Were you aware that he manifested a Siberys mark during his imprisonment?"

"Yes. House Kundarak has kept me informed of developments."

"You have seen the reports of his ravings?"

"Ravings?" Arnoth said. "You think he is mad?"

"His mind hardly seems stable, if you'll pardon my saying so."

"You underestimate his mind, Sentinel Marshal. He is not all brawn."

Evlan shrugged and tried another tack. "Does the name Haldren ir'Brassek mean anything to you?"

"Ir'Brassek?" Arnoth scratched the side of his face. "Wasn't he an Aundairian general? Tried for war crimes?"

"Yes. Are you aware of any connection between your son and ir'Brassek?"

"Gaven and Haldren?" Arnoth seemed genuinely confused. "No. I can't imagine that Gaven would associate with such a person."

"They occupied adjacent cells in Dreadhold," Evlan said, a reminder that Gaven was no less a criminal than Haldren.

Arnoth shook his head and looked back at Thordren. "No, I've never heard their names connected." He looked back at Evlan. "Did Haldren escape with Gaven?"

"Yes, they fled Dreadhold together. Mounted on wyverns."

Arnoth raised his eyebrows and sank back down to the bench, to Thordren's obvious relief. "Gaven is free," he muttered, running a hand through his short gray hair.

Thordren spoke for the first time. "Sentinel Marshal, my father is in poor health. I must ask—"

Evlan cut him off. "He has escaped, but he is hardly free. He is a fugitive from justice, and the combined efforts of Houses Deneith, Tharashk, Kundarak, and Thuranni will locate him eventually."

"House Thuranni?" Arnoth said. "They'll kill him!"

"Probably. Certainly you can appreciate that it would be better for Gaven if I find him before Thuranni's assassins do. If you have any information that might help me locate him . . ."

"If I knew anything, I would certainly tell you, Sentinel Marshal," Arnoth said, and Evlan believed him. "And if I hear from him . . ."

He trailed off. He couldn't quite bring himself to promise that he'd turn in his son. Evlan would have marshals watch the house.

"Thank you. I have just one more question for you. Do you know where I might find Rienne ir'Alastra?"

* * * * *

The shadows pooled and thickened in a corner of the little room. A sword blade took shape out of the darkness, glinting dully in the dim light that filtered through the shutters of the room. Then the hand that held it appeared, covered in a black glove. Phaine d'Thuranni stepped out of the shadows, lowering his sword as his eyes swept the empty room. Another form took shape in the dark corner, and Phaine made a hand signal: Stand down.

Either they had received bad information, or they had arrived too late. Phaine shifted his sword to his left hand and used his teeth to pull the glove off his right hand. He bent over the bed beside the window, placing his palm on the mattress. A trace of a circle rumpling the blankets showed that someone had been sitting there not long before. Very recently, in fact—Phaine could still feel the heat.

Phaine shot Leina another hand signal, and she stepped to the door, pressed an ear to it, and shook her head. Then something on the door caught her eye, and she examined it. She knelt and looked at the floor, then stepped away from the door, signaling to Phaine: Look here. She pointed at the door and the floor.

Phaine crossed the room in two steps and looked where Leina had pointed. There was a mark on the door as if something had struck it. Perhaps the metal head of a mace, but not a hard blow. The floor was scuffed.

"A warforged," he whispered. "Pacing here beside the door, and the door hit him when it opened." The other elf nodded. Search it, Phaine told her.

Phaine pressed his own ear to the door then opened it silently. There was no one in the hall, and the opposite door stood open. Taking his sword in his right hand again, he stepped quickly across to the other room. Empty. The two beds were pushed together, their blankets piled on the floor. He found white hairs on the bed—presumably ir'Brassek's—and curly black hairs that must have belonged to the woman the innkeeper had described, the beautiful elf. Phaine snorted. He didn't like to imagine an elf dallying with an old human like ir'Brassek.

He stepped back across the hall, no longer making an effort at silence. "What did you find?" he asked Leina, who knelt on the floor beside the window.

"Come have a look," she said.

Phaine crossed the room and looked over her shoulder. The window sill was thick with grime—except where a fingertip had traced patterns in the dirt.

Without thinking about it, Phaine reverted to hand signals: Over there. Leina got out of the way, and Phaine knelt on the floor to study the patterns. At first, they were incomprehensible, but he knew there was something—the shapes hinted at letters, in the ornate Draconic script. But they'd been written on top of each other, and he found it almost impossible to distinguish them. He breathed the words of a simple spell, and the letters slowly resolved themselves in his mind.

He read them aloud, translating them from Draconic to Elven. "The Bronze Serpent seeks the face of the first of sixteen."

"What?" Leina said.

"The Prophecy. Come. Let's get out of here."

The shadows in the corner darkened again, and Phaine stepped into them. When he vanished, Leina took one last look around the room, then followed.

* * * * *

Rienne ir'Alastra whirled on Evlan, a picture of righteous fury. "I assure you, Sentinel Marshal," she said, "if I had any idea where Gaven was, I'd tell you, just as I did all those years ago."

She set her jaw, trying to make herself believe the words she spoke. Back then, she had honestly believed that she was helping Gaven by leading the Sentinels to him—she thought they would help him, restore him to his right mind. Instead, they had locked him in Dreadhold, and she had spent two and a half decades blaming herself for all the tortures she imagined him enduring there. Now he had escaped, and this Evlan d'Deneith seemed a little too skilled at reading the ambivalence she felt.

"I am sure you will do what's right," Evlan said. He smiled slightly, but his eyes fixed on her like a hawk.

She turned her back on him again. "I appreciate your confidence," she said.

"I spoke to his father this morning," Evlan said. The sound of his voice drew a little closer. "Master d'Lyrandar does not believe that Gaven is mad."

"Love blinds him."

"Perhaps. Although he was careful to remind me that, technically, he has only one son."

"The censure of House Lyrandar means little to Arnoth."

"And what about you, Lady?" he whispered, uncomfortably close now. She could feel him behind her.

Rienne stepped forward and whirled on him again, resting a hand on the hilt of a dagger in her belt as she did so. "What about me, Sentinel Marshal?"

"You were engaged to be married. Gaven has been in Dreadhold for twenty-six years, and you have not married anyone else. Might love be blinding you as well?"

"My marriage to Gaven would have been advantageous both to my family and to House Lyrandar. It was a political allegiance. After Gaven's arrest, my value in such a bargain diminished significantly. House Lyrandar has made other alliances with other noble families, and the ir'Alastras have waned in influence. Surely you, a scion of House Deneith, can appreciate what is involved in such an alliance."

Evlan raised his palms as if to deflect the force of her anger. "I married a woman I loved."

"Well, aren't you lucky?"

Evlan met her glare and held it for a long moment. "Very well," he said at last. "If you hear from Gaven, please contact me immediately. I don't imagine that I need to remind you of the consequences if you do not."

"I would hate to imagine that a Sentinel Marshal is leveling petty threats at a member of Aundair's nobility, however much my family's influence has fallen."

"Farewell, Lady." Evlan turned and strode out of the hall.

Rienne watched his back until the servants had ushered him out the front door and closed it behind him. Only when she heard the satisfying slam of the door did she turn and run to her chambers.

* * * * *

Bordan looked up through the shattered ceiling of Dreadhold's tower to the dazzling arc of the Ring of Siberys overhead. He tried to imagine the force it must have taken to break through the thick stone, the size and sheer strength of the dragon that had done it. Blinking several times to clear the dust and drowsiness from his eyes, he set a thick sheaf of papers down on the bed beside him and stood up to stretch his back.

He walked around Gaven's tiny cell, reading whatever words his eyes fell on, hoping that something would leap out at him that would help him understand. He could certainly see why so many people thought Gaven was at least halfway across the Sea of Rage, practically lost to madness. Disjointed fragments full of strange imagery and obscure descriptions covered the walls. Bordan had been wrestling for hours with numbers: twice thirteen years, the first of sixteen, shards of three dragons, thirteen cycles of the Battleground, nineteen turns of the thirteenth moon.

The thirteenth moon? Bordan thought. To the best of his knowledge, there were only twelve. And he could only guess at references for most of the rest of these numbers.

His eyes fell on a scrap of writing at his eye level, and he read the words aloud. "The cauldron of the thirteen dragons boils until one of the five beasts fighting over a single bone becomes a thing of desolation." Bordan stroked his beard. "Very well, Gaven, let's play this game. Five beasts fighting over a single bone—is that your code for the Five Nations? Are we talking about the Last War here? And Cyre, bless it, has become a thing of desolation. So Galifar is the boiling cauldron of the thirteen dragons? It's a boiling cauldron because of the war. Thirteen dragons—thirteen dragonmarked houses!"

He looked up at the Ring of Siberys again. "But there were only twelve dragons before House Phiarlan split, Gaven. Is that why you conspired against them? Did you orchestrate the schism so there would be thirteen dragons and your precious Prophecy would make sense?"

He looked around the room again, at all the writing on the walls, the rubble on the floor, the crack in the ceiling through which Gaven, formerly of House Lyrandar, had escaped.

"So your Prophecy would come true?"

CHAPTER
7

The Aerenal jungle teemed with life. Even discounting the insects that swarmed around them, the sounds of movement were everywhere—gibbons leaping through the canopy overhead and whooping at each other, the hiss of an emerald-scaled snake coiled around a nearby branch, the harsh cries and elaborate songs of a dozen different birds. More alarming, something large rustled in the undergrowth not far enough away, off to Gaven's right.

"Welcome to Aerenal," Haldren announced. He swept his arm grandly around him, taking in the jungle, then pointed behind Gaven. "The City of the Dead lies in the valley in that direction."

"The City of the Dead?" Darraun paled, but Haldren ignored him, shouldering past Gaven to walk in the direction he'd indicated.

Gaven followed, falling into step beside Cart. Senya slipped between them as she hurried to catch up to Haldren, and Darraun brought up the rear, grumbling to himself. Gaven saw a clump of ferns shake slightly, opposite where he'd heard the rustling a moment before. Without thinking, he reached over his shoulder to where his sword should have been, and cursed softly when his hand met only empty air.

"What is it, Gaven?" Cart said, slowing his pace. "Did you see something?"

Senya darted forward, shouting, "Haldren, look—"

Another rustle in the undergrowth, then a creature collided with Haldren, knocking him to the ground. It was covered in sable fur like a panther and resembled a cat in its general form—a cat the size of a horse. Two long tentacles arced up from its shoulders, trying to rake at Haldren's flesh even as it clawed him with six feet and bared long fangs. Gaven found that looking at it was like peering through a curved glass—it seemed to shift position without moving.

Haldren did not cry out or make any exclamation. Calm and sure, he chanted a few words of power that grew in volume until they became a thunderous shout that blasted the beast off him, sending it sprawling on its back. As Haldren got to his feet—a little unsteadily, Gaven noticed—the beast flailed its six legs in the air for a moment before managing to right itself. Senya had already reached it and swung her sword toward its head in what should have been a deadly blow, but her weapon failed to connect. To all appearances, it passed right through the creature's head.

Cart took up a position between Haldren and the beast, waiting in case it threatened his commander again. Darraun produced a slender wand from his belt and reached toward Haldren, working magic to stanch the bleeding. For a moment, Gaven thought about running—getting as far away from Haldren and his team as he possibly could, and making his way on his own. Then he saw the rest of the beast's pack emerge from the ferns, forming a wide circle around them. He cast his eyes around for a branch or even a stone he could use as a weapon, but then the beasts closed the circle. One pounced at him, rearing up to plant its front paws on his shoulders, trying to knock him down. Gaven planted his feet and stayed upright, raising his hands to grab the thing's head just as it tried to bite at his neck. Its middle pair of legs tried to tear at his chest and sides, but it couldn't quite reach him.

His dragonmark was burning. The shadows around him deepened, and the sky grew dark. Gaven growled with the effort of wrestling the beast, and a rumble of thunder rolled overhead. He felt disconnected from the struggle—he was in the storm brewing in the sky, looking down at his tiny form far below—and the storm brewed in his blood. Lightning flashed in the clouds above, and Gaven felt it jolt across the Mark of Storm on his chest.

The beast's tentacles bludgeoned his back, but he barely noticed. His hands held its jaws open and twisted its neck around. With another rumble of thunder overhead, he snapped its neck and roared as he threw its corpse away.

Gaven had become the storm. He was killing with his bare hands, a primal force of nature, and the sky met his savagery with equal fury. Unbound, no longer locked within the walls of

Dreadhold, not restrained by convention or decorum, not con-fined by the limits of his flesh, Gaven's fury flashed across the sky, making shadows dance across the forest.

Two beasts lunged for him, but he held them off, one with each hand. His muscles screamed in pain, but he exulted in the raw physicality of it. For the first time in years, he was completely in the moment, ancient memories and prophetic nightmares exorcised from his mind. An ear-splitting crash of thunder made one of the beasts flinch slightly, and he pressed the advantage, pushing it off him. Finally able to bring two hands to bear on the other beast, he grabbed it and swung it around him, crashing its hips into the snarling maw of the first creature. Darraun appeared at the edge of Gaven's awareness, bringing his heavy mace down hard into the ribs of the beast he'd thrown.

A monstrous roar answered the thunderclap, and another beast crashed through the jungle to enter the fray. If the beasts they'd been fighting were the size of horses, this one was a small elephant, though it was as wiry and compact as the others. Trying to follow its movements made Gaven's eyes ache.

Gaven's eyes rolled skyward, and he lost himself in the storm. The dragonmark that covered his chest was a mirror of the thundercloud overhead, surging with power and flashing with lightning. The wind howled around him, and he let it hold him upright as he gave himself over to the tempest. The rain began to fall.

He was aware of shouts and bestial howls of pain, but if the downpour fell on him, he did not feel it. He opened his eyes, but he felt so far away, so high above the battle that he could barely make sense of it. Darraun stood in front of him, hefting his mace in both hands as if to protect Gaven from the great beast. Haldren was at the artificer's shoulder, his magic searing flesh from the beast's skull, and Cart drove his axe again and again into the creature. The beast's tentacles thrashed through the air, but its roars of pain and rage were drowned out by the howling wind.

The wind lifted Gaven off the ground, and light exploded around him. Gaven felt rather than saw the location of each remaining beast, and bolts of lightning impaled each one, tying them briefly to each other, to the churning clouds above, to the burning dragonmark on his chest.

The world fell silent, and the wind set Gaven back on his feet. Small hailstones pelted him, but the storm's power was spent. He shook his head, trying to make sense of the ground beneath his feet, the fire in his muscles, the frenetic movement around him. Haldren's mouth was open wide as though he were shouting in Darraun's ear, but there was no sound. Darraun nodded to Haldren and ran somewhere behind Gaven, just as Cart's axe felled the great beast.

Then Haldren's red face was inches away, apparently yelling at Gaven. The half-elf shrugged and tried to turn away, but Haldren grabbed his shoulders and continued his tirade. Gaven watched little flecks of saliva form around Haldren's mouth, and he remembered all the times he'd seen that mouth through the shutters in their cell doors. Nausea gripped his stomach, and he curled around it. Haldren released his shoulders and let Gaven drop to the ground.

The silence was strange. With his eyes open, Gaven could perceive the chaos left in the wake of their battle, but when he closed his eyes it was gone. The jungle was silent, and he might have been alone. The earth was warm beneath him, and the ferns made him a soft bed. He felt himself start to drift, so he opened his eyes, and found himself embroiled in chaos again.

Darraun and Haldren stood over him, apparently bickering. Haldren no longer looked like he was yelling, which probably meant that he was getting angry. Darraun rummaged through a large pouch at his belt. Gaven had seen scrolls in there before, so he supposed that Darraun was looking for a spell that would restore his hearing. He closed his eyes again, relishing what might be his last taste of peace and quiet.

His ears started ringing, and Gaven looked up. Darraun was still rummaging, so he wasn't responsible. Gaven rolled onto his hands and knees, letting his head hang between his arms for a moment, then he pushed himself shakily to his feet. Darraun said something.

"Just ringing," Gaven said, pointing to one ear. He heard the sound of his voice, but it was muffled and strange.

Darraun frowned, and Haldren crossed his arms impatiently. Haldren said something—Gaven could hear his voice now—and stomped away. Gaven watched him help Senya to her feet while

Darraun talked, a rapid stream of syllables that didn't quite resolve themselves into language in Gaven's ears.

Senya moved slowly, and Gaven noticed a lot of blood staining her clothes and armor. But something about her suggested that something besides her physical injuries slowed her down—she looked distant, almost vacant, as she got to her feet and looked around. Her eyes didn't seem to linger on Haldren at all, almost as if she didn't see him there. She turned slowly where she stood, as if she could see through the thick growth of trees to scan the horizon.

Gaven's ears cleared enough that he could hear Haldren's voice, coaxing her, almost pleading in its tone. Senya lifted an arm to point into the distance, and Gaven could clearly hear her words: "The City of the Dead awaits us."

CHAPTER
8

aven took an involuntary step backward as the weight of Senya's words—the weight of what they were doing here—finally registered in his mind. He was no longer in his cell, dreaming of the Prophecy and remembering all the research he had done into its mysteries. No, he was in the jungle of Aerenal, outside the City of the Dead, waiting for the Eye of Siberys to fall in fulfillment of the Prophecy. He was helping to bring it about.

That was what had landed him in Dreadhold in the first place.

Haldren's eyes narrowed and rested on him. "What is it, Gaven? Did you see something?"

"With respect, Haldren," Darraun said, "I'm particularly interested in what Senya is seeing right now." Senya took a few steps in the direction she had indicated, her eyes still fixed on some distant point.

"Senya will guide us to the City of the Dead," Haldren said. "But the Prophecy—Gaven, what did you see?"

Gaven didn't answer. Instead, he lifted his eyes skyward. The clouds of his unnatural storm had cleared, but the sky was beginning to darken. Even in the deepening blue, the Ring of Siberys was visible, glowing faintly. By the time the sun's light faded, the ring would be as bright as the sun—turning the night into day.

Haldren followed Gaven's gaze, and remembered the words Gaven had uttered before. "When Siberys turns night into day," he muttered. "Yes, Gaven. The Time of the Dragon Above is here. All is coming to pass as the Prophecy declares."

Gaven shuddered. Some part of him wished he were back in his cell with his nightmares. That seemed preferable to living them out.

* * * * *

Senya led them through the jungle as though following a distant call, and as they crested a hill, the forest cleared before them. The City of the Dead lay exposed to their wondering gazes. Wide streets ran straight and long between hulking buildings—sloping pyramids crowned with pillared temples, squat ziggurats decorated with elaborate skull motifs, graceful domes with chiseled arches, winged pillars, and flying buttresses. Great eldritch fires leaped skyward atop towering columns and danced inside the galleries of ancient temple-tombs.

Gaven saw no sign that the jungle encroached into the city—no trees adorned the streets, no vines clung to the ancient stones. No wall surrounded it, either, but the line between the vibrant life of the jungle and the calm stillness of the City of the Dead could not have been more clear. Where ferns and grasses ended, stone began. People walked the streets, though not in any great numbers—and Gaven couldn't be certain whether those people were themselves alive. In the elven homeland, the spirits of long-dead ancestors still inhabited their desiccated corpses, speaking to the living within their ancient tombs. The City of the Dead was the center of the elves' ancestor worship, where the Undying Court continued to guide the spiritual and political affairs of the elves, unhindered by the death of their mortal bodies. Even the guards at the gate might be undying soldiers conscripted to guard the elders' rest.

Senya insisted on leading them to a towering arch set up as an entrance. Two guards wearing helms decorated to resemble skulls crossed their spears in the archway as Senya approached, and easily a dozen more stood beyond. One spoke in Elven. Gaven couldn't make out any words, but the hostility in his voice was unmistakable. Senya stepped forward proudly and replied in the same language. She spoke more slowly, and her voice wasn't muffled by a helmet with a skull mask, so Gaven caught a few words: "the right of counsel," "revered elder."

The guards looked at each other and moved their spears out of the way slowly, as if it caused them pain. Gaven watched them stare at Cart as the warforged lumbered past, and he thought he heard one of them make a spitting sound as he followed Cart through the arch.

Then he was surrounded by the monumental buildings of Shae

Mordai, the City of the Dead. He felt as though he had stepped into a tomb.

"Haldren?" Darraun said.

Darraun had been lingering behind as they entered the strange city of monuments, but now he hurried to catch up to the front of the group, where Haldren walked beside Senya. Gaven noticed that he still seemed pale, and wondered if the necromancy of the elves unsettled him. Haldren barely glanced over his shoulder to acknowledge Darraun.

"Why are we entering the city? Didn't Gaven say that we'd find what we need near the City of the Dead, not in it?"

Haldren stopped and turned around. "Indeed he did, though I was not aware you had overheard that part of our conversation." His pale blue eyes burned into Darraun. "However, Senya has access to an unusual store of knowledge here within the city, and I would not miss the opportunity to tap it while we're here."

The Right of Counsel, Gaven thought—the privilege to confer with her ancestors within their tombs. The tradition of the elves attached so much weight to that right that the elders would be compelled to answer her questions. He wondered what they might have to say about the Prophecy and Haldren's plans to fulfill it. The elves were the ancient foes of the dragons, sporadically warring with them since their first arrival on the island continent of Aerenal. The elves studied the Prophecy as a matter of survival.

For that matter, what would they say about him? He had not missed the hostility of the guards at the gate, and he felt certain that elves more ancient would share that distaste for a half-elf violating the sanctity of their tombs. And what of a half-elf who carried so much knowledge of the Prophecy?

The sound of his name drew Gaven out of his reverie. Darraun had stepped closer to Haldren and lowered his voice, but he was gesturing in Gaven's direction.

"Yes, we do have Gaven," Haldren said, turning his icy gaze on him. Gaven looked away. "But Senya's additional information could corroborate what Gaven has told us—or contradict it. Or it could expand our understanding further. Besides, we have time. The Ring of Siberys is at its brightest, and the Eye should fall tonight. It might turn out that our hasty departure this afternoon was actually advantageous. Now come! Senya's family is waiting."

"Family?" Darraun said. He looked slightly relieved and turned to Senya. "You have family living here?"

"The living members of my family left Aerenal many decades ago," Senya said, her voice little more than a whisper. "But the dead remain."

She started walking again, and Haldren took her arm. Darraun stared after her. Cart clapped him on the shoulder as he and Gaven walked past, and Darraun trailed behind them.

Senya led them down a wide, quiet street into the city's heart. The city seemed almost normal as they passed through—merchants beginning to pack up their wares for the evening, loading their carts and rolling up the tents they'd erected in front of the gigantic stone buildings. Most of the people on the street were alive, Gaven could see now, though a few had painted their faces to resemble skulls or corpses. All were elves, and they clustered together as Senya passed with her non-elf allies in tow. The hostility on their faces was clear.

They turned a corner, and the trappings of life fell away. Twin rows of towering monuments stretched before them, many-tiered pyramids topped with thick columns, each column supporting a blazing beacon in honor of the dead who resided within. The air was thick with incense, wafting out the open doorways of the temple-tombs. This was the heart of the City of the Dead, where the Aereni priests performed the Ritual of Undying, which bound the spirits of revered elders to their bodies so they could continue sharing their wisdom with their descendants through the ages. Gaven stopped in his tracks.

He had been here before.

The power of the memory overwhelmed him. He had stood on this spot—seen the same line of ancient temples, heard the roar of the blazing beacons, breathed the thick, scented air. He had been here with a friend, an elf, who sought the counsel of his ancestors just as Senya did now.

No, he told himself, that was not me. That was the . . . other.

"What is it, Gaven?" Darraun tried to follow Gaven's gaze. Cart had stopped a few paces ahead and turned to see what held them up, while Senya and Haldren walked further ahead.

"Nothing," Gaven said, shaking his head quickly. "Sorry." He started walking again, and Darraun stayed close beside him.

Senya started up the stairs of one of the great pyramids. Haldren lingered just long enough to look back at the others and hurry them with an imperious gesture. Cart hustled forward, and Gaven quickened his pace, pushing the memories aside.

He climbed the stairs slowly, with Cart on one side and Darraun on the other. Two more elves wearing skull helmets flanked the open doorway, holding their spears apart so the three could pass. Their stares told Gaven that he was not welcome here. He also remembered that from before. He had been nervous that these guards—or their ancestors, more likely—would see through his disguise and try to prevent him from entering, bring the wrath of the city on his head. His heart started pounding, but this time, as before, he passed through the entrance without incident. The guards crossed their spears across the entrance behind them, and the ancient stone swallowed them.

They climbed a narrow staircase inside the temple-tomb, so long that Gaven began to feel the walls close in around him, until they finally emerged onto a high balcony overlooking the street they had just left. Haldren stood in a narrow doorway, his back to the room behind.

"We'll wait here," Haldren said. "There are certain rites Senya needs to perform. We'll all go in when she's finished." He looked at Gaven for that last sentence, and Gaven thought he heard an emphasis on the word all. He also heard Darraun swallow hard at Haldren's words.

Gaven turned around and stepped to the edge of the balcony. The air was clearer up here, above the clouds of incense that settled at street level. The western horizon was blood red—"Evening red, clear skies ahead," he whispered, remembering the old sailor's proverb. The Ring of Siberys shone across the sky like a million tiny suns, lighting the night sky in a pale imitation of day. As he looked, a shooting star darted down from the Ring and disappeared above the distant forest.

More memories surfaced in his mind. He had climbed the dark and narrow stairs beside his friend, Mendaros, and waited on this balcony as the elf made his petitions to his ancestor. Then Gaven had knelt in the small room behind him, and learned much that was still locked in his mind. Mendaros Alvena Tuorren had been his friend, probably Senya's great-uncle or cousin far removed. And now Senya and her lover had brought Gaven here because of the knowledge he possessed.

"Gaven, we're ready," Haldren said behind him.

Gaven turned to see Cart and Darraun shuffling into the chamber. Haldren extended a hand, inviting Gaven to join them, a broad smile on his face. Gaven's pulse quickened. What did Haldren hope to learn here?

Gaven followed Darraun into the small stone chamber. It smelled of death, clouds of incense unable to mask the acrid scent of the embalmed corpse that stood and watched them enter. Pale flames flickered in empty eye sockets, and Gaven felt them burning into him as he approached. Senya's ancestor was draped in ancient finery, rich velvet and brocaded silk cloaking her withered flesh. Long black hair fell around her desiccated face, pale paper-thin skin stretched tight over her bones, and her clawlike hands held a slender gold rod. Senya knelt on the floor before her ancestor, and Cart took a similar position behind her.

Gaven cast a sidelong glance at Darraun as they sank to their knees, noticing his wide eyes and the sweat beading on his brow. He'd seen this reaction on the battlefield during the war. Soldiers faced with the undead soldiers of Karrnath, animated from the corpses of earlier battles, often suffered more from their own fear than from the blades and arrows of their enemies. He wondered if Darraun had fought in the war, perhaps suffered at the skeletal hands of Karrnathi forces. He gave the man credit for facing his fear at Haldren's command. Haldren knelt in front of Gaven, just behind Senya's elbow.

"Senya Alvena Arrathinen," the deathless thing said. Her shriveled lips barely moved, as though the cold, clear voice emerged magically from somewhere inside her head. Gaven was surprised at the purity of the voice, a far cry from the rasping whisper Gaven had expected. "What are you doing here? You are not a credit to your family." She spoke in Elven, and Gaven wondered who else in the room understood her words.

Senya held her head high. "I am a warrior, and my skill at the blade brings honor to my ancestors."

"Martial skill is not honorable when it is used for the pursuit of profit."

"The Valaes Taern would not agree," Senya said.

Gaven held back a smile. The warriors of the Valaes Taern had been mercenaries in the Last War until they annexed part of southern Cyre to form the nation of Valenar.

"Your family is not of the Valaes Taern."

"Nevertheless, I fight with honor in a worthy cause."

Her ancestor made a sound like a long sigh and stepped closer to where Senya knelt. "You have invoked the Right of Counsel, and tradition requires that I answer your questions, as much as I might wish to deny you. What counsel do you seek, Senya?"

Senya glanced over her shoulder at Haldren, and Gaven caught his first glimpse of fear in her eyes. Haldren put a reassuring hand on her shoulder, and she turned back to her ancestor. "I seek knowledge of the Prophecy of the Dragons," she said. Her voice sounded high, strained.

"The knowledge of the dragons should be used only as a weapon against the dragons."

"I have invoked the Right of Counsel, as you said. Grant me the knowledge I seek."

"There is more to wisdom than knowledge. You would do well to heed my counsel."

Gaven watched Haldren take his hand from Senya's shoulder and bring it to his mouth. The old man had to restrain himself from jumping into the argument. Gaven rather enjoyed seeing Haldren faced with someone he could not charm, bully, or dominate. He hoped to see many more examples of Haldren caught powerless.

"Give me knowledge, and trust my wisdom and that of my allies," Senya said. Haldren nodded approvingly behind her.

"You have given me no cause to trust either." The ancestor cast her burning eyes over Senya's companions. Gaven was sure she dwelled longest on him. Was she studying his dragonmark, perhaps? Or did she somehow recognize him? "On the contrary," she continued, "to all appearances you are rushing headlong into folly and destruction. I would not assist you in this."

"You must," Senya said.

Gaven was impressed at how Senya handled herself. For a moment he wondered if Haldren had established a magical connection between his mind and Senya's so that he could speak through her. But Gaven decided it was more likely that Haldren had fallen in love with a woman who shared some of his talent for debate.

The undying ancestor drew herself up, bristling with anger. "I am bound to give counsel to deaf ears and show the path to blind eyes."

Triumph rang in Senya's voice. "Tell me, revered elder, how the Storm Dragon shall claim the place of the first of sixteen and become a god."

CHAPTER
9

The Storm Dragon?" The elder's voice was quiet, and the fire in her eye sockets dimmed. She fixed her gaze on Senya, then on Haldren for a long moment. Gaven watched the old man hold her gaze without flinching. Then the deathless elder turned her burning eyes on Gaven, and he forced himself to meet those eyes.

"Who is this, Senya?" the ancestor said, her eyes still locked on Gaven's. "Who is this hybrid you have brought into the city of your ancestors?"

Senya rose to her feet and stood between her ancestor and Gaven. Gaven looked at the floor and took a deep breath.

"Answer my question," Senya said.

"Kneel!" The ancestor's shout rang with supernatural power, and Senya dropped back to the floor. Gaven saw that Haldren had been about to rise as well, but he planted both knees back on the floor at the elder's command.

"You came to ask my counsel," the ancestor said, "but you have proven yourself unwilling to heed it. I will give you the knowledge you seek because I must, but I will not tolerate insolence from the likes of you, Senya Alvena Arrathinen."

She turned her back on them, and Haldren shot a glance over his shoulder at Gaven. Gaven looked away.

"It can be no accident that you have come here on this night," the ancestor continued. "You seek the Eye of Siberys, and your question suggests that you would help the Storm Dragon rather than hinder him. So be it." She turned to face them, and again her eyes burned into Gaven's. "The Eye of Siberys lifts the Sky Caves of Thieren Kor from the land of desolation under the dark of the great moon, and . . ."

Gaven found himself speaking the rest of the sentence in

unison with the ancestor. ". . . the Storm Dragon walks in the paths of the first of sixteen." The Draconic syllables of the Prophecy coiled and snaked through his mind as he spoke them in Elven. Those words had become a part of him.

The ancestor stepped closer to Gaven. "I have told you this before."

Gaven shook his head slowly, trying to wrench his eyes away from the ancestor's piercing stare. "I am just a man," he gasped.

I am not the other, he thought—I am not the one who was here before.

"In the first age of the world," said Gaven, "sixteen dragons transcended their mortal forms to become like the Dragon Above who had made them. These are the first ascendant. In the second age of the world, the first elders of Aerenal transcended their mortal forms to become the second ascendant. In the last age of the world, the Storm Dragon takes the place of the first of sixteen, the Gold Serpent whom the world has long since forgotten. The third ascendant." Words spilled from Gaven's mouth without thought, the narrative of his nightmares: "A clash of dragons signals the sundering of the Soul Reaver's gates. The hordes of the Soul Reaver spill from the earth, and a ray of Khyber's sun erupts to form a bridge to the sky."

Images filled his mind as if summoned by the words he had spoken: the gibbering hordes of tentacled monsters, the brilliant column of light bursting up from the ground.

"The Storm Dragon descends into the endless dark beneath the bridge of light, where the Soul Reaver waits. There among the bones of Khyber, the Storm Dragon drives the spear formed from Siberys's Eye into the Soul Reaver's heart. And the Storm Dragon walks through the gates of Khyber and crosses the bridge to the sky."

The deathless elf stared at Gaven in silence for a long time, and Gaven could not turn his eyes away. He was dimly aware of the others—Haldren glaring at him, Senya gaping in amazement, Cart watching with curious interest. Darraun's eyes were elsewhere, probably avoiding contact with the undying thing he seemed to fear.

Finally the ancestor turned her gaze away from Gaven and wheeled on Senya. "Your question is answered, my counsel given.

Depart from here, and may you bring honor and not shame to your family."

Senya pressed her forehead to the ground then stood and busied herself around the brazier that burned in the corner of the room—Gaven had not noticed it before—but the ancestor interrupted her.

"I do not care for your prayers and offerings. Be gone!"

Startled, Senya hurried from the chamber, Darraun right on her heels. Haldren and Cart followed. Gaven tried to avoid the ancestor's gaze as he moved to the door, but she placed herself in his path.

"Who are you?" she demanded.

"I am just a man," he said again. "Gaven, once of House Lyrandar."

"Go then, Gaven. Twice you have come to me now. The third time, you will finally find what you seek."

Gaven hurried after Cart. He did not think he breathed until he was back on the street.

When he reached the street, Haldren snarled at him. "What in the Realm of Madness was all that about?" The sorcerer's face twisted in rage.

Gaven shrugged, his eyes darting everywhere but in Haldren's direction. He wasn't sure what had happened, but he certainly didn't want to tell Haldren what he suspected.

"How did she know you?" Senya asked. "Why did she say you'd been here before?" Her voice held none of the fury of Haldren's outburst, and Gaven allowed his eyes to meet hers. But he quickly looked away, and shrugged again.

"Who did she think you were?" Haldren demanded.

Gaven sat on his haunches and stared at the ground.

Darraun put a hand on Haldren's arm. "Why are you so angry, Haldren?" he said. "What did you expect to happen in there?"

Haldren straightened and seemed to calm down a bit, but his eyes were still narrowed in suspicion, and he didn't answer Darraun. "Have you been here before? Is that how you learned about the Prophecy?"

I have not been here before, Gaven thought. I just remember being here. He ran a finger along a groove between the cobblestones. But what had the ancestor meant with those words? The third time, you will finally find what you seek?

Senya fell to her knees in front of Gaven, trying to make him meet her eyes. "Gaven, that was my ancestor in there, and she said you had been there before," she said. "Why did she say that? What's your connection to my family?"

Gaven kept his eyes on the ground. Senya Alvena Arrathinen, he thought. What is your relation to my old friend Mendaros? No—I never knew him, he reminded himself, shaking his head. That was the other.

"Damn you!" Senya drew her hand back as if to slap him, but Cart's words stopped her.

"It seems those showers of light have begun," the warforged said.

Gaven looked up at the night sky. The Ring of Siberys made it look like an overcast day; the sky was dark blue gray and studded with points of golden light. Streaks of fire crossed the sky as dragonshards fell from the ring and rained to earth.

A few dragonshards clattered on the stone streets nearby, and Gaven heard others striking the buildings above them. He had been a prospector—that's what he'd told Darraun. To a prospector's mind, there was a small fortune to be made here. Siberys shards were the most precious dragonshards, useful primarily to the dragonmarked houses, who sent prospectors to Xen'drik to find the products of showers like this one. Properly attuned, a Siberys shard could enhance the power of a dragonmark in a variety of ways. House Lyrandar built them into the helms of their galleons—probably their airships as well—so that a dragonmarked heir of the house could control the elemental spirit bound into the ship. Clearly many of the living residents of the City of the Dead shared that point of view. They were scrambling after the shards that landed in the street like chickens after a handful of seed.

But Gaven was not here to make a fortune, and the shard they sought was no ordinary dragonshard. As he looked, one shard flared brighter than all the others and streaked across the sky. It grew brighter as it fell, stinging his eyes. When it landed, he heard its impact, like a great spear striking the earth. It was close, no more than a mile outside the city.

"The Eye of Siberys," Haldren said. "Move!"

Gaven did not need Haldren's command—he was already on his feet and three strides ahead of Haldren. Darraun kept pace with him at first—spurred, no doubt, by his eagerness to leave the City of the Dead—but Gaven soon left him behind.

The guards at the gate started to close ranks as he approached, probably assuming that he was fleeing the scene of a crime or trying to escape an angry watch patrol. Gaven prepared himself to barrel right through the guards if necessary. It proved not to be necessary—either the guards noticed the lack of any pursuit or they figured the city was best rid of the foreigners anyway.

It felt good to run. For so many years he had been confined to a small cell or given his exercise in a tiny yard where he just walked, slowly, counting his paces like the passing of years. Now the wind whipped his hair behind him, cooling the sweat from his face. His arms and legs pumped hard, his muscles protesting the exertion but also exulting in his speed. He remembered riding on the wyvern's back behind Cart, feeling the dragon's muscles as it flapped its wings hard to propel them through the air, and for a moment he felt as if he were flying.

A hundred yards outside the city, he realized he didn't know where he was running. Three more steps, and he realized he didn't care. He would run until he reached the sea, and then he would take flight and run across the waves. The wind blew at his back, and he could almost feel it lifting him off the ground.

In the jungle ahead of him, he saw a flicker of golden fire lighting a wisp of smoke, and he remembered why he ran. He turned toward the glow. The wind blew his hair into his face, and he lifted a hand to brush it aside. Then he was upon the source of the golden fire, and he stopped running.

The wind billowed around him, lashing the ferns and the leaves of the overhanging trees like a tiny cyclone, then it blew itself out. Gaven looked down at the Eye of Siberys where it lay, nestled in the tiny crater of its impact, where the earth had formed a sheltering hand to hold it. Blackened ferns lined its bed, burned from its heat, still blowing out wisps of smoke that twisted and danced in the dying wind. He fell to his knees and stretched out a trembling hand to touch it.

It was warm, not hot as he'd feared. Its yellow surface shone with light reflected from the Ring of Siberys high above, and veins of gold in its heart pulsed with a light of their own. He scooped it up with both hands, holding it in front of him like a chalice full of holy water. As he stood, he heard thunderous footsteps behind him, and he pulled it close to his chest as he turned to face his companions.

Darraun reached him first, wild amazement in his eyes. He was breathing too hard to speak, and he bent over double to catch his breath before Haldren and the others reached them.

Gaven cradled the Eye of Siberys close. Its warmth spread through him and set his dragonmark tingling.

CHAPTER
10

"That was quite a run," Darraun said, trying to smile as he panted.

Gaven ignored him, his gaze fixed on the pulsing veins of gold in the heart of the dragonshard.

"Gaven?" No answer.

Darraun shot a nervous glance over his shoulder at Haldren, who ran as fast as his old legs could carry him. He was still a bow-shot away, though Senya and Cart were closer.

Stepping closer to Gaven, Darraun tried to get a good look at the crystal, good enough to analyze the magic in it. "Gaven, if you'll let me look at that . . ."

Gaven turned away, shielding the dragonshard against his chest, his eyes still glued to it.

Darraun put a hand on Gaven's shoulder. "Gaven, look at me." He shook him gently, then harder. Gaven pulled away but didn't raise his eyes.

"This is not good," Darraun muttered. "I'm sorry about this, Gaven." He swung his fist at Gaven's chin as hard as he could, hoping to snap Gaven out of this trance.

A deafening clap of thunder shattered the air, and Darraun found himself on his back two strides away from Gaven, gasping for breath. His ears rang, but he could still hear the footsteps approaching.

Senya and Cart stopped dead near where Darraun lay. Cart fell to one knee beside him.

"Are you injured?" the warforged asked, his voice heavy with concern. Darraun shook his head. "What did he do to you?"

Darraun sat up. Gaven still held up the hand he had used to block Darraun's punch, but his eyes remained focused on the dragonshard in his other hand. Senya stood behind Cart, staring at Gaven as if she were entranced. A clap of thunder rumbled somewhere in the distance.

"I'm not sure," he said. "I think the dragonshard is enchanting him somehow, so I tried to wrench his attention away from it. Evidently he's got some attention to spare—enough to defend himself anyway."

"Evidently," Cart said. He lifted Darraun to his feet and shifted his shield on his arm, his right hand coming to rest on the head of his axe.

"Do we need to take him down?" Senya whispered.

Darraun turned around just as Haldren caught up with them, breathing heavily from the exertion. "I don't think—" he started to say, but Haldren cut him off.

"Gaven!" Haldren stepped forward, extending a hand to Gaven. "Give me the Eye of Siberys now!"

To Darraun's surprise, Gaven looked up at the sorcerer, holding the dragonshard in his left hand, as far from Haldren as possible.

"Not until you tell me exactly what is going on," Gaven said.

* * * * *

Seeing the Eye of Siberys and touching it, Gaven's mind flooded with memories. There could be no doubt that it was the dragonshard of his visions—he had seen that crystal shard carved to a point and bound to an ash-black staff to form a spear. He'd seen it plunge into the twisting shadow body of the Soul Reaver, in fulfillment of the Prophecy—

There among the bones of Khyber the Storm Dragon drives the spear formed from Siberys's Eye into the Soul Reaver's heart.

As he continued gazing into the dragonshard's liquid depths, Gaven found himself very aware of the present. The Eye had earned its name. Staring into it was like opening a great eye onto the world. He saw Darraun approach, with the others straggling behind. He saw Darraun pulling his hand back for a punch, and it took little more than a thought for him to react, blocking the punch and knocking Darraun away, without ever looking up from the dragonshard. He saw as he had never seen before—he saw every living thing nearby, from the gibbons in the trees to the ants crawling along the ground. He saw each tree, the orchids nestled in their branches, the lianas coiled around their trunks, and the ferns shielding the earth.

And then he saw himself, far more clearly than ever before. He remembered who he was, the man he'd been before Dreadhold, before the memories of the other came and coiled in his mind. And he saw the man he'd become, stumbling along behind Haldren's lead in a fog of confusion or madness. He realized that he did not want to be that man any longer. It was time to confront Haldren, who had reached him and demanded the dragonshard.

"Not until you tell me exactly what is going on." Gaven stared into Haldren's pale blue eyes, which were open wide in surprise.

"Very well, Gaven," the sorcerer said. Gaven enjoyed seeing Haldren caught off guard. "Very well. We have no secrets here. What do you want to know?"

"You think Vaskar is the Storm Dragon of the Prophecy," Gaven said. "You're helping him raise the Sky Caves of Thieren Kor so that he can walk in the paths of the first ascendant and become a god. What's in it for you?"

"A noble enough goal in itself, don't you think?" Haldren had recovered his wits, and his voice was smooth.

"I don't know about Vaskar, but most people don't aspire to seize godhood out of a benevolent desire to make the world better," Gaven said.

"On the contrary, Gaven, most of us believe that the world would be a better place if we had the power to shape it according to our will."

"I'm sure you'd like the same power. How do you plan to get it?"

"In exchange for my aid in acquiring divine power, Vaskar has agreed to help me acquire power that is more temporal in nature."

"Which throne do you plan to seize?"

Haldren smiled. "The only throne worth holding."

Something gnawed at the edge of Gaven's mind—a fragment of the Prophecy, a flash of a vision or a nightmare, but he banished it. He would not be the madman any longer. "Thronehold?" he said. "A new Galifar?" Before the Last War, all Khorvaire had been united in a single empire ruled from Thronehold. The scions of old Galifar had warred for a century over the right to sit in that throne.

"Something like that, yes. You know that I appreciate your assistance, Gaven. I can assure you of a position of power in the new world."

"Why were you in Dreadhold?"

"For no worse crime than yours," Haldren whispered. Gaven could tell that he had struck a nerve. "I disagreed with our Queen Aurala over the way the war should be prosecuted."

"Sounds like you should have been stripped of your command, maybe thrown in an Aundairian jail. Why Dreadhold?"

Haldren's voice dropped to an urgent whisper, and he stepped closer to Gaven, speaking right into his face. "You were already imprisoned at the time, Gaven, but at the end of the war the nations decided they could put the horrors of the war behind them if they locked some people up. I was a scapegoat—they locked me up so they could believe that all the death and destruction was the work of criminals. I was fighting a war, damn it!"

"And now you're going to start the war all over again."

"It will be different this time. With Vaskar's help—"

Haldren reached out suddenly and tried to snatch the Eye of Siberys from Gaven's hand, but Gaven yanked the Eye back away from Haldren, simultaneously thrusting his other hand forward. There was another thunderclap, but this time Haldren only stumbled back a few steps, while Gaven flew backward, landing hard a few paces away.

Haldren smirked and strode to stand over Gaven. "I won't underestimate you again, Gaven." He crouched and took the Eye of Siberys from Gaven's limp hand. Gaven stared wildly up at the sorcerer, every nerve in his body tingling. "I expect the same consideration in return." He turned away, stowing the dragonshard in one of the many pouches he wore.

Gaven sat up and glared at the sorcerer's back, embarrassed that Haldren had gotten the shard from him so easily. Then he slowly got to his feet and looked around at the others. Senya had Haldren's arm, apparently congratulating Haldren, though she kept glancing back at Gaven too. Cart stood near Haldren as well, demonstrating his loyalty to his commanding officer, awaiting orders. Darraun had turned his back on the group and was looking at the surrounding jungle.

Gaven reviewed his situation. He was stuck on an unfriendly island with a war criminal who wanted to rule the world. And who, Gaven reminded himself, was his only means of getting back to the mainland. His most likely ally was Darraun, who was clearly hiding something, maybe a great deal. The warforged was completely loyal to Haldren—Darraun had said as much, and Cart's behavior reinforced it.

His eyes lingered on Senya. She was still something of a mystery to him, but the prospect of unraveling that mystery was starting to grow more interesting. She glanced back at him, caught his stare, and flashed him a coy smile before looking back at Haldren.

* * * * *

Haldren conferred briefly with Senya, then announced his plans.

"Tonight we'll make camp in the jungle," he said, "but not here. We need to get far enough from the city that the elves will leave us alone."

"And far enough that we won't be bothered by treasure-seekers scouring the jungle for dragonshards," Senya added.

"We need supplies," Haldren said with a glare at Darraun, "so Senya will return to the city and secure them. The rest of us can relax for a short time. As soon as Senya returns, we march."

With that, he settled himself onto the ground. He was still breathing heavily from his exertion, Gaven saw, which gave him a slight feeling of satisfaction. Cart stood guard by his general, and Darraun busied himself with his pack, preparing for another march. Gaven sat as far away from Haldren as he thought the sorcerer would allow—still in sight and earshot.

He closed his eyes and imagined that he still held the Eye of Siberys, trying to remember the thoughts and feelings it had stirred in him. He'd seen the man he was before, and he clung to that memory—a sense of self that kept him in the present. But over and over he found his thoughts straying to what he had not seen: the man he could become.

In his youth, before he'd taken and failed the Test of Siberys, he'd had a clear idea of his future, even if it was not one that he would choose. His father expected him to manifest the Mark of Storm and work for House Lyrandar. Arnoth had groomed his eldest son to take over his dynasty, ignoring every indication that Gaven would have preferred a different life.

Failing the Test of Siberys had given Gaven an excuse to pursue something different, and Rienne had given him the opportunity. Together they explored the depths of Khyber—still working for House Lyrandar, but in a way of his own choosing. With Rienne at his side, he had never worried much about his future, as long as she was in it.

He saw Rienne at his side in Khyber's depths, holding a flickering torch up so he could read the words scratched into the cavern wall.

The Eye of Siberys lifts the Sky Caves of Thieren Kor from the land of desolation under the dark of the great moon, and the Storm Dragon walks in the paths of the first of sixteen.

He saw a great mass of stone suspended in the air, floating above a blasted wasteland. A storm churned the sky above him, and he thought he saw a dragon wheeling in the air. A flash of lightning showed him bronze scales.

"We march, Gaven. Come!" Haldren's barked command jerked him out of his vision, and for a moment he was in his cell in Dreadhold. Then the walls dissolved into jungle, and he scrambled to his feet.

* * * * *

They walked through the jungle in the cold light of the Ring of Siberys, Cart and Senya leading the way. Gaven counted his footsteps as he'd done in the exercise yard in Dreadhold, trying to keep his mind from straying. His count approached three thousand before Haldren finally called a halt and ordered Cart to pitch their tents.

Gaven helped Cart set up the camp, partly to keep his mind off other things, and partly because he simply enjoyed the quiet company of the warforged. They built a fire, which Darraun used to cook another fine meal. Gaven realized that he hadn't eaten since their luncheon in Whitecliff that afternoon, and just the smell of Darraun's cooking was a delight.

"In the morning we return to Khorvaire," Haldren announced as they ate.

"Where are we going next?" Gaven asked.

"Senya and I discussed that question earlier, and I am of the opinion that Darguun is the best possible destination for tomorrow's journey."

"Darguun?" Gaven asked. "The goblin lands?"

"Indeed," Haldren said. "Are you aware of the rebellion that carved the lands of Darguun as an independent entity?"

"I knew of the rebellion, yes. But I assumed that those lands were destroyed along with the rest of Cyre."

"They were not. And the goblin leader, Haruuc, was recognized as ruler of a sovereign nation in the treaties that ended the war. It remains something of a frontier land, though, which is why it suits our purposes. We should be able to do business there without interference from the dragonmarked houses and their agents, who are presumably still searching for us across the length and breadth of Khorvaire."

"Darguun it is, then," Gaven said.

Haldren scowled at him. "I am glad you approve. And now we are going to bed." He got to his feet and extended a hand to Senya. "I suggest you all do the same—it has been a very long day."

Senya took his hand and kissed it. "I'll be there in a moment," she said, indicating the remainder of her meal. Haldren's scowl deepened, and he disappeared into his tent. Darraun took his pots over to a nearby stream to clean them, and Cart started patrolling a wide circle around the campsite. Gaven supposed he'd do that all night.

With a glance at the tent where Haldren waited for her, Senya set down her platter of food and reached for a large bundle beside her. Gaven watched as she pulled out a greatsword in a fine leather sheath and brought it over to him.

"I picked this up in the city," she said with a smile. "I thought you'd like to be armed before we get into another fight."

"Thank you, Senya," Gaven said. "That was very thoughtful." He pulled the blade a little way out of the sheath and admired the fine edge and elegant scrollwork. The pommel bore a skull decoration, which seemed fitting—given both the elves' preoccupation with death and the purpose of any weapon.

Senya stared into the dying fire. "I'm still a little confused about what happened back there," she said, pointing over her shoulder toward Shae Mordai. "Have you really been here before?"

"I think your ancestor mistook me for someone else."

"That hardly seems likely, does it? We go to them for their wisdom."

Gaven shrugged.

"Do you think Vaskar is really the Storm Dragon, Gaven?"

Gaven looked at her, and she turned from the fire to meet his eyes.

"I don't know," he said. "I think I've seen him in my dreams, the color of his scales." The color of his scales—that thought sparked something in his mind. The Bronze Serpent . . .

He shook his head. Here and now, he told himself. Stop living in dreams and memories.

"I thought he was at first," Senya said, "but I don't think so any more." She looked back into the fire.

"You think this is all a fool's errand?" Gaven said. "Then why go along with it?"

"Well, even if Vaskar fails, Haldren still has a chance at getting what he needs. And besides," she said, "I didn't say it was a fool's errand." She looked at him sidelong. "Want to know what I think?"

"What do you think, Senya?"

Haldren bellowed from inside the tent. "Senya!"

She leaped to her feet but stopped to look down at Gaven again. "I think the Storm Dragon is you."

CHAPTER
11

W hen Darraun returned from the stream, he found Gaven staring into the embers of the fire. He saw Cart walking his tireless circle outside the camp, and waved to him as he came near. He sank down on the fallen log beside Gaven.

"Quite a day," he said.

Gaven made a sound a little like a laugh and nodded.

"This time last night I was landing a wyvern on top of Dreadhold."

"How did you end up a part of all this, Darraun?"

"Haldren figured the group needed someone with my skill set, to work on Dreadhold's defenses. And help keep everyone alive, I suppose. He planned the whole thing from his cell, you know."

"How did he do that? We were kept in the Spellward Tower—he couldn't use any magic there."

"Not in his cell, no. Except the magic of his tongue. You've probably noticed by now that he could talk a sphinx into answering its own riddle for him. So partly he persuaded the guards to help him out. And he also used some magic to talk to Vaskar, when he was out of his cell for exercise and such. Again, he talked his way out of the usual restraints and the constant supervision."

Gaven shook his head. "So he told Cart and Senya to find an artificer, and they got you?"

"Senya talked to people in Aundair who were loyal to Haldren, and my name came up."

Gaven turned to look at him—a little too closely, Darraun thought. "You made sure your name would come up," Gaven said.

Darraun let a trace of a smile show on his face. "What do you mean?" he said.

Gaven shrugged. "So are you a true believer in Haldren's cause?

Anxious to see him sitting on the throne of a new Galifar? Or are you just along for the ride?"

"Something like that."

"Something like which one?"

"What were we talking about?"

Gaven arched an eyebrow at him and stopped asking questions.

"So," Darraun said, "now that you know all about Haldren's plans, what are you going to do?"

"Do?" Gaven scratched his chin. "At this point, it seems I'm along for the ride whether I like it or not."

"I take it you don't like it."

"It's better than Dreadhold, but I don't look forward to spending the rest of my life on the run from Sentinel Marshals. If I'm going to be free, I'd like to be really free."

"And you think helping Haldren will get you there?"

Gaven scoffed. "No. I think helping Haldren will get me dead."

"So you're along for the ride for now. Not long-term."

"Why am I telling you all this?"

"Because I could talk a sphinx into answering its own riddle for me."

"I thought that was Cart."

Darraun laughed. "Don't underestimate Cart's powers of persuasion."

"Believe me, I don't. I saw the way he jumped at that . . . thing." Gaven gestured out toward the surrounding jungle.

"The displacer beast? Yeah, Cart can handle himself in a fight."

Gaven stared into the dying embers.

Darraun shifted so he could see Gaven more easily. "What would you do if you were really free?"

Gaven raised his eyebrows, but he didn't look away from the fire. "I have no idea," he said.

"You didn't spend the last twenty-six years making plans?"

Gaven shook his head. "It never occurred to me that I might get out of there. I spent that whole time . . . I don't know. I wasn't thinking about the future." His brow furrowed. "Well, I wasn't thinking about my future."

"Just the Prophecy."

"Right."

"The future of the world, the future of countless people whose names you don't know. Great events and terrible cataclysms. And no idea where you fit in to it all."

"I never would have thought it had anything to do with me," Gaven said, looking up. "The Prophecy was just a hobby for me, until—" He broke off and looked back to the fire.

"Until what?"

"I don't know. Until I was in Dreadhold and had nothing else to think about."

Darraun cursed to himself. He'd been so close, but he'd pushed too hard and Gaven had shut him out again. Until . . . what? he wondered. What had made the Prophecy take such a hold over Gaven's mind?

And how could he not know his own part in it?

* * * * *

Haldren roused them early and set Cart to work packing up the camp. Gaven found it increasingly difficult to sit around the campfire and eat with these people. He'd fought with Haldren when he found the Eye of Siberys, and he was chafing under the sorcerer's barked commands and patronizing explanations. He'd shown a little too much of his thoughts to Darraun last night. And Senya kept looking at him in a way that made him distinctly uncomfortable. After eating as quickly as he could, he got up to help Cart roll up the tents.

All too soon they stood in a close circle again. Senya held Gaven's right hand and Darraun his left, and both seemed as though they believed Gaven could understand a secret language of squeezing his hands. He almost pulled both hands free in frustration just as Haldren completed the spell and brought them, in the blink of an eye, to Darguun.

The hobgoblin lands presented a stark contrast to the steaming jungles of Aerenal. The air was no less sweltering, even so early in the morning. But the towering trees and lush ferns were replaced by dry grasses, stunted shrubs, and barren outcroppings of red and gold rock.

"The Torlaac Moor," Haldren announced.

Gaven surmised that Haldren was the only one of the group who had been here before. The rest looked around at the alien landscape with curiosity and perhaps fear.

Haldren gestured to the rising sun. "To the east is the Khraal rain forest, which is not too different from the jungle we just left on Aerenal." Gaven could see a green haze on the horizon he supposed might be the canopy of a distant jungle.

"Jaelarthal Orioth," Senya said. "The Moonsword Jungle."

"I'm not sure what Khraal means in the Goblin tongue," Haldren said. "It probably describes a peculiar form of disembowelment, knowing their language. And knowing the jungle, for that matter." He turned and pointed in the opposite direction. "To the west, the Seawall Mountains divide this land from Zilargo. Just north of here, the Torlaac River marks the end of the moor, and wide plains make up the rest of the goblin lands. Far to the north, goblins dwell in ruined cities built by the good people of Cyre. Beyond that region, to the east, is the Mournland."

"I see no settlements nearby," Gaven said. "Where are we supposed to get supplies?"

"Have faith, Gaven," Haldren said with a patronizing smile. "As I did when we journeyed to Whitecliff and Aerenal, I chose a destination outside of a settlement and out of sight, lest our sudden appearance startle the natives. And far better to startle an elf in Aerenal than some bugbear going about his business in Darguun."

He laughed at his own joke, and Senya smiled at him. Darraun and Cart were busy scanning the horizon.

"In any case," Haldren continued, "there's a small town on the river just down in the valley there, to the north. It carries the rather quaint name of Grellreach."

"Grellreach?" Gaven said. "I don't understand."

Haldren started walking to the north, with Senya and Cart falling into place beside him. Clearly, Cart was not going to allow Haldren to fall victim to another surprise attack.

"Grells are hideous aberrations said to dwell in the Seawalls near here," Haldren explained as he walked. "They've been described as flying brains with beaklike mouths and long, barbed tentacles. Can you imagine living in a town named after such a thing?"

"I take it that it was not originally a Cyran settlement," Darraun said with a wry smile.

Haldren laughed. "No, it was not."

* * * * *

The spell had set them down a considerable distance from Grellreach, despite Haldren's easy confidence. They walked through the morning, with the sun growing hotter as it neared its zenith, before they even came into sight of the town. They walked through fields of grain nestled between the wreckage of ancient settlements and monuments. Wheat stalks brushed up against weather-beaten blocks of reddish stone, the vague outlines of long-fallen buildings. Here and there a farmhouse stood at the feet of an ancient colossus, clearly built from stone salvaged from the toppled statue. Gaven had to remind himself that, as easy as it might be to think of the goblins of these lands as brutal savages, they had once ruled a mighty empire that stretched across the length and breadth of Khorvaire.

Farmhouses appeared more often, and at last the party came within sight of the town's wooden palisade. Haldren called a halt. "We need to be careful how we approach," he said. "I'm certain I can get us all inside, if we're careful and play it right. People of Darguun are not generally fond of elves—and I have no idea how they'll react to Cart. So Darraun and I will draw near the gate first. And I will do the talking," he added, with a commanding glare in Darraun's direction.

Darraun nodded, and the two of them closed the remaining distance to the town. Cart took a few long paces after Haldren, then dropped to one knee to wait and watch. Gaven found himself more or less alone with Senya. She gazed after Haldren too, and Gaven shifted uncomfortably.

"It's funny," she said, without turning toward him. "Haldren was in Dreadhold for three years, and he's basically had only one thing on his mind since he got out. You were there, what? Twenty-six?" She turned to face him now. "And you're afraid to look at me. I'm starting to wonder if you found a way to become deathless while you were locked up."

Gaven felt his face flush, and he turned away from her.

"Or is it your destiny that keeps you focused on higher things?"

she said. He heard her step closer behind him, and he swallowed hard. "The Storm Dragon must have more important concerns—the realm of the spirit, not the flesh." Another step, and he could feel her presence close to him, electrifying, like a storm brewing overhead.

Gaven found it strangely hard to speak. "I'm not the Storm Dragon, Senya," he said. "I'm just a book in which the Prophecy is written."

He heard the creak of her leather coat behind him and felt her light touch on his shoulder, tracing his dragonmark where it disappeared beneath the collar of his shirt. "And written on," she said. Her finger tugged on his collar as she traced the dragonmark downward. "But who wrote it, I wonder?"

Gaven closed his eyes, and Rienne was there with him, touching him, letting him lose himself in her skin. He felt Senya's hands on his chest, and she pressed herself against his back. He pulled away, whirling to face her again.

"You don't want me," he said, shaking his head violently and looking down at the ground. "You want the power you think I represent. You're wrong about me, Senya."

She stepped close again and breathed into his ear. "So what if I am? What do you want, Gaven?" She put a hand on his chest and started to slide it downward.

He took her shoulders in his hands and gently pushed her away, looking straight into her bright blue eyes. "I don't want you," he said.

He couldn't quite read the expression that twisted her face. It was clear that she wasn't used to being refused, and her hurt pride made her angry and defensive. But her eyes held something else, something that her anger couldn't quench.

"Senya!" Cart's voice surprised them both, and Gaven saw Senya's pale skin flush red. "Gaven!" the warforged called. "Haldren is signaling! Time to move!"

Gaven wondered how much Cart had seen or heard, and what he'd tell the Lord General. His mind filled with a string of curses directed at Senya and himself, even as his feet carried him quickly to the gate of Grellreach.

CHAPTER
12

D arraun took in the scene while he waited with Haldren for
Gaven and the others to catch up. His travels had taken
him over most of Khorvaire, to Xen'drik a couple of times,
and now to Aerenal, but Darguun was a new experience. It wasn't
uncommon to see the three races of goblinkind—the burly bugbears, proud hobgoblins, and sniveling goblins—in the rougher
parts of many cities, and they were more common the closer you
came to the fringes of civilization. Here, though, they were everywhere, from the guards at the gate to the merchants hawking their
wares in ramshackle stalls that lined the main street.

Four hobgoblins stood proudly at the gate, wearing piecemeal
armor—mismatched plates and bits of chain over a basic suit of
leather—that was at least clean and well maintained. They leaned
on polearms that were as motley as their armor, watching impassively as Haldren led the group through the gate. The guards were
all almost a head taller than Darraun and looked considerably
stronger, so he was glad that Haldren had so easily talked his way
past them. Just past the gate stood a bugbear who looked like he was
normally kept chained and as if he might begin a savage rampage
at any moment—head and shoulders taller than the hobgoblins,
covered in matted fur, and armed with a wickedly serrated sword.
Despite his appearance, he too let them pass without incident.

If one could forget that all the citizens of this town were
goblinkind, Darraun reflected, it would not seem very different
from Whitecliff. The buildings were constructed from stone
blocks salvaged from the surrounding ruins, but they were well
made. Street vendors hawked food, clothing, and tools from
push-carts and wagons pulled by donkeys or oxen. Many of the
buyers were women, and children ran and played on the rutted
dirt streets.

One thing made this place different from Whitecliff in a way that Darraun didn't like. People stared at them wherever they walked—particularly at Cart, he noticed—and Darraun squirmed under their curious gaze. He had made a living out of blending in, and to be attracting so much attention made him nervous.

"Senya and I will get the supplies," Haldren said as they made their way down the town's main street. "We won't spend the night here, so there's no point in getting a room—even assuming we could find one that would take us." He called a halt in front of an open-air building—some sort of restaurant or tavern by the looks of it—crowded with rowdy hobgoblins, probably drunk even in the early afternoon. "Why don't you three find a table here and pass the time until we're finished?"

Some of the nearby hobgoblins stared at Cart and pushed out their chests in a way that Darraun recognized as a sign of aggression, so he wasn't sure Haldren's idea was a good one. But the sorcerer was already walking away, his arm locked around Senya's waist. "And watch your tongues," Haldren said over his shoulder, shooting a glare at Gaven.

With a sigh, Darraun led the way to a table in the quietest corner of the place, making a wide circle around the aggressive hobgoblins near the street. "Do either of you speak Goblin?" he mumbled as they took their seats.

Gaven shook his head, and Cart said, "A few words—the kind soldiers throw around."

"Let me order, then," Darraun said, as a rail-thin goblin woman approached the table.

"Azhra dam?" Her voice was a high growl.

"Two ales," Darraun answered in Goblin, and the goblin woman vanished in the crowd.

"I hope Haldren comes back quickly," Gaven muttered.

"I agree," Darraun said. "Cart, some of these men were looking at you in a way I didn't like."

"I noticed that," the warforged said, "but I'm used to it."

"Kak-darzhul!" Three of the hobgoblins Darraun had seen before stomped to their table, and the one in front addressed Cart. The warforged turned to face the one who had spoken. He was almost as big as Cart, and his arms were as thick as Darraun's legs.

"He doesn't speak Goblin," Darraun said, pronouncing his words carefully to avoid any insult.

"Tell him I think his ancestors' swords couldn't cut the tail from a lizard," the hobgoblin said.

Darraun started to explain the hobgoblin's insult to Cart, but the warforged interrupted, rising to his feet. "Your ancestors couldn't sharpen sticks to use as spears," Cart said in perfect Goblin.

Darraun bit back a laugh. Naturally, the language of insults would be what Cart had learned from goblin soldiers.

The hobgoblin pounded his chest with one fist, raising the other hand toward Cart. Cart mimicked the gesture, and the onlooking goblins backed up, making a wide circle with Cart and their leader at the center. Cart and the hobgoblin clasped hands and started to push.

Darraun had never seen this form of contest before, but it was easy enough to see what was going on. Right palms together, each man pushed to his left, trying to force his opponent off balance. Their feet were firmly planted on the dirt floor, so Darraun surmised that a single step would mean defeat.

He also quickly saw what he hoped none of the goblins could discern: Cart was holding back. He would win eventually, but he was letting the goblin feel that the contest was a close one. Darraun smiled. Cart continued to impress him, demonstrating an amazing sympathy for the emotions of flesh-and-blood people.

A dozen goblins circled the contestants, shouting, laughing, and making wagers on the outcome. Cart showed no sign of exertion, of course, but his opponent grunted as his biceps bulged, veins pulsing. He leaned in closer, baring sharp fangs in Cart's face and snarling to intimidate him. Unfazed, Cart bent his legs to lower his center of gravity, and with one last push he sent the hobgoblin sprawling on the ground. Cart gave his chest one more resounding thump and returned to his seat, among the yells and jeers of the onlookers.

A quick glance around confirmed Darraun's suspicion that a lot of money had just changed hands. He figured that meant that their chances of nursing their drinks in peace were almost zero, and his fears were confirmed when a big bugbear stepped into the circle, drawing a chorus of loud cheers.

The bugbear pointed at the defeated hobgoblin, who tried to

slink away. "Prax is so stupid he doesn't know that the kak-darzhul have no ancestors," the bugbear growled.

Many in the crowd laughed, but several looked with wide eyes toward Cart, wondering how he would respond to what they considered a grievous insult.

Cart leaned close to Darraun and whispered, "What did he say?"

Darraun translated, and Cart stood up. "Well, I wasn't drinking anyway," he said with a sigh. In Goblin, he addressed his challenger. "I'd rather have no ancestors than have ancestors too weak to throw stones."

The crowd murmured a mixture of approval and offense, and the bugbear roared as he pounded his chest. Cart seized his outstretched hand, and the contest began. Darraun could see that the warforged had found a closer match, but he predicted another victory. From what he could hear of the wagering, it seemed the bettors favored the bugbear, and Darraun briefly considered placing a bet.

Again, Cart gave the appearance of a good fight before forcing the bugbear off balance. The big man took two steps and didn't fall, but it was no less humiliating a defeat. More money changed hands, sending the music of clinking coins all around the circle. Challengers began to line up. Darraun looked around for the ale he'd ordered—if he was going to watch fights all afternoon, he wanted to do it with a drink in his hand.

He didn't see the goblin who had taken his order, but Gaven caught his eye. The half-elf watched intently as the next contest began, and Darraun watched the muscles in his arm flexing. Did he want to get in on the action? he wondered.

Cart defeated four more challengers, and the crowd grew boisterous. The next one in line showed some hesitation, to the derision of the onlookers, and Gaven got to his feet before Darraun could stop him.

"All right, Cart," Gaven said, "I don't know the formalities of the challenge here, but I know how to do the wrestling." He beat his chest as he'd seen the goblins do and raised a hand to Cart.

"Well, I should think of some way to insult your ancestors," Cart said, "but I'm afraid I'm running out of ideas. And I have nothing but respect for House Lyrandar, in general."

"Chaos take House Lyrandar," Gaven said, "and your makers in House Cannith, for that matter. Let's do this."

Cart beat his chest, seized Gaven's hand, and started to push. Gaven pushed back, hard, and Cart had to stop holding back. Darraun's mind flashed back to the jungle, the previous night, when he'd tried to punch Gaven and ended up flat on his back. He imagined for a moment that he heard a rumble of thunder in the clear blue sky.

The bets favored the warforged now. "I could have made a fortune here today," he muttered to himself, shaking his head. "I've never seen people so eager to make losing wagers."

It was over quickly. Cart's left foot shifted slightly, then he stepped back with his right. A silence fell over the crowd, then the few spectators who had won money started to cheer, and then the circle closed. Hobgoblins and bugbears swarmed around Cart and Gaven, jabbering at them in Goblin, throwing out a few words of congratulations—and curses—in Common. Darraun smiled. They'd won their acceptance.

They had also attracted a great deal of attention, which had been exactly what Darraun had hoped to avoid. Still, there was no sign of Sentinel Marshals appearing on the scene, no city watch coming to investigate the disturbance, no brawl breaking out. He was starting to like Darguun.

* * * * *

Gaven spotted Senya first, peering around the edges of the bar, looking for them. Haldren hung back, wearing new clothes. Both of them carried new backpacks loaded with goods. Gaven looked down at his own worn shirt and breeches, the same clothes he'd been wearing in Dreadhold before his release. At least he had a sword.

Haldren and Senya were having a hard time finding him, surrounded as he was by rowdy goblins waiting their turn to buy him a drink. Gaven stood, prompting some shouts from people nearby.

"Haldren!" he called. "Over here!"

Haldren looked around, spotted Gaven, and scowled. He hit Senya's shoulder and pointed at Gaven, started toward the unruly crowd, then thought better of it, waving impatiently in Gaven's direction.

"Cart, Darraun," Gaven said, "our escort has returned."

Cart leaped to his feet, breaking the hold of a trio of inebriated hobgoblins who had been draping themselves over his shoulders, trying to get the warforged to drink. Darraun was not thronged by as many admirers—his command of Goblin and his ready wit had won him some friends, but those qualities were not as impressive to the goblins as the sheer strength Gaven and Cart had demonstrated—so he was able to extricate himself from the crowd and get over to Haldren quickly.

Gaven waded through the crush. With every step, goblins grabbed at his hands and jabbered at him, making him wish he could understand a word of Goblin. He hoped it was compliments or well-wishes they threw his way, rather than insults and challenges, but he figured he would never know. The crowd closed behind him as he passed, and he realized with a smile that their departure wasn't going to quiet the party.

"Would you care to explain that spectacle?" Haldren said to Darraun as Gaven drew near. His voice was a threatening whisper.

"Well," Darraun said, "a hobgoblin challenged Cart to a kind of wrestling match, which Cart won. Then he beat a bugbear, then people were lining up to challenge him. Then Gaven—"

"Relax, Haldren," Gaven interrupted. "We kept our mouths shut, and no one here cares a damn who we are or who wants to find us. Looks like you two got what we need. We stayed out of trouble and had a little fun. No harm done. Let's get on our way."

"I will be the judge of what incidents are important or otherwise," Haldren said. "And I will remind you, Gaven, that I am in command of this expedition."

Gaven took a step toward Haldren and looked into his weathered face. "I don't like taking orders, Haldren. I'm not a good little soldier. I never obeyed my father. And the fact that you orchestrated my escape from Dreadhold doesn't mean that you own me."

Haldren's face went purple with fury as he returned Gaven's stare. "Perhaps it would be best if you continued to think of yourself as a prisoner, then. I wouldn't want you getting ideas that you are free to travel about as you please. You are part of this expedition whether you like it or not."

His eyes rested on the pommel of the sword slung on Gaven's back, as if he were noticing it for the first time.

"Where did you get that sword?" he whispered.

Gaven reached over his shoulder and drew the blade out of its sheath, without moving away from Haldren. "You like it?" he said. "Senya got it for me in Shae Mordai."

"Senya?" Haldren whirled on her. "You armed this madman?"

Senya stood her ground to Gaven's surprise—and, evidently, to Haldren's as well. "I thought it would help our cause if he didn't get torn to shreds by another pack of displacer beasts," she said.

Haldren's fury was palpable as he turned back to Gaven. "Clearly, I underestimated you. I took you for an idiot with nothing in your mind but the Prophecy, and now even Senya is doing you favors. But listen to me, Gaven—all of you, listen well. This isn't about the Prophecy or Vaskar's dreams of godhood. It's about my destiny, and I will not be denied what is due me. If you think for a moment of standing in my way, I will crush you. Any of you," he added, with a glance toward Senya. "Don't question whether I can or really will." He thrust a finger into Gaven's chest. "I will snuff your life like a candle."

In his mind, Gaven saw himself bringing his sword around, cutting right into Haldren's belly so he would die slowly and in great pain. The hand holding the sword tightened, the muscles flexed, his other hand itched for a grip on the smooth leather of the hilt. Something held him back, though. Perhaps it was just his better judgment, or the stares of the goblins who were circling them, watching the argument even if they couldn't understand the language. But some part of Gaven's mind whispered words of the Prophecy.

Gaven growled as he slid the sword back into its sheath. He took some pleasure, at least, in seeing the briefest flinch cross Haldren's face as the huge blade swung past. Several people in the crowd groaned with disappointment.

Gaven pushed his way through the encircling goblins and strode toward the gate of Grellreach. "Lead on, then, Haldren," he said.

CHAPTER
13

Haldren led them a short way outside of town, then gathered them into a circle. Gaven brooded as he walked, and the others seemed happy to share his silence.

"What's our next destination, Lord General?" Cart asked. The warforged was the only one who didn't seem subdued after the confrontation, and Gaven wondered what he had thought of Haldren's threats.

Haldren didn't answer. He seized Senya's hand in his left and Darraun's in his right and began the now-familiar chant of his spell without waiting for the others. Cart and Gaven quickly closed the circle. Senya clung fiercely to Gaven's hand before Haldren completed the spell that yanked them through space once again.

They stood in a mountain valley, barren rock stretching up on two sides. The bands of red and gold in the cliff faces suggested that they had not traveled far from the Torlaac Moor with its outcroppings of similar stone. Haldren gazed upward at something behind Gaven, so Gaven spun around, pulling his hand from Senya's grasp.

A towering ruin loomed before them, what had once been a grand city nestled among the mountains. A broken wall formed a ring at the head of the valley, each end blending seamlessly into a cliff wall. A gate was built into the wall on a massive bridge straddling a dry river bed. Colossal statues flanked the gate, mostly crumbled away but still showing traces of what looked like gnome features. The carvings were odd, and Gaven stared at them for a long moment trying to puzzle them out.

"Paluur Draal," Haldren announced. "We are high in the Seawall Mountains now, in land claimed by Zilargo. This city is one of the most important ruins of the ancient goblin Empire of Dhakaan in Khorvaire. Scholars from the Library of Korranberg have explored and catalogued it extensively, but they say there are many secrets yet to uncover."

"And what are we doing here?" Gaven said.

"We are looking for a map," Haldren said. "Specifically, one that will point us to the Sky Caves of Thieren Kor."

"So if this is a Dhakaani ruin," Senya said, "why are there gnomes guarding the gates?" She was staring at the same carvings that had puzzled Gaven.

"Those carvings were originally hobgoblins, or perhaps bugbears. However, several races inhabited Paluur Draal over the centuries—kobolds, humans, and gnomes most recently. By the time the gnomes settled here, the original statues were worn to mostly smooth pillars, so the gnomes carved them again in their own image."

"And where are we going to find this map?" Gaven said.

"We're going to look for it, as I said."

"Out here?"

Haldren didn't answer, but started walking toward the gate. Cart followed on his heels, with the others trailing more slowly after.

Heavy drops of rain began to fall as they entered the ruins, forming tiny craters in the dry earth. Gaven glowered up at the slate gray sky with a sense of satisfaction. Anger brewed like a storm in his mind, furrowing his brow and hunching his shoulders, and the rain seemed like a proper complement to his mood. He flexed his hands and arms as he walked, itching for a fight—for anything that would let him give vent to his frustration. He was tempted to attack Haldren outright, but he doubted he could take the sorcerer, Senya, and Cart by himself. He wondered which side Darraun would take.

So intent was his glare at Haldren's back that he barely saw the ruined city as they walked through it. He had an indistinct impression of stone buildings in varying states of ruin, none too different than what they'd passed in the fields outside Grellreach. They wandered along streets paved with shattered cobblestones and clambered over piles of rubble that blocked their way, and slowly made their way toward the cliff face at the back edge of the ancient city.

But Gaven noticed no details, took in none of the grandeur. His attention was solely on Haldren's back, imagining his new blade striking the sorcerer down. Despite his rage, Gaven couldn't swallow striking anyone in the back. He'd draw the sword, call for Haldren's attention, give the man a moment—no more—to ready himself, then bring the blade across and down. No. A quick death would be too good for Haldren. Gaven imagined summoning the fury of the storm itself, lightning falling to blast the sorcerer's smug grin from his face.

Thunder rumbled in the distance, and Gaven could feel the burning tingle of the storm coursing through him. He smiled and opened his mouth to call for Haldren—

A mountain troll emerged from a fissure in the cliff face. The troll's gray hide was covered with warty bumps like gravel. It was three times Gaven's height when it reared up, bellowing a rumbling roar, then it shambled forward using one rubbery hand to help it over the slippery ground, a splintered log held in the other hand.

At last! Here was the chance Gaven had been craving. The attack of the displacer beasts had caught him unprepared, the argument with Haldren had filled him with rage; but now he had a sword in his hand and a reason to fight. Gaven looked up at the enormous creature. A grim smile lit his face, and lightning flickered above them.

Then the creature's smell—a mix of carrion and excrement—hit him and nearly knocked him off his feet. Gaven was glad for the sword in his hand but nervous about his lack of armor. He circled to one side and let Cart take the brunt of the troll's initial charge.

With a word, Gaven made crackling lightning erupt along his elven blade. He ran forward, put all of his rage and frustration into his swing, and brought the sword around in a wide arc. The blade bit deep, and the lightning coursed up the creature's body. It howled in pain. Gaven glanced behind it—and noticed two smaller trolls emerging from the cave entrance. Perhaps that first roar hadn't been anger but a command, summoning the creature's followers to its aid.

"More on the way!" Gaven shouted.

The mountain troll's club came at him, and Gaven ducked, feeling the wind from the massive limb sweep over him. His attack had drawn the troll's attention. Either that, or the creature was smart enough to recognize an unarmored foe as a soft target. Following the big troll's lead, the other two moved in.

Gaven looked up at the trolls surrounding him. The big one was twice the size of the other two, but even the smaller ones were head and shoulders taller than him. Their claws reached for him even as the mountain troll raised its club.

Gaven kept his sword up, batting aside the smaller trolls' tentative slashes and grabs. The trolls stepped back, and Gaven dodged as the massive club came crashing down. He knew he couldn't outlast them in a hand-to-hand fight. They were too big, too fast, and too damned strong.

He focused his mind and chanted the syllables of another spell. Gaven's body erupted in violet flames, and the rain hissed into steam as it touched him. All three trolls recoiled.

The mountain troll turned from Gaven with a grunt and swung its club hard into Cart. The warforged took a couple of steps back, then shook off the blow and renewed his assault. Senya darted around the mountain troll's feet, finding its most vulnerable spots, the weaker parts of its thick, stony hide, and slashing at them with her light blade.

The two smaller trolls overcame their initial shock at the appearance of flames around Gaven, and one took a swipe at his back. The claws raked his skin, but the troll roared in pain as the violet flames engulfed its claws, searing its rubbery flesh. Both trolls backed away. Gaven brandished his sword with a roar of his own, and they scurried further back, unwilling to be seared by Gaven's fire.

"Gaven!" shouted Haldren.

Gaven tumbled and rolled back the merest instant before an eruption of flame struck the trolls, Even so, it seared him badly—the flames around his body burned the trolls that attacked him, but did nothing to protect him from other fires. He got back to his feet in a fury. Haldren had cast the spell, he was sure, and didn't seem to mind that Gaven had been caught in the blast. Despite his rage, Gaven had to admit that the spell had been effective. Both smaller trolls lay on the ground, their unmoving bodies charred black from the flames, and the mountain troll showed signs of serious injury. It could have been much worse.

Thunder rolled overhead, and Gaven leaped at the giant troll, channeling all his anger into each swing of his blade. It dropped to one knee, nearly overwhelmed, and Senya ran up its back to drive her sword into the base of its skull. The troll fell hard, throwing Senya to sprawl on the ground, but it did not move again. The fight was over. As Gaven tried to catch his breath, silence fell back over the ruins of Paluur Draal.

Gaven whirled on Haldren. "So what is it, Haldren? Are you dragging me along to help you on your fool's quest, or do you want to get rid of me?" He stood nose to nose with the old man again, and grabbed a fistful of Haldren's shirt. "Because if you want to get rid of me, I'll go. There's no need to kill me."

"Don't be absurd, Gaven."

"Absurd? You nearly blasted me into the fires of Fernia!"

"Hardly," Haldren said.

Gaven suddenly felt like a small child getting a scolding, and his anger boiled. He pulled Haldren up so his toes just dragged on the ground. "I'm not an idiot, Haldren."

"Of course, Gaven." No trace of fear came through in Haldren's voice. "I wasn't trying to hurt you, certainly not kill you. I simply realized too late that you had moved into the area of my spell. I did try to warn you."

Gaven realized that his threatening steps toward the retreating trolls had taken him closer to the center of the fiery blast, so Haldren's excuse might have been true. That possibility did little to diminish Gaven's rage, though. He pushed Haldren away and stalked over to Darraun, who crouched on the ground beside Cart.

It seemed the troll had gotten one good blow in before it fell. Cart's left arm looked badly hurt—or did it hurt? Gaven realized he had no idea if the warforged felt pain. In any event, Darraun ran his hands over the damaged arm, and his touch straightened bent plates and knotted broken cords back together. It was amazing and strangely fascinating—although, he realized, it wasn't too different in principle from the way a healer's magic knit flesh and bone back together. That was just a magic he was more used to seeing.

While Darraun tended to his injuries, Gaven traced a finger in a groove that ran through the stone on which he sat. He didn't like to watch a healer's magic when it was his flesh being knit together. A flash of light drew his eyes up to Haldren, who had just cast a spell to brighten the darkness inside the cave from which the trolls had emerged.

"Finished," Darraun said, and he rose to join the others, who were gathered around the cave entrance, staring upward.

Gaven started to get to his feet, but the groove he'd traced caught his attention. He had run his finger along a straight part of the groove, but it was not straight for long—it traced the outline of Kraken Bay.

"Behold!" Haldren announced, sweeping his arm across the cave entrance. "The sixteen gods of Dhakaan!"

Gaven brushed a thin coat of mud away from the stone, his heart racing. He glanced up at Haldren, but the sorcerer was completely absorbed in the spectacle within the cave. He looked back at his work, smiled, and tried to sweep mud back over the map he had uncovered.

* * * * *

Darraun looked over Haldren's shoulder at the cavern beyond. The cave might have been natural in origin, but the ancient builders of the place had carefully enlarged it, hollowing the ceiling and smoothing the walls. The debris of a thousand years and the more recent remnants of the trolls' habitation littered the floor, but as Darraun's eyes followed the arches up he realized that the grandeur of the ancient city was far better preserved here than anywhere else they had been so far.

Sixteen enormous figures stood around the far wall, their stone heads near the ceiling and their feet a troll's height above the floor. Most of the figures were proud hobgoblins, dressed in archaic armor and carrying ornate weapons. Two loomed taller than the others, bugbears with their hairy hides and fang-filled mouths, and one goblin crouched near the center of the frieze, half the size of the burly bugbears. As Darraun looked, Haldren started naming them.

"On the left end is Norrakath the Hunter, who slew the great serpent and roped in the sea with its corpse. When humans first came to Khorvaire, they identified him with Balinor."

Norrakath was a fearsome bugbear, leaning on a bow that seemed to be made of the bones of some beast—perhaps the ribs of the great serpent. He was a far cry from any representation of Balinor Darraun had ever seen, though the god of the hunt was sometimes depicted as a half-orc. Balinor smiled in every depiction Darraun had seen. Norrakath, on the other hand, snarled like a beast.

Haldren continued. "Beside him is Uthrek the Keeper. He was so fearsome a god of death that the early humans adopted him completely into their beliefs, though his Goblin name disappeared. He remains the evil god of death, the Keeper."

Uthrek was so gaunt as to be almost skeletal, perhaps intended to be an undead hobgoblin. Darraun had seen the Keeper depicted in similar fashion, but he was more commonly shown as a grossly fat human, hungry for the souls of the dead and a god of greed as well as death.

"Kin to Uthrek, beside him is Korthrek the Devourer, likewise adopted into human myth as one of the Dark Six." The god of the stormy sea was a hobgoblin with the many-toothed jaws of a shark.

"Next is Tauroc the Hammer, god of the forge. Obviously identified with Onatar." Darraun was used to seeing Onatar depicted as a dwarf, but he could easily see the similarities between this hobgoblin smith and the burly Onatar. The god's hammer, in particular, appeared the same as in many modern depictions of the god.

"Then we have Kol Korran, or I should say Rantash Mul, the Thief." Darraun started in surprise—this hobgoblin bore no resemblance whatsoever to any depiction of Kol Korran. Perhaps modern humans valued trade more highly than the ancient hobgoblins did, because Rantash Mul was sickly, sinister, and unpleasant. Kol Korran, by contrast, was usually shown as fat and cheerful.

"Next is Dukash the Lawbringer, sort of a culture hero of the Dhakaani. I'm afraid we humans neutered him when we identified him with Aureon. His exploits as a hobgoblin are something to read about."

Darraun could see the contrast. Aureon was the god of knowledge as well as law, and he was usually depicted as a somewhat frail, elderly wizard—sometimes even as a gnome. Dukash, in contrast, was the most vibrant figure before them now. He looked ready to leap out of the frieze, and his craftiness shone in his eyes.

"And now we come to the great mystery of the Dhakaan Empire," Haldren said, pointing at the figure in the middle. Its body had the erect posture of a hobgoblin, though it was taller even than the hulking bugbears at either end. Its face, however, had been completely obliterated. "This god was the greatest of the goblin pantheon. When the humans conquered Khorvaire, they identified some goblin gods with their own gods—Aureon and Kol Korran, Onatar and the other Sovereigns. Six goblin gods worked their way into human myth as the Dark Six. This one alone was suppressed, forgotten, struck from written legend, and wiped from memory."

A voice at Darraun's shoulder startled him. "The first of sixteen." Darraun had not heard Gaven come up behind him.

"Yes, Gaven, the first of sixteen," Haldren said. "The Gold Serpent whom the world has long since forgotten."

It took Darraun a moment to remember where he had heard the words before, but then he could hear the cold, clear voice of Senya's deathless ancestor in his mind. Snippets of that strange conversation between Gaven and the undying elder flashed through his mind.

In the first age of the world, sixteen dragons transcended their mortal forms to become like the Dragon Above who had made them.

"Wait," Darraun blurted, causing Haldren to turn and face him. "Senya's ancestor said that sixteen dragons became gods in the first age of the world. So you're suggesting that these sixteen dragons were the gods of the goblins, and fifteen of those gods are also the gods of the Host and the Dark Six?"

"Indeed," Haldren said. "That is exactly what I am saying."

"But why was that sixteenth god forgotten?"

"That is the great mystery of Dhakaan. It might be that the god was so closely identified with the Dhakaani that the humans obliterated any record of him in order to quell any resistance from the goblins they conquered." Haldren paced as he spoke, and he sounded as though he were thinking out loud. "Perhaps they believed that wiping out all memory of the god would also extirpate all memory of the goblin empire. On the other hand, the words of Senya's ancestor suggest that the god himself abandoned the world. Perhaps he stopped granting spells to his clerics. Or perhaps the goblins grew convinced that their god had abandoned them in allowing their defeat at human hands, and they themselves obliterated his memory. It could be that he abandoned the world because the world forgot him."

"I'm still not clear on what happened with the other fifteen," Senya said. "You said the humans identified some gods with gods of the Host, and adopted others like the Keeper? Those are the Dark Six?"

"Exactly," Haldren said, putting a hand on Senya's back. "As far as we know, the first humans to come across the sea worshiped nine gods—the Sovereign Host. They encountered the goblin pantheon of sixteen gods, and apparently they were willing to believe that they had lived in ignorance of six more. But those six were the most destructive and evil of the fifteen, the Dark Six, and they were made inferior to the Sovereigns."

Darraun shook his head. "And all sixteen of these gods—the nine Sovereigns, the Dark Six, and the missing one—all of them were actually dragons who became gods during the first age of the world?"

"Correct. And according to the Prophecy, there's a vacancy in that roster of sixteen gods. Khorvaire will have a new god—Vaskar, the Storm Dragon. Right, Gaven?"

Darraun looked at Gaven. He was staring up at the statue with its marred face, apparently lost in a trance. Then his lips moved, but no sound came out.

"What was that, Gaven?" said Darraun. "What did you say?"

Gaven's voice was a whisper. "The Bronze Serpent seeks the face of the first of sixteen," he said. His voice trailed off, though his lips kept moving.

Haldren stepped forward, his face purple with rage, and slapped Gaven hard across the face. "Speak," he said, "so I can hear you."

Strong and clear now, Gaven repeated his earlier words. "The Bronze Serpent seeks the face of the first of sixteen." A wind stirred the stale air in the cave. "But the Storm Dragon walks in his paths. The Bronze Serpent faces the Soul Reaver and fails. But the Storm Dragon seizes the shard of heaven from the fallen pretender." The wind swirled around Gaven, kicking up a whirlwind of dust and pebbles around his feet and whipping his hair around his face.

The color drained from Haldren's face, and he took two steps backward, away from Gaven. "No," he murmured. "The Bronze Serpent . . . Vaskar is the Storm Dragon! He must be!"

Senya grabbed Haldren's arm. "But what if he's not, Haldren?"

"No!" Haldren's eyes were wild, and he stumbled backward. Cart took up a position between Gaven and Haldren, as if to ward his commander from an attack. Darraun stayed out of the way, watching and waiting to see how the situation played out.

"What if it's Gaven?" Senya clung to his arm, her voice an entreaty. "Look at him—the Mark of Storm he wears. The wind blows at his command, the rain outside—"

With another crash of thunder outside the cave, the wind swirling around Gaven died. Gaven slumped to his hands and knees and stared at the ground, shaking his head.

"You old fool," Gaven said, then lifted his eyes to Haldren. "Vaskar's not the Storm Dragon. You've hitched your chariot to the wrong horse."

Haldren found his feet and pulled his arm away from Senya's grasp. "And you think you're the one?"

Darraun couldn't read his voice—it might have been an accusation, but there was a hint of genuine wonder.

Gaven scoffed. "The Storm Dragon? No. No matter what Senya says."

The mention of her name made Haldren wheel on Senya. "You have betrayed me," he whispered.

"I'm trying to help you," Senya said. Darraun had expected her to cower in the face of his wrath, but she stood her ground and met his gaze. "Abandon Vaskar, Haldren. He's doomed to fail. It's not too late! If we work with Gaven—"

Senya broke off as Haldren turned his gaze back to Gaven, fury burning in his eyes. Gaven had dropped his head again and was staring at the ground. Haldren shook his head.

"No," he said. He grabbed Senya's hand and yanked her toward him, then reached out for Cart's hand. "Take hands. We're leaving."

Cart took Darraun's hand, and Darraun bent over Gaven, helping him to his feet and holding on to one hand. Senya gently took Gaven's other hand in hers.

Haldren began the words to his spell, and Darraun found himself lost in the rhythm of them. He looked around the troubled little circle. Haldren's eyes were closed as he focused on his spell;

he was suppressing his anger in order to keep his mind clear. Cart stared impassively ahead. Senya's eyes were on Gaven, her brow furrowed, and she clung to his hand. Gaven's head hung down, and Darraun couldn't see his eyes.

The spell built to its conclusion, and Darraun felt the first tugs that would carry them across hundreds of miles. In that instant, Gaven's hand wrenched free of his. Haldren shouted the last syllable of the spell as if he couldn't choke it back, and they were gone.

PART
II

In the Time of the Dragon Above,
when Siberys turns night into day,
and showers of light fall from the sky,
the Eye of Siberys falls near the City of the Dead.

A fragment of celestial light,
the Eye sees, and in it all is seen.

The Eye of Siberys lifts the Sky Caves of Thieren Kor
from the land of desolation
under the dark of the great moon,
and the Storm Dragon walks in the paths
of the first of sixteen.

The shard of heaven falls to earth a second time,
and its light brightens Khyber's darkness.

Chapter
14

Rienne stood at the railing of the small airship and gazed at the churning waters of Scions Sound far below. An unnatural storm blew out of the Mournland, churning the dead gray mist that marked the borders of that desolate wasteland into a roiling frenzy and sending long tendrils of smoky gray reaching for them. So far, the skill of the ship's windwright captain had kept the air around them calm—and free from the grasping reach of the mist. Rienne shuddered. The mist stood in her mind as a symbol of the mystery that cloaked the destruction of Cyre near the end of the Last War. It was impenetrable, inscrutable, and deadly. Within its embrace, nothing could survive for long. Wounds did not heal, plants did not grow, and horrible creatures born of flesh and metal warped by magic stalked the deserted ruins of the nation that had once been the jewel in Galifar's crown.

Securing the use of the Morning Zephyr had been a little tricky, but she'd managed it. It was primarily a matter of convincing her friends in House Lyrandar that Arnoth had authorized it, without letting Arnoth know that she'd borrowed the vessel. If Gaven's father knew that she was looking for Gaven, he'd want to be involved. And if he was involved, that Sentinel Marshal who had barged into her house would be involved soon after.

She told herself she would probably get the Sentinel Marshals involved soon enough anyway. After all, Gaven was a fugitive from Dreadhold. Whatever reservations she had about her role in getting him captured and convicted, the fact remained that he was a criminal. For all she knew, he might prove dangerous—even to her. Perhaps especially to her—the one responsible for turning him in to House Deneith in the first place. She might have to call in another favor once she reached Vathirond, to ensure her safety in case she actually found him.

"Lady Alastra?" The first mate's voice stirred her from her thoughts. She turned to see that the young man's face, normally smiling broadly, was creased with worry. "The storm is growing worse, and the captain isn't sure she can fend it off much longer. We might need to alter our course slightly, which could delay our arrival in Vathirond."

Rienne sighed. "A slight delay will probably not matter," she said.

"Yes, lady. In the meantime, the captain suggests you take shelter below." The young man smiled briefly, nodded a small bow, and disappeared back into the wheelhouse.

Rienne looked around the deserted deck. She had not even realized that the crew had left her alone, either in deference to her or in fear of the brewing storm. She turned around again and stared into the gray mist. Something stared back, she thought—something powerful and malevolent. She shuddered and made her way below.

Back in her cabin, the bundle of silk propped against her bed caught her eye immediately. She lifted it and sat on the bed, tenderly resting the bundle on her lap and carefully pulling at the wrappings. Beneath the silk was a fine leather scabbard tooled in gold, and she drew out the gleaming blade of her sword, the weapon she called Maelstrom. She removed a scrap of silk that caught on the blade as she drew it, and ran her finger carefully along the razor-sharp edge.

Rienne had not wielded Maelstrom in battle since the Sentinel Marshals had taken Gaven into custody. She had adopted the dress of a noblewoman and settled down in Stormhome. She had made herself useful to her family and lived a quiet and profitable life, making the most of her connections to House Lyrandar despite what she had done to Gaven.

But at least once a week, sometimes every night, she had closed the door to her chambers and brought out Maelstrom, polishing the blade and oiling the leather that wrapped its hilt. She kept it carefully wrapped and secure, in case she ever needed it. She hoped this journey wouldn't be such an occasion, but she was glad to have Maelstrom with her. Some part of her soul sang as she touched it again.

* * * * *

The storm threatening from the Mournland diminished as they made their way farther south, though their route took them alongside the dead-gray mist all the way to Vathirond. Rienne watched the city as it came into view—stone buildings forming tiers and bridges at the bases of its many tall towers, a gray metropolis set in stark contrast to the surrounding green hills—but her mind was consumed with thoughts of how she might find Gaven.

She started her search in the docking tower. A larger airship had docked at roughly the same time as her vessel, and she scanned the disembarking passengers carefully, on the off chance that Gaven was among them. She tried to anticipate the effects of twenty-six years in Dreadhold on his appearance, as well as any magic he might use to hide his face. More than a few passengers responded with nervous stares or angry rebukes as she tried to peer into cowls and under the wide brims of hats meant to conceal.

After one passenger drew steel, Rienne abandoned that approach, making her way through the crowds to the city streets. She ran down her mental list of contacts in Vathirond—distant relatives, people who owed favors to her family, and a few very old friends—and chose the most likely suspect. Looking around the streets, she quickly got her bearings and made her way to Subsidence, the neighborhood perched along the stream that flowed alongside the city, carrying its filth into the Brey River.

Krathas was a half-orc she believed had some connection to House Tharashk, though he didn't carry the Mark of Finding. His residence in Subsidence suggested that he didn't benefit much from this connection, and Rienne wondered if he were an excoriate like Gaven. She had never met Krathas, but Gaven had spoken of him a few times, and she had the impression that Gaven trusted him.

Setting foot in Subsidence reminded her of descending into Khyber. Danger was near—she could feel it—and she loosened Maelstrom's silk wrappings.

"Look, Marsh," an oily voice purred from an alley to her right, "we found ourselves a noble mouse. A half-elf mouse. Half elf, half mouse." The man laughed, loud and grating.

Rienne sank into a combat stance, and she could feel the hesitation already taking root in her opponents' minds. A quick glance showed her two assailants, emerging from the alleys on either side of her, and she heard a third trying to sneak up behind her. Keeping her attention on the position of the three attackers, she pulled again at Maelstrom's wrappings, trying to free the hilt so she could pull the blade loose.

"Ooh, the mouse has been to fencing school." It was the same one that had spoken before, foolishly drawing attention to himself before he was close enough to attack. He was a lanky human with a weirdly asymmetrical look to him, like one side of his body had grown just a bit faster than the other. He sort of half limped, half shuffled toward her, a leering smile spread across his angular face.

"I'm not sure about this, Jad." The one coming in from her left was an orc, clearly brought in on the operation for his size and strength, though he displayed more sense than his leader at that moment.

Jad responded to Marsh's hesitation the best way he could imagine: he shouted, "Get her!" and sprang forward, his gangly arms flailing wildly. He held a wavy-bladed dagger in each hand.

Rienne managed a firm grip on the hilt of Maelstrom but didn't have time to draw the blade. She didn't need to. She ducked slightly, batted Jad's left arm aside with her sword—silk, scabbard, and all—and pushed his right arm so the dagger slashed across Marsh's chest. Marsh yelped in pain and surprise, and Jad staggered backward. She could see the doubt gnawing at his mind, and she used their hesitation to quiet her mind.

While her eyes kept careful watch on the two assailants before her and her ears listened for the approach of the man behind, her innermost mind quieted, opened—like a flower opening to the new sun—then focused, channeling her inner energy into a fine point, a sharp edge of energy that flowed into her limbs. She focused the energy and held it, waiting.

The one behind her hung back for that first instant, but then he came charging in. Without turning, Rienne crouched, gathered her soul energy, then released it, springing straight upward. She slammed down on the back of the third attacker, cracking his skull with Maelstrom in its sheath, then landed on her feet behind him. The third assailant fell like a stone, and his head bounced once off the stone walkway.

Jad and Marsh stood flanking the prone body of their

companion and gaped at her. Marsh started backing away first, keeping a wary eye on her in case she decided to charge after him. Rienne took the opportunity to draw Maelstrom from its sheath.

That was enough. Marsh and Jad turned tail and ran, leaving their unconscious ally to Rienne's mercy. She touched her lips to Maelstrom's blade and slid it back into the sheath. She started to return the blade to its silk wrapping, then thought better of it. She unrolled the silk and wound it around her waist, then carefully placed the scabbard into its folds so she could draw the blade more easily if she were attacked again.

Only then did she check on the third attacker, the one whose face she'd never seen. She rolled him over onto his back—he was a handsome young man—and checked the pulse in his throat. Aside from a large bump on his head, he'd be fine when he woke up.

He was lucky she'd never freed her blade.

* * * * *

Krathas stared at her across a filthy desk covered with scraps of parchment, and Rienne stared back. The sign on his office door had identified him as an inquisitive affiliated with House Tharashk's Finders' Guild. Rienne wondered what kind of business he attracted in Subsidence—certainly not jobs that paid very well, if his office was any indication. He was clearly past his prime, his hair thinning and white and his face deeply lined, though he was still muscular and tall—very tall. He had made a show of welcoming her in and clearing a chair for her to sit on, though he fell silent as soon as she mentioned Gaven's name. That was when the staring began.

At last he broke the silence, though he didn't look away. "Last I heard, Gaven was in Dreadhold," he said, watching her carefully. "In fact, I heard you were the one who put him there."

She held his gaze. "I thought he was possessed and needed help."

"You thought his actions might disgrace your family and get in the way of your social climbing."

Rienne felt a surge of anger but held it down, making sure no trace of it showed on her face. "Is that what he told you?"

"Something like that."

"When did you talk to him last?"

"Sixteenth of Zarantyr."

"Zarantyr? Three months ago?"

"Sorry, was I not clear? Three months and twenty-six years ago. Just before they locked him up."

Rienne sighed and looked away. She remembered that month, all those years ago. It had been a cold winter, and she'd spent many hours staring out windows at snow-draped fields and blank white skies. She looked sharply at Krathas again.

"Just before? The sixteenth?"

"That's right."

"That was after his trial. Was he here? In Vathirond?"

Krathas stared at her for another long moment. "Not then, no. I spoke to him at a Sivis message station. They let him put his affairs in order before they locked him up."

"What did he ask you to do?"

"I'm afraid that's between him and me, Lady Alastra. I'm sure if he had wanted you involved, he would've contacted you."

"Krathas, if you're not inclined to help me, I shall be forced to consult with another member of your esteemed House Tharashk. It would be unfortunate if I accidentally mentioned to them how a certain half-orc inquisitive used to give Gaven leads on finding dragonshard deposits for House Lyrandar. I understand that's a business House Tharashk would rather keep a tight hold on."

She had hoped to avoid playing that card. She wasn't positive that Gaven's information had come from Krathas—Gaven had always been very cagey about revealing his source. And she wasn't sure that House Tharashk hadn't known about it, perhaps collected large fees from Gaven for that information. She had leaped from a couple of hunches, and she dearly hoped they proved accurate.

Krathas's face registered nothing, but he was silent again for a long moment, studying her. When he spoke again, his voice was much quieter. "He told you that?"

"Something like that."

"There's no way you can prove that."

So her hunches had been on the mark. "Do I need to?"

Krathas took a deep breath and let it slowly out through his nostrils. "Very well, Lady. What is it you want from me?"

"Gaven has escaped," Rienne said, watching Krathas carefully. His eyebrows raised, but she couldn't judge whether he was genuinely surprised. "I have a hard time believing you hadn't heard that already."

"My sources aren't what they once were."

"I hope that won't diminish your usefulness to me. I want to find him before the forces of the four dragonmarked houses who are scouring Khorvaire at this moment do, and that's where I need your help."

"If I didn't know he escaped, how can I possibly know where to find him?"

"I know he was arrested here in Vathirond, and you just told me he contacted you after his conviction and had you do something for him. I assume there's something here he cares about, maybe even something he'll come back here for. What is it?"

"It's been almost thirty years, Lady."

"I assume he planned for the possibility that it would be even longer before he was able to return. That's why he contacted you."

For the first time, Krathas smiled, revealing uneven rows of broken teeth. "I begin to see what Gaven admired in you, Lady Alastra."

Rienne returned his smile. "Wait until you see me in a fight."

CHAPTER
15

Gaven found himself staring up into the face of the Traveler.

At least, he assumed it was the Traveler. A goblin was carved in the great frieze, crouching at the feet of the mysterious sixteenth god, stepping out of the line formed by the other fifteen gods. She wore a quirky smile that seemed out of place in the ancient sculpture of Dhakaan—an expression that made this one goddess seem more real than the others in their majestic stillness. Gaven shot a grim smile back at the trickster-god and sat up.

His smile fell from his face when he saw that he was not alone. "Senya!"

"Come," she said, "we need to get out of here." She stepped over to him and extended a hand to help him up. He stood without her help.

"What do you think you're doing?"

"I think I'm helping you achieve your destiny. Now move!" She started out the cave entrance, and he followed, reluctantly.

"Senya, wait a moment—"

"No! Haldren could be back any second. We need to be out of sight and as far away as we can get."

That got Gaven moving. He followed Senya as she retraced their steps out of the ancient city. Gaven cursed to himself all the way. He had hoped to make a clean break with Haldren and all his business. He wanted to be rid of them all, certainly including Senya.

They made their way down the rocky valley, following the dry riverbed as it wound between the cliffs. The ground sloped steadily downward along the ancient river's course to the sea. Soon the wall of Paluur Draal with its enormous carved guardians was out of sight behind them.

Feeling they'd put enough distance between them and the city, Gaven lunged forward and grabbed Senya's arm, pulling her to a stop. "How many times do I have to tell you that I am not the Storm Dragon?"

"You can say it all you want," she said. She stepped closer and looked up into his eyes. "Sooner or later you'll realize you're wrong."

"I also made it clear that I'm not interested in you."

She put a hand on his face and pressed herself closer to his chest. "You'll come to recognize that mistake as well."

He stepped back and pushed her away. "Listen, Senya, you are the one making a terrible mistake here. Go find Haldren. Maybe Vaskar's not the Storm Dragon, but you can still go with Haldren. Maybe you'll end up the queen of something."

Senya scoffed. "A queen at Haldren's side? I'd rather spend the rest of my life in the Realm of Madness."

"I thought you loved him."

She threw her head back and laughed. "Love him? That old man?"

"You only stayed with him because of the power you thought he could give you."

"He was much more exciting when he was younger."

"I have nothing to offer you, Senya. I can't even pretend to love you, and I have no plans to seize any throne, mortal or divine."

"What are your plans, then? Maybe I have something to offer you."

Gaven threw up his hands and continued down the valley. "I don't have any plans. I didn't think past getting away from all of you, and I even failed at that. You want to come with me? Fine. We'll end up dead or back in Dreadhold together."

Gaven walked for a while in silence before looking back over his shoulder. Senya trailed behind him, her eyes fixed on the ground as she picked out a path on the rocky trail. She was smiling.

* .* * * *

"Damn you to the outer darkness, Gaven." Haldren quivered with fury. Darraun was nervous that he might end up taking the brunt of the sorcerer's anger again. After all, he was the one who had let go of Gaven's hand.

They had appeared on the shores of a lake, large enough that the opposite shore was nearly invisible. Darraun's hunch was Lake Brey, somewhere near the uneasy border between Breland and Thrane. The wind blowing off the water was cold, and Darraun pulled his cloak around him.

"We're going back," Haldren announced. "Join hands."

Darraun cast his eyes around, looking for a distraction, anything to buy Gaven more time. Nothing caught his attention. "Wait a moment, Haldren," he said.

"Join hands now." Haldren was not going to wait. Cart had already seized one of Haldren's hands and held the other out to Darraun.

"I'm just thinking—"

"Stop thinking and join hands. If he harms her because you're too busy thinking, I will reduce you to dust and scatter your remains across the Ten Seas."

Darraun took Cart's hand, and Haldren intoned his spell. Darraun considered yanking his hand away at the last second as Gaven had done. A world of possibilities began to form in his mind, then Haldren finished the spell and they were back in Paluur Draal, staring up at the sixteen goblin gods.

No sign of Gaven or Senya.

"Senya!" Haldren yelled. His voice echoed around the cave, but that was the only reply.

Cart moved immediately to the cave entrance and looked outside, while Darraun made a show of examining the floor.

"I was just thinking, Haldren," he said, scanning the ground as if looking for tracks, "what if they were still caught in the magic of your spell and got shunted through space, just not to the same place we were?"

Haldren snorted. "I thought I told you to stop thinking. And you know the spell doesn't work like that."

"On the contrary, I've seen teleportation spells go horribly awry."

Haldren moved to stand beside Cart, turning his back on Darraun and looking out at the ruins nearby. "It would have been one thing for the spell to carry us to the wrong location, but quite another for it to transport us correctly while taking them elsewhere."

Darraun stood behind the others. He couldn't see much past the corpse of the mountain troll they had slain earlier.

"Senya!" Haldren shouted again.

Darraun grabbed his shoulder. "Don't! You'll draw every troll and wyvern in the city down on our heads."

"I don't care!" Haldren whirled around as he shouted, and emphasized his last word by shoving Darraun backward, simultaneously blasting a gout of fire from his hand.

Darraun fell to the ground and clutched his arms to his body. His shirt and cloak smoldered but didn't ignite, and his leather cuirass protected his chest, but his face and eyes stung with the heat. Haldren turned away and started out into the city. Darraun sat up and glared after him.

"Are you hurt?" Cart extended a hand to help him stand, and his voice was full of concern.

Darraun took his hand and pulled himself to his feet. "Not badly, no." He scowled. But I'll make him pay for that, he thought. When this is all over.

"Let's go, then." Cart hastened after Haldren, his sense of duty to the Lord General replacing his concern for Darraun.

Darraun lagged behind, watching his feet as he walked. He didn't want to be the one to spot Gaven or Senya, and if Haldren did find them, Darraun wanted to be as far away as possible.

Something on the ground caught his eye, and he stopped. There was a groove, either cut into the stone or marking the space between two ancient cobblestones. Drying mud covered the ground around it—mud that had been smeared across the stone. He crouched and traced his finger along the groove. It was the shape of Kraken Bay—he'd found the map they were looking for.

"Haldren!" he called. "You need to see this!"

Haldren wheeled around and walked back to within a few yards of Darraun. "Did you find their tracks? Are we on their trail?"

Darraun brushed mud away from the region northwest of Kraken Bay. "Not them," he said. Haldren threw up his hands and started to turn away. Darraun pointed to a strange symbol carved into the stone, where he had cleared the dust away. "But I think I've found the Sky Caves of Thieren Kor."

* * * * *

As the western sky grew red, the valley opened up, and a stream poured out from under the mountains. Gazing down the valley, Gaven saw other mountain streams joining its flow, and it widened into a river far ahead.

Senya spotted a grassy patch near the stream bank and threw herself down. "This river should lead us all the way to Korranberg," she said, starting to remove her boots.

"Is that where you're heading?" Gaven asked.

"There's a lightning rail station there. We could get from there to pretty much anywhere west of the Mournland." Senya got both her boots off and started massaging her feet.

"The Mournland," Gaven echoed.

Words from the Prophecy echoed in his mind: Desolation spreads over that land like a wildfire. Haldren and Vaskar had taken those words to refer to the Mournland. He saw it, briefly, in his mind—a barren plain, unbroken by any sign of life or civilization, the earth itself reduced to ash. Then he saw his hands half buried in the scorched soil, tasted the acrid air. He shook his head, trying to dispel that image. Senya was watching him curiously, and he forced himself to look at her. She is here now, he reminded himself. The rest . . .

"So that's what they call Cyre now?" he said. His mouth was dry, and the words scratched his throat.

"It was a beautiful land, before," Senya said. "Did you ever go there?"

"Many times." Faces sprang to Gaven's mind, people he hadn't seen in many years. How many of them were dead?

"Cart and I went there once after the Mourning. Just a short way in." She shuddered. "Far enough. I don't ever want to go back."

"Haldren's going there—or Vaskar, perhaps. Or both of them."

"Looking for the Sky Caves. Haldren told me."

"Thunder!" Gaven sighed. "I'm glad to be done with Haldren and his schemes." Even as he said it, though, it rang false. Looking for the Sky Caves of Thieren Kor in the Mournland sounded like quite an adventure—and to explore them would be the chance of a lifetime. The knowledge they must hold . . .

He sat down on the stream bank, a few paces downstream from where Senya had started dipping her feet into the water. The stream showed him the Ring of Siberys overhead.

"Shall we stop here for the night?" Senya asked.

Gaven looked up at the sky. The red in the west had faded to a narrow band above the mountains, while the Ring of Siberys shimmered gold above him. It wasn't as bright as it had been the night before in Shae Mordai, but it still shed enough light that they could make their way farther down the valley if they wanted to. Realizing that the previous night they'd been in Aerenal made him feel exhausted.

"Yes, it seems quiet enough," he said. "And open. Less chance for anything to sneak up under cover."

Senya rummaged through her pack and tossed Gaven some dried meat. "I have to say, I'll miss Darraun's cooking."

Gaven scowled, thinking of the fragments of conversation he'd had with Darraun. "Haldren said he was a more recent acquaintance. How long have you known him?"

"Darraun? Only a few weeks. Cart and I recruited him to help us break into Dreadhold."

"How did you find him?"

Senya shrugged. "We asked around. Haldren still has a lot of friends in Aundair. In the army mostly. I think Darraun has friends in intelligence."

"Intelligence? The Royal Eyes?"

"Mm-hm. It was almost like he'd planted his name at the end of every trail we followed. He knows what he's doing."

"Does Haldren know that?"

"I don't know. Why?"

"I'm not sure I'd trust someone who went to such lengths to make sure you chose him for the task."

"Oh, Haldren doesn't trust him."

Gaven laughed. "Of course not."

* * * * *

The sky grew dark over the ruins of Paluur Draal. Cart paced slowly back and forth, watching for more trolls or any other trouble. Darraun finished copying the map he'd found. Haldren knelt beside him, pointing out details and criticizing his work.

Darraun entertained himself with thoughts of strangling the sorcerer as he put the finishing touches on the paper.

Haldren stood, brushed dried mud from his knees, and looked up at the darkening sky. "Damn," he muttered. "We're not going to find them now."

Darraun double-checked his map and rolled it up. "At least we found what we came here for."

"Indeed, and the information in the Sky Caves could very well make Gaven irrelevant to us. As for Senya . . . well, I shall have to trust that she can free herself from his clutches eventually."

"Free herself? You think he's captured her?"

"Of course. What else?"

Darraun opened his mouth but closed it again, remembering Haldren's temper. He would not be the one to shatter Haldren's delusions.

"Cart," Haldren said, "find a secure location and set up camp. Darraun, I'd be grateful for some of your cooking, if you can make something palatable from the supplies we have left. I need to contact Vaskar and inform him of our progress." He glanced around, then pointed to a small stone house near the trolls' cave that was mostly intact. "I'll be in there."

Haldren went into the little house without a backward glance, and Cart busied himself inspecting other structures nearby. Few of the ruined buildings offered much shelter, and Darraun suspected that the trolls had kept the area around their lair clear of competing predators. All the same, something emitted a horrible dying shriek from the house Haldren had entered.

Darraun started to throw a meal together while Cart checked on Haldren. Darraun shook his head as Haldren rebuked the warforged for disturbing his privacy. Darraun waited until Cart had returned and busied himself setting up their camp in another little house. Then he rummaged in a pouch at his belt until he found the right scroll. He spared a quick glance at the warforged, who was rummaging through their supplies, then began to whisper the words inked upon the scroll. A final glance at the warforged, then Darraun uttered the final syllable. With a slight tingle across his skin, Darraun became invisible.

The spell didn't quiet his footfalls, so he moved as quietly as he could up to the house Haldren had claimed. He crouched in the doorway and peered in to where Haldren stood before a shimmering image of the bronze dragon's head. The image was speaking.

". . . than the Lyrandar whelp could anyway. Meet me as we planned, give me the Eye, and everything will be fine. You will receive your reward."

"What about Senya?" Haldren's voice was agonized, and Darraun almost felt sorry for him.

"She is irrelevant."

Vaskar's head vanished in a shower of sparks, and Haldren sank to his knees, his chin on his chest. Darraun watched him for a moment, but the sorcerer didn't move. Darraun slunk away, glanced around to make sure he wasn't in Cart's sight, and dismissed the spell of invisibility.

Waste of a good scroll, he thought.

He finished preparing the meal and ate some. The rest was cold before Haldren emerged.

CHAPTER
16

A splashing in the stream jolted Gaven from his sleep, and he scrambled to his feet. The sky was growing bright in the east, shedding enough light into the valley that he could see Senya kneeling on the bank. She had removed her leather coat, baring her shoulders, and she washed her face and hair in the stream.

Gaven sighed and lowered himself back to the ground. "You startled me."

Senya spun around, surprised by Gaven's voice. Her startled look dissolved into a laugh. "I didn't hear you move. Sorry I disturbed your sleep."

"That's all right. We should get a start on the day."

Senya sat on the ground, stretching her legs out in front of her and leaning back on her hands. Her wet hair clung to her cheeks and neck. She had washed the pigment off her eyelids and lips, which to Gaven's eyes enhanced her beauty. Gaven was painfully aware of the smooth, bare skin of her shoulders, the gentle curve of her collarbones, the graceful arc of her throat. She teased one corner of her mouth with her tongue and smiled. "It's still early."

Gaven turned away. "You never give up, do you?" He pulled his boots on.

"Not when I know what I want."

He stood and shouldered his pack and his sword. "Get dressed. It's going to take days to get to Korranberg." Without waiting for a response, he started walking downstream.

Subdued by his rebuff, Senya trailed behind him in silence, and he lost himself in the monotonous rhythm of walking. Step after step, mile after mile—the scenery changed little, and nothing distracted him from the thoughts that surfaced and subsided in his mind. It was a bit like sleep, especially when the nightmares began—

Enormous wings beat the air, and the morning sun gleamed on scales of every color—red and black and blue; silver, gold, and copper. Dragons wheeled and dived, grappled each other, furies of claws and teeth. Raw elemental power spewed from their mouths—fire and lightning, searing acid, virulent poison, and bitter cold.

He felt the earth tremble beneath his feet and saw a column of blinding light spill up from the ground, casting sickly shadows on the dragons fighting overhead. And he knew what was coming: the hordes of the Soul Reaver.

"Gaven!" Senya's voice jolted him back to the present, and he caught himself just before he slipped over the edge of a low cliff. Off balance, he fell backward and sat on the rocky ground. Beside him, the stream tumbled over the cliff and began to broaden, forming a wide, slow river as it left the valley and wound among the foothills of the Seawalls.

"Are you all right?" Senya clutched his shoulder.

He didn't feel all right. His skin was clammy, and his stomach churned. He dropped his chin to his chest, trying to keep his head from swimming. He cursed under his breath. The Eye of Siberys had given him clarity, but it was slipping away.

"What is it?" Worry creased Senya's face.

"It's nothing," he croaked, but Senya was clearly not convinced.

"Here, why don't you lie down for a moment?" She wrapped an arm around his shoulder, trying to guide him into a more comfortable position.

"It's nothing!" he repeated, pushing her away. "Don't mother me." Rienne had mothered him from time to time, and he'd accepted it from her. Not from Senya.

"I'm sorry," she said. She looked hurt, so much that Gaven almost regretted his words.

He stood, slowly, with Senya hovering nearby. He was a little unsteady on his feet, and Senya put a hand on his arm as if to steady him. He decided against brushing her hand away, and let her help him down the little cliff. Then they continued, side by side, along the river.

* * * * *

Darraun gazed at the brightening sky as Haldren finished his spell. He blinked, and the ruined city disappeared around him, replaced by the churning waters of Lake Brey. The sun, no longer hidden behind the surrounding mountains, shone in his eyes and glared off the lake so that he had to look away.

Darraun shivered as he surveyed the near shore. They stood on a rocky bluff overlooking the lake. To the north, the land sloped down to the water, and in the distance he could see a small fishing village. Shielding his eyes against the sun, he looked to the south, where the shore curved off to the east. Darraun figured that the city of Starilaskur, one of the larger cities in the north of Breland, stood in that direction, not too far beyond the lake. That meant they were probably not far from Hatheril, a tiny hamlet that was only important because of its position at the intersection of a caravan route stretching west from Starilaskur and a lightning rail line heading north to Aundair.

A gateway to anywhere I want to go, he thought. He shook his head. *Maybe when this is over.*

Haldren shielded his eyes and looked out over the lake as Cart stood watching, impassive.

"What are we looking for?" Darraun said.

"Vaskar, you fool."

Darraun looked back over the lake, squinting into the glare. The sky was light blue and clear of clouds. A flock of gulls swarmed near the village to the north, stealing from the fishers' morning catch, and what might have been pelicans soared over the waters to the southeast. Nothing in the sky was large enough to be a dragon. Then something in the water caught Darraun's eye.

A moment later, the shape rose up from the water, leaping into the air and beating its wings fiercely to stay aloft. The sun gleamed on Vaskar's bronze scales and shimmered in the drops of water cascading off his body and spraying from his wings. He caught the air under his wings and glided over to the bluff where they stood, alighting gently near Haldren.

Haldren smiled, though it seemed to require an unusual effort. "Hail, Storm Dragon!"

"Show me the Eye of Siberys," Vaskar said.

The smile fell from Haldren's face, and he reached into a

pouch. He produced the Eye of Siberys but held it close to his chest as he displayed it to the dragon.

"Here is the Eye," he said. "We found it outside the City of the Dead, as Gaven predicted."

"Excellent." Vaskar hissed. "And Paluur Draal? Did you find what you sought there?"

Haldren winced at the mention of the city, as if its name was enough to remind him of what he had left behind there. "I did."

Sure you did, Darraun thought, I was just along for the ride.

"The map, Darraun." Haldren held a hand out to him without taking his eyes off Vaskar, still clutching the dragonshard to his chest.

Darraun slid the map he had copied from the ruins out of its case and handed it to Haldren. The sorcerer fumbled to unroll it while keeping a grip on the Eye of Siberys. He pointed to the map as Vaskar lowered his enormous head to see it.

"We found a map carved in the pavement of a plaza in the city," Haldren explained. "The outline of Kraken Bay was very clear. Naturally, the locations on the map were marked with their ancient Dhakaani names, when they were labeled at all. But certain geographical features are unmistakable." He shifted his grip on the map and traced his finger over it. Darraun noticed that the Eye of Siberys disappeared at some point in that process, and he wondered if Vaskar noticed it too. "The Seawall Mountains run parallel to the western edge of Kraken Bay. They turn to the east here, at Marguul Pass, then there's the gap where Kennrun stands now—a Brelish fort on the border of Darguun. Then more mountains rise up from the plain—and that's where the Mournland begins now. If you continue following the line of the mountains, you hit Lake Cyre, here. But the map indicates the Sky Caves here, to the southeast of the mountains." With a flourish, he indicated the strange symbol Darraun had transcribed on the map.

"You seem reluctant to deliver the Eye as we agreed, Haldren," Vaskar said. "Why is that?"

"What? Reluctant?" Haldren stammered. "Not at all!"

"Where is it, then?"

"Well, I returned it to its pouch so I could more easily hold the map."

"Give it to me."

Haldren drew it out but cradled it to his chest again. "I will deliver it as I promised, Vaskar. I'm a man of my word. But—"

"Give it to me now."

Darraun could see Haldren struggling against the command, which must have carried a magical weight. In the end, his resistance failed, and he extended the Eye to Vaskar. The dragon plucked it from Haldren's outstretched hand with a gigantic claw. Darraun couldn't see what Vaskar did with it.

"What about your end of the bargain?" Haldren said. "The aid you promised me?"

"Don't worry, Haldren," the dragon said. "My promises are as good as yours. A flight of dragons is on its way to Aundair as we speak, ready to do battle at your command."

Haldren's face lit up. "A flight? How many dragons?"

"More than enough for your purposes. No army in Khorvaire will stand against you."

* * * * *

"Tell me about the Prophecy."

The Ring of Siberys was bright enough to shine through a thin layer of clouds. Gaven and Senya had laid out their bedrolls in a bend of the river, so their camp was surrounded by water on three sides. Gaven was exhausted from the day's march, but so far he'd been unable to sleep. Apparently Senya had the same problem.

"What about it?"

He heard Senya's bedroll rustling, and glanced over to see her propping herself up on her elbows. "Well, how does it work? I mean, does it describe events that are sure to happen? Is the path of my life spelled out in advance? Am I just following a story that's already been written, like . . . like a stage actor or something? Is that what life is?"

Gaven laughed. "An actor trying to follow a script you've never read, fumbling your way through lines you're making up as you go? That feels about right."

"But you can read the script."

"No. I see bits and pieces of the script, as if it's been transcribed by a madman. Unconnected scenes. Lines here and there, with no idea who's supposed to be speaking."

Senya put her head back down and was silent for a long time.

Just as he began to think she'd fallen asleep, she said, "I don't believe it."

"What?"

"I don't believe there is a script."

"But you believe in destiny. You seem set on making sure I fulfill mine."

"That's different. Destiny is . . . it's like the highest hopes the universe has for you. Like—like my mother wanted the best for me. And you can either fulfill your destiny, or you—" Her voice became strangled, and she stopped trying to speak.

A wave of thicker clouds drifted across the sky, and the night grew darker. Gaven brought his hand up to his neck and traced the lines of his dragonmark. Suddenly he was an adolescent again, adrift at sea at the mouth of Eldeen Bay. This was his Test of Siberys, a rite of passage of the dragonmarked houses, a trial meant to force his dragonmark to manifest, if he was to bear one. Heirs of the houses usually developed their marks in times of great stress in their adolescent years, so the Test of Siberys had been developed to create just the right stress.

Most children spent the Test straining in the desperate hope of forcing a mark to manifest on their skin. Gaven saw himself on his knees, pouring out desperate prayers to each god of the Sovereign Host that no mark would appear on him. The sea was calm, under the command of a Lyrandar windwright, and he drifted for days, pouring out his prayers. Some dragonmark heirs would call up a wind to move their little boats, while others would develop a protective mark that would inure their bodies to the burning sun. Still others would call up great billowing banks of fog to shield themselves from the heat. Gaven did not. Day after day he knelt in prayer under the sun's unblinking gaze, and his prayers were answered.

At the end of the test, an elemental galleon came to his rescue. Some strong cousin lifted his body, weak and weathered from the scorching sun, and carried him aboard. He was feverish, and most of the faces surrounding him were blurred together, indistinct. But one face was clear in his memory—his father's, trying to smile at him but unable to hide the disappointment etched into every line.

At least there could be no doubt that this memory was his and not the other's.

CHAPTER
17

Noon sunlight glittered on the domes and spires of Korranberg, the oldest and one of the most important cities in the gnome nation of Zilargo, nestled among the foothills of the Seawall Mountains. From his perch at the edge of a cliff, Gaven could see the whole city spread out before him, and miles of fields stretching out to the sea. The city was a fascinating mix of old and new; the ancient buildings of the city's great library pressed between the more recent construction of shops and markets. He was struck by how green the city looked from his vantage point—ivy clung to gracefully arched walls, gardens sprawled over spacious courtyards, and flowers burst in a rainbow of colors to celebrate spring's height.

Behind him, Senya snorted. "Gnomes," she said. "How do they defend this place? It's right next to Darguun, and these mountains are full of kobolds."

"I suspect the city isn't as defenseless as it looks," Gaven answered. He pointed at the city wall nearest their position. "Look at the holes along the top edge of the wall. I'd be willing to bet there's some kind of mechanism that will pump boiling oil or acidic fire out of those holes in case of an attack. In fact, I'll bet the jets shoot out far enough that the ivy is unharmed."

Senya snorted again, adjusted her pack on her shoulders, and started along the winding path that would take them down the cliff and into the city. Gaven took a last look at the city and the sea then followed her down.

* * * * *

Gaven was glad he had taken the time to admire the city from a distance. From inside, the elegant spires and sprawling gardens were lost in the bustle—much of which occurred at waist level.

He was not the tallest of men, but in Korranberg, making his way along streets crowded with gnomes, he felt like a giant—and he attracted about as much attention as a real giant would have. Senya only reached Gaven's breastbone, but the majority of the people on the streets only reached her chest. Gaven noticed that she kept her arms in front of her chest as they moved through the city, and he couldn't blame her. He kept his hands at waist level, making sure to maintain a space between himself and any nearby gnomes.

They were not the only "tallfolk," as the gnomes referred to them, walking the streets of the city, but there were few enough that Gaven felt acutely self-conscious. As he had in Whitecliff, he found himself constantly wondering who might be watching him, ready to turn him in. Considering the Zil reputation for trafficking in secrets, he felt sure that word of his escape had reached even distant Korranberg. It was probably just a matter of time until someone identified him and summoned the authorities, so he decided to give them as little time as possible.

Trying not to attract any more attention than absolutely necessary, he seized Senya's hand and pulled her through the streets toward the lightning rail station he'd spotted from his vantage point above the city. He would get them on a carriage and out of Korranberg before any wheels could be put in motion to stop him.

Unfortunately, their great height relative to the natives didn't help them part the crowds on the streets. It was midday, and many people seemed to be taking a respite from the day's work to eat, socialize, and shop. Gaven and Senya's progress was painfully slow, but no one tried to arrest them or actively hinder their progress. The lightning rail station came into view as they rounded a corner, and Gaven let out a long sigh.

The sight of armored guards at the station sent a jolt of panic through him. He pulled Senya to a sheltered spot on the side of the street and stopped his headlong rush.

Senya fell into a ready stance, dropped a hand to her sword hilt, and stared around looking for enemies. "What is it?" she whispered.

"Relax. You're drawing stares."

She straightened and leaned close to him, transforming their appearance from nervous fugitives to amorous lovers. She brought her lips close and murmured, "What's going on?"

Gaven felt his face flush, but passersby were averting their gaze, so he went along. He lowered his head to speak right in her ear. "It just occurred to me—what if Haldren gave up on finding us in Paluur Draal and came here instead? What if he had Cart or Darraun alert the authorities here? There could be Sentinel Marshals waiting for us in there. I don't want to just stroll in."

Senya reached behind his neck and started twirling her fingers in his hair, which seemed to him to be taking the ruse too far. "It's not Haldren's style," she whispered. Her lips touched his ear, and her warm breath sent a tingle down his neck. "He'll want to find us himself. I can't see him relying on the Marshals or anyone else to do it for him. Besides, we know too much. If we're captured, we could tell them about his plans and make his life very difficult. He doesn't want us caught."

"That makes sense. Let's go, then." He started to pull away.

She held him, keeping him close. "Not before you kiss me."

"Senya." He put his hands on her waist and pushed her back, a little less gently than before.

Her mouth was half pout, half smile as she followed him into the station.

* * * * *

"I'm sorry, master, but I can't sell you a ticket without seeing your papers. If you've lost your papers, House Sivis has an outpost in the upper story where they will gladly help you replace them."

The agent at the ticket counter was a human woman attached to the Transportation Guild, a branch of House Orien. The scions of House Orien carried the Mark of Passage, which enabled some to transport themselves instantaneously across great distances, making them ideally suited for courier work. The Transportation Guild operated caravan lines as well as the lightning rail, competing fiercely with House Lyrandar's overseas shipping lines.

The woman was cheerful enough, but Gaven could tell that she was already calculating how to deal with him if the situation got ugly. It wasn't until Senya produced her papers to buy her passage that Gaven had even considered this possibility, which irked him most of all. Securing new papers would be impossible. The gnomes of House Sivis, whose Notaries' Guild issued important documents like identification papers, would send him back to Dreadhold in a heartbeat.

"Look," Senya said beside him, tugging the neck of his shirt open, "he's a dragonmarked member of House Lyrandar. Don't you think you could make an exception?"

The Orien agent stared at Gaven's huge, elaborate mark. "An heir of Siberys," she breathed, not really speaking to them.

"Yes, I'm an heir of Siberys. I'm just trying to get to Vathirond to see my family. Can't you help me?"

Her eyes narrowed. "House Lyrandar has an outpost here. Why not appeal to them?"

Gaven sighed, leaned on the low counter, and spoke in a low voice. "I came here to work for my cousin in the Lyrandar outpost," he said. "But . . . well, it didn't work out." He looked meaningfully at Senya, hoping to convey some sense of scandalous behavior. "So now I'm not in any position to ask a favor from my house here—so I've come to House Orien." He could see the young woman starting to soften. "And it's not any great favor I'm asking. I'm paying for passage, after all."

The agent's eyes shifted between Senya and Gaven, then she gave a resolute nod. "Very well."

Gaven smiled warmly. "Thank you so much. I'll remember your kindness."

Senya put down the money, and they walked toward the lightning rail. A row of decorated wooden carriages, strung together like pearls on a string, hung suspended in the air above a line of glowing blue stones set in the ground. Lightning danced between the stones and similar stones embedded in the bottoms of the carriages, giving the lightning rail its name. Even the empty air shimmered with magic.

The carriages in the rear were meant for passengers—passengers of means, who would ride in luxurious comfort. At the front of the long line, the crew cart held the bound elemental that would propel the coach in the same manner as bound elementals propelled the galleons of House Lyrandar. The conductor stones kept the carriages suspended in the air, but the elemental moved it forward, unhindered by wheels grinding against the earth.

Senya clung to his arm as they walked, evidently enjoying the ruse they had adopted, but Gaven noticed that she kept glancing behind them. After a moment, she stretched up and planted a kiss on his cheek, then whispered in his ear, "There might be a problem."

Gaven kept walking without looking back. "What is it?"

"The agent has summoned a pair of men, half-elves I think, which might mean your house."

"Or House Medani, which could be worse."

"And they're coming after us now. Pretty quickly. Yes, they're Medani. I see the basilisk emblem now."

Gaven quickened his pace, seizing Senya's hand as he hustled to the waiting coach. Senya showed their tickets to the coachman as Gaven looked back. They were close—two half-elf men, as Senya had said, with the basilisk emblem of House Medani on the lapels of their long coats. The coats billowed behind them as they walked, showing the long, slender blades both men wore at their belts. Medani's Warning Guild provided a wide range of services, from tasters employed to detect poison to inquisitives trained to root out lies. Assuming these two were the latter, Gaven hoped to avoid any contact with them.

Making sure the Medanis were watching, Gaven boarded the lightning rail coach. He saw them start to run toward the coach, then he hurried in after Senya. "Quick. Get to the front of the coach."

Senya obliged, pushing her way past a handful of other passengers who were waiting politely to get into their private compartments. Gaven followed her, peering into the compartments they passed. Each was like a small but elegant sitting room, with three lushly upholstered chairs, a small table, and walls paneled with matching mahogany.

At the far end, a door led into the next coach forward. Gaven checked over his shoulder again. One of the Medani agents caught his eye and held up a hand. Gaven nudged Senya forward, and they went through the door.

"Master Lyrandar!" Gaven heard the agent call.

"Off the coach," Gaven told Senya. "Now."

She pushed her way through more boarding passengers then paused at the bottom of the stairs, looking back at Gaven for more instructions.

"Stop them!" one of the agents shouted.

Gaven took off at a run. He moved toward the crew cart at the front of the lightning rail. Senya's boots clomped on the marble tile behind him, and shouts arose farther behind them. Seeing Gaven's size and bulk, the passengers and House Orien workers in his path stepped out of his way, rather than obeying the Medani agents' orders to stop him. One man looked like he might try to stop Senya, but Gaven heard Senya's sword slide from its sheath, and her footfalls didn't falter behind him.

They reached the cart immediately behind the crew cart, and Gaven threw himself beneath it, hoping Senya would follow. He scurried forward on his hands and knees, crawling between two columns of sparking lightning that danced between the conductor stones, then Senya crashed into him. Lightning erupted around him, connecting the two conductor stones and arcing up around the cart. The force of Senya's body sent him hurtling forward along the underside of the cart, propelling him between two more pairs of orbs, sending up three more bolts of lightning before he managed to roll free to the other side of the cart.

The lightning had knocked the wind out of him, and he lay on the hard floor for a moment trying to catch his breath. Senya ran and fell to her knees beside him.

"Ten Seas! Are you hurt?"

He still couldn't speak, but he sat up in answer. She scrambled to her feet and grabbed his arm to help him stand.

"Now what?" Senya's voice was frantic, and there was a commotion coming from the other side of the cart.

Gaven pointed weakly at the cart they'd come under. Senya seized his hand and dragged him to the door of the cart.

His nerves started to reawaken, and they screamed in protest.

They had climbed aboard the steerage cart, where dozens of people—gnomes, goblins, orcs, humans, and a very subdued-looking minotaur whose horns had been sawed off—squeezed onto narrow benches. These were people who couldn't or didn't want to pay standard fares, which would have entitled them to comfortable seats, sleeper bunks, and meals in the galley cart. Here they could get where they needed to at a fraction of the cost, but they had to endure close quarters—increasingly close as the lightning rail made its way through Zilargo and into Breland, picking up more passengers on the way—and sleep in their seats.

Gaven led Senya to the empty seats near the minotaur, and he felt the cart lurch forward as the lightning rail started its journey. He collapsed on a bench, while Senya crouched beside him.

"Well, they didn't keep us in the station," she whispered. "So did we leave them behind? Or did they come back aboard to search for us on the carts?"

"I guess we'll find out," Gaven said. Pain started to cloud his vision. He closed his eyes, feeling consciousness swirling and slipping away.

* * * * *

"Gaven?" Senya's voice was close and urgent. Gaven fought to open his eyes. The pain had diminished, though one shard of it seemed to have traveled to between his eyes and taken up residence there. His dreams had been echoes of what his body had endured—lightning coursing through his body—though in the dream there had been a taste of exhilaration in the midst of the pain.

Senya had disguised herself as best she could—her leather coat was stowed somewhere, replaced by a more or less formless linen shift. She had pulled her hair back into a short ponytail that made her look almost like a young human girl—except for the shape of her ears and eyes. Her sword was nowhere to be seen, though Gaven couldn't imagine that it was far from her reach.

"How are you feeling?" she said.

"Well enough. Head's pounding a little." He winced as he spoke. "A lot."

She held a waterskin to his mouth and poured some water in. It was warm but clean, and it helped the pounding in his head.

"I've walked every cart," she said. "I didn't see the men who were chasing us. Vond says that a couple of Orien men came in here while I was gone, but he made sure they never laid eyes on you."

"Vond?"

Senya pointed behind him, and Gaven turned slowly around. The minotaur was planted on the bench behind him, staring fixedly at the door that led to the next cart back.

"This is Vond," Senya said. "Vond, this is Gaven."

"Know that," the minotaur growled, not shifting his eyes from the doorway.

"Nice to meet you," Gaven said, feeling awkward. Vond didn't respond in any way, so Gaven turned back to Senya, arching an eyebrow at her.

"Vond has been very helpful, keeping an eye on you while you slept," Senya said. "Not to mention scaring the Oriens away."

"I can imagine," Gaven muttered.

"Anyway, I think we're safe."

"Safe? Maybe until we get to Zolanberg. Then they'll send a team of inquisitives or Sentinel Marshals or gnome soldiers or something to search every cart until they find us. Seems to me we're trapped. But at least we're safe here in this cozy little cage."

"How far to Zolanberg?" Senya asked.

CHAPTER
18

The only reason the village of Bluevine appeared on maps of Aundair was its wine: a fine vintage with a distinctive indigo color. That claim to fame made it perfect for Haldren's purpose, Darraun reflected, which seemed to be getting all his old friends drunk enough to pledge their support to his cause.

Ten people gathered around a table in the back room of a Bluevine winery might not seem like much to a casual observer, Darraun thought. The guests Haldren had gathered, however, represented a significant concentration of power in Aundair. If he wanted to start another war, he could do worse.

Darraun sat at the foot of the table, trying to avoid drawing notice. That was easy enough, as Haldren commanded attention—preaching his vision of a new Galifar reunited under his rule as if it were a message of salvation. Many of the assembled notables received the message as if their salvation did depend on it, nodding or grunting or sometimes shouting their approval of the Lord General's words. Darraun was almost certain Haldren had woven some magic into his words, though subtly. Sometimes even he felt swayed by the rhetoric.

Looking around the table, Darraun made sure he had fixed every participant in his mind. Most were officers who had served under Haldren in the war. None of these were a surprise. Colonel Kadra Ware, Lord Major Parron ir'Fann, Major Rennic Arak, and Lord Colonel Deina ir'Cashan. Ir'Fann and ir'Cashan were not old noble families—the officers or their parents had earned titles during the war. All four of them had lost any importance they might have had when Haldren was stripped of his rank and imprisoned, so they all had good reasons to support Haldren's return to power. Ware and ir'Fann were the most vocal in their approval of Haldren at this gathering, but all four nodded at times and seemed very receptive to his message.

General Jad Yeven was also not a surprise, though he had been Haldren's equal rather than his subordinate. The two had collaborated a great deal during the war—sometimes in actions that, while showing initiative and ability, landed them in trouble with the crown. Unlike Haldren, though, Yeven had reined in his insubordinate streak at the end of the war, which had probably saved him from Dreadhold. Yeven sat with his arms crossed and a thoughtful scowl on his face—clearly, he would need more convincing, but he was willing to listen.

The other two were the interesting ones, and Darraun watched their reactions carefully. Darraun knew of Arcanist Wheldren only by rumor. He was supposed to hold great influence among the researchers of the Arcane Congress. Any involvement of those wizards was interesting, not least because Queen Aurala's brother, Lord Adal, maintained close ties with the Congress in his role as minister of magic. Adal was also the chief warlord of Aundair, however, and was well known to want the throne of Aundair—and, indeed, of all Galifar—for himself. Wheldren's involvement in Haldren's schemes could mean that Adal was also involved, or there could be a personal connection between the two that Darraun wasn't aware of, perhaps dating back to Haldren's magical education. The wizard was completely inscrutable. His face didn't move as Haldren spoke, and he never uttered a word.

And then there was Ashara d'Cannith. By law and longstanding tradition, the dragonmarked houses generally stayed out of political affairs. Their neutrality allowed them to pursue their activities across national boundaries—and to avoid too much government interference in their business. House Cannith was in a fragile state, though, with three branches of the house working almost independently. There was some speculation that the house would split the way House Phiarlan had during the war, with Merrix d'Cannith of Sharn going his own way. Jorlanna d'Cannith led the northern branch of the house from an enclave in Fairhaven, and Darraun had heard rumors that Jorlanna was interested in seeking closer ties with the throne of Aundair. Darraun had no idea what Ashara's relationship to Jorlanna was, but she had warmed quickly to Haldren's speech.

"Dragons."

Darraun realized he'd been so caught up in gauging the reaction of Haldren's audience that he had barely heard a word Haldren had been saying. Someone had asked Haldren a question, and that had been his answer—and it had left the rest of the table speechless.

"That's right, friends," Haldren went on. "At this moment, a flight of dragons is making its way from Argonnessen to a rendezvous point in the Starpeaks. The dragons are coming to Khorvaire to fight at my command. And no army will stand in their way."

Arcanist Wheldren spoke for the first time. "The dragons of Argonnessen do not fight for human causes."

"Do you doubt my words, Arcanist Wheldren?" Haldren said, smiling. He gestured around the table. "Those who know me will attest that I do not make idle boasts."

"I have no doubt that the dragons are coming as you claim. I question only their reasons for doing so."

"You prove yourself as astute as your reputation suggests," Haldren said. "You are correct, Wheldren. The dragons have their own reasons for fighting in our cause. Will that make their breath less deadly, their teeth and claws less sharp, their presence less fearsome to our foes? No." He slapped the table for emphasis. "They will drive our enemies before us in terror."

Colonel Ware shouted her approval, and Darraun noticed a smile behind General Yeven's hand as he stroked his chin thoughtfully.

Haldren leaned forward, planting his palms on the table, and a conspiratorial tone entered his voice. "But in the dragons' view, greater events are afoot than the reunification of Galifar. The dragons act in accordance with their understanding of a great prophecy, which they see revealed in the movements of the stars and moons, in the bones of the earth, and even in the flesh of the races of Khorvaire, in dragonmarks. They would not be coming to fight on our behalf were it not for their belief in the Prophecy."

"Our victory is foreordained!" Lord Major ir'Fann laughed, pounding his fist on the table.

Darraun noted how carefully Haldren responded. He smiled and laughed slightly. He did not confirm the Lord Major's interpretation of his words, but neither did he correct it.

And his audience was won. The four loyal officers clinked their wine glasses together, already celebrating their victory. General Yeven was smiling openly now, his eyes not quite focused in the room, as if he were seeing the dragons flying in front of his armies, breathing terror and devastation before them. Ashara d'Cannith leaned in to share a joke with Major Arak, clearly caught up in the excitement. Only Arcanist Wheldren seemed to have noticed Haldren's careful choice of words. He was not, perhaps, fully won over to the cause, but neither was he going to run back to Arcanix and tell Lord Adal all about this treasonous gathering.

Darraun stared into his glass, swirling the wine. Greater events afoot, indeed, he thought. Haldren had no idea.

* * * * *

Bordan hated Zilargo. It wasn't the gnomes themselves, but the constant feeling of being watched, almost overseen. There was a reason he worked alone—he'd worked hard in his house to earn the privilege of working without supervision. Among the gnomes, he felt as though every step he took was being watched and evaluated, and at any moment he could be judged a threat to the social order and dealt with. He knew only too well that the agents of the Trust, responsible for maintaining peace and stability, didn't look kindly on people like him.

On the other hand, that constant watchfulness proved helpful sometimes. After Gaven and his elf companion ran through the lightning rail station in Korranberg, evading the idiotic Medani agents, dozens of gnomes could describe everything the fugitives had done from the time they entered the city to their hasty departure. They came in from the north, but walked around to the west gate to enter by the main road. Gaven's eyes had lingered on a well-crafted suit of plate armor, but he hadn't bought it. The pair had shared an intimate moment just outside the rail station—or had they? The elf had looked wary a moment before, as if expecting an attack, so the intimacy might have been a cover. Bordan couldn't argue—the eyewitness reports were thorough and useful.

There was much they couldn't tell him, though. Who was Gaven's elf companion? He'd only been out of Dreadhold a few days, which didn't seem long enough to persuade some new romantic interest to risk her life running from the authorities in a lightning rail station. She didn't match descriptions of Gaven's betrothed. It might be possible to mistake a half-elf for a full elf, Bordan supposed, but he had been told Rienne had brown skin, not the pale ivory of Gaven's current companion. He figured she must be part of the group that had broken him out of Dreadhold, but that left plenty of questions unanswered. Starting with where Haldren ir'Brassek was.

In contrast to the detailed reports of Gaven's activities, there was no indication that Haldren had been in Korranberg at all. Even though Gaven had evidently made no effort to alter his appearance, Bordan tried to imagine every possible way that Haldren might look different than he did in Dreadhold, but the basics—a male human about sixty years old—drew a blank from the gnomes of the city council. It seemed clear that he had not been here at all. He and Gaven must have split up—and perhaps split up the rescue party as well. Certainly there had been no dragon sightings in the region.

Bordan left the city council hall and made his way through the crowded streets to the lightning rail station. He didn't expect as much detail from the Orien and Medani witnesses to the event, but there were certainly some things they could tell him that the gnomes couldn't. Starting with the agent who sold them passage.

"Of course I remember them," the young woman said. "He was an heir of Siberys with the Mark of Storm. Hard to forget."

"You checked their papers?"

The woman flushed crimson. "I checked hers. You'll see her in my log, there." She pointed to the sheaf of parchment Bordan was idly flipping through while he listened. "Both her identification papers and her traveling papers were issued in Fairhaven. I remember thinking she'd come a long way."

"And the man?"

Her color deepened, and she spoke as if to get the painful truth out as quickly as possible. "He had no papers."

"He had no papers," Bordan repeated, his voice flat.

"He was an heir of Siberys! He hardly had to prove his identity. I could see the dragonmark right there!"

"Calm down. I'm not here to challenge your decision. I'll leave that to your house. What was their destination?"

"They bought passage to Vathirond."

"Did they say why?"

"He said he was going there to see his family. He came here to work for his cousin, he said, but something happened between his cousin and the woman, I think, so they were going home. Or that's what he said."

Bordan found what he sought on the parchment pages. "Is this her? Senya Arrathinen?"

The woman leaned forward to see where Bordan pointed. "Yes, that's the one."

Bordan picked up his pen, jabbed it into the ink, and scrawled what little information the log held into his notebook. Senya Arrathinen, citizen of Aundair, residence in Fairhaven.

"This shows her destination as Vulyar," he said.

"Does it? Hm. Well, that makes sense."

"It does?"

"Certainly. When traveling papers show a destination on the other side of the Mournland, I don't pay much attention. We're obviously not carrying you across on the lightning rail, so I assume whatever your destination may be is just your next stop on the way to where you're going. And Vathirond makes sense, being just this side of the Mournland."

"But he told you Vathirond was their final destination."

"He did, but that was after she bought her passage. Didn't register in my mind."

"I see. So they're on the lightning rail, bound for Vathirond. Where does that cart stop?"

"Zolanberg first, then Sterngate, where Breland will check the passengers pretty carefully. Then up to Starilaskur, then Vathirond."

"Four stops. That should be more than enough. They can't run like that every time."

CHAPTER
19

The steerage cart grew dark as the sun sank over the forests of Zilargo. No lights would come on, Gaven knew—ever-bright lanterns might shine in the other carts, but steerage passengers went to sleep when the sun went down and rose at dawn. Or else they sat awake in the dark.

Gaven sat up through the first watch of the night, thinking they were probably the longest three bells of his life.

The lightning rail came in to Zolanberg at the start of the second watch. Gaven sat on a bench, cradling a gnome woman on his lap as if she were his young child. He tried to remember her name as he stared at the cart door, waiting for it to open. Lightning flashed along the length of the car as it came to a slow stop, and Gaven allowed himself a quick glance at Senya. She was mostly hidden behind Vond's huge, hairy body, but he could see her legs draped along the bench on one side. This was the best plan Senya could come up with. Her idea was that a man traveling with a small child would not be suspect, and a woman traveling with the minotaur would be carefully avoided. For his part, Gaven had been too sore and tired to think of anything better. He shook his head, trying to prepare himself for what would probably turn into a terrible fight—or at least another headlong flight.

It seemed to take forever for the door to open. Gaven supposed that made sense. If they were searching for him, they wouldn't want a rush of passengers disembarking all at once. There were many travelers, mostly gnomes, standing by the door, waiting to get off, and if Gaven hadn't been twice the height of most of them he might have tried getting lost in that crowd. It would have been a mistake. When the door finally opened, the people standing nearby agitated toward the door, but a loud voice commanded them to form a single line to get off and have identification papers ready.

Gaven's heart beat a rhythm of panic. He still had no identification papers. What would he do if someone asked to see them? It would have been smarter, he reflected, to bluff the staff at the Sivis enclave into giving him papers instead of bullying the Orien agent. Probably harder, but safer.

The disembarking passengers filed off slowly. As their numbers thinned, Gaven could see past them to the gnome guards who scanned the faces of each passenger. Gaven let out a cautious sigh. Zil soldiers were one thing—one he suspected he could deal with. Medani inquisitives or Sentinel Marshals would have been another matter. The guards mostly waved the passengers through with no more than a cursory glance at them and their papers, though Gaven did see one gnome who looked like she might be scanning for magical auras. They paid more attention to the few orcs and humans who got off the cart, staring closely into their faces and checking their identification.

When all the departing passengers were off the cart, a gnome with a lantern climbed in and walked around. He made a wide circle around Vond, though Gaven saw his eyes linger on Senya's legs for a while. He peered more closely at the remaining tallfolk on the cart, pausing to harass a half-orc with completely irrelevant questions. Then he stood in front of Gaven, shining the light into his face.

"That your child?" the soldier demanded.

"Yes." The gnome in his arms gave a small cough, sounding very much like a sick child. "She's not feeling well."

"Poor thing, crowded into the steerage cart. What's her name?"

Gaven swallowed hard, then blurted out the first name that popped into his head. "Rienne."

"Pretty name." He leaned in close, trying in vain for a better look. "You have your papers?"

Gaven jerked his head toward the bench he sat on. "In my pocket."

The soldier chewed his tongue, trying to decide whether to insist on seeing the papers. Then he laid a gentle hand on the gnome woman's shoulder. "Feel better, sweetheart," he said. Then he was gone.

Passengers were finally allowed to board, and the steerage cart grew crowded. Only when the new passengers were getting settled, the door was closed, and the lightning rail finally started moving did Gaven release his hold on the gnome in his arms, setting her down on her feet beside him.

"Rienne?" she said. "That is a pretty name."

Gaven shrugged. "Thank you so much for your help. You probably saved my life."

"Yeah, me and the fact that the guy they sent in to look for you was a family man." She no longer sounded like a child, but like a streetwise woman of middle age. "Whew! It was getting hot in there." She fanned herself with one hand to emphasize the point. "Not that I'm complaining, mind you. It's been a good long time since I had a pair of strong arms around me." She noted Gaven's discomfort, and put a hand on his arm. "Oh, don't worry, sweetheart, you're not my type." Her eyes widened. "Way too big."

* * * * *

He stood overlooking a blasted canyon, desolate of life, like a wound that refused to heal ripped into the earth. Wolves that were not wolves howled, too close at hand, but he did not move. The only sign of life was a churning cloud of smoke and steam that billowed up from a rift in the floor of the canyon.

He fell until he was in the canyon, peering through hot smoke to a great furnace below. He felt a steadying hand on his shoulder. He clasped it in his own hand without tearing his eyes from the eldritch machine, the source of all the smoke. Dragonfire fed the furnace, and fiendish figures tended it.

Beside the great machine, whose great canisters and ichor-filled tubes were too bizarre for his mind to comprehend, a mass of crystal jutted up from the cavern floor. A silver serpent writhed and coiled in the heart of the crystal, as if it were the largest dragonshard ever seen. Caught within its coils was a smear of darkness. Gaven could feel the serpent's rage, a palpable fury radiating like heat from the crystal far below him.

A quiet voice came over his shoulder, words lost in the noise of the furnace like the haziness of dream. Words sprang to his lips in answer—

"Two spirits share one prison beneath the wastes, secrets kept and revelation granted. They bind and are bound, but their unbound whispers rise to the Dragon Between, calling to those who would hear."

A great blast of flame erupted from the furnace, jetting upward to engulf him.

* * * * *

"Gaven!" He struggled to wake up, images and emotions from his dream slow to clear from his mind. Senya was on her knees next to him, shaking him awake. She seemed deeply concerned. "Gaven, are you all right?"

"I . . . I think so." Gaven sat up, rubbing his forehead. "I was asleep."

"You were?" Senya looked perplexed. "But your eyes were open, and you were saying . . . something."

"What did I say?"

"I don't know. Half the time, I think you were speaking another language. You sounded confused, and then you screamed, and that's when I shook you."

Gaven looked around. The other passengers tried not to stare, but everyone glanced his way from time to time. He wondered how many of them understood Draconic, assuming that was the language he had been babbling.

He turned back to Senya. "Thank you for waking me," he said. "It wasn't a pleasant dream."

"You're welcome." The worry melted from Senya's face, and she smiled, then looked up at the window. "Sun's almost up anyway. I think we're due at Sterngate around noon."

Gaven groaned. He felt like he had barely slept, and he didn't feel up to another confrontation of any kind, let alone a border crossing. His body was still recovering from its brush with the rail, and sitting upright proved to be a greater effort than he could manage. He slumped back down on the bench. He didn't think he'd be able to sleep again, but he could at least rest his body.

Despite the sun beginning to peek in the windows, darkness swallowed him again.

* * * * *

Gaven opened his eyes to see Senya leaning over him again, anxiety on her face. He woke quickly, feeling clearheaded and almost well rested.

"Was I shouting again?"

"No, but we'll be at Sterngate soon. I didn't want to wake you any sooner than I had to."

"Thank you. I needed sleep."

"I talked to Vond and Juni, and they're both willing to help us like they did at the last stop, assuming the guards board the cart again. Might be best to be consistent, especially if they're comparing what they see to a passenger list compiled in Zolanberg."

Gaven shook his head. "It'll never work. They're never going to let me across the border without papers."

Senya looked like she was about to argue, then thought better of it. "So what do we do?"

"How far to Sterngate?"

"Not far. We've already turned east toward Marguul Pass, I think."

"So the thing to do is to make sure I'm not on the lightning rail when they come looking for me." He got to his feet and strode to the door leading to the next cart back.

"What are you doing?" Senya asked.

Gaven opened the door and looked around. A small platform jutted out the end of the steerage cart, separated by a short gap from a similar platform at the front of the next cart. "I'm not sure yet." He pulled his head back in and looked at Senya. "Your papers are in order, right? They'll stand up to border scrutiny?"

"Yes."

"Good. Stay here. Stick with Vond if you want. They'll be so busy going through his fur with a comb that they'll barely look at your papers, if I know border guards. I'll see you once we're across."

"What are you doing?" she asked again.

"Still not sure. But I'll figure it out."

* * * * *

Evlan d'Deneith watched the lightning rail approach Sterngate. He stood tall, his arms folded, two good marshals at his back, confident that he was about to make the arrest that would put the final flourish on a long and distinguished career. He'd capture Gaven, who would lead him to Haldren ir'Brassek, and the two would lead him into a comfortable retirement.

Silent lightning arced around the crew cart and along the trailing coaches, flaring blue as they slowed. He watched carefully, in case his quarry tried to jump from the cart before it reached the station, and he had two marshals on the other side doing the same. Two more marshals walked the length of the station. He had spread a net that Gaven could not possibly escape. Evlan drummed his fingers on his arm, impatient.

The carts came to a stop. A platoon of Brelish soldiers stepped forward to open the doors on each cart, barking orders to the passengers inside. All passengers would disembark and file through a checkpoint where their papers would be examined before they would be allowed to leave the station or reboard the lightning rail.

Evlan signaled to one of the marshals behind him, and she followed him aboard the crew cart. They would make their way backward, searching every cart until they found him. The other five marshals would stay in place, watching for any escape attempt.

The crew cart was a maze of arcane devices, cramped quarters, and storage areas. There were hundreds of places a man could hide, but Evlan searched every one. Satisfied that Gaven could not be aboard, they moved to the next cart back, the steerage cart. The passengers had already cleared out, but Evlan could guess from the smell that it had been crowded on the journey from Zolanberg. He wrinkled his nose as he moved through the cart, peering under every bench.

When he reached the rear of the cart, Evlan stuck his head out the door. The marshal he'd left outside gave him an all-clear signal, and he scowled. If Gaven hadn't been seen leaving the lightning rail, then he must still be aboard. He returned to his search.

He opened the door leading to the next cart back, and was struck by the pungent smell of ozone, presumably from the lightning discharges that occurred as the lightning rail moved along its line of conductor stones. He thought it was strange that he hadn't noticed it when leaving the crew cart, but he attributed it to the stench of the steerage cart—the ozone smell was a striking contrast. All the same, he lingered in the space between the carts, peering to the sides and down. He glanced up, and noticed dark clouds blowing in from the west. A storm on the way.

"What is it?" the marshal behind him asked.

"Nothing." He slid open the door to the next cart and went through, ready to search every compartment until he found the fugitive.

* * * * *

Gaven shifted just slightly, looking up from under the small platform at the end of the steerage cart. He saw the door sliding shut behind the Sentinel Marshals, and he let out a long, slow breath.

That was close, he thought. Something made that marshal suspicious.

"Lord Marshal!" a voice cried from the station, very close. Afraid he'd been spotted, Gaven pulled his head back down, clinging to the underside of the platform. His heart pounded, and his muscles started to shake from the exertion of holding himself in place.

The marshal's next words hit him like a punch in the stomach. "We've got the woman!"

CHAPTER
20

Lightning flashed along the crew cart as it started moving again, and a long rumble of thunder answered it in the sky. Gaven took advantage of the sound to jump to the roof of the next cart, where he'd seen them take Senya. His feet slipped on the damp surface, and he started to fall before his hands caught the beam that ran the length of the cart. He hung there for a moment, breathing slowly, before pulling himself back up to a crouch, straddling the beam.

He still hadn't decided what he wanted to do. A loud voice in his mind told him to forget Senya. It seemed clear that the Sentinel Marshals were trying to lure him out of hiding by holding her, and he wasn't eager to fall into their trap. She had chosen to follow him around. He had made no request of her, and he told himself he owed her nothing.

On the other hand, the ruse that had kept him safe at Zolanberg had been her idea. And more importantly, she was at the moment the only person in Khorvaire who was actively trying to keep him out of Dreadhold. That thought had brought him as far as the roof of the cart she was in.

But he stopped there. The lightning rail was just out of Sterngate and wouldn't reach its next stop, Starilaskur, until the middle of the night. If he was going to attempt some kind of rescue, it made more sense to do it under cover of darkness and closer, at least, to his destination. He tried to find a position that would let him relax without slipping off the cart's roof and shield him from the brunt of the wind. He ended up lying facedown on the beam with his arms and legs spread wide to keep him balanced. It wasn't very comfortable, and the rain was coming down harder. At least it was warm. He sighed. It would be a long ride to Starilaskur.

He closed his eyes, suddenly exhausted again. But every time he started to drift into sleep, he felt as though he were slipping off the beam and he woke up with a start. The third time that happened, he opened his eyes and saw a pair of booted feet planted on the roof beside him. Then something hit his head, and everything went black.

* * * * *

A sharp crack of thunder startled Evlan, and he glanced out the window. The storm raged. Trees bent over in the wind, and from time to time a particularly strong gust set the lightning rail to rocking. He'd never heard of high winds blowing the lightning rail off its conductor stones before, but that didn't mean it couldn't happen.

He looked back at his prisoners and was pleased to see Gaven stirring. The marshal had hit him too hard. Still, Gaven was lucky Phaine d'Thuranni hadn't found him first. At the hands of House Thuranni, he'd be dead instead of nursing a headache.

Gaven groaned and looked around. His eyes fell on the elf woman first—he looked at her face, which was set in a grim expression, then to the ropes binding her to her chair. He tested the strength of the ropes binding his own wrists, without putting much effort into breaking them. Only then did he seem to take in the rest of the compartment—the wood paneling, the upholstered chair, the ceiling ornamented with filigree. And then he saw Evlan.

Evlan took that opportunity to introduce himself. "Ah, Gaven," he said. He watched Gaven's eyes drop to the dragonmark on Evlan's neck, then flick over his armor and the heavy bastard sword at his belt. "I am Evlan d'Deneith, Sentinel Marshal of House Deneith, and you are under arrest."

Evlan wasn't sure what to expect from his prisoner—resigned defeat or spirited defiance. He'd seen fugitives go both ways, and a range of emotions in between, upon finding themselves captured and bound. Sometimes they pleaded for their lives or for the lives of their companions. He certainly did not expect the reaction he received.

"A clash of dragons signals the sundering of the Soul Reaver's gates," Gaven said, his eyes wide but fixed on Evlan's neck. On his dragonmark. Evlan found himself looking at Gaven's own mark—a huge, sprawling Siberys mark that extended from his jaw down beneath his shirt.

"Ah, yes," Evlan said. "They did tell me that your mind was off in the Realm of Madness." He sighed and sat down in the seat next to Gaven. He glanced at the woman, whose face had not changed. "Listen, Gaven. Your friend here has been singularly uncooperative. She didn't tell us where to find you, and she says she doesn't know where Haldren ir'Brassek is. So I need you to think very hard in that warped little mind of yours and see if you can tell me where he is."

Gaven stared at the woman.

"Gaven?" Evlan said. "Look at me, Gaven."

Gaven turned his head.

"Where's Haldren ir'Brassek?"

"A clash of dragons signals the sundering of the Soul Reaver's gates." Gaven didn't look at Evlan's dragonmark this time, and Evlan thought he detected the faintest hint of a smile.

"Yes, you said that already. Are we the dragons, Gaven, you and I? Two heirs of dragonmarked houses? Is our confrontation cosmically significant?" Evlan got to his feet and spat on the floor. "I'll tell you what's significant, Gaven. You're going back to Dreadhold, and you're going to rot there. I haven't decided yet what to do with your friend Senya, but I'm fairly certain it will involve rotting in a cell somewhere too. This is no clash of dragons. I'm a Sentinel Marshal, and you're a criminal and a fugitive from justice. You're mine now. Can you understand that? You're mine."

"The hordes of the Soul Reaver spill from the earth, and a ray of Khyber's sun erupts to form a bridge to the sky."

Evlan spun on his heel and left the compartment. He barked an order for another marshal to relieve him, and he started toward the galley cart to get something to eat. He would need to keep his strength up to deal with this one.

As he reached the door at the front of the cart, a gust set the cart rocking again, and Evlan nearly lost his footing. He gripped the handle mounted beside the door, cursing the storm under his breath, and yanked the door open.

A brilliant flash of light exploded in his face with a crash of thunder, sending him sprawling backward into the cart, blind and deaf. The cart shivered from front to back. Evlan lay on his back, gasping for breath. Someone grabbed his hand and tried to pull him up, but he couldn't seem to plant his feet on the floor. He heard shouts—quiet, as though they were far away, though he could feel breath on his face. His sight started to clear at the same time, though blue-green lights danced across his vision. He found his feet at last, mumbling his thanks to whichever of his marshals had helped him stand.

And then he saw Gaven. The prisoner had broken his bonds and forced his way out of the compartment. Two Sentinel Marshals lay on the ground by his feet, unmoving. The storm wind howled through the cart, entering by the door that Evlan had opened. It swirled around Gaven where he stood before blowing out a broken window beside him. Hail drummed the roof, and constant flashes of lightning engulfed the cart like a slow, steady heartbeat of the storm.

Evlan drew his sword and charged. The cart lurched to starboard, sending him careening. His shoulder slammed into the wall of the corridor, but he kept his feet. A few more steps and he was there—at the heart of a churning maelstrom of wind and thunder. The air itself buffeted him backward, thunderclaps ringing in his ears.

"Merciful Sovereigns," he shouted. "What are you?"

"Don't you remember?" Gaven's voice was a peal of thunder. "I'm a criminal and a fugitive. And I'm yours. Your doom."

He stretched out his hand, and lightning coursed outward, swallowing Evlan in another burst of blinding light.

* * * * *

Gaven looked up at a purple-gray sky. Wind lashed the tall grass across his field of vision and blew rainwater onto his face. He sat up with effort and watched the last cart of the lightning rail disappear behind a curtain of rain in the distance. A few yards away, a conductor stone sparked with the memory of the carts' passing, as if imitating the angry sky. He looked around, saw another depression in the grass nearby, and crawled over to where Senya lay flat on her back, staring blankly up at the sky.

He tried to speak, but his voice came out a croak. He coughed, sending a jolt of pain through his throat.

Senya's eyes flicked to his face, then back to the sky. "What does the Prophecy say about me, Gaven?"

He watched her face for a long time, watched her eyes follow the clouds as the sky slowly began to clear. Finally he stood up, bent down to take her hand, and lifted her to her feet.

"I think that's up to you," he said, his voice still gravelly.

"How do you know so much of the Prophecy?"

Gaven found his sword, liberated from the Sentinel Marshals' custody, a few paces away, and Senya's pack nearby. They shouldered their gear and walked to the conductor stone, then to the next one on the line, leading them slowly toward Starilaskur. Gaven thought about his answer for a long time before speaking.

"Years ago, I made it my life's work to learn all I could about it."

"My ancestor said she'd talked to you before."

"That's what she said."

"Well, did she? Had you been there before?"

Memories flooded Gaven's mind, recent past and ancient history blurring together. "I don't know," he said.

"You don't know? Why not?"

"Maybe you can help me," he said. "Does the name Mendaros mean anything to you? Mendaros Alvena Tuorren?"

Saying the name conjured his old friend's face in Gaven's memory—even as he realized that those memories were not his. Mendaros had never known Gaven, though Gaven remembered him clearly.

"The name's a blot on my family's honor," said Senya. "He's reviled as a traitor to Aerenal."

"Why?"

"He conspired with dragons. He opened a door for one of the most devastating attacks against Aerenal in a thousand years."

"Did he? That's a story I'd like to hear sometime."

"Why are you asking about Mendaros? He's been dead for centuries."

Centuries, Gaven thought. That helped put the memories in context. "How many centuries?"

"I'm not sure. Four, maybe five?"

"And he was a relative of yours?"

"Fairly distant, but yes. Naturally, my family would like to emphasize the distance, not the relation."

"How long has your family lived in Khorvaire?"

"About as long as Mendaros has been dead. Coincidentally." Senya stopped, grabbed Gaven's arm, and whirled him to face her. "But it's your turn to answer questions now. What does Mendaros have to do with you and the Prophecy?"

Gaven sighed. "During the war, I worked for House Lyrandar, hunting for the dragonshards they needed to build galleons—or, rather, to bind elementals to power the galleons. Khyber shards are found underground, so I spent a lot of time crawling around tunnels. And the Prophecy was sort of a hobby of mine, something to think about as I traveled. It turns out that Khyber holds a lot of secrets about the Prophecy, maybe even some things the dragons don't know."

"And Mendaros?"

"Well, at one point I found . . . something—a record left by another scholar of the Prophecy. Evidently it was an ancient record, at least four centuries old, because it mentioned Mendaros. As a contemporary."

"What did it say about him?"

Gaven remembered his laugh—a loud, easy laugh. "Not much. It indicated him as a source for some information about the Prophecy. Much the same information that your ancestor gave us in Shae Mordai."

"You knew what he was going to say, you recited the words along with him, because you'd read this ancient record. And that's why my ancestor thought you'd been there before?"

"Something like that."

"I see."

They walked in silence, conductor stone to conductor stone, following the magical line that stretched off past the horizon. The sun broke through the clouds, and Gaven pointed out the hint of a rainbow over the mountains to the east.

"How far to Starilaskur, do you think?" Senya asked.

"Got a map?"

"No."

"Well," Gaven said, "I figure we must have been about half the way from Sterngate when we jumped off. At least six days on foot."

"Six days! I'm exhausted just thinking about it."

"I agree. I suppose we could just wait for the next lightning rail and try to jump aboard."

"People die doing that."

"I know. I was joking."

"Wait—we're near the end of the Seawalls, right? We can't be far from New Cyre."

"New Cyre?"

"A refugee town, more or less. After the Mourning, Breland gave a little patch of land to surviving Cyrans. It can't be more than a few days east, nestled up against the mountains."

"New Cyre it is, then." Gaven turned his steps away from the next conductor stone, setting his course to run along the line of the mountains instead. "From there, we'll try to find a carriage or something to carry us to Vathirond."

"And what's in Vathirond, anyway?"

Gaven shrugged. "After twenty-six years? Who knows? Maybe nothing but memories."

CHAPTER
21

V ery well, Gaven," Senya said, "if you're going to be a fugitive, we're going to do this right."

Senya's hunch had proved accurate, and they had reached New Cyre after dark on their third day of travel. Now she was dragging Gaven through the tiny village.

"What are you talking about?"

Gaven was exhausted. They had pressed hard to reach New Cyre before resting for the night, and he wanted nothing more than to find a comfortable bed. Despite their stops in Shae Mordai and Grellreach, the last time he'd slept in an inn had been White-cliff, and he was almost ready to go back to Dreadhold just for the beds.

"We're going to get you some papers."

"How are we going to do that in a town this size? I think it might have a pickpocket or two, but a forger?"

"Would you mind keeping your voice down?"

"Sorry." Gaven glanced around at the darkened windows.

"And trust me."

Gaven watched in bemused wonder as Senya—heir to a noble warrior line of Aerenal—found the few people in New Cyre who were still awake, asked just the right questions, and led him to what must have been the only house anywhere between Starilaskur and Darguun that could get him forged papers. He stayed up through the night watching the forger—a gnome with a thick accent who must have been a renegade offshoot of House Sivis—carefully tracing the lines of a magical sigil that would convince any inspector that his papers were authentic. The sun brightened the sky behind the Seawalls by the time they finally left the forger's house, Gaven admiring his new identification and traveling papers.

"Keven d'Lyrandar," he said, trying to get used to the name.

"This makes me really uncomfortable, pretending to be a legitimate heir of my house."

"It's either that or wrap yourself like a mummy to hide that dragonmark," Senya whispered.

Shutters were starting to open in the village, and Gaven was suddenly aware of the stares they drew as strangers who had arrived in the night.

"Well, it might work, as long as I don't show these papers to any other Lyrandar."

They stood at the door of one of the village inns—New Cyre, though small, had enough transient residents to support a handful of inns—and found it locked. Undaunted, Senya pounded on the door until a sleepy-looking woman opened the door.

"Respectable folk aren't about at this hour," she said, scowling at Senya.

"Please," Gaven said, cutting off Senya's retort, "we've been traveling for days and just need beds."

"Time for sleeping's done."

"We understand, but—"

"If you understand, then why are you asking for a place to sleep? Why don't you go to the Jorasco place? The halflings'll take anyone who shows enough silver."

They'll also look over my papers with too close an eye, Gaven thought.

Senya interjected, "Silver? We'll pay gold." She produced two galifars to emphasize her point, and smiled as the woman's eyes fixed on the gleaming coins.

"And will you be needing one room or two?"

"Two," Gaven said.

"Please, come in."

* * * * *

New Cyre by daylight was a strange experience. To Gaven's mind, it was easy to imagine that he was in Cyre. The fashions and architecture he'd seen on his previous visits to that nation were on proud display, and the people spoke with the lilting accents of Cyrans. In his cell in Dreadhold, Gaven had heard only vague and conflicting reports of what had happened to Cyre, the nature of the magical cataclysm that had engulfed the nation. Most of Cyre's residents had been killed in an instant, he had heard, but here was a village full of refugees who had been lucky enough to escape the Mourning, presumably because they had been traveling or fighting abroad when it occurred.

As they walked to House Orien's enclave, Gaven found himself thinking of his own home, House Lyrandar's island refuge of Stormhome. When he was convicted and sent to Dreadhold, his family had declared him excoriate, cut out of the house, and he was no longer welcome in Stormhome. He felt an odd sort of kinship with these displaced Cyrans, who spoke so lovingly and passionately about the home they had lost.

Gaven hardly dared to breathe as another agent of House Orien examined his papers. She stared at them a long time, reading each word carefully, and Gaven felt sure she would recognize the forgery. When she handed the papers back to him with a smile, saying, "Enjoy your trip, Master Lyrandar," he could scarcely believe it. He shot several glances back over his shoulder as he walked to the coach, certain that she was summoning a Sentinel Marshal to arrest him. But apparently the forgery was a success. He and Senya boarded the coach, settled into a pair of comfortable seats, and began to relax as they started to move.

Only when they were up to full speed did Gaven stop looking out the windows and actually look around the coach. It was similar to the lightning rail coach—the well-appointed ones, not the steerage cart—but on a smaller and slightly less lavish scale. Instead of a private compartment, they had a cushioned bench with a high back, affording them some privacy. The ceiling was elegantly carved with the unicorn seal of House Orien. There were no passengers in the only other seats Gaven could see, the ones across the aisle to his left.

He drew a deep breath, savoring the woody smell of the coach, and let it out slowly. He turned his gaze back out the window, trying to ignore the warmth of Senya's body beside him, and watched the mountains drift slowly past. The effect was hypnotic, and his eyes started to droop.

"Who's Rienne?" Senya's question jolted him fully awake. He didn't remember ever having mentioned Rienne to Senya.

"You tell me," he said. He wasn't going to give more information than he had to.

Senya laughed at his guarded answer. "That's what you called Juni, remember? The gnome on the lightning rail? The guard asked your daughter's name, and you said Rienne." She watched his face, and he concentrated on keeping it impassive. Her smile faded. "Do you have a daughter?"

"No," Gaven said. "I just gave him the first name that popped into my head."

"But whose name is it?"

Gaven turned to look out the window again. "Before . . . all this happened, I was to be married." He glanced at Senya and saw her eyebrows rise. "Rienne came from a minor noble family, and our marriage would have been advantageous to both our families. House Lyrandar is always looking for political alliances while officially maintaining the neutrality demanded by the Edicts of Korth, and the families it makes connections with stand to gain a great deal of wealth and prestige." He paused. "So that's who Rienne is."

"A nice arranged marriage, then?" she said, leaning closer. "Loveless? Passionless?"

Gaven turned to look past Senya out the windows across the aisle.

"Was she human? Is she an old woman now?"

"She's a Khoravar, elf-blooded like me."

"And she's in Vathirond? All this time I've been helping you reunite with your long-lost love?"

"No, she lives in Stormhome, as far as I know." He scowled. "Seeing Rienne again is not a priority."

"Oh, I see." A mischievous smile crept onto Senya's face. "The romance ended badly?"

Gaven scowled, and Senya's smile disappeared. "My life ended badly," he said. He waved his new papers in her face. "I'm living someone else's now."

He turned back to the window and smiled grimly at the clouds darkening the afternoon sky.

* * * * *

As soon as she stepped into Krathas's office Rienne knew that there was news of Gaven—and that it wasn't good news. The old half-orc's face spoke volumes.

"There's been an incident," he said.

Rienne put a hand on a chair back, then stumbled around it to sit down. "What happened? Is he dead?"

"I don't think he's dead, and I'm not even sure what did happen. There are people working hard to keep this quiet."

"Tell me."

Krathas took a deep breath, then plunged in. "What I hear is that a team of Sentinel Marshals captured Gaven on the lightning rail near Sterngate."

"Captured him? But he escaped."

"Apparently. There was some kind of storm between Sterngate and Starilaskur, and one carriage was blown open."

"Blown open?"

"Sort of funny, isn't it? They call it the lightning rail, but then a lightning storm does this." Krathas smiled weakly.

"One carriage—the one where Gaven was?"

"It appears so."

"So he called in the storm and used it to escape. That means he's in Breland somewhere."

"Probably. Quite possibly trying to get here—that lightning rail line runs through Starilaskur and on to Vathirond."

"There's something else," Rienne said. Krathas's eyes were fixed on his desk.

"One of the Sentinel Marshals was killed," he said.

CHAPTER
22

The coach stopped too often, but never for long. At some point in the night, they had a longer stop to bring a new driver aboard and change the magebred horses that pulled the cart, but even so, Gaven figured they were moving most of the day. And within two days of leaving New Cyre, the coach pulled into Starilaskur, eastern Breland's largest city. They stayed in a hostel that night, which was a vast improvement over trying to sleep sitting up on the coach's bench. The next day, they boarded a new coach bound for Vathirond.

Another two days of endless rolling and bouncing, punctuated with fitful attempts at sleep or conversation, brought them almost to Vathirond's gate. Gaven awoke from another nightmare to a child's loud voice in a bench near the front of the cart.

"What is it?" the boy said.

"I'm not sure, sweetie." The child's mother kept her voice low, trying to calm him. "Probably a dragonhawk."

"But dragonhawks live in Aundair. We're still in Breland." He sounded as though he couldn't believe his mother's ignorance.

"But we're in northeast Breland now, actually not far from Aundair."

That seemed to satisfy the child, and Gaven closed his eyes, settling back into his bench with a smile. Then Senya, sitting by the window, hit his chest. She was staring intently out the window.

"What is it?"

"Look." She pointed out the window and up, skyward.

He leaned over her and peered out, trying to follow the direction of her finger. At first he saw nothing but the gray clouds that had been hanging in the sky for days, glowering but never quite getting around to storming. Then he saw a shape flying in the clouds. Presumably, the same shape the child had seen.

"That's no dragonhawk," he whispered.

"Vaskar?"

"Probably. It's big enough."

"Where's he going?"

Gaven glanced at the sun, still low in the sky. "More or less eastward. To the Mournland. To raise the Sky Caves of Thieren Kor."

They watched the dragon soar in and out of the clouds for a long moment.

"What do you think it will be like, if the Storm Dragon succeeds?"

A vision from his nightmare flashed into Gaven's mind: numberless legions of soldiers marching beneath bone-white banners bearing a blasphemous rune, leaving carnage and devastation in their wake. Senya and the coach around him suddenly fell away, and he stood on the desolate plain in the army's wake. Vultures flapped their heavy wings and peered at him sidelong before returning to their grisly feast. In the distance, above the marching legions, dragons soared among the clouds.

"Gaven?"

He was back in the coach, though he still felt the clammy air of the battlefield on his skin. Senya stared at him, eyes wide, her back pressed against the window. He curled around his stomach, resting his forehead against the smooth wood of the bench in front of him.

"Are you all right?" Senya whispered.

"Do I look all right?"

"What is it? What did you see?"

He turned his head back and forth, feeling the wood against his skin. Senya put a tender hand on his back, and he tried to concentrate on the sensation of her touch.

"I don't want to see any more," he said. "I just want to be here, now. Blind like everybody else."

* * * * *

"Lady Alastra?"

Rienne looked up from the cup of warm wine she cradled in her hands. The messenger was a young half-orc cursed with a face that could break mirrors, with wide-set black eyes and a nose and mouth that were both like ragged holes in his gray skin. He wore a sleeveless shirt that showed off his muscles, and his black hair was cropped close to his head.

"Yes?" she said, trying to smile.

He looked awkward, uncomfortable around women perhaps. She noticed a flush in his cheeks, and he didn't meet her gaze. "Krathas sent me," he stammered.

"Of course he did. You have news?"

"I'm to tell you that he has arrived by Orien coach. Er—not Krathas. He's the one who told me. But I don't know who he is. Uh, I mean, I know who Krathas is. I don't know who has arrived by Orien coach."

A brain to match his face, Rienne thought. "I do. Thank you."

The messenger's smile revealed jagged rows of crooked and broken teeth, and did nothing to improve his looks. Rienne returned the smile as best she could, then ignored the boy as he murmured some pleasantry, bowed, and made his exit. She sipped her wine, trying to calm her nerves and her pounding heart.

Gaven is here, she thought. Now what?

* * * * *

Gaven was dimly aware of Senya saying something beside him, just as he had vaguely noticed the busy plaza they stood in. But the thing that had captivated his attention since they emerged from the Orien station was a ship, ringed with a circle of dancing flame, floating in the air across the plaza. She was moored to a tower that proudly flew the kraken banner of House Lyrandar. A Lyrandar airship.

He had to fly one.

His mind spun, trying to remember all he had learned about the research his house had been doing, trying to make these ships work. The ring of fire must be a manifestation of a fire elemental bound to the ship, probably granting her propulsion rather than levitation. Piloting the ship, then, was almost certainly just a matter of imposing one's will on the elemental bound into her, not too different from piloting an oceangoing Lyrandar galleon. He wondered if his dragonmark would help him do that—his lack of a mark had hindered him in his previous attempts to pilot galleons.

"Gaven!" Senya pulled on his arm. He tore his eyes away from the ship—the most beautiful thing he'd ever seen—and looked at her.

"What do we do now?" she said.

Her question jolted him back to the present, and to something that he had been turning over in his mind for days. "I'm not sure we do anything."

"What?" She arched an eyebrow at him.

"Listen, Senya. I meant to have this conversation with you back in Korranberg, but we got so caught up in . . . things, and I never got around to it. But now that we're here, you could go anywhere you want, do anything you want. It doesn't make any sense for you to shackle yourself to me, especially since there's a strong possibility of real shackles in my future. I have no idea what I'm going to do, and I don't want to tangle you up in whatever mess I end up making. I think we should go our separate ways."

"Without me you'll be bound for the cold northeast in a week's time."

"I can handle myself. And besides, I know people here."

"After all these years? People move, you know. Or die."

"That's not the point."

"The point is you want to get rid of me."

"Yes," Gaven said. He watched her eyes narrow and her nostrils flare in anger.

"Too bad. I'm not leaving."

Gaven sighed. "Senya, I appreciate all you've done for me already. I have enjoyed your company these last couple of weeks. But I couldn't—I don't want you to suffer because of your association with me."

"It's too late for that. Ever since the lightning rail, they know me."

"Those people won't be bothering us again."

"No, but I'm sure they checked the passage records in Korranberg. They know who you're traveling with—they know my name. And that's all they need."

Gaven put his hands to his temples. "I'm sorry, Senya. I wish—"

"You seem to have forgotten that I chose this. Not just in Darguun, either. I was in this up to my neck when I got on that wyvern's back in Q'barra. I've made my choicees. So what do we do next?"

He shook his head. "Let's see if Krathas is still alive."

* * * * *

"Lady Alastra, there's one more thing you should know." Krathas spoke cautiously, and Rienne moved her hand to Maelstrom's hilt instinctively.

"What?"

"Gaven has not been traveling alone. He has a companion." Rienne raised her eyebrows, and Krathas flushed. "A woman."

"That's his business," Rienne said, trying to ignore the icy claw touching her heart.

Krathas was visibly relieved. "Just thought you should know."

"I appreciate your concern, wasted though it may be."

Krathas inclined his head in a small bow.

"So where is he now?" she asked.

"On his way here."

"Krathas, would you do me the favor of allowing me to greet Gaven alone?"

"Of course, Lady." Krathas got to his feet and worked his way around his desk. He laid a hand on her shoulder and smiled. "Olladra's fortune."

Rienne returned his smile warmly. "Thank you."

As Krathas shuffled out the door, she sank into his desk chair, her heart racing. She'd been in Vathirond nearly two weeks, working with Krathas, waiting for this day. She had rehearsed her eventual meeting with Gaven in her mind so many times, but it was different each time—she had no idea how he would respond to her, what he might say to explain his behavior, whether he would forgive her for hers. And in her mind, it had always been the two of them, trying to pick up where they left off all those years ago. She'd been so naïve.

"Here it is, right where I left it."

It was his voice, just outside the door. Her mouth went dry.

"Looks like it hasn't been painted in thirty years." A woman's voice.

Rienne drew a deep breath through her nostrils and let it out slowly through pursed lips. Then the door swung open.

In her mind, this encounter had always started the same. She was cool, a little distant, aloof. Her voice low, she said, "Hello, Gaven," and he was thunderstruck, surprised. She began with the upper hand. The reality was drastically different.

He stood framed in the doorway, so beautiful to her eyes. She was overwhelmed with a rush of the love she'd felt so strongly, so long ago, and had worked so hard to suppress these last decades. Then came a wave of remorse—this was what she had done to him. The weight of twenty-six years in Dreadhold was clearly visible on his face and in his posture. His hair was long and unkempt, and his face looked haggard. Then she saw his dragonmark, and she gasped.

"Rienne." His voice was flat, betraying no surprise or emotion.

The woman stepped into view behind him, peering over his shoulder into the office. She was an elf, pretty in a fey sort of way, with eyes too big for her face and stained with blue makeup. Her lips were full and also painted, the bright red of a streetwalker, and she wore heeled boots and a chest-hugging coat to match. Rienne scowled.

"Rienne?" the woman said. "So she is in Vathirond after all. What a nice surprise!" The red lips twisted into a sardonic smile as she looked at Gaven.

This was nothing like Rienne had imagined.

"Where's Krathas?" Gaven said.

Rienne stood. " 'Where's Krathas?' Hm. It's good to see you, too."

Gaven stepped into the room. "I'm s—no, I'm not sorry. What do you expect me to say?" His voice and his face came alive with anger. "The usual pleasantries don't seem to fit. The last time I saw you, a pack of Sentinel Marshals were dragging me out of the room. You put on quite a show of grief, as I recall. No, Rienne, it's not good to see you. I didn't come here to see you, I came to find Krathas. Where is he?" Without waiting for an answer, he stepped into the room and started peering into the shelves that lined the walls.

"Well said, Gaven," the streetwalker chimed in.

Rienne put her hand on Maelstrom's hilt and stepped around the desk to face the woman. "Would you leave us? We have a lot to talk about."

The red lips pouted, but the mocking smirk lingered at their corners. "And miss all the fun?"

Rienne noticed the woman's hand settling on the hilt of her own sword, which she hadn't seen before. Perhaps she wasn't a streetwalker after all.

"We haven't been introduced," Rienne said. "I am Rienne ir'Alastra."

"Yes, I know. The one Gaven was to marry. I gather it ended badly."

"And your name?"

"Senya Alvena Arrathinen." Rienne heard the first hint of an elvish lilt in her voice.

Gaven began looking around the desk.

"Pleased to meet you, Senya," Rienne said.

"Remember what Gaven said about the usual pleasantries?" Senya smiled and blinked her too-long eyelashes at Rienne before dropping the smile and stepping past her into the room. "What are we looking for, Gaven?"

"An adamantine box, about the size of a small book, but thicker. Maybe two small books."

Rienne felt a surge of fury replace the love and guilt she had felt on first seeing him. "You will not ignore me, Gaven."

He glanced at her, then bent to open a desk drawer. "I'm not ignoring you, Rienne. I just have nothing to say to you."

"Well, I have some things to say to you."

"Go ahead." He slammed the first drawer shut and slid another one open.

"Don't you think I deserve an explanation?" she said.

He glanced up at her again, then back down. "No."

"I think I do. I loved you once, Gaven, and you made me believe you loved me."

He straightened and folded his arms. His mouth was a thin line as his eyes bored into her. "Funny way of showing your love," he said, "turning me over to House Deneith."

"I had to! You were out of control!"

Rienne heard the window behind her shake in its pane as Gaven bent to the desk again. "You had to," he said with a snort.

"Gaven, please talk to me." Rienne had lost any shred of control she might have had over the situation, and she resigned herself to pleading with him. "I need to understand what happened—and what's happening now. What is going on?"

Gaven stood again and looked at her. She saw something in his eyes—pity, maybe, or compassion—and thought for the first time that all might not be lost.

"A great deal has happened, Rienne. I . . . I do regret your part in it."

Rienne felt her face flush as tears sprang to her eyes. "I do as well."

He held her gaze for a moment, then pushed past her to search the drawers on the other side of the desk. "So I think it would be best if you don't have any part in what's happening now," he said. Rienne felt the breath squeezed out of her chest. "You should go."

He was so close, she could just reach out and rest a hand on his back. For a moment she thought that if she did, her touch would bring everything back to normal, would bring him back to her. Just as she began reaching for him, the elf woman interrupted.

"Didn't you hear him?" Senya said. "You should go." Her hand was back on the hilt of her sword.

Rienne walked around the desk and stopped in the doorway. She turned back to Gaven and produced a thick box from beneath her outer cloak. "Is this what you're looking for?"

Gaven leaped around the desk and snatched the heavy metal box from her. "Krathas gave it to you? Or did you steal it from him?"

"Steal it?" Blood pulsed at her temples as fury surged in her heart again. "I have done things I regret, Gaven—a great many things. But I have not stooped to theft. Or murder."

"Murder?" Gaven barely glanced up from the box, which seemed to consume his attention. She wondered again what was inside. What was so important to him that he asked Krathas to keep it safe?

Her throat was tight, and she blinked back a fresh wave of tears. It was too much to bear. "Goodbye, Gaven." She kept her pace tightly under control as she strode out of the room and down the hall, without a backward glance. Only then did she break into a run. She ran down the stairs, out of the building, and into the street, and a shadow detached itself from an alley to follow her. She pulled Maelstrom from its sheath and turned to face this new attacker. The poor fool would bear the brunt of her fury.

"Lady Alastra!" His voice brought her up short, and she lowered Maelstrom's point. A dwarf hurried up to her, dressed for the neighborhood except for a signet ring that gleamed in the starlight. "Are you hurt?"

"I'm fine," Rienne answered. "Who are you?"

"A friend," the man said, but his tone was not convincing. "Gaven in there?"

Rienne's eyes darted back to the building that held Krathas's office, and that was apparently the only answer the dwarf needed. He turned and ran back the way he'd come.

CHAPTER
23

S he's going to turn us in, you know," Senya said. "We need
to get out of here."

"In a moment." Gaven had set the adamantine box on
the desk and was on his knees in front of it, carefully manipulating a set of dials set in the front. For twenty-six years he had
clung to these numbers, the key to unlocking the one thing
he still owned in the world outside Dreadhold. They were the
numbers of the Prophecy, and as he set the dials to open the
box the Draconic verses danced through his mind: the land of
thirteen dragons, three ages of the world, sixteen gods. Then
five beasts at war, three shards of three dragons for nine, and
another thirteen—thirteen moons. He stared at the numbers
before opening the box. "And the Storm Dragon emerges after
twice thirteen years," he whispered. Then he shook his head and
opened the box.

Senya gasped, and Gaven felt a chill wash over him. It had
been haunting his dreams, but he had not seen it in so many years.
Cradled in black velvet, the clear crystal glowed with a purple-
black light from a writhing vein of color at its heart. It mesmerized
him as it had when he had first found it, and he stretched out a
hand to it without consciously willing it. His hand brushed against
Senya's as they both touched its surface, which seemed to jolt them
both out of a trance.

"A nightshard?" Senya said, drawing a hand across her eyes.
"What's this all about?"

"It's called the Heart of Khyber," Gaven said quietly, "sort of a
dark twin to the Eye of Siberys. It—" He stopped, listening. Yes,
there were footsteps in the hall, slow and heavy. "They're here.
Come on."

Gaven shut the adamantine box and spun the dials. Senya

moved to the door, still open from Rienne's departure, and quickly jumped back, taking cover behind the jamb.

"Stay where you are!" a gruff voice shouted from the hallway. "Gaven the excoriate, surrender yourself to the Ghorad'din!"

"Dwarves," Senya whispered as Gaven leaped to cover on the other side of the open door and slammed it shut. "House Kundarak."

"Elite dwarf soldiers, no less," Gaven muttered. "How many?"

"I saw two, but they were just coming around the corner. Might be more."

The footsteps were right outside. "Open this door!" the same voice yelled.

"Surrender? Open the door?" Gaven's tone was mocking. "Just like dwarves to expect someone else to do all your work for you." He slid his sword out of its sheath, holding it in one hand and the box in the other.

The words were barely out of his mouth when a body slammed hard into the door on the other side. The door was strong, but not strong enough to withstand an angry dwarf. It slammed open toward Senya, who knocked it back into the dwarf charging through. The dwarf stumbled, and Gaven brought the hilt of his sword down to ring on the man's helmet, sending him staggering backward into his companions.

That moment of confusion provided Gaven a chance to size up his foes. Three of them, all dwarves, two women. They all wore the manticore sigil of House Kundarak, the Mark of Warding, but Gaven didn't see a dragonmark on any of them. The man and one of the women were dressed to fit in to the slum where Krathas's office was located, which suggested that they had been here for a while, ready for him. Gaven silently cursed both Rienne and Krathas for this new betrayal. The third dwarf, evidently the leader, was a handsome noblewoman wearing a silk shirt of a rich red that complemented her marble-black skin. House Kundarak didn't send inexperienced warriors far from their mountainous home in the east—these would be elite warriors, a real challenge.

I'm going to need both hands, Gaven thought. He tossed the adamantine box behind him, where it landed with a heavy thud on Krathas's desk.

Senya stepped out from behind the door to face the dwarves,

the tip of her sword pointing at the face of the nearest foe. The dwarf glowered at her, evidently incensed at having had the door pushed in his face. He hefted his spiked mace and charged. Senya smiled, shifting her sword ever so slightly.

The dwarf threw his weight sideways and crashed into Gaven, knocking him to the floor and sending his sword clattering to the floor. Gaven barely had time to roll to the side before the mace crashed down where his chest had been. He rolled with his momentum and came up on his feet, but his sword was on the other side of the angry dwarf.

He glanced at Senya as she parried the other soldier's short sword. "Come to think of it," he said, "I like your plan. Let's get out of here."

The leader of the dwarves planted herself in the doorway in response, her grim smile seeming to indicate that she looked forward to Gaven's attempt to get past her. Gaven spat a few arcane words, sheathed his body in crackling blue flame, then lunged toward the dwarf who had knocked him down.

"That's right, knock into me now," he said with a grin.

As he had hoped, the dwarf avoided his lunge, which provided Gaven the opening he needed to reach his sword. He lifted the blade and swept it in a wide arc that forced the dwarf back another couple of steps. That gave Gaven room to reach the desk and pick up the box with the Heart of Khyber in it.

He glanced at Senya, who was still on the defensive, warding off a flurry of cuts and jabs. "Come on," he said. He jumped onto the desk and threw himself at the window.

Heavy shutters splintered around him, and he fell. Another syllable of a spell brought his fall under control, and he floated gently from the second-story window to the street below. He looked up just in time to see Senya hurtle out the window, somersaulting in the air and landing hard on her feet nearby.

A crossbow bolt bit into Gaven's shoulder, and he glanced around. He hadn't seen a crossbow on any of the dwarves upstairs, which meant there was at least one more waiting here on the street. He heard one of the dwarves follow Senya out the window, and he knew the others wouldn't be far behind. Shaking his head, he broke into a run.

Rain hissed into steam as it made contact with the flames

wrapping his body, and he laughed as he ran. He felt the wind at his back, and he willed it to carry Senya along with him, and it obeyed his will. His feet barely touched the ground—he felt the cobblestones brushing the soles of his boots as he ran. Then the cobblestones ended, and it was rocks and grass that kissed his feet as he ran along the river out of the city. He let the fire wash off his body and felt the rain splatter on his face and drench his clothes. No more thought of pursuit entered his mind. He was the wind, carrying Senya as he blew—he was the rain, dancing in the wind and pattering on the ground. He was the storm.

When he finally stopped running, he stood with his face to the rain, his arms outstretched, and laughed. Senya collapsed on the ground at his feet, and still he laughed.

* * * * *

Rienne watched the dwarf approach through the rain, and she knew that Gaven had escaped. The dwarf's scarlet shirt stuck to her skin, revealing the outline of her dragonmark beneath it. Her shoulders were hunched, and she walked slowly despite the downpour.

She came close to the doorway where Rienne stood out of the rain and gave a small bow. "I am Ossa d'Kundarak," she said. "You should have come to us first."

"I know." It was an effort to speak. "You followed me?"

"You were followed from Stormhome, yes. We had a suspicion that you might try to contact him."

"What happened?"

Ossa shook her head, as if she weren't at all sure what had happened. "We found him, of course, in Krathas's office, with the elf woman. They refused to surrender, drew arms against us, and then jumped out the window. They got away," she added, quite unnecessarily.

"You had someone on the street, surely."

"Kerra hit both of them with her crossbow. She thinks the woman must be pretty badly wounded. But it didn't slow them." She shook her head again, bewildered. "They ran fast. Impossibly fast. And when we ran after, it was like—" She looked away, into the sky where lightning danced among the dark clouds. "Clearly, he used magic to impede us. The wind blew in our faces, slowed us down. Thadar was struck by lightning."

"Is he badly hurt?"

"He's at the House of Healing now, but he'll be fine. Thank you."

"It's quite a storm," Rienne said, turning her eyes to the sky as well.

"Unnatural, surely. Must be related to his dragonmark."

"I suppose. I've never seen anything like it, and I've worked with House Lyrandar most of my life."

"Let me say again, Lady Alastra, you should have come to us. He's clearly dangerous."

Rienne nodded.

"Did you talk to him at all?"

"A little, yes."

"Did he say anything important? Anything that might suggest where he is going, what he's up to?"

"He said precious little. I was hoping for some kind of explanation, anything that would help me understand what happened to him. I got nothing."

"What was he doing here?"

Rienne was not ready to betray him again. She answered as vaguely as she could. "Looking for Krathas."

"Do you know why?"

She shrugged. "Krathas was his only friend left after his trial. I think he was looking for someone he could trust."

"What about the woman? What's she doing with him?"

"Isn't it obvious?" Her stomach tightened, and she felt a bit light-headed.

"I suppose it is. You look pale. Are you unwell?"

"It's been a trying evening. I think I'd better get inside, warm up, get some rest."

"I understand." Ossa bowed again and started to turn away. She stopped and looked back over her shoulder at Rienne. "You will contact us if you should run into him again?"

"I will." As she said it, some part of her thought she actually might. The idea saddened her more than her encounter with Gaven had.

"Good night, Lady Alastra."

"Good night."

CHAPTER
24

T he wind blew itself out in cyclonic eddies once Gaven stopped running. Lightning blasted the ground near where he stood, and his laughter died with the winds. He looked around at the river, the fields of grain on either side, and the city in the distance. Only then did he notice the small pool of blood spreading from Senya's body, and he fell to his knees beside her.

Several crossbow bolts had hit her as they ran from the dwarves. Some had fallen out, but three penetrated deeply enough that they remained firmly lodged—one in her lower back, one in her shoulder, one in her thigh. The one in her leg had gone deepest, and Gaven couldn't imagine how she had continued running so far. Her breathing was shallow, her skin bone-white, and her eyes wide and staring. Murmuring a prayer to Olladra, the goddess of good fortune who watched over healers, he set to work extracting the bolts.

It was grim work. Senya had lost a good deal of blood, and she barely had strength to groan as he pulled the first one out. Fortunately, the bolts were little more than sharpened sticks with fletching, so they didn't take more flesh with them as he pulled them out. By the time he got the second one out, her eyes were closed.

"You shouldn't have left Haldren," he whispered as he set to work on the third. "Darraun would have had you closed up and back on your feet in no time."

To his surprise, Senya managed a weak smile, and her eyes fluttered open. Her lips moved a bit, but no sound came out.

"I know," Gaven said. "If you were still with Haldren, you probably wouldn't have been hurt. I told you it was dangerous to come with me. I'm surprised you made it this long."

He suddenly felt very alone. He missed Darraun's conversation, even his prying questions. He worried that Senya might not recover from these wounds. And he had driven Rienne away.

He took off his shirt and tore it up to make bandages, binding Senya's wounds to the best of his ability. He pulled a blanket from her pack, spread it over her, and sat beside her, watching the sun's last glow fade from the western clouds. When it was dark, he opened his adamantine box and turned the Heart of Khyber over and over in his hands, watching the vibrant coil of purple-black twist and pulse in the crystal's depths.

* * * * *

The night was well into the fourth watch, and part of Gaven's mind reasoned that he was hallucinating. Even so, the inky coil of color in the heart of the nightshard seemed to have taken on a draconic face, and he had the distinct sense that it listened to him and might answer. So he asked the question that had haunted his mind for most of thirty years.

"Why have you done this to me?"

"You were the one who found me," the dragon said, though Gaven's lips moved as it spoke.

Gaven remembered stretching his broken hand out, despite the pain, to touch the perfect nightshard. The Heart of Khyber.

"You've ruined my life."

"I've given your life purpose." Its voice was Gaven's, but lower.

"I don't want that purpose," he spat. Chasing the Prophecy, manipulating history so that he—Gaven!—could become a god.

"Then choose a new one. But you can't carry on without one."

"Who are you?" Another memory—a draconic face reflected back at him in the swirling waters of a dark pool.

"Who do you think I am?"

Senya stirred in her sleep. Gaven thought she looked better.

"You're me," he muttered. "And you're a dragon who's been dead for five hundred years. With your dying will, you stored your memories in this damned nightshard—you gave them to me. Without having any idea what you were doing to me."

Choose a new one, he thought. He turned the Heart of Khyber over in his hands, thinking of its bright twin.

* * * * *

Senya emerged from unconsciousness to the sensation of warmth spreading through her shoulder—a warmth that brought chills in its wake, like the kisses of a lover. Her eyes fluttered open, and she saw a halfling man crouched beside her on the ground, smiling at her. His hand was the source of the warmth, and the dragonmark visible on his bare upper arm confirmed her first guess: he was a healer of House Jorasco. She returned the smile briefly, then looked around in a panic.

"Where's Gaven?"

The healer's smile flickered but didn't die. "Good afternoon, Senya," he said. "You're safe now. Don't worry."

A couple of other halflings busied themselves around a wagon nearby, but there was no sign of Gaven.

"What happened?" she said. "How did you find me?"

"You were attacked by bandits," the halfling said, a look of concern on his face. He put a hand on her forehead, checking for fever, but seemed satisfied. "You suffered some serious wounds, but you're going to be fine now. Your traveling companion, Keven d'Lyrandar, summoned us and paid for our services. I expect he'll be waiting for you at the House of Healing in town." He watched her reaction carefully.

"I understand," she said. "Thank you."

He shifted his attention to the wound in her leg, effectively hiding his face from her view. "You mentioned someone named Gaven?"

"It wasn't bandits that attacked us," Senya said. "It was Keven's cousin, an excoriate of his house named Gaven."

"I see," the healer said. Senya could only see the back of his head. "And he loosed the crossbow that wounded you?"

Senya's pulse quickened, and she was suddenly sure the halfling saw through her lie. "No, he wasn't alone. There was an old man, a sorcerer I think, and a warforged, and another human with a crossbow. He's the one that wounded me."

"I see," the halfling repeated. Senya felt the warmth spreading through her leg, unknotting the muscles and washing away the ache.

The healer smiled and pulled his hands away. "I think you're ready to be moved." He looked up and signaled to the other halflings, still avoiding Senya's eyes. The others brought a stretcher over and gently rolled Senya onto it, then carried her over to the wagon. When they had loaded her in and carefully strapped her down, they clambered aboard, and the wagon started rolling.

Senya watched the clouds drift across the sky and wondered where Gaven was. She knew that the chance he lingered in Vathirond's House of Healing was next to none.

* * * * *

Gaven crouched on the horse's back, thrilling to the feel of its muscles as it galloped along the road. He hadn't ridden in more years than he could remember, and it had taken a while to get his body into the rhythm of the horse's stride. Once he did that, though, he felt like he was running, his muscles moving in perfect synchronization with his mount's. The wind blew his hair back from his face and cooled the sweat from his skin. Best of all, his mind was completely submerged in the pounding hooves and flexing muscles, the rush of speed and wind. Any time his thoughts began to stray toward Rienne or Senya, he forced them back to the horse and the run.

Hours and miles sped by under the mare's stride. Vathirond—along with Rienne and Senya—fell farther and farther behind him, and he thought as little as he could about what lay ahead. He lost himself so completely in his flight that he nearly fell from the saddle when his mount abruptly slowed.

They had reached the Mournland. A wall of gray mist hung in the air like a funeral shroud, swallowing the road ahead, and the horse would not get any closer.

"It's all right, lady," he murmured as he dismounted. "You've done well. You see if you can find your way back to the barn I stole you from, huh?"

He lifted a bag from the mare's saddle and slung it over his shoulder. It held the scant supplies that would sustain him in the Mournland—journeybread that would keep him nourished and full, and a magic waterskin that would never run dry. He regretted the theft, but there would be enough threats to his life in the Mournland without adding the worries of starvation or thirst.

He patted the mare's flank and let her go. She loped away from the wall of mist without a backward glance. He watched her until she was out of sight, then turned back to face the mist. He had the fleeting sense of a presence in there, something watching him. Waiting for him—impatient, hungry.

A chill ran down his back, and he drew his sword. He was suddenly struck by a feeling of awesome solitude. No one was here to cover his back, no one to share his anxiety—or to make him feel brave, like Rienne used to. No one at all, except perhaps the creatures lurking in the mist.

He checked the sky for the hundredth time, looking in vain for any sign of Vaskar. He took a step closer to the wall of mist, then extended his sword until the point sank into it. The blade met no resistance—in fact, for just a moment, Gaven felt as though something were gently pulling the sword into the mist. He stepped forward, sinking the sword all the way into the fog, bringing his face to within a hand's breadth of the vaporous pall. His movement didn't stir it; even his breath made no eddies in the mist.

He looked around as if taking a final survey of the living world before crossing into the land of the dead, then stepped in. The mist was cold on his skin. He stepped forward again before he dared to take a breath, letting the clammy mist into his lungs. There was an odor to it, not putrid exactly, but definitely a smell of death. The mist closed in around him, and he hurried forward, eager to push through to the other side.

Tendrils of mist coiled around his limbs as he moved, tugging at him. With every step, he felt a weight of exhaustion settling on him. He stopped, shook his head to clear it, and pressed ahead, but he began to wonder why he bothered. He could see no end to the mist ahead, and when he looked over his shoulder it seemed to stretch forever behind him. He dropped to his knees, his heart heavy, his muscles too tired to move.

An old dream filled his senses. Staggering across a blasted landscape where nothing lived. Falling to the ground, seeing his hands sink into earth that was half dirt, half ash. The taste of the air, bitter like bile.

"Have I been here before?" he asked the mist. "Or did I dream of this moment?"

He lifted one knee out of the dust and planted a foot on the shifting ground.

"It doesn't matter," he said. "Either way, I'm here now." He shifted his weight forward and pulled himself up until he stood with his chin on his chest. "And I have work to do."

The mist began to swirl around him. He smiled as he felt the air stir—the breath of wind restored his strength. Great gusts cleared the air around him, showing him the ground at his feet and a path ahead. He walked between receding walls of billowing fog, and soon the dead-gray mist was gone.

The land around him was a desolation. He had crossed into another world—the verdant landscape of Breland was lost in the mist, far away, unreal. Beneath his feet, the ground was a layer of fine sand or ash on top of smooth rock. He saw nothing alive on this side of the mist. No trees, no birds overhead, not even weeds. The sun hung low in the east, its feeble light drowning in a distant fog. Above him, the sky was the gray of a corpse. Even the wind around him died.

Gaven stepped forward, visions from his dreams crowding his mind. Another step, and the sand around him stirred, jolting him back to his senses. Something formed itself from the ground beside him, taking on a vaguely human form, gaunt arms and a gaping mouth and eyes of sickly green fire. The sight of it sent a wave of unreasoning terror through his body, and he stepped back—right into the grasping claws of a second ghoulish creature.

"Thunder!" He wrenched himself free of the creature's grasp and hefted his sword in his trembling hands.

A third monster surged up from the sand, and Gaven swallowed his fear. He swung his sword in a full circle around himself, biting into each one, sending three sprays of ash into the still air. The creatures didn't flinch—they were upon him, their claws tearing his skin and pulling him in three different directions.

With a single arcane word, Gaven pulled a cloak of fire around his body, its warmth dispelling the lingering chill of the awful mists. The creatures drew back in obvious pain, giving him an opening to slip through, to put all three in front of him. As they tried to circle him, he sent a crackle of arcane lightning into his sword, then lunged to his right to intercept the creature moving around that side. The blade bit deep, and the thing's form lost some definition, but it didn't slow its advance. It slammed into Gaven's shoulder, one claw cutting a gash down his chest. The wound flared with green fire, and Gaven shouted in pain. The creature clung to him, even as Gaven's fiery armor engulfed it. It brought its face right up against his, its eyes staring into his. In an instant, Gaven thought he saw a distillation of all the pain and misery that filled the Mournland.

Desolation spreads over that land like a wildfire, he thought—like a plague. In the creature's eyes, he saw a roiling gray mist spreading across the verdant land, leaving nothing alive in its wake. More, he felt the despair of every living thing that was swallowed in that mist, every spirit that lingered in this graveyard, every person who had lost a relative or friend to the Mourning. He fell to his knees, the creature still staring into his eyes.

Then he brought his sword around, cutting right through the thing's waist, making it dissolve back into the sand.

The other two creatures came at him from opposite sides, stalking in cautiously. Gaven stood and stepped backward, a little unsteady on his feet. A soft breath of wind blew up his back, chilling his sweat, and he filled his lungs as though to draw strength from the moving air.

The creatures pounced, and Gaven exhaled. The breeze at his back swelled, and he became the wind. He stretched out his hands, and the wind blasted forth to tear at the creatures' sandy forms. They staggered backward as the wind continued to drive at them, ash streaming out behind them. He was the fury of nature, all wrath and destruction. He smiled grimly as the power of the storm coursed through him.

A crack of thunder rent the air, and Gaven became the lightning, joining blasted earth to gray sky. His feet lifted off the ground, and the lightning shot out of his hands with the wind. The instant of the lightning strike stretched into an eternity in his mind—he was storm, and he was everywhere at once. This was power like he had never tasted before, and he exulted in the destruction he wreaked.

The instant ended. He came down hard on his back, a few paces from where he'd been standing, staring up at the clear, dead sky. He lifted his head with a tremendous effort, just long enough to make sure that the creatures were gone. Two patches of sand were blackened and smoking, but there was no other sign of the monsters. He let his head fall back on the ground.

The magical flames around his body had gone out, but his body still burned with pain where the creature had raked his chest.

His dragonmark also stung, as though lightning still coursed along its intricate tracings. He groaned, tried to lift his head again, and failed.

"Welcome to the Mournland," he said.

* * * * *

Gaven rested for only a moment—long enough for the sting to fade from his dragonmark, though the wound on his chest still burned. He struggled to sit up, every muscle in his body protesting, then slowly got his feet under him and stood up.

He looked at the sun as it disappeared below the horizon, scanned the sky again for any sign of Vaskar, then turned to look for Nymm, the largest moon. It was just rising out of a gray haze to the east, orange and round.

"The Eye of Siberys will lift the Sky Caves of Thieren Kor from the land of desolation under the dark of the great moon," he said to himself. "The great moon's full now. I've got two weeks."

He put his hands on his knees and let his head hang.

"Two weeks to reach the Sky Caves. If I can stay alive that long."

He found his sword where it had fallen on the ground, heaved it onto his shoulder, and started walking.

CHAPTER
25

Vaskar perched on an eruption of stone, overlooking a plain of jumbled rock and sand. He had been watching the great moon's ascent through the sky, and his patience was rewarded as it neared its apex. A hint of shadow appeared at the edge of its disk. He clutched the Eye of Siberys tighter in his great claw and rumbled deep in his throat.

"The eclipse is beginning," he murmured, "the dark of the great moon." He stretched his neck and his wings to the sky and roared. "The time is at hand!"

He watched, waiting for the perfect moment, as Nymm slowly disappeared in the world's shadow.

When its light was completely quenched, he raised the Eye of Siberys high, holding it gingerly between his two front claws. "Do your work," he whispered. He gazed into the golden crystal, and he saw.

He saw the desolation of the Mournland and the life-leaching energies that still permeated the land. He saw the twelve moons arrayed in the sky above him, Nymm shrouded in its eclipse, and he perceived the forces aligned to make this moment possible. He saw the Sky Caves slumbering beneath the ground, and he called to them. He felt them begin to stir, responding to his call.

For a moment, he saw himself—small and insignificant among the events of the moment. But he did not like to see himself, and he certainly didn't like feeling small.

"The Storm Dragon has emerged!" he cried. "I will walk in the paths of the first of sixteen!"

He closed his eyes, and the earth began to shake. The ground trembled so violently that Vaskar took to the sky, pounding his wings in the still air to rise above the tumult. The plain below him looked like a troubled sea, sand erupting in geysers and boulders rolling wildly in every direction. He flew in widening circles, watching the earth churn in an area the size of a large island.

Soon there was direction in the movement below him—a general tendency toward the outside of an enormous circle. The ground swelled, sand sliding and boulders rolling downhill from the center of the bulge. Vaskar flew to the edge of the swell, not wanting to be directly above whatever emerged.

As he continued his flight, the sand at the crest of the swell fell away, revealing a jagged dome of reddish stone. Slowly it rose higher and higher above the surrounding earth, and Vaskar caught sight of a cave entrance in the face of the rock, sand pouring out of it as it lifted into the air.

"The Sky Caves of Thieren Kor!" he roared.

The more rock emerged from the earth, the faster it rose, and in another moment it had broken free entirely. The rumbling thunder of the earth below came to an abrupt stop. In the sudden silence, an enormous island floated a hundred feet up in the air, rounded at the top, a jagged point at the bottom like an inverted mountain. Sand and rubble poured from dozens of holes, spilling down the sides and trickling into a great crater in the ground below it.

Vaskar tightened the circle of his flight, surveying the Sky Caves from every side, trying to decide where to enter. The cave mouths seemed to form patterns, characters of the Draconic script, but every time he tried to read them he thought they shifted, aligning themselves in different patterns. Finally, impatient, he chose a cave near the top and landed on its lower lip, scrabbling at the edge until he could get all four claws on solid ground.

"The Storm Dragon walks in the paths of the first of sixteen," he said. "I am here. Reveal your secrets to me!"

He advanced into the winding tunnel.

* * * * *

Gaven felt the earth rumbling and hefted his sword, expecting an attack—something springing from the ground, perhaps, or some enormous monster that shook the earth with its steps. The rumbling grew until it threatened to knock him off his feet, and in that moment he glimpsed the eclipsed moon above his head.

"No," he breathed.

Exhausted as he was, he ran. The wind cradled him and sped

him on. The sky darkened as clouds rolled in—the first real clouds he'd seen since entering the Mournland—and covered the Ring of Siberys, the stars, the eclipsed moon. His steps and the wind around him kicked up a storm of sand and ash in his wake.

He occasionally glimpsed creatures moving in the night around him, from scavenging vermin the size of dogs to an enormous war construct he spotted in the distance, lumbering across the landscape. One spiny crab-spider thing snapped at him with fangs and pincers as he ran, but he didn't slow at all, and it quickly grew tired of the chase. Nothing else came close enough to threaten him.

Rain began to fall. It cooled him as he ran and soothed the burning wound across his chest. He saw it form craters in the sandy ground and drain away.

The land around him was flat and featureless. The map he'd found in Paluur Draal and committed to memory was his only guide, and he had no better way to navigate than trying to keep his path straight in the direction he'd first chosen. The bank of gray mist hung off to his right, sometimes nearer than others, but otherwise he could see nothing to indicate where he was, where he'd been, or where he was headed. He slipped in and out of an illusion that only the ground moved at all, that he hung in the air, running in place. He lost all sense of time and distance—he could have been running for hours, days, weeks.

But then a darkness appeared before him in the distance. At first it looked like a dark cloud, a heart of a storm in the midst of an overcast sky. As he drew closer, though, it began to take shape. The first feeble daylight illuminated the clouds overhead, casting it in silhouette. It was huge, like a mountain hanging upside-down in the air above the blasted landscape. It floated over an enormous crater, the remains of the cyst from which it had burst forth.

A part of Gaven's mind that was not quite his knew all about the Sky Caves of Thieren Kor. In a different life he had learned all he could about them, poring over fragments of the Prophecy collected in great draconic libraries. He had waited a dragon's long lifetime for the opportunity to explore them and plumb their secrets, and when that lifetime had ended, he—that other he, the dragon of the nightshard—had made sure that what he had learned would someday be remembered.

So Gaven remembered, and the knowledge flooded back to him. The Sky Caves were ancient—they had floated above the untouched wilderness of Khorvaire when dragons first ventured forth from Argonnessen to challenge the fiends that ruled the world. Thieren Kor was a placename in the language used by the fiends, meaning "mountain of secrets." Countless battles had raged beneath that floating mountain, in the skies around it, and within its twisting tunnels—dragons and demons tearing at each other, spilling oceans of blood to gain control of its secrets. When the dragons emerged victorious from the eons-long war, the first dragon to explore the Sky Caves in their entirety became a god, the first of sixteen.

Now Vaskar hoped to follow where that ancient dragon had led. And Gaven felt, for the first time, a surge of envy—he wanted that knowledge, and that power, for himself.

He roared, giving vent to the frustration that had simmered in him since he felt the earth rumble and saw the darkened moon that had propelled him across the Mournland. The brooding clouds thundered in answer to his roar, and lightning danced around the floating mountain. And the wind that had blown at his back swirled in a whirlwind around his feet, lifting him into the air. Higher and higher it carried him, until he stepped forward and alighted in one of the many mouths of the Sky Caves of Thieren Kor.

"Vaskar!" he shouted, sending echoes dancing through the twisting network of caverns. He tensed, gripping his sword in both hands, expecting an attack at any instant. All that emerged from the darkness before him was his own voice in a hundred fragments.

Gaven limned his blade with a pale blue glow, lighting the cave ahead, showing him three tunnels converging on the same mouth—one leading up and to the left, one up and to the right, and one more or less straight ahead. The tunnels were like the boring of some enormous worm—round, smooth, and wide. Stretching his arms wide, he could not touch the walls on either side, and the walls curved together far above his head. He started along the right-hand passage, following it as it wound in an upward spiral. At each branch, he bore right, ensuring that he could find his way back to where he started if the need arose.

After the fourth branch, he found himself teetering at the edge of another cave mouth, his momentum almost carrying him over the brink. He threw himself backward, sending his sword clattering to the floor and sliding toward the cave mouth. He stopped it with his foot then scooted forward to grab it. He got back on his feet and turned around, continuing to follow the right wall.

The next cave opening didn't catch him by surprise, but it did make him stop and think. He'd been blindly following the right wall, as if it would lead him to some destination. But what was his destination? He didn't recall any mention of a specific location within the Sky Caves that might be important—a vault of knowledge or library of some sort. Finding Vaskar seemed like a hopeless endeavor, especially if the dragon were trying to avoid him—he could never hear or see the dragon before Vaskar noticed his approach. So what was he trying to do?

He moved back into the passage he'd just left. The walls were striated in broad patterns of dark and light stone, which he had noted only casually before. As he examined it more carefully, he realized that there was a definite shape to it. He couldn't see it all at once, but as he moved farther in to the tunnel, the parts formed a whole in his mind, a Draconic character representing either a hard th sound or the sixth of some sequence. He continued slowly along, reading more characters—short "a" or a moon, a "sh" sound or a beast, or horns. *Thash,* meaning storm—or the horns of the sixth moon, the crescent phase of Eyre.

He stopped, retracing the tunnel he'd been following in his mind. He turned and followed it again, his eyes closed, trying to visualize the path he was walking. It, too, took shape in his mind—another Draconic character, a long e sound or the number nine. Was that part of another sequence, or an attachment to the word and phrase he'd already pieced together? The number nine could be part of a calendrical expression connected to Eyre's crescent phase. Or *thashe* would turn "storm" into an adjective—he had a feeling there might be a "dragon" attached to that somewhere. Or this character could be connected to other symbols formed by the other passages of the Sky Caves.

His mind reeled, and he put a hand out to rest on the solidity of the cavern wall. He had suddenly gained a new depth of respect for the Prophecy. He had learned endless passages of it in Draconic lifetimes ago, and he'd translated them so often in his mind that they spilled out of his mouth in his own language quite naturally. But he began to appreciate what a poor vehicle language was to convey the meaning of it all, how feeble these words and phrases seemed in comparison to the layers of meaning he was experiencing.

Trailing his hand along the cavern wall, he turned and walked farther into the tunnels. He no longer cared about finding his way back. He opened his mind and explored the Prophecy.

CHAPTER
26

When Gaven was a young man, a casual hobby of collecting snippets of the Draconic Prophecy had given him the merest glimpse into its intricacies and complexities. It had made him think that perhaps there was more to life than working and sleeping, eating and getting drunk, getting married and having children—some greater purpose beyond the mundane activities of life, something unfolding behind the scenes. Many people he knew who shared his interest in the Prophecy found that it gave their lives a sense of immediacy, of urgency—life lived against the context of impending catastrophe. Some of the best-known fragments of the Prophecy did seem to concern the most earth-shattering events—the death of empires and the decline of races, natural disasters on an enormous scale, battlefields where thousands upon thousands fell. And he had understood it then as most people did: as sort of a script for the unfolding events of history, preordained and unalterable, revealed through the gods of the Sovereign Host or perhaps binding even them to its dictates.

Discovering the nightshard, the Heart of Khyber, had given him a better sense of the scope of the Prophecy and of the age of the world. He had learned pieces of the Prophecy that had been fulfilled before humans or elves ever walked the earth, and phrases that could not be fulfilled for another thousand thousand years. His earlier sense of immediacy had largely washed away in a dragon's perspective on the Prophecy: the world would not end that year, or the next, or during Gaven's lifetime, but individual events on a smaller scale still carried enormous weight. The appearance of the Storm Dragon seemed to be a central point in the Prophecy from this perspective—possibly the most important event that any human, elf, or dragon alive would ever experience.

Walking the Sky Caves of Thieren Kor showed Gaven the

Prophecy in its proper context. In some sense, Senya had been right. If the Prophecy had anything to do with destiny—the destiny of individuals or of the world—it was destiny as Senya had described it. The Prophecy was not a foreordained sequence of events but an infinity of possibilities. Most people used their limited understanding of the Prophecy to justify their action or their inaction, but Gaven came to understand it as a context for action. The Prophecy was reason to act, to watch for opportunities and seize them when they came.

But after days spent tracing the winding tunnels of the Sky Caves, a greater wisdom seemed to dance at the edges of his understanding, like the layers upon layers of meaning in the words of the Prophecy. Exactly like that—to one way of understanding, the words of the Prophecy weren't even Draconic anymore, they were their own language. The Prophecy seemed, in his mind, like the language of creation, the words that called the world into being and spoke it through its course, the tongue in which all things were named. Then, somehow, it was no longer about fulfilling what had been predicted, but about continuing the course of creation that had been established in the beginning, acting in such a way as to become a creator in one's own right. A co-creator alongside all the beings, mortal and divine, who had heard and understood and spoken that mystic language in the past, and all who would do so in ages yet to come.

With that greater wisdom came power, enormous power—the power of the Storm Dragon, whether he chose to accept that title or not. What he decided to do with that power, though, was up to him.

* * * * *

Gaven closed his eyes and walked a stretch of tunnel for the sixth time, trying to get a sense of its convoluted path, the meaning it tried to convey to him. He stopped. Something had changed. He felt the hair on the back of his neck standing up, his skin tingling, and his mouth had gone suddenly dry. The dragon approached.

He stood still, waiting for it. I am the lightning, he thought.

Then lightning engulfed him, flowing through his body and out through his limbs. It sank away into the tunnel floor and sputtered harmlessly out his hands.

He opened his eyes and turned to face Vaskar. The dragon

filled the tunnel, wings pressed against his body, legs pulled in close. He crawled forward, more snake than dragon, his emerald eyes fixed on Gaven.

"You shouldn't have come here, Gaven," the dragon said. "The secrets of the Sky Caves belong to me, the Storm Dragon. I don't need you anymore. The Prophecy is laid bare to me now."

Gaven hefted his sword. If that were true, if Vaskar had learned as much from the Sky Caves as he had, the dragon would be a deadly foe.

"Did you hope to thwart me?" Vaskar said. "Would you prevent me from unlocking the secrets of this place? You pathetic creature."

"You arrived before I did. You've been here for days. What have you learned?"

Vaskar roared. "Insolent hatchling. I shall tear you open and feast on your bones!"

Gaven remembered seeing those gaping jaws closing on a wyvern's neck. Suddenly the dragon seemed like nothing more than a ravening beast. Vaskar had learned nothing. "Will you usurp the Devourer?" Gaven said. "Does the world need two gods who eat without thinking?"

"You dare mock me? Are you too dim-witted to fear me?"

"I know better than to fear you, Vaskar."

Another roar, and another blast of lightning from the dragon's mouth coursed across Gaven's skin, through his bones, and harmlessly out his hands and feet. All his hair stood on end, and his dragonmark tingled, but he felt no pain. I am the storm, he thought.

"It appears I underestimated your magic," Vaskar growled. "But will your spells ward you from my teeth?" He lunged, faster than Gaven would have thought possible in such a tight passage.

Gaven stumbled backward, surprised. The dragon's snout knocked him to the floor, the teeth slashing his shoulder. Vaskar pressed his advantage, pinning him to the ground with one massive claw. The dragon brought his mouth close to Gaven's face.

"Now the Storm Dragon will feed." Vaskar hissed.

Gaven grimaced. The dragon's claw was tearing at the wound in his chest, and fear seized his gut. He saw death in the dragon's jaws, and pictured his own neck severed like the wyvern's had been. Then his eyes fell on the ceiling behind Vaskar, its bands of light and dark, and he perceived what he had missed before—a new word in the language of creation.

"No," he said, and a clap of thunder exploded in Vaskar's face, knocking his head back and shaking the tunnel around him. The dragon growled and pulled back, but he found himself stuck in the tunnel.

Gaven scrambled to his feet and drove his sword into the dragon's mouth, cutting a deep gash.

Vaskar pulled his head back as much as he was able, spitting blood that sizzled and hissed where it splattered on the rock. He narrowed his eyes at Gaven. "What has happened? These are not your spells or even your dragonmark at work. What power do you wield against me?"

"If the Prophecy had opened itself to you, you wouldn't need to ask."

Vaskar lunged again, his head lowered this time. Gaven's sword glanced off the armored plates on top of the dragon's head, which hit him full on. He managed to dodge out of the way of the two curving horns, but the force of Vaskar's charge carried him off his feet and backward. With no ground under his feet, nothing solid in his reach, there was nothing he could do but ride it out.

The tunnel fell away behind them. Vaskar emerged into the open air and spread his wings. Only then did he let Gaven fall.

Days had dawned and passed since Gaven had entered the Sky Caves, and the sun was somewhere high overhead, hiding behind a towering mass of thunderclouds. Storm winds swirled around them, and Gaven couldn't see the ground through a cloud of dust. It was enough to note that the dust was a long way down.

Gaven's stomach lurched as he fell, but he closed his eyes and calmed his mind, calling upon the power of his dragonmark. The wind tugged at him, slowing his descent, and he spread his arms and legs wide to catch it. Power surged through him, and he harnessed it, summoning wind and storm and bending them to his will. He stopped, cradled in the palm of the wind, and he exulted as it lifted him. He looked up to where Vaskar wheeled in triumph, and he gripped his sword tightly in both hands as he soared toward the dragon.

Seeing him, Vaskar recoiled in surprise. Then Gaven was on him, swinging his sword back and forth. The heavy blade clanged against Vaskar's bronze scales, catching flesh behind and between them. The dragon's claws batted at him, almost as though Vaskar hoped to knock him from the air. Gaven rewarded his efforts by cutting another bleeding gash between two of the dragon's claws.

The clouds rumbled with thunder, and the wind howled as though it echoed Vaskar's pain. The dragon gave a mighty flap of his wings and pulled away from Gaven's assault, but the wind snatched him and dashed him against the side of the Sky Caves. For a moment his claws scrabbled at the sheer rock face, then he pushed off and into the air again, swooping directly at Gaven, his enormous teeth bared, his wings folded to cut through the gusting wind.

Again, power surged through Gaven's dragonmark, and he funneled it outward. A cyclone lifted Gaven up and out of Vaskar's path. When the dragon hit the whirlwind, he veered hard to the left, rolling over on his back as he swerved, stretching his wings out wide to bring his flight back under control. As he rolled, he spat a bolt of lightning at Gaven, but it flowed through Gaven's body to dance in the clouds, touching off a cascade of light and thunder.

I am the storm, Gaven thought. He stretched his arms out then brought his palms together in a great clap. Winds buffeted Vaskar from either side, crumpling his wings, and another blast sent him reeling backward. The dragon was clearly working hard to stay aloft, and one of his wings looked oddly bent, perhaps broken. He beat his way through the wind to perch in one of the cave openings. Snaking his neck around, he let out a roar that drowned out the dying thunder.

"Thief! Betrayer!" he cried. "I freed you from your prison, and this is the gratitude you show? You stole my prize! Usurper!"

"The prize is not yet won," Gaven said, his voice echoing in the thunder. He stretched out a hand, pointing at the characters formed by the gaping cave mouths. "The Crystal Spire has not yet risen, bridging the realm of mortals and that of the gods."

"What?" The dragon drew his head back, evidently surprised at Gaven's words. "But the Sky Caves—'The Storm Dragon walks in the paths of the first of sixteen!' What have I not fulfilled?"

"Have you learned nothing? Are you blind? The Prophecy is written plain before you, and you have no eyes to see it. On a field of battle where dragons clash in the skies, the earth opens and the Crystal Spire emerges."

As he spoke, the characters of the Prophecy danced in his mind, the layers of meaning that language couldn't capture weaving themselves behind his words.

"A ray of Khyber's burning sun forms a bridge to Siberys's heights."

Images flashed in Gaven's mind from the tortured dreams of his last night in Dreadhold. Gibbering hordes rising up, following the brilliant light up from the depths of the earth. The hordes of the Soul Reaver.

"I will cross that bridge, Gaven! Not you!" Vaskar's rage was all the more unsettling because the dragon's face lacked any human expression. "I am the Storm Dragon!"

The bronze wyrm leaped into the air, lurching toward Gaven on his bent and broken wing.

The wind swelled into a hurricane with Gaven at its eye. Lightning flashed all around him, engulfing Vaskar and limning his scales in brilliant light. The winds battered the dragon and swept him off his path, carrying him around Gaven in a wide arc. Vaskar flailed his wings helplessly. The wind grew, howling through the cave tunnels, sending tremors through the whole mountain. Vaskar whipped around in the wind until he crashed into the side of the Sky Caves, sending a shower of rock in a whirling cascade to the ground.

Vaskar clung weakly to the rock face for a moment, then he let himself fall. He folded his wings and plummeted through the whirlwind, disappearing into the blooming dust cloud below. Gaven lifted his arms to the lightning-scarred sky.

"The Bronze Serpent has fallen," he said, his words disappearing into the wind. "Must I then be the Storm Dragon?"

The wind carried him higher and higher, until he looked down on the top of the Sky Caves. At the same time, the wind lifted the dust and ash from the ground below into a whirling sandstorm that grew to engulf the floating rock.

Gaven lowered his hands, and the wind began to die. The whirling column of air that held Gaven aloft carried him down. As he sank, the sandstorm lost its fury—but even as it settled, it pulled the Sky Caves of Thieren Kor back down to earth with it.

Gaven came to rest on a level, featureless plain of dust. Somewhere beneath his feet, the Sky Caves slumbered again.

PART
III

The cauldron of the thirteen dragons boils
until one of the five beasts fighting over a single bone
becomes a thing of desolation.

Desolation spreads over that land like wildfire, like
plague,
and Eberron bears the scar of it for thirteen cycles of
the Battleground.

Life ceases within its bounds,
and ash covers the earth.

CHAPTER
27

Darraun stayed in camp, staring into the fire. It was easier that way. Earlier, he had made the mistake of wandering out to look at the dragons.

On every ledge jutting out from the cliff they perched or wheeled through the air like seagulls. More huddled in circles on the ground outside the camp. Great four-legged lizards—some squat and strong, others long and sinuous—with wings folded alongside their scaled sides or fanning out above and behind them. Long tails lashed along the ground, and teeth like swords tore the flesh of the game and fish they caught. And these monsters, these dragons . . . they spoke.

It was the speech that really unnerved him. It was one thing to see a score of dragons as something like a flock of birds, riding the wind and roosting on the cliffs as if they jockeyed for the best roosting places and squabbled over fish. It was something very different to recognize them as a collection of intelligent creatures, gathered in this place for a purpose—a purpose they took very seriously. It made them less like a flock of animals and more like an army.

Of course, the closer Darraun got to any dragons, the larger he realized they were. Again, as they circled in the sky above, it was easy to imagine they were no larger than eagles. But when he rounded a corner and found himself face-to-flank with a red dragon, it struck him that many of these creatures were the size of a horse, and a few were larger than Vaskar. He stumbled away from a blast of flame that he was pretty sure had been meant merely as a warning, and retreated to the camp.

He caught enough snippets of dragon conversation on his brief stroll outside the camp to confirm that the dragons gathered here shared Vaskar's philosophy, more or less.

"We're not mercenaries," a large black dragon had protested within his earshot. They spoke Draconic, of course, which made Darraun a little unsure of his understanding.

"Of course not," a smaller silver had answered. "This isn't about serving a human army. It's about the Prophecy."

Darraun stared into the fire. What part of the Prophecy did the dragons think they were accomplishing by fighting for Haldren? He thought he remembered Gaven saying something in the City of the Dead about a "clash of dragons," but that seemed to imply dragons fighting other dragons. Or dragons fighting people with dragonmarks. Or dragons fighting the Storm Dragon. Or the Storm Dragon fighting Vaskar, for that matter.

"Thinking about the Prophecy makes my head spin," he muttered.

"That's why I don't think about it," Cart said. His voice startled Darraun, who had been so wrapped up in his thoughts he'd forgotten the warforged was there.

Darraun arched an eyebrow. "Just do as Haldren says, and trust everything to work itself out?"

"Trust Haldren to make everything work out. That's why he's a general."

"What's that all about, Cart? You're anything but stupid. You could think for yourself, but you choose not to."

Cart stood a little straighter, still staring away from the fire as if he were on watch. "I think for myself where it's appropriate, and I obey orders where that's called for. That's why I was part of the general's trusted staff."

"But you're not in the army anymore. And Haldren isn't a general any more. By obeying Haldren, you're disobeying his superiors. You're disobeying the queen."

"My loyalty is to Haldren, not to Aundair or Queen Aurala."

"I see." Darraun picked up a stick and stirred the embers of the fire.

"It's what I was made to do," Cart added.

Darraun watched the sparks rise from the coals and climb into the sky, glowing with all the brightness they could muster before winking out.

* * * * *

The first light of dawn gleamed in the sky when Haldren's grand pavilion opened, vomiting a stream of drunken generals, majors, and captains, staggering and weaving their way to bed. Their tents were safely away from the dragons' roosts, so there were no ugly encounters between belligerent commanders and short-tempered dragons. Darraun watched them emerge and disperse, making sure to keep his disgust from showing on his face.

"Well, I suppose that's my cue to go to bed," he said to Cart.

The warforged nodded, still staring into the distance. Darraun stood and shuffled out of Cart's sight. With a tent between himself and the warforged, Darraun rubbed the fatigue from his eyes and circled back as quietly as he could manage. As he approached the pavilion, he heard Haldren's voice, and he hurried closer.

". . . interested in celebrating," the sorcerer was saying. "Now that they've seen the dragons, they have no doubt of our victory."

There was another voice, this one quieter—but Darraun couldn't make it out from behind the tent. He made his way to a flap, dropped to the ground, and crawled inside, disturbing the fabric of the pavilion as little as he could. He stayed on the ground, behind the great table Haldren had set up for the feast.

"I am exceedingly grateful," Haldren said. It was a protest. "You have certainly fulfilled your end of our arrangement, and I believe my plans are assured of success as a result. And in turn, I have performed my obligations to you. If your plans are not turning out as well—"

A harsh growl cut him off. "You let him get away from you." The voice was Vaskar's. Darraun risked raising his head above the table to scan the inside of the tent. He was relieved to see an image of Vaskar's face floating in a large silver mirror, not the dragon himself.

"You hardly seemed concerned about that at the time," Haldren said. "You told me the Sky Caves would render him obsolete."

"I admit that I did not consider the possibility that he would appear at the Sky Caves and wrest their secrets from me."

Darraun's mouth fell open. No, he thought, I didn't consider that possibility either. Well done, Gaven.

"And you did not destroy him?"

"Do not mock me, Haldren. He acquired tremendous power in the Sky Caves, power that should have been mine. He could not have done that if he had remained in your custody."

Haldren's voice dropped to barely a whisper. "In case you have forgotten, he kidnapped Senya when he made his escape. I would have pursued him across the Ten Seas, but you dismissed them both as irrelevant. I owe you nothing."

"Idiot," Vaskar snorted. "I have seen two mates and half a dozen hatchlings die. They are irrelevant. We seek greater things. Would you abandon the throne of Khorvaire for her? Should I put aside a chance at godhood for the sake of your lust or love or whatever you call it?"

Darraun heard the rustle of cloth. Haldren did not answer for a breath—two breaths, five. Darraun began to panic. Had Haldren heard him somehow? His heart beat so hard he was sure Haldren could hear it in the silence.

Ten breaths, and still neither Haldren nor Vaskar had spoken. Keeping his head sideways, Darraun raised one eye above the table to see what was going on.

Vaskar's head still hovered in the mirror, but Haldren had turned away from it, his hands clenched over his temples. Unfortunately, that meant he stared right at the table where Darraun hid. Darraun ducked his head back down, but it was too late.

"A spy? Darraun?"

Haldren's confusion lasted only an instant, and in the next, a blast of fire exploded around Darraun, engulfing him as well as the table and the wall of the tent behind him. Searing pain shot through his body as he rolled away, under the flaming edge of the tent, and up to his feet outside. Clenching his teeth to quell the pain, he scrambled to the nearest tent.

"Darraun!" Haldren cried behind him. "Traitor! Coward!"

Darraun ducked into the nearest tent, hoping Haldren's cries hadn't woken the occupant.

"Who's there?" A man's voice came from the ground at his feet—very close. The inside of the tent was pitch dark, and the man's voice was thick with sleep and drink.

Darraun took a deep breath, focused his mind, and changed.

Quickly. Hair long, height the same in case the tent's occupant could make out his outline. Breasts, waist, hips—the face could wait a moment. The new form made certain parts of his clothing too tight, but in this case that was an advantage. Voice—soft, husky, seductive. "Haldren sent me to see if you need anything." Pose—chest out, one hand on a cocked hip.

"Sovereigns, is he trying to kill me?"

Darraun heard the man lie back on his furs. He changed his face—round and soft, with full lips and heavy-lidded eyes. It was a face he'd used many times, and it had proven its effectiveness. He started peeling off his clothes, glad he hadn't been wearing his leather cuirass.

"No, no. Go away, girl."

Darraun stepped out of his breeches. Haldren hadn't shouted again, but Darraun knew that didn't mean he'd abandoned the chase. Haldren was too smart and too angry to continue yelling. There was some commotion outside, a susurrus of voices trying to stay quiet.

"What's going on out there?" the man on the ground murmured. "Is something burning?"

"Give me a blanket," Darraun said. "I'll go see."

The man grunted. Darraun bent down and felt around for a blanket. He pulled one off the pile and wrapped it around himself, making a few adjustments to his body as he did so. His new identity complete, he stepped out of the tent.

* * * * *

"How much did he hear?" Vaskar asked.

"I have no idea," Haldren said. "He certainly wasn't there during the feast, and I made sure I was alone in the pavilion before I contacted you. But he could have come in at any point after that."

"We spoke mostly of Gaven. Why should he care?"

"I don't know."

"Perhaps your success is not as certain as you believed," Vaskar said.

"Nonsense. Everything is set in motion. Nothing can rob me of victory now."

"Nothing? You've had a spy in your midst since you escaped from Dreadhold. How many other conversations has he heard? You told me yourself he had intelligence contacts. It's possible the queen knows every detail of your plans."

"Indeed."

"Perhaps now you will reconsider my request."

Haldren sighed. "Very well, Vaskar. We will choose a different field of battle. We'll conform to your damned Prophecy."

* * * * *

Getting away from Haldren had been easy enough. Finding a new suit of armor to fit a new body shape and blending in among the hundreds of camping soldiers was not too difficult. The real challenge would be getting out of a military camp located miles from civilization and surrounded by dragons.

The changeling who had been Darraun was getting comfortable in her new body, new identity, and new name—Private Caura Fannam, an enlisted soldier under the command of Major Rennic Arak. She wore her tawny hair pulled awkwardly into a tail down her back, a fashion popular with many female soldiers. A long shirt of leather studded with heavy steel rivets was standard issue for Aundair's light infantry. She carried a short spear—not her favorite weapon, but easy enough to use: "Put the sharp end into the enemy," she'd heard a training sergeant say once. In practice, she knew the hard part was pulling it back out in time to put it in the next enemy, which was why she preferred shorter weapons. But if all went well, she'd have no reason to use her spear as anything but a part of her disguise.

Even with dragons surrounding the camp, soldiers couldn't abandon military protocols—sentries were posted at various spots around the edge of the camp and patrolling the perimeter, probably at least as much to make sure no one left as to intercept anyone coming in. Caura knew they'd be on heightened alert since Haldren had discovered Darraun spying on him. She smiled—how easy it was to think of Darraun as another person entirely.

"Where are you supposed to be, soldier?" A sentry's voice rang out nearby, and Caura started. She'd thought she was well hidden in the shadow of a supply cache. She couldn't see the sentry.

"Uh—I . . . I . . . ." The voice was a young man's, just on the other side of the supplies. The pieces of a plan started to come together in her mind. Jumping to a decision, she stepped out of her hiding place.

"I'm ready," she announced. She looked expectantly at the other young soldier, hoping he would follow her lead. She spotted the sentry at the edge of her vision, but tried to act as if she hadn't noticed him.

"What's this?" the sentry demanded. "What are you two up to?"

Feigning surprise, Caura turned to face the sentry. She stood at attention and gave a salute. "Private Caura Fannam, sir."

"Answer the question, Private, since your lover here seems to have lost his tongue."

"Lover?" An instant of concentration brought a flush of color to her cheeks. "Oh, no, sir. We're on our way to report for sentry duty, and I had to stop to, ah, use the latrine, sir. He was just waiting for me." She saw a second sentry hanging back from the scene, ready to get help if a situation developed.

"What's your name, soldier?" The sentry addressed the man beside her, who had fumbled his way to attention as well.

"P-p-p—"

"Do you have a problem with your tongue, Private?"

"Yes, sir, he does," Caura interjected. "A terrible stutter. That's why he's not in Communications."

That drew a harsh laugh from both sentries, and a blush she suspected was genuine from the other soldier. But it covered her new friend's initial hesitation in responding to the sentry—one more step toward getting out of the camp alive.

"Private Jenns Solven, s-s-sir." Jenns saluted. He seemed to be warming up.

"All right," the sentry said, "get where you're supposed to be. Don't let me see you sneaking around like that again, Solven. And keep your eyes open tonight, the both of you. Word is a spy's been discovered—pretty high up, too. So don't go fooling around when you're supposed to be on watch! The Lord General's depending on you."

"Yes, sir!" Caura and Jenns said in unison, saluting again. The sentry returned the salute and turned to rejoin his partner. She and Jenns stayed at attention until the two sentries were well on their way. She heard more laughter, then the sentries were gone. Jenns let out his breath and visibly sagged.

"Thank you," he said. "I don't know who you are or why you helped me, but I think you just saved my life."

"Well, now it's time for you to return the favor," Caura said with a smile.

CHAPTER
28

Bluevine was exactly the kind of place that Phaine despised. A village small enough that everyone knew each other meant that strangers like him drew attention. The people loved to talk, they were never satisfied with terse answers, and they took umbrage at his habitual silence. On top of that, the weather stayed warm and bright. He vastly preferred the shadowy alleys, darkened skies, and comfortable anonymity of Khorvaire's large cities.

The flip side, though, was that even a secret meeting like the one Haldren had held in Bluevine could hardly be kept secret in such a small town. The fugitive had admitted only a few people inside the room during the feast and had sworn them to silence, which of course meant that everyone in the village knew some version of what had happened inside. Getting information wasn't difficult; just sorting out the truth from the wild speculation and rumors was problematic.

Almost everyone he interviewed claimed to know someone who knew someone who had been in the room, but few could name the source of their information, and those that were named denied that they'd been present. Several times, between interviews, he told Leina he wished he could just find a throat to slit and be done with Bluevine for good.

Through all the gossip and exaggeration, some hints of a consistent picture eventually began to emerge. Haldren had clearly stayed in Bluevine for several days. He had been accompanied by another human man, younger, and a warforged. There was no indication that the elf woman or the Lyrandar excoriate had been there. After the first day, other strangers had arrived: seven men and women, some of them clearly of noble birth, though all of them acted like they were entitled to royal treatment.

Beyond those bare facts, Phaine found little agreement, which made sense to him. Many people in the town would have had occasion to interact with these ten outsiders in various ways, so it was natural that a consistent picture of them would emerge. He had yet to find anyone who claimed they had actually been present at their gatherings, though, which would explain why there were so many different stories about what had actually taken place.

Given that all the stories were probably the inventions of various villagers, it amused him that every one attributed some sinister purpose to the gathering. He figured that adequately summarized the village's attitude toward outsiders. If a group of strangers came to town and met in secret, it was almost certainly for a cultic ritual, a political conspiracy, a depraved orgy, or an arcane summoning. At least, those made for better stories, more likely to get repeated. Phaine supposed that if it had been a casual gathering of old military friends sharing war stories over glasses of Bluevine's famous vintage, that story would hardly have captured much interest.

Finally, Leina pointed him to a promising lead—a dour old farmer who acknowledged, after some badgering, that his grandson had been pressed into service pouring wine for the strangers. He refused to come into the village center, so Phaine followed Leina out to his farmstead. He knocked at the door and waited, knocked louder and waited more, and finally saw the farmer for himself as the door swung open. The man's face was leathery and deeply lined, and one big hand was clutched around the handle of a scythe.

"What do you want?" the farmer demanded.

"Good afternoon," Phaine said, forcing a smile. "My associate tells me that your family has some information about the strangers who visited your charming village a few weeks ago."

The man's hand clenched his scythe harder. "I told her we don't want to talk about it."

"Perhaps Leina neglected to mention that some of these people are fugitives. One of them escaped from Dreadhold."

"She told me. I'm not surprised."

"It is very important that I learn everything I can about these people and what they were doing here. If your grandson has information that might help find them, it's imperative that I speak to him."

The farmer's knuckles whitened on this handle of his scythe.

"Listen. My boy was there, and maybe he heard things that would help you. But we'll never know, see? The bastards cut out his tongue."

* * * * *

Under normal circumstances, Senya did not sleep. She was an elf, and four hours spent in quiet meditation rested her body and mind like a full night's sleep. During this trance, her mind would run through a series of mental exercises of memory and reflection that she had practiced tens of thousands of times. Humans would call them dreams.

But circumstances were not normal. She had been badly injured, and her body needed a great deal of rest. She entered her trance in the late morning, and her mind wandered strange paths of fevered dreams. She surfaced from her trance in a panic and stared wildly around the room, trying to remember where she was. Darkness surrounded her, and something held her down where she lay. "Gaven?" she whispered, but then she remembered seeing him, spread-eagled on a great stone slab, covered in blood. Was that memory, or fevered imagining?

Panic welled in her chest, and she started thrashing to escape whatever held her. To her surprise, the bonds came away easily, and she realized that she was lying in a soft bed, swathed in linen sheets and warm blankets. Other memories returned to her—their flight from the dwarves in Vathirond, the wind that carried her when she couldn't run any more, the healers who tended her and loaded her into their wagon. And the knowledge that Gaven had abandoned her.

At least he's not dead, she thought—but the thought gave her little comfort.

She fumbled her way out of the sheets and sat up in the bed. She wore something soft and loose, a nightgown or something very different than the leather she'd been wearing last. She swung her feet down to the bare wooden floor and slid along the bed until her outstretched hand touched the wall. Then she got to her feet and slowly shuffled along the edge of the room, keeping her right hand on the wall and her left stretched out low in front of her. She felt ridiculous, but the darkness was so complete that she still couldn't make out the room's dimensions or features.

Her left hand brushed something she quickly decided was a nightstand, and she worked her way around it. She'd no sooner reached the other side of it than she found another wall, then heavy curtains. She fumbled at the windows, and her eyes finally came alive as dim starlight filtered through thick glass into the room. She was about to turn back to survey the room, but something in the sky caught her attention.

It was Nymm, the largest of the twelve moons. It hung high in the sky, right near the top of her view out the window. At first she thought it was just in a crescent phase, nearly new or just beginning to wax again. But its shape was strange—its color, too—and she realized that a shadow blocked its light, an eclipse. Words danced at the edge of her memory, something about the great moon, something her ancestor had said in Shae Mordai. But it eluded her, and she returned her attention to her immediate surroundings.

The room was small and simply appointed, but cozy in its way. She'd already discovered the bed and the nightstand. One chair stood near the other side of the bed. There was one door, opposite the window. Her coat and her sword hung from a hook on the back of the door.

A good start, she thought. Now where are the rest of my clothes?

Her eyes fell on the nightstand again, and she noticed the two drawers it held. She stepped to it and opened the top drawer. Sure enough, her clothes were there. She pulled them out and set them on the bed.

My boots, my pack—where are they?

A few steps took her to the other side of the bed, and there they were. Her pack was neatly arranged beside the bed, with the elegant, impractical boots standing perfectly next to it. She breathed a sigh of relief and sat down on the bed.

"Well now, Senya," she whispered to herself, "what are you doing?" She ran her fingers through her hair. It felt clean, silky. "They're taking care of you here. Are you going to bolt out in the middle of the night?"

Her thoughts ran back over her conversation with the halfling who had tended her, the way he avoided her gaze as he asked about Gaven. She thought about their ride on House Orien's lightning rail, the House Medani inquisitives they'd avoided at the station in

Korranberg, and the Sentinel Marshals of House Deneith who had captured her when the rail stopped in Starilaskur. Was it unreasonable to fear that House Jorasco's healers might turn her over to the Sentinel Marshals or some other house?

The more she considered the possibility, the more she convinced herself that the halflings would almost certainly hand her over as soon as they saw that she was recovered. She took off the nightshirt the healers had put on her, stuffed it into her pack, and put on her own clothes. She was lacing her boots when she heard a creak outside her door. She froze and listened, but the sound did not recur. Was there a guard posted outside her room? Had he heard her moving around?

Taking care that her boots made no sound on the wooden floor, she crept to the door and lifted her sword belt and coat off the hook. She pressed her ear to the door, cringing as it jiggled in its frame. She heard nothing but the pounding of her blood in her ears.

She started to inch away from the door again, but another creak from outside stopped her. She tried to bring her breath and her racing pulse under control and listen. She heard voices whispering outside. With agonizing slowness, she stepped back from the door and tugged at the hilt of her sword. It didn't come free of its sheath, and she almost swore out loud. A glance confirmed her suspicion—the halflings had peace-bonded it, attached it to its scabbard with leather straps designed to make it impossible to draw in anger. It would take too damned long to undo the knots holding it in place. She reversed her grip on it and readied herself to swing the weighted hilt as a club, if the need arose.

The metal latch clanked softly as it moved, and a sliver of light spilled into the room from the hallway. The hinges squeaked softly as the shaft of light grew wider. When the light fell on the empty bed, there was a pause, and Senya coiled, ready to strike.

The door flew open, and a man rushed in, holding a longsword in his left hand. Senya stepped up to meet him, swinging the pommel of her sword as hard as she could. The attack had caught him by surprise and might have been deadly if she'd managed to pull the blade free, but instead it glanced off his mailed shoulder. He whirled to face her, but his eyes were clearly still adjusting to the darkness. Pressing that advantage, Senya batted at his sword with the basket hilt of her blade, trying to knock it from his hand for her own use.

He kept his grip on his sword and used that moment of connection to swing Senya around until the light from the hall fell full on her face, reversing her initial advantage. Only then did he wrench his sword free, sending Senya's sword skittering across the floor.

Blinking into the light, Senya put her hands up in a gesture of surrender as she tried to size up her opponent. He was not a tall man, but his body was strong. He looked to be about Gaven's age, but he was human, which probably meant he was considerably younger than Gaven's sixty-odd years—certainly younger than Haldren, though his hair was lightly dusted with gray. His armor was gleaming mail, and he wore the black surcoat of the Sentinel Marshals.

Behind this man, an armored halfling in the gold and green of House Jorasco held an everbright lantern—the source of the light shining into her eyes. His other hand was on the hilt of his sword, still in its sheath.

"Senya," the Sentinel Marshal said, "I am Sentinel Marshal Arrakas d'Deneith. You are under arrest. Stop trying to fight."

"Why?" Senya demanded. "So you can give me a quick and painless death?"

"The murder of a Sentinel Marshal is serious business, Senya. But frankly, I'm more interested in finding Gaven and Haldren than in punishing you for your part in it. If you cooperate, I can make sure your sentence is light."

"Hm. A very considerate offer." She shifted almost imperceptibly closer to where her sword lay on the floor, but Arrakas raised his sword as he stepped between Senya and the blade.

He jerked his head toward the halfling in the doorway, without taking his eyes off Senya. "Pick up the lady's sword, will you?"

The halfling scurried into the room and snatched Senya's sword off the floor, clutching it to his chest as if he were afraid she might leap at him and try to wrest it from his grip.

Senya smiled and started toying with the top of her bodice. She might not have her sword, but she'd found in the past that her body was often a more powerful weapon. "Well, Arrakas," she said, her voice low and breathy, "it seems you've bested me. Now I'm yours."

She saw the blood rise to his face, and noticed that even the halfling seemed to be having some trouble swallowing. She stepped closer to Arrakas, letting her coat fall to the ground and trail behind her. His eyes locked onto hers, which was not where she wanted them. She reached up to brush her hair back from her face, and slowly trailed her hand down the side of her face to her neck, her bare shoulder, her collarbone. To her satisfaction, his eyes followed her hand downward, and she stepped closer again, close enough to feel the warmth of his body.

She cupped his face in her hand, felt the flush in his cheek. Men were so easy to manipulate. She let her fingers slip softly down his chin, tracing the thin line of his beard, then down his neck, and she smiled slightly as his eyes closed. She ran her fingers along his shoulder, which he probably couldn't feel through his armor, and squeezed his upper arm to make sure his attention stayed on her hand.

The halfling watched her with undisguised excitement in his eyes, which made her slightly sick, but suited her purposes. She dropped her hand to stroke the back of his, and saw him shiver slightly from the light touch.

This is it, she thought. Last chance.

She stepped forward again, pressing the softness of her body against his armored chest and letting her breath brush his neck. At the same moment, she deftly slipped the sword out of his hand and started bringing it up to strike.

Arrakas's other hand was behind her, though. Before she could bring the sword to bear, something hard came down on her head, and she crumpled to the floor.

CHAPTER
29

"What do we do now?" Jenns looked at Caura with wide eyes and bit his lip as he waited for her answer. He might be nervous, but so far he'd proven more than willing to follow Caura's lead.

"Act like sentries," Caura said. "We'll walk the perimeter, insert ourselves between two real patrols."

"Then what?"

"Did you have a plan at all before I found you? Or were you just going to make a break for it?"

"I hadn't really thought it through," Jenns admitted with a smile.

"Good thing I found you, then." Caura returned the smile. He might have been young and naïve, but he was endearing. "At the right spot, we'll alter our course and slip out. I think I know a place where we'll be out of sight and mostly avoid the dragons."

"Can I ask you something, Caura?"

"You can ask, but I won't promise you an answer."

"How do you know so much about the camp and things?"

"I pay attention."

"Sure, but they keep us on a pretty tight leash. Like they want to make sure we don't figure out too much."

"I'd say that's a pretty accurate assessment." Caura had heard Haldren give instructions to the commanders who followed him, a long list of rules to make sure that the rank and file didn't learn too much.

"You're not really just a private, are you?"

Caura smiled at him again, chastising herself. She shouldn't have answered the innocent questions—her answers clearly led right up to a question she didn't want to answer.

They walked in silence for a moment, then Caura guided Jenns into an excellent imitation of a sentry patrol around the perimeter.

"Want to hear my crazy thought?" Jenns said.

"Can I stop you?"

"I think you're the spy that sentry was talking about."

"What on earth makes you say that?" Caura carefully modulated the tone of her voice, making sure that her face did not flush. A perfect lie.

He shrugged. "I told you it was a crazy thought."

"How do I know you're not the spy? Why are you running out of here?"

"Me?" Jenns chuckled. "You saw me back there. I'd be a pretty pathetic spy."

True, Caura thought. But you'll do for now.

"So why the daring escape?" she said.

"Do I have to answer that?"

"I guess not. Fair is fair."

Caura entertained herself trying to imagine the reason this innocent young soldier would desert his post and flee the camp. A romantic entanglement struck her as the most likely reason, although abject terror seemed like another strong possibility. She wouldn't ask again, mostly because she didn't want to put herself in a position of feeling obligated to reveal anything more to him.

The western side of the camp was bounded by cliffs overlooking the stormy Eldeen Bay. Their path took them alongside the cliffs briefly, and Jenns gasped when he saw the dragons wheeling in the air over the water and perching on the cliffs. He walked in silence, wide-eyed, until they turned their backs on the bay and the dragons, heading along the northern perimeter.

The sun appeared over the horizon, shining in their eyes as they walked, and the camp was coming alive. Bugle calls roused soldiers from their tents, and the shouts of sergeants assembled them into formations for inspection.

"You'll be missed soon," Caura observed.

Jenns raised an eyebrow. "What about you?"

"Me too," she said. "We'd better get moving." She pointed to the line of trees in front of them, blocking part of the rising sun. "That's the Whisper Woods up ahead. Our best chance of getting out of here." Alive, she added silently.

Caura kept their pace slow and steady until they got within bowshot of the trees. At that point, instead of continuing southward around the perimeter, they veered toward the woods and picked up the pace. They had only covered half the distance when a shout arose behind them.

"What did he say?" Jenns said, a panicked look in his eyes.

Caura turned to run. "Not sure, but it sounded a lot like 'Halt!' " she yelled. "Come on!"

"We're going to die," Jenns groaned as he hurried behind her.

A few arrows flew lazily overhead, then a few more thunked into the ground near their feet as the archers found their range. More shouts erupted from the camp, and Caura thought she heard the tromp of pursuing feet far behind, but she didn't dare slow down to look backward. Jenns had caught up his initial lag and kept pace with her. A quick glance confirmed the terror she expected to see on his face.

"We'll make it," she gasped.

But the trees didn't seem to be getting any closer, and they weren't dense enough to guarantee cover from their pursuers. She started to feel guilty for leading Jenns to his death, then she reminded herself that she'd already saved his life once. So she hadn't caused his death, merely delayed it.

The arrows started falling short, the shouts faded in the distance, and no one seemed to be gaining on them. Caura saw a look of hope begin to dawn on Jenns's face as they came closer to the sheltering trees. She shot him what she hoped was a reassuring smile, but he wasn't looking at her. As she watched, the color and the hope drained from his face, and his steps faltered.

"Sweet Sovereigns, protect us," he breathed, stopping his headlong run and falling backward onto the ground.

Caura slowed her pace but didn't stop, searching the forest ahead for a sign of what had terrified him. The forest's edge was thinly scattered with trees, but a covering of ferns and bushes promised more cover, and just a few yards in the trees grew more closely together. Everything was lush with spring growth, and a gentle breeze stirred the branches in a soft susurrus.

Then she saw it: a dragon snaked among the trees. Its green scales helped it blend in among the leaves and ferns, but its eyes were fixed on her. It was one of the smaller dragons she had seen around the camp, but that still meant it was roughly horse sized. And it looked hungry.

Caura stopped dead. She cast a glance over her shoulder. Jenns was still on the ground, looking desperately back and forth between her and the dragon. Far behind him, a clump of soldiers from the camp had stopped to watch—they had evidently spotted the dragon before Jenns and didn't want to approach it any more than he did.

"Caught between the Kraken and the Hydra," she muttered. The expression made her think of the two rocky islands that marked the entrance to the dangerous straits of Shargon's Teeth, poised like twin monsters waiting to devour ships passing between them. "Well, that's nothing new."

"What do we do?" Jenns shouted.

"Follow me!"

Caura ran, turning her course just to the right, aiming for a spot a little south of where the dragon waited. She saw the dragon whip around, keeping even with her, but after a moment it disappeared into the heavier trees. She glanced back and saw the soldiers move again, ready to catch them if they circled back toward the camp.

Caura and Jenns reached the woods, charging into the undergrowth with a clamor of rustling leaves and branches. When they were out of sight of the camp and the pursuing soldiers, Caura put up a hand to stop Jenns. The forest settled around them. She listened. Birds fluttered, a few squirrels or chipmunks scurried at their feet, and something large stalked nearby. Too near. It stopped when it couldn't hear them moving anymore.

Caura was painfully aware of how loud she and Jenns were breathing after running so hard. She held a finger to her lips and tried to catch her breath. After a moment, though, she heard the dragon resume its stealthy movement toward them.

She realized the flaw in her thinking. She'd been treating this dragon as a strange reptilian leopard or something, a big predatory animal stalking them through the woods. This was not an animal—not any more than Vaskar was.

"All right, dragon, you've got us," she said.

Jenns goggled at her, but she held out a reassuring hand. If dragons could argue with each other over the Prophecy, then certainly they could talk to her before eating her. Maybe this one could be talked out of eating her.

The rustle of its approach grew louder. It wasn't trying as hard to sneak up on them. Getting closer. Caura saw branches bending and swishing back into place as it passed—thirty paces, then twenty, fifteen. It must have been crawling along the ground to remain so well hidden, and it used the trees for cover as much as possible. But at ten paces it couldn't possibly keep out of sight any longer, and it reared up on its hind legs like a bucking horse, revealing itself in its terrible majesty.

Jenns let out a tiny whimper and took two steps away from it. It was much smaller than Vaskar, more like a sleek, agile tiger than the lumbering behemoth she was more familiar with. Its scales were mottled green and gray, resembling the patterns of light and shadow on the forest growth. Its head bore a crest that stretched high as it reared up, and it spread its wings to look larger, breaking branches and pushing saplings aside. For a moment, Caura wondered if she had misjudged—its behavior was not too different from that of a threatened predator ready to strike. But then she noticed its eyes. They watched her with evident curiosity, flicking occasionally to the terrified Jenns behind her.

The dragon's snout was long and narrow, tipped with a wicked point that made it look almost like a bird of prey. As it looked at them, the flesh at the corners of its mouth stretched back to reveal its sharp teeth. Caura's heart leaped, but then she recognized the expression—the dragon was smiling.

"And now that I've got you," it said, "what am I to do with you? A pair of deserters, are you?" Its voice was low and smooth, almost seductive.

"That's right," Caura said. Jenns whimpered again. "We don't have the stomach for the coming battle."

"I think my course is clear, then," the dragon said, its grin growing wider. "You'll be my main course. I do have the stomach for you."

Caura resisted the temptation to groan at the dragon's awkward wordplay. At least it hinted at a strategy for keeping the dragon busy, and she leaped at the opening. "But if we're deserters, shouldn't we be your dessert?"

The dragon opened and closed its mouth in a gesture Caura

discerned as a laugh. "Well spoken, meat. But who ever heard of eating meat for dessert?"

"Don't you think it's sweet to meet us?" Caura glanced over her shoulder. Jenns stared at her with his mouth hanging open, incredulous. But the dragon was still enjoying the game.

"Perhaps I'll eat your sweetbread for dessert."

"Oh no, we're not well bred."

"Are you suggesting I was born in a well?" The dragon fanned its wings, breaking more branches. Caura thought she detected an impatient tone in its voice. At the thought, her mind went blank.

Jenns stepped forward to stand beside her, then bowed before the dragon. "We hope your offense doesn't run deep."

The dragon laughed again, and furled its wings. "The male joins in the game!"

Caura shot Jenns a smile and picked up the thread. "There must be tastier game in the forest."

Jenns added, "I fear you'll find us too gamey for your taste."

"I think perhaps you're too tasty to let this game continue." The dragon's tongue flicked out and brushed its lips.

"No, not at all," Caura shot back. "Haven't we amply demonstrated our bad taste?"

Again the dragon flapped its lower jaw. "You have indeed. I suggest you flee before I change my mind."

Caura almost retorted, but Jenns grabbed her arm and pulled her away from the dragon as fast as their legs could run.

CHAPTER
30

I s there news?" Rienne sat in Krathas's office, her elbows on her knees, looking at the floor to avoid the half-orc's gaze.

The half-orc shifted some rolled papers on his desk. "There is. The woman who was with him—she's been captured."

"Really?" Rienne hated the tone of her voice, but she couldn't keep the spite from her voice.

"Indeed. As I understand it, she was badly injured while she and Gaven fled from the dwarves." A twinge of guilt pricked Rienne's heart—she had unwittingly led the dwarves to Gaven. "Somehow, Gaven sent healers from House Jorasco to find her and bring her back to the city for care. A Sentinel Marshal apprehended her at the House of Healing."

"Where's Gaven?"

"I don't know." He paused, but something on his face indicated that there was more. Rienne waited.

"At about the same time as the Jorasco healers set out to find Senya, a horse was stolen at the eastern edge of town. It's possible that was Gaven."

"The eastern edge? Is that near the House of Healing?"

"Not particularly, no. Gaven might have ridden east."

"East—toward the Mournland."

"Right." He rubbed the side of his face. "There's one more thing. The horse—it found its way home."

Rienne sat back in her chair, trying to absorb that information. Krathas found something interesting on his desk and kept his eyes low.

"Well, that might not mean anything," she said after a moment. "I can't imagine a horse would willingly ride into the Mournland. Perhaps he just let it go and made his way in on foot."

"Maybe so." He didn't say any more, but Rienne could read his thoughts on his face: he didn't like Gaven's odds of surviving in the Mournland on foot.

"Why would he go in there?" She remembered her view of the roiling gray mist from the airship deck, the sense of a malevolent presence in the Mournland. The thought of walking into the Mournland made her shudder.

"I hoped you might have some idea."

Rienne shook her head, replaying her conversation with Gaven and Senya in her mind. "He didn't say anything." She shrugged, feeling helpless. "It was so hard to see him. Not at all what I expected—or hoped for. He seemed so strange."

"Strange how?"

Rienne considered her words, trying to express the thoughts that had been nagging at her since her encounter with Gaven. "He was . . . absent. He had no interest in talking with me. He didn't ask me for an explanation or offer me one. I thought he would be angry. I didn't expect him to just not care."

"He's had years to get over his anger."

"So have I. But all he cared about was that damned box. What was in it, anyway?"

Krathas shrugged. "I don't know."

"He never told you?"

Another shrug. "I never asked."

"He accused me of stealing it from you." The memory stirred her anger.

"I promised him I'd keep it safe. He came to my office and found you holding it. I think I can see why he might have been upset."

"And as soon as I left, those dwarves ran in. He probably thinks I summoned them."

A look of profound sadness settled on Krathas's face as he stared at his desk.

Rienne's anger melted away. She reached out and clasped the half-orc's folded hands. "I can't see him go back to Dreadhold, Krathas. It's my fault he went there in the first place. I want to help him, but I don't know how."

Krathas looked into her eyes. "Don't you?" His voice was gentle.

Rienne sat in silence for a long time. Krathas held her gaze for a while, then looked back down at his desk. Finally, Rienne sighed.

"I suppose that means I'm heading to the Mournland."

* * * * *

"Desolation spreads over that land like a wildfire," Gaven muttered. He lurched forward and fell into the dust. "Like a plague." He spat dirt out of his mouth. "A plaguefire, a virulent plague, a wasting sickness, a spreading cloud that burns and wastes and destroys."

He scooped up a handful of the sandy ground and let it spill out between his fingers. A shadow of a dream flitted through his mind.

So many thoughts were in his mind, he couldn't cling to one. He slowly got to his feet.

"Two spirits bound in one prison beneath the wastes," he whispered, his eyes unfocused. Twisting caverns forming letters, letters bound together in infinite combinations of words, words that danced unfettered in his mind. "Secrets kept and revelation granted, the Secret Keeper and the Messenger." He started to walk forward, stumbled, stopped and stared at the sky. "They bind and are bound, but their whispers are unbound."

"Destroyer!" he shouted. "Tearer and reaver and flayer of souls, the Soul Reaver." He staggered in a different direction beneath the featureless sky. "The Soul Reaver waits in the endless dark, where it is forever night, the un-day. Beneath the bridge of light, there will descend the Storm Dragon, the Dragon of thunder and lightning and wind and rain and hail."

Something dark jutted up from the barren ground, tracing jagged lines against the gray horizon. Gaven turned and reeled toward it. It meant something, he knew.

"There among the bones of Khyber the Storm Dragon will drive a spear—the Eye of Siberys bound to a branch of ash, an ash tree's branch charred with ash, a victim of the storm."

The object began to take shape as he drew nearer—blackened branches stretching up from the earth to the sky, a memory of life where nothing else grew.

"Drive the spear into the Soul Reaver's heart!"

A distant rumble of thunder testified to the storm that had passed and left the tree scorched by lightning.

"Where is the Eye of Siberys now, Gaven?" Gaven's voice was suddenly clear and coherent, though lower than usual. As if startled by the sound of it, he fell to the ground again. He tore at the pouch at his belt until he got it open, then pulled out the heavy adamantine box and opened it.

The nightshard captivated him, pulsing with its purple-black light, and he mumbled at it as if answering its question. "The Storm Dragon seizes the shard of heaven, a tiny fragment of Siberys's glory, from the fallen pretender, the bronze serpent."

"Where is it now?" he said, clear and low again.

"Vaskar. The Bronze Serpent used it, it lifted the Sky Caves of Thieren Kor from the earth, he had it."

He scrambled to his feet once more and lurched to the burned tree. He started to fall when he reached it, but he caught himself on its blackened trunk, smearing his hands with ash.

"Drive the spear into the Soul Reaver's heart," he murmured again.

He walked his hands up the trunk, stretching as high as he could, just barely managing to get his hands around the lowest branch. In one smooth movement he pulled himself up onto the branch, then climbed until he was near the top of the tree. He planted himself on a high branch and reached up to another one that seemed the right size. It broke off easily in his hand, almost throwing him off balance. He steadied himself and hefted the branch in his hand.

Perfect.

"There among the bones of Khyber the Storm Dragon drives the spear formed from Siberys's Eye into the Soul Reaver's heart." Shadow given twisting form writhed in his thoughts, a distant echo of a long-ago dream. "It was my hand on the spear," he whispered.

He climbed slowly back down to the ground, his mind suddenly clear. Studying the sky to find his bearings, he set his face to the west and started walking.

* * * * *

Rienne patted her new horse's nose as the stable hand cinched the saddle. The mare hadn't come cheaply, but she had a House Vadalis pedigree—she was magebred for speed, and the previous owner had boasted that she ran as fast as a Valenar horse. Rienne doubted that claim, but felt sure the mare would be fast enough for her needs.

Rienne checked the saddlebags, loaded with the journeybread and water she'd need for her journey. She had also secured a sizable amount of cash from the bank operated by House Kundarak, knowing that the dwarven house might soon block her access to her accounts. She smiled wistfully. It was like the old days, setting off on another dangerous adventure, and a far cry from the settled life of a sheltered aristocrat that she'd adopted without Gaven.

"She's ready, Lady," the stable hand said with a small bow. "Safe travels."

"Thank you," she said, dropping a few copper coins into the girl's hand. She led the mare out of the stable and mounted on the street. Reaching over her shoulder to make sure Maelstrom was securely strapped to her back, she gave the horse a gentle nudge with her heels and started riding out of town to the east.

She was happy to put Vathirond behind her. She couldn't help but identify the city with her disastrous encounter with Gaven, a meeting she preferred to forget. As soon as she cleared the gates, she urged the mare to a gallop, exulting in her speed.

"I'm sorry I doubted you," she whispered in the mare's ear. "You put the steeds of Valenar to shame."

* * * * *

"She must know something." Ossa d'Kundarak glared across the table. "People don't ride off this close to the Mournland for fun."

Bordan shook his head, staring down into his wine glass. "It doesn't make sense. Senya told the Sentinel Marshals that Aundair is where the action is, and the last I heard from Phaine he was there, close on Haldren's tail. Anyway, if she knows where he is, why not just contact you or the Sentinel Marshals? Why chase after him herself?"

"She doesn't want to see him go back to Dreadhold."

Bordan looked up and met Ossa's gaze. "She turned him in twenty-six years ago."

Ossa shook her head. "She only turned him in because she thought he was possessed and hoped to get him cured."

"And what happened the other day?"

"I think she hoped for a happy reunion, picking up where they left off before he went mad. Then he appeared in town with his new elf ladyfriend, and there went her hopes for getting married at last."

"Oh, come now." Bordan swirled the wine in his glass.

"I'm serious. Twenty-six years, she never gets married? I tell you, she's been pining for him. So she ran out into the street, angry. You should've seen her—Natan said she was ready to cut him in half. But she didn't want him to get caught. She knew he'd escape, somehow. Ten Seas, maybe she helped him escape."

"Damn," Bordan breathed. "You're a suspicious one."

"I'm still alive."

"So what do you suggest?"

"I suggest we follow her, and I'll bet you fifty crowns she leads us right to Gaven."

Bordan drained his glass. "I'm not a betting man. And following her will be no easy task—she rode out of here on a magebred horse, remember, and not the draft kind."

Ossa tugged at one of her long braids. "Then what's your suggestion, d'Velderan? Following people is supposed to be your specialty."

"Well, if I told you my suggestion was that we forget about Rienne and join Phaine in Aundair, you'd accuse me of not listening to you. And I have been listening. I'm just not sure I believe your reasoning."

"Sovereigns! What's it take, man?"

"Hold on," Bordan said quickly. "I didn't say I don't believe you. I'm just not convinced yet. But if I were convinced, I think I'd suggest that we secure the use of a small airship from House Lyrandar. An airship can at least keep pace with a magebred horse, though she's a little obvious. But if I'm going into the Mournland, I'd rather do it in the air than on the ground."

"I happen to know," Ossa said with a grin, "that House Lyrandar has a small airship in town at this moment that would be ideal for that purpose."

"And if this turns out to be a chase after the dragon's tail, it'll be easy enough to turn the ship around and take her to Aundair."

"Have I convinced you, then?"

Bordan smiled. "Close enough."

CHAPTER
31

The moment Gaven pushed through the gray mist, leaving the Mournland behind him, his chest erupted in stinging pain. One of the ghoulish creatures had slashed his flesh when he first entered the Mournland, and Vaskar's claw had torn him further. But the wounds had gone numb in the dead air of that desolate land, neither healing nor festering as long as he remained there. At first he was afraid that some contagion in the mist had contaminated the wounds, entered his blood, and started an assault on his body from the inside. He washed the wounds carefully in the first clear stream he could find, and the bright red blood he rinsed from them reassured him that they were still, somehow, fresh and relatively clean.

The wounds taken care of, though their sting remained, he climbed up a hill near the streambank to get the lay of the land. Putting the wall of dead-gray mist behind him, he surveyed the surrounding landscape. To his right and ahead, gentle hills, some covered with tilled fields, others painted with wildflowers and prairie shrubs, rolled on as far as he could see. To his left, the horizon was shaped by mountains—a small range fairly close—then a level gap, then more mountains. As best as he could figure, that put him somewhere southeast of Vathirond, looking at the northernmost extent of the Seawall Mountains. A careful study of the northwestern sky showed him what might be the smoky haze of the city, far in the distance.

The thought of returning to Vathirond gave him pause, and he sat down on the hill to eat some dry journeybread and consider it further. Since cutting the wood from the ash tree, his mind had been fixed on his destination, and he'd given little thought to how he would get there. Going through Vathirond presented numerous dangers: the Kundarak dwarves who had nearly arrested him on his last visit, Senya, whom he'd abandoned in the House of Healing there, and of course Rienne. He groaned. No, that was a city he would prefer not to see again.

He scanned the horizon, trying to think of another city he could use to launch his journey. But this time, something in the sky caught his attention.

"Vaskar!" he spat. But looking again, the dark shape in the clear blue sky did not resemble a dragon at all. Far too large to be a bird, though he supposed a dragonhawk was a distant possibility. But the air shimmered around it—

No, a ring of fire. An airship!

Gaven rested his hands on the ground behind him, damp with dew, and watched the airship soar closer, all his plans pushed aside. How high she flew! And there were people aboard! People who could stand at the rail and peer down, see the whole country spread below them like a grand banquet. His eyes drifted down to the hills and fields, trying to imagine what they would look like from so high in the air, but his gaze always returned to the majestic ship, the pinnacle of House Lyrandar's achievements.

As she flew closer, he could make out more details of her shape and construction. She was about the same size as the one he'd seen moored in Vathirond—he wondered if she might be the same one. She came from the right direction, from the north along the wall of mist. Then he wondered what different sizes existed—how large was the largest airship? How majestic a vessel something like a flying galleon would be!

A sudden thought put an end to his speculation, and he stared blankly into the sky as he ran through its implications. An airship coming from Vathirond, coming closer to where he was, southeast of the city—where was she bound? Would she continue along the mist, heading somewhere in Darguun? Or soar over the Mournland to reach Valenar, perhaps? One of those possibilities, certainly, because otherwise . . .

Otherwise she was coming for him.

He scrambled to his feet and raced down the hill, no other thought in his mind than finding cover to get out of sight. What a splendid view the airship's decks must offer, indeed! The whole landscape spread out below—one might even be able to make out a person on the ground! Especially if the crew had sighted him while he was still in the Mournland, where he would stand out from the barren ground like an ogre at a society gala.

Unfortunately, the land offered little in the way of cover. Crawling or crouching his way through tall grasses or crops might have helped him elude a pursuer on the ground, but it would do little to conceal him from the view of watchers on the airship. What shrubs there were held little more promise: they were scattered widely, so while he might be able to hide under one, he couldn't move from there. So if they had already spotted him, hiding would just give them more time to reach him.

He jumped back down to the streambank and stopped, surveying the land again. The stream tumbled through a narrow, rocky ravine on its way down from the mountains. It probably passed very near Vathirond by the time it joined up with the Brey River and poured into Scions Sound. The ravine didn't offer much in the way of cover, but it might be better than nothing. Gaven looked up to the sky.

The airship was much closer, and she flew considerably lower. That probably meant her crew had spotted him. He crouched back against the side of the ravine, trying to get out of sight. But he couldn't find a position that blocked his own view of the airship. He cursed and clambered back up to the grassy bank.

"What am I doing?" he wondered aloud. "I have walked the Sky Caves of Thieren Kor. I sent Vaskar flying away with his tail between his legs. I will not hide any longer."

He stood and waited as the airship drew closer.

* * * * *

"Fifty crowns!" Ossa slapped her hand on the bulwarks. "I told you we'd find him here!"

"And I told you I'm not a betting man," Bordan retorted, peering through a spyglass. "But I have to admit that you were correct. It certainly seems that we've found our man." He watched as Gaven tore down the hillside and crouched in a ravine. "He's seen us. And he thinks to hide."

"Where can he hide out here? Nothing but open field as far as the eye can see."

"He appears to have reached the same conclusion." Gaven had

climbed out of the ravine and stood on the streambank, head high, watching the airship approach.

"Ha! We've got him!"

Ossa was a little too pleased with her victory, in Bordan's opinion. Certainly it was reasonable to be concerned about the honor of House Kundarak after the dwarves allowed Gaven's escape from Dreadhold. But part of the reason for Ossa's crowing seemed to involve the fact that she had been right and Bordan—an heir of House Tharashk who bore the Mark of Finding—had been wrong. With every exclamation of triumph, Bordan heard an undertone of condemnation, as if the dwarf said, "If we'd taken the course you suggested, we'd still be chasing the dragon's tail." He had very quickly grown tired of Ossa's voice.

"We don't have him yet," Bordan said, a little too sharply. "Remember what happened to the Sentinel Marshals."

"What did happen to the Sentinel Marshals? I heard some sketchy reports, but I'm not clear on the details."

"No one is. I think House Orien and House Deneith are trying to keep it quiet. I can hardly hold it against them. If they blame the storm, House Orien loses business—people won't want to ride the lightning rail in a lightning storm. If they blame Gaven, House Deneith looks bad for letting such a dangerous fugitive escape again, and we all come under tremendous pressure to recapture him. The whole reason we're in on this chase is that House Kundarak"—*your House,* he added in his mind—"wanted to keep the facts of his escape quiet as long as possible."

"So it's true," Ossa breathed. "Just like when I chased him in Vathirond. Gaven caused the storm? Or he brought it down to the lightning rail?"

"So it appears. Evlan was definitely killed by lightning, and there was significant evidence of wind blowing through the cart. But just the one cart. It seems that Gaven was the center of the storm—and I don't mean the calm eye of the hurricane."

"These storm clouds, then . . ." Ossa gestured at the sky.

"Churning chaos!" Bordan swore. "The sky was clear when we spotted him!" He and Ossa gaped at each other for a moment, then Bordan whirled around and shouted to the pilot, "Take us down! Now!"

A roar of thunder overhead drowned out his last word but

made his point just as effectively. Lightning danced around the prow of the airship as a gust of wind set her rocking wildly in the air. Bordan had to clutch the bulwarks to keep his feet as the pilot steered her in a sharp descent. The ground rushed up beneath them, and as they turned in their descent, Bordan lost sight of Gaven.

Instead of looking overboard, which made his stomach lurch, Bordan found comfort in watching the pilot. All around him, the crew retied broken ropes and retrieved spilled cargo, a whirlwind of activity. But the pilot was a still point in the chaos. His hands were white as they gripped the wheel, but no trace of panic was visible in his eyes. He exuded confidence and competence, which helped Bordan keep the terror from welling up in his own chest.

Thunder rolled and lightning crackled, and the pilot seemed locked in a war with the wind over control of the ship. Her timbers creaked, the ring of fire leaped wildly around her, something in the prow snapped loudly, but the pilot managed to keep her under control and bring her to the ground. A bump rocked the ship as some part of her keel touched the earth, then an ear-splitting crack as that something broke. The fiery ring disappeared as though the ship had sucked it in, and Bordan had to pull his hand off the bulwarks as it flared hot. The ship groaned loudly as she settled, then everything fell silent. Bordan watched a smile start to form at the corners of the pilot's mouth.

A great shout went up from the crew, celebrating a safe landing. Their roar was answered by a rumble of thunder, then a series of deafening cracks as lightning struck the earth around them. Bordan's eyes went wide as gouts of flame reached out from the ship toward each lightning strike, as if trying to join the heat of the lightning, before disappearing back into the wood. Bordan put a hesitant hand back on the bulwarks, found it perfectly cool and wet with rain, then jumped up to stand on it and look for Gaven.

A blast of wind dashed him from the bulwarks and clear of the grounded airship, landing him flat on his back in a field of rain-drenched grass. For a moment he could only lie there, staring up at the angry sky, straining to breathe and then to sit up. He raised his head, finally, just in time to see two bolts of lightning strike the airship. Flames leaped up on the deck in the lightning's wake, and an instant later the entire ship erupted in an inferno. Bordan threw his arm across his face to shield it from the fire's heat, and he rolled farther away from the ship.

Sailors jumped off the ship, some of them trailing flames or smoke as they came. Ignoring them, Bordan leaped to his feet and ran to the prow of the ship. As he neared it, the source of the attack finally came into view: Gaven hovered in the air, riding a column of swirling wind that blew dirt, leaves, and smoke in a cyclone around and beneath him. The fugitive's long hair whipped around his face, and the dragonmark on his bare chest and neck crackled with lightning.

CHAPTER
32

Gaven was the storm—raw, destructive fury. Some part of him regretted wrecking the airship, damaging a thing of such beauty. Somewhere in his mind a voice cried out for the safety of the people on board. But that voice was drowned in thunder and roaring wind.

Lightning struck the downed airship, sparking new fires on the deck, splintering timbers and sending sailors hurtling overboard. He felt a knot of anger in his gut, rage that lashed out in great gusts and rumbling thunder to smash and burn and destroy. Fury that silenced every voice of reason and compassion in his heart.

Something caught his eye, movement at the edge of his vision, and he turned his head to see a man on the ground, running toward him. He held a sword in each hand, as though he thought he could cut through the cyclone that held Gaven aloft. Lightning followed Gaven's glance, splitting the ground just behind the man, who tumbled into a forward roll across the grass, found his feet at the end of the roll, and kept running. Gaven scowled, and another bolt struck right in the man's path. That made him falter. The man leaped to the side and came down hard, one of his swords skittering away across the grass. Gaven looked back at the airship and frowned.

Destruction was so easy. He had acquired the power of the Storm Dragon, and it would be so simple to take up that mantle and become a god of devastation, a rival to the Devourer. Simple and so tempting. He looked back at the man. He was still advancing—so determined to meet his doom.

"Curse you," Gaven muttered. "Don't make me kill you."

With a breath, Gaven sent a gale to blow the pest away. The man faltered in the face of the wind, turning his head to draw breath, but he strained, still pushing his way forward. Gaven waved his hand, and the wind whipped into a cyclone. Gaven sent it for the man, hoping to lift him off his feet and carry him away.

But the idiot dropped to his knees, sank his fingers into the earth, and held on tight to wait out the wind. Gaven roared his frustration, and the wind howled in answer before blowing itself out.

Gaven tried to swallow his rage, and he forced the wind around him to set him down. He was tired, and he clutched the ash-black staff in both hands, leaning on it as his feet settled to the ground. The man looked up, grabbed both swords, and got to his feet.

"What's your name?" Gaven called.

The man gave a small salute with his twin swords. He stood a head shorter than Gaven. He was not strongly built, but his movements were quick and precise. His hair and his neatly trimmed beard were dark brown, but his temples were gray. His armor was well-worn leather, and the shoulders of his cloak had been bleached almost white by the sun.

"Bordan d'Velderan, heir of House Tharashk," he said. "I assume the formalities of declaring your arrest and demanding your surrender are pointless."

Gaven sighed. Surrender—the idea held some appeal. To stop running, stop fighting for his freedom and whatever feeble hold on sanity he still had. Surrender and let fate run its course.

No. He shifted the staff to his left hand and drew his greatsword.

"You're all alike, you know," Bordan said, stepping a few paces closer. "You criminals and fugitives. You all think you're better than the law, more important. You think you've done nothing wrong, you're just misunderstood, you've been treated unjustly. You think the law should make an exception for you. Every petty thief and small-time thug thinks the same way you do."

"Don't be so sure you can see into my mind," Gaven said. At the same time, he wondered—should he not return to Dreadhold and pay for his crimes?

Bordan stepped closer. "See? That's exactly what I mean. You all think you're different than the others. Sure, Gaven, you're unique—just as every dragonshard that falls from the sky is unique. But they're all the shattered parts of the same dragon."

Gaven saw the sky above the City of the Dead, the Ring of

Siberys shining bright as dragonshards rained down, clattering on rooftops and cobblestones. Then the bright streak that was the Eye of Siberys. A shattered part of the same dragon? Perhaps, but one with a part to play.

Bordan leaped for him, his swords moving in a deadly, whirling dance. Gaven swung his greatsword reflexively, cutting a low arc toward the other man's legs. Bordan adjusted the pattern of his blades to deflect the blow, their clashing blades sparking, and the momentum of his charge carried him past Gaven.

No, Gaven decided. He would not surrender. He had a part to play. He jammed the staff into the sheath on his back, then stepped forward, his greatsword whirling toward Bordan's head. Bordan crossed his blades to stop Gaven's sword and hold it, trembling against the bigger man's tremendous strength.

"You think you're better than all the others," he said, "but you're not."

Gaven wrenched his sword free and swung it in another low arc. Bordan stumbled back out of his reach, unable to parry in time. Gaven pressed his advantage, trying to keep him off balance by driving him farther backward. Unable to recover his footing, Bordan threw himself backward into a roll. As he came up, he batted Gaven's greatsword aside and found a balanced stance again.

"I don't want to kill you," Gaven said.

"Why not?" Bordan's swords blurred as they parried Gaven's swings and exploited every opening, putting Gaven on the defensive. "Would that violate your criminal's code? You've murdered before, Gaven. Why not kill me too?"

"I didn't say I won't. Just that I don't want to." Gaven stomped one foot on the ground, unleashing a thunderous blast of air that knocked Bordan backward, battering him off his feet. He raised his greatsword and advanced. Destruction was so easy.

Bordan lolled on the ground, still reeling from Gaven's concussive blast. Thunder rolled overhead, and Gaven growled his fury.

An axe clanged against his sword as he swung it down, then the dwarf holding it barreled into him and knocked him to the side. He recognized the scarlet-shirted, long-braided leader of the dwarves from Vathirond. He staggered under her weight, and wrestled to free his body and his sword from the tangle.

Bordan had found his feet and his swords, and was circling

around him for a clear swing. With a heave, Gaven swung the dwarf around, planting her between Bordan and himself.

"Bastard," Bordan growled. He lunged and cut a long line in Gaven's arm, the only exposed skin he could reach.

With a growl of pain, Gaven pushed the dwarf to the ground and sent her axe flying, bringing his sword up to block Bordan's flurry of steel.

He was floating, disconnected from the blur of steel, the sweat, the straining muscles. He saw it all—saw it so clearly. The flurry of Bordan's swords resolved itself into weaving patterns, just as the tunnels of the Sky Caves had revealed their patterns to him. Seeing the paths of the whirling blades, he had no trouble blocking the strikes, cutting through the defenses. The dwarf found her feet and joined Bordan's assault, but his sword was fast enough to block them both.

"Velderan," he mused. "Part of House Tharashk. Do you carry its mark, the Mark of Finding? Is that how you found me?"

Bordan's eyes narrowed, and he paused before answering.

"Rienne led us right to you," he said.

Rienne. A fresh surge of rage welled up in Gaven's chest. A blast of lightning exploded around Bordan, lifting him off his feet and hurling him away. The dwarf staggered back as well, though she kept her feet this time.

Rienne led them to him. Rienne summoned the dwarves to Krathas's office in Vathirond. Rienne sent for the Sentinel Marshals who arrested him twenty-six years ago. Why?

"Rienne is here?" Gaven said. He pushed past the dwarf—she and Bordan no longer mattered—and strode toward the fallen airship.

Apparently Bordan didn't realize that he'd become irrelevant. Gaven heard him charge up behind him, and swept his sword behind him in a half-hearted, one-handed swing. He half turned around, thrust a palm toward Bordan, and drove him back in a blast of wind. Then he broke into a run, carried by the wind.

* * * * *

Rienne hunched down in the saddle and urged the magebred mare to greater speed. The cloudy sky ahead of her grew blacker by the minute, and lightning flashed among the clouds. That probably meant that her pursuers had found Gaven.

She had first spotted the airship shortly after leaving Vathirond, and she kept telling herself that it was unreasonable to assume the ship was following her. Even so, she had tried to choose paths that blocked her from the sky. She didn't suppose it mattered—if they were trying to follow her to Gaven, they would have a better chance of finding him than she did.

And she suspected that was exactly what had happened. When she reached the edge of the Mournland, she turned to the south mostly on a hunch, and she saw the airship do the same. Not long after, though, she lost sight of the ship. When storm clouds had started to form over the sky ahead of her, fear clenched her heart.

What am I afraid of? she thought. That they'll catch Gaven? Or that he'll kill more innocent people?

She reached the crest of a hill and almost fell out of the saddle in surprise. The land sloped gently down the other side of the hill to a wide, bowl-shaped valley, then rose up into steeper hills, the foothills of the Seawalls. On the far side of the valley, she saw the airship lying askew on the ground, an inferno of leaping flames and splintering wood. Lightning danced in a ring around the ship, occasionally striking a high point on her shell. An enormous thunderhead towered in the sky above the conflagration, as though the smoke billowing up from the ship were somehow feeding the storm.

As the mare charged down into the valley, Rienne's stomach sank—the airship was the Morning Zephyr, the same ship she'd taken from Stormhome to Vathirond. The smiling face of the first mate appeared in her mind, and she strained to remember his name. This disaster was her fault. The ship wouldn't have been in Vathirond if she hadn't borrowed her for this journey.

But who had commandeered her for this voyage?

Rienne settled back into the saddle and urged the mare to even greater speed. She assumed Gaven was responsible for this disaster, which meant he was probably down there. She didn't know what she'd do if she found him, but she knew she had to be there.

As she drew closer, she could make out people around the wreck of the airship—and even people still on her deck, trying to get the fire under control. With each pounding hoofbeat, she called on the Sovereign Host to protect the innocent people who were caught up in this maelstrom. A new burst of fire erupted on the deck, sending a group of people scattering, jumping over the bulwarks, shouting.

While still a bowshot from the wreck, Rienne saw two people running toward her. One was a dwarf—possibly Ossa d'Kundarak, if the scarlet shirt were any indication. That would explain the Morning Zephyr being here: a dragonmark heir on such important business could probably call in favors to secure the use of a Lyrandar ship. And if the human beside Ossa were also an heir of a dragonmarked house—well, that would be twice as many favors.

"Lady Alastra!" Ossa stopped running and shouted at her, waving his arms wildly over his head. "Stop! You're in great danger!"

Danger? From Gaven? But how did he know she was there?

She reined in the mare right in front of Ossa and her companion. She noticed the human eyeing her carefully, but she ignored him and spoke to Ossa. "What did you tell him?"

"Tell him?" It seemed Ossa had been unprepared for her leap ahead in the conversation.

"Gaven. If he knows I'm here and wants to hurt me, I can only assume you told him that I led you to him, which might be technically true but could give the wrong impression." She saw Ossa and the human exchange a surprised look. "But he thinks I came here with you on the Zephyr, so he's probably looking for me there." She nudged her mare forward. "Thank you for the warning."

"Wait!" Ossa called, but Rienne ignored her. She urged her mount to an easy gallop and didn't look back.

She rode up beside the airship. Another gout of flame burst from the hull—reaching for her, it seemed. Her horse screamed, reared, and backed away from the ship. She guided her mount in an arc around the ship, keeping their distance from the flames.

"Gaven!" she shouted into the roar of the inferno. She could barely hear herself.

No one moved on the deck any longer. She saw a clump of people moving away from the ship's bow, but she didn't see anyone who looked like Gaven—or any sign of a fight going on among those people. She looked behind her and saw Ossa and the human man running toward her again. She didn't have much time.

She guided her mare as close to the airship as she dared, then brought her to a stop. With a word and a calming hand, she steadied the horse then nimbly jumped up to stand on the saddle. The mare shifted slightly, and Rienne teetered, but she found her balance, tensed, and sprang into the air. She somersaulted through the air and landed on the airship's bulwarks.

"Gaven!" she cried. Where was he?

As if in answer to her unspoken question, the deck before her exploded outward in a shower of sparks and splinters. A gust of wind carried tongues of flame and clouds of smoke up from the cabin below, and she threw her arms up to shield her face from the sudden heat. As soon as she dared, she lowered her arms and peered through the billowing smoke.

He stood on the deck before her, silhouetted by the raging flames. He took a hesitant step toward her, accompanied by a crash of thunder and a bright flash of lightning from above. She couldn't see his face, and she wasn't immediately sure whether he intended to use the sword in his hand.

"Gaven, please hear me out," she said, holding her palms out to him.

He took another step then slumped to the deck.

CHAPTER
33

S o where do we go now?" Jenns said. He licked his fingers, savoring the last taste of the meal Caura had cooked.

"Where do you want to go?" Caura avoided his expectant gaze, staring into their little campfire.

"I hadn't really thought about it."

"Churning Chaos, man! Did you have any thought in your head besides getting out of that camp?"

"Not really."

"Well then, Jenns," Caura said, leaning back on her hands. "We seem to be safe for the moment. Tell me about yourself. Why were you in such a hurry to get away from the camp?"

"Do I have to?"

"I think you'd better."

Jenns sighed and leaned forward, gazing into the fire. "I'm Jenns Solven, from Passage. You ever been to Passage?"

Caura nodded, remembering the bustling city, and the person she'd been there.

"So you know it's a pretty big city, sort of a hub for the lightning rail and caravan routes. And of course House Orien has their big enclave there."

"Are you attached to House Orien?"

"I'm the youngest of three brothers. My father works for House Orien. Both of my brothers work for House Orien. I fled. I joined the army a week before the signing of the Treaty of Thronehold."

Caura arched an eyebrow. "How old are you?"

"Twenty. You don't look any older. How long have you been in the army?"

Caura suddenly remembered that the face she wore was a great deal younger than Darraun's, and quickly covered her mistake. "No, I'm twenty-one. I joined up when I was just sixteen, though, so I thought maybe you were younger than you are."

"Just sixteen? What drew you in?"

Caura tilted her head and glared at him. "We're talking about you, remember?"

"I can't help it," Jenns said with a sheepish grin. He avoided her eyes. "I find you fascinating."

Oh, here we go again, Caura thought. "I think you're just dodging the question."

He looked up and smiled. "Fair enough. I joined the army when I was eighteen. I was still in training when the war ended, and I never saw combat. Truth is, that suited me just fine. I wanted to get out of my parents' house, and the army was all I could think of. Well," he added with a mischievous grin, "it was the best way I could think of to make my father crazy."

"Did it work?"

"Oh yeah. He wrote letters, he got various Cannith heirs to write letters, he pulled all the strings he could to bring me home. So one day my sergeant comes to my barracks, sends everyone else away, and asks me if I want to go home. I said, 'No, sir,' and that was that. Sergeant Kessel was a good man." The smile slowly faded from Jenns's face as he stared into the fire. "So I joined the army to get away from my father. I never wanted to fight. And then the treaty was signed, and I thought I got lucky—I never had to fight."

His smile reappeared for a fleeting moment. "Except that for some people, the war wasn't over. Lord General ir'Brassek ordered my unit into the Reaches, in violation of the treaty. I saw combat after all, which mostly meant that I pissed myself and hid when those damn huge Eldeen bears started tearing into our ranks. Sergeant Kessel was killed."

"I'm sorry," Caura murmured.

Jenns tried to smile.

"So the Queen called us back—I still don't know how she got the Lord General to listen. They put the Lord General up before the Tribunal and sent him to Dreadhold, gave all the units below him drudge duty as far from the borders as possible, and that was that. Two years I've been in the army now, and that one assault into the Reaches is my only combat engagement. And that doesn't bother me a bit."

"And then, out of nowhere, you're mobilized and sent to the middle of nowhere on the coast, no idea why, and you learn that the Lord General's back and about to violate the treaty again, and you want no part of it."

"Pretty much. Though I'm less concerned about the treaty than I am about the bears."

"Not to mention the dragons," Caura added.

"Please don't mention them again." He smiled.

"So you fled in panic, without taking the time to put a plan together?"

"Well, yeah. I figured I had to get out before we started to march."

"What?" Caura sat up. "I thought we weren't marching for another week yet."

"You didn't hear? No, the orders came down just before you found me in the camp. I guess it wasn't widely known yet, since most people were still asleep. Change of plans, straight from the Lord General."

Change of plans, Caura thought. So everything I learned is useless.

"What's wrong?" Jenns asked, his voice full of concern.

I am really slipping tonight, Caura thought. He must have seen me scowl. Control, Caura—it's all about control.

She smiled, erasing the tension from her face. "I must just be tired," she said. "It's been a long day, and I didn't sleep much last night."

"You sleep, then. I'll keep watch."

"Don't bother. I'm a very light sleeper. I'll hear anything coming through the woods toward us. And if you're walking around on watch, I won't get any sleep."

"All right, then. It won't be the first time today I've put my life in your hands."

Caura returned his smile, then pulled her cloak around her and lay down facing the fire. She closed her eyes and felt the exhaustion grip her, pulling at her consciousness and stilling every movement of her body.

"Caura?"

Her eyes shot open.

"I'm sorry," Jenns said. "I just wanted to thank you."

"I'm glad for your company, Jenns. We'll make plans in the morning."

"Good night."

"Night."

* * * * *

Poor boy, Caura thought.

She stood by the fire, looking down at Jenns as he slept. She thought he looked like a child, though he was only ten years her junior—his body curled tightly around the warmth of the dying fire, his face unlined, untroubled.

How long will you search for Caura Fannam? she wondered. Will you think I've been kidnapped or killed, like a fool? Or are you smart enough to discern the truth?

"Safe travels, Jenns," she whispered. His brow twitched, and Caura hurried away, afraid he might awaken.

As she walked, she made herself a new person, ensuring that neither Jenns nor anyone from Haldren's camp would ever find a Caura Fannam in all Khorvaire. Of course, Haldren might suspect he was searching for a changeling, but that wouldn't make it any easier to find the spy who had been in his midst so long.

Constrained by armor made to fit Caura's slender body, the changeling decided on a male elf—fewer hearts got bruised when he took male forms, it seemed. Elf eyes were hard to do right, especially without a mirror, but he enjoyed the challenge. He decided on long hair, raven and straight, figuring he'd braid it back when he got a chance. A slim but muscular body, pushing at the limits of the armor. He found a strap he could loosen to give him more room in the chest—room in the right places, anyway. He sketched the face—bright blue eyes in an almond shape, chin a little angular, smooth, fair skin, high cheekbones. He'd fix details when he found some still water or a mirror. He hated traveling without a mirror, but he had left Haldren's camp rather abruptly.

That would do for the time, he decided. Except for a name. He passed the time as he hurried through the night turning name ideas over in his mind. By the time the sun came up, he'd settled on Vauren as a given name, and fell back on a family name he'd used as an elf before—Hennalan. Vauren Hennalan. It was funny, he reflected, how the name he chose shaped the persona he adopted.

Vauren shared its consonants with the name of a paladin he'd known, lifetimes ago it seemed, and that made him want to act nobly. The last time he'd been a Hennalan, he had been a little mischievous, though, so those two streams flowed together and began to shape a personality for him.

Crafting a personality took a lot longer than shaping a face and body. He hadn't really had time to figure Caura out. That seemed to be the time when he was most vulnerable: while he was still deciding what kind of person to be, he was faced with temptation to be the kind of person who opened up, who shared secrets, who cared about people. That probably explained his slips at the camp-fire the night before.

Perhaps Vauren wasn't the best name. How could he be as noble as the name demanded and still be a spy?

Chapter
34

G aven!" Rienne rushed forward and gathered him in her arms, trying to get him back to his feet. He seemed unconscious, and he was probably twice her weight even after his stay in Dreadhold. She glanced around, frantic for anyone who could help, but the Morning Zephyr seemed deserted. Worse, flames began to engulf the upper deck, spreading out from the hole Gaven had blasted through it. "Gaven, you've got to help me get you out of here."

He didn't stir, and Ossa and the human were too far away to help. Rienne took a deep breath, steadied herself on one knee, and slid her weight beneath Gaven, shifting his limp body onto her shoulder. She groaned. "I must be out of practice, because I know you haven't gotten any heavier."

The heat stung her eyes and face, and she heard the deck creaking beneath her. "Here we go." She tried to imagine she was deflecting a charging enemy, using his momentum to throw him, but the only momentum Gaven had was what she gave him. So she leaned forward as much as she dared, then quickly rocked back, using the movement of his body to roll her up onto her feet. She staggered backward under the weight, but managed to find her balance.

Something gave way, and the airship rolled hard to starboard, nearly throwing Rienne back into the flame-ringed hole in the deck. Just trying to keep her feet beneath her got her moving, and she managed to run around the shattered planks to reach the starboard bulwark and struggle over it. Her feet kicked open air. With Gaven on her shoulder, she couldn't see how far she was above the ground, so she tried to brace herself for a hard landing and protect Gaven as much as she could.

To her surprise, the ground wasn't far at all. Her feet hit first, and she toppled forward, sending Gaven sprawling. The impact knocked the breath out of her. She rolled onto her back to look at the inferno behind her. The airship's hull started collapsing under its own weight, devoured by flames, but she had landed clear of the snapping timbers and leaping flames. She fought to fill her lungs again, panted to catch her breath, then scrambled over to where Gaven lay. The position of his limbs looked awkward, and his head seemed twisted around too far—panic rose in her throat.

"Sovereigns, no, he can't be dead," she said.

He coughed weakly, and she breathed again. Eyes still closed, he turned his head to a more natural position and shifted one leg.

She clutched his face, leaning in close. "Gaven? Wake up, Gaven."

To her amazement and relief, his eyes fluttered open. It was a moment before recognition registered on his face, then when he tried to speak no sound came from his throat.

"Come. We need to get away from this ship."

"Are you—?" Gaven began, then he broke into a fit of coughing.

"Take it easy," she murmured, stroking his cheek.

"Are you going to turn me in again?"

"What?" she said. "I just saved your life. Can you get up?"

Gaven lifted an arm and tried to lift his body after it, without much luck. Rienne got to her feet and took his hand, and managed to get him sitting up. He held up a finger and took a deep breath, trying to steady himself.

"Why are you doing this?" he said.

Rienne put her hands on her hips and looked down at him. "Because I love you, damn it. I'm not going to turn you in again. But I need you to tell me what's going on. If you can do that, I'll get you out of here, I'll join you on the run, I'll make myself a criminal for you. Just let me in."

Gaven lifted his eyes to meet hers. "I'll explain everything," he said.

"Wonderful. Now let's get out of here."

He held his hand up. She took it and heaved him to his feet, then wrapped his arm around her shoulder. "Lean on me," she said, and they hobbled as quickly as he could manage away from the burning wreckage of the Morning Zephyr.

Rienne spotted her mare—as well as Ossa and the human, trying to grab the mare's reins as she bucked and neighed. "That's a good girl," Rienne whispered. "Don't let the bad people catch you." She whistled, high and long and loud, and the mare's ears pricked. The horse reared up again, backing away from the others, then ran past them to reach Rienne.

As the mare ran by, the human saw his opportunity. He grabbed the horn of the saddle and leaped onto the mare's back. The horse tossed her head and screamed, but the man held on. His feet found the stirrups and he clutched the reins, but he let her keep running to Rienne.

"No!" Rienne shouted, waving her arms over her head. "Go back or throw him or something!"

"Bordan d'Velderan," Gaven muttered. "And his Kundarak friend." His hand went over his shoulder to his scabbard, but he found the ash staff instead of his greatsword's hilt. He looked at Rienne with wide eyes.

"I'm sorry," she said. "It must still be on the Zephyr." As she spoke, she drew Maelstrom from its scabbard.

She saw the man, Bordan, draw back at the sight of her steel, but then he hunched over the mare's back again, guiding the horse directly toward her.

"He's going to try to use you to get at me," Gaven said. "Clearly, he doesn't know you very well."

Rienne shot him a grim smile and focused her thoughts as she settled into a ready stance, Maelstrom poised over her head. She waited, utterly motionless, as Bordan drove the mare forward, faster and faster. As he drew near, he leaned out, reaching down as if to grab her waist and hoist her up.

Rienne only wished she could see his face as she grabbed his arm and used the mare's speed to throw herself into the air. Her feet went up in a wide arc, and her body followed. Suspended above her would-be captor, she slammed both feet into the side of his head, sending him tumbling from the saddle. She landed astride the mare and pulled on the reins. The mare wheeled around and trotted back to where Gaven stood over Bordan.

"Leave him, Gaven," she said, reining in the mare beside him.

Rienne clutched Gaven's arm and helped him swing up behind her. He put his arms around her waist—a little hesitantly, she thought—and she had to stifle a gasp. It had been so long since she'd felt those arms around her, she had all but forgotten how it made her feel.

She urged the mare back to a gallop, no destination in mind but away. This time, though the hoofbeats filled her ears, all she felt was Gaven pressed against her, holding her. After almost thirty years, she had finally come home.

CHAPTER
35

"I think it's time to honor your promise," Rienne said.

She sat on the edge of a hard, lumpy bed in a squalid inn, somewhere in northern Breland. She didn't know the name of the town, and she didn't care. Gaven stretched in the bed, and for the first time in two days, he didn't wince in pain. That confirmed her assessment that he was well enough to start talking.

"Rienne," he said, "I promised to marry you a long time ago and under very different circumstances. I think—"

"Not that promise, you ogre." She slapped his shoulder. "Don't pretend you don't remember. You promised to explain everything."

"Can I eat breakfast first?"

"No. Get started."

"It'll be time for luncheon before I'm done explaining, and you won't be able to hear me over the rumbling of my stomach."

She quirked her mouth at him, then broke into a full smile. "Very well, we'll get some food, and you can tell me everything while we eat. And if I'm pleased with the story, we'll buy you a new sword before we head out of town."

Gaven grinned. "Thanks, Mama."

She cupped his cheek in her hand and smiled at him. How long since he had called her that? It was an old joke between them—he complained that she mothered him, but she knew he appreciated it. And no matter how many times she reminded herself that she had many reasons to be angry at him, she couldn't help but thrill at every such recollection of their old life together. And to savor the feeling of his skin under her fingers.

He insisted that she turn away while he stood and dressed, which made her smile even more, thinking of the evening she had bathed him, tended his wounds, and dressed him when he was too weak to do it himself. But she resisted the temptation to nettle him further by peeking over her shoulder.

* * * * *

They were quiet as they left the inn and went in search of a fruitseller. Rienne couldn't think of anything to talk about besides the coming explanation, and Gaven seemed deep in thought, as if composing the words he would say. Her mind raced through all the things she thought he might say to her, and her mood grew darker. Her thoughts kept circling back to the elf woman in Vathirond, the one who had been arrested.

She watched Gaven pick out fruit. He checked each piece over for bruises or rot, used his thumb to test its firmness, and finally brought it to his nose before deciding whether to buy it. They bought a small bag of plums, a block of sharp cheese, and a fresh loaf of bread, then started back to the inn. By the time they reached the corner of the building, Rienne scowled down at the dirt road beneath her feet, tormenting herself with thoughts of Gaven testing the fruit of that elf strumpet.

"Hey," Gaven said, coming to a sudden stop just outside the door to the inn.

Rienne's sword flew into her hand as she whirled around to face him; it whistled softly as it bit through the air—and neatly cut through the plum that Gaven had tossed at her. She caught one half in her left hand, and the other landed in Gaven's outstretched palm. He laughed, and she couldn't help but smile again.

"I see Maelstrom hasn't lost its edge," Gaven said, pulling the pit out of his half of the plum and holding it up to her. Rienne's cut had divided the pit in half. His eyes found hers. "And you haven't lost yours, either."

She brought the point of her sword right under his chin. "And don't you forget it," she said, trying to scowl again.

He winked, and her face dissolved into a smile. She returned Maelstrom to its sheath, took a bite of her plum, and started up the inn stairs.

Back in the room, she sat cross-legged on her bed while he sprawled across his, devouring a plum.

"Where to start?" he wondered aloud, wiping juice from his chin and tossing the pit aside.

Rienne cut a piece of cheese from the block. "Perhaps at the point where you started acting like a madman?"

"Hm, no. I think I need to go further back." He pressed his palms to his eyes and drew a deep breath. "All right," he sighed. "Our last descent together, those caves in the Starpeaks. Remember?"

"How could I forget? I was so worried when you fell. I tried so hard to catch the rope! I was about to grab it, and then a swarm of bats came up from the shaft, thousands of them. I couldn't see my hand, let alone the rope, and by the time they'd flown by, the rope was gone."

Gaven let his hands fall to the bed and stared at the ceiling. Rienne waited, but he didn't continue. She stood and leaned over him. His eyes didn't register her presence.

"Gaven?"

His voice was distant, dreamy. "I fell. Down and down through endless dark. The pain . . ."

She sat beside him on the bed and put a hand on his chest. "You were so badly hurt."

His head jerked up, and she saw his eyes come back to focus on her face. "You found me. But not until after—" He sat up, taking her hand in his.

"After what?"

"Did you look in that box that Krathas gave you?"

"No. What was in it?"

Gaven reached into the pouch at his belt and produced the adamantine box she'd given him in Vathirond, the one he'd left in Krathas's care so long ago. As she watched, he opened it, his eyes gleaming as he peered inside. He stared so intently that she grew worried and started to push the lid closed. Only then did he turn the box so she could see its contents.

Her breath caught in her throat. A long time ago, a very different Rienne had made a career out of exploring the depths of Khyber, far below the sunlit world, searching for the dragonshards that formed there. Legends held that Khyber shards were formed from the blood of the Dragon Below, one of the three primordial; dragons who had shaped the world at the dawn of time, the progenitor of fiends and the father of all evil. Those legends gave nightshards their other common name: demonshards.

Legends aside, nightshards were valuable—especially during

the Last War. The dark crystals were suffused with magic, making them extremely useful in the creation of certain magical items. They carried a particular affinity for magic of binding, which made them essential for the artificers and magewrights who crafted elemental vessels for House Lyrandar: seafaring galleons early in the war, airships in more recent years. She and Gaven had made a small fortune procuring nightshards, because they had been good at finding them and good at selling them to the right people at the right price.

But she had never seen a nightshard like the one in Gaven's adamantine box. It was larger than her fist, and the swirls of midnight blue in its heart pulsed with barely contained energy. She reached out and touched its hard surface, and it seemed for an instant as though her fingers might sink into the crystal to touch the writhing serpents of color inside.

"The Heart of Khyber," Gaven said, and his hushed tone gave voice to the awe in Rienne's heart.

She moved her fingers slowly over the smooth facets, then suddenly jerked her hand back, wrenching her eyes away from the crystal to Gaven's face. The largest nightshard she'd ever seen—the largest demonshard. Her original suspicions about Gaven's behavior resurfaced—could the exorcists have been wrong? A shard this large—perhaps it held a spirit powerful enough to hide its presence from their examination.

Gaven must have read the fear on her face, because he snapped the box shut and took her hand. "I'm not possessed," he said, his eyes searching hers. "But in a way, you were right. Something was in the shard, something that entered me when I touched it." Rienne tried to pull her hand away, but he held it tight. "Not a spirit, though—it didn't dominate me, control me. Just knowledge. Memories. A whole lifetime of memories, incredibly ancient and wise."

The mystery that had haunted Rienne for nearly three decades was starting to unravel. She felt dizzy. "But whose memories, Gaven?" she said.

"A dragon's."

A dragon's memories. She tried to imagine the thoughts and experiences of a dragon's long lifetime, and found that her mind wasn't up to the task.

"So many memories, Ree. I still can't keep them straight." His eyes were staring, out of focus again.

"Which ones are really yours, you mean?" Sometimes, before all this happened, she would remember doing something as a child, or thought she remembered—it turned out Gaven had done it in his childhood. They had been that close, once. They had shared so many stories and memories that they had forgotten whose were whose.

He nodded. "At first, it seemed like the dragon's memories were mine, and the memories of my life as Gaven were the figments. I knew you, but it felt like I knew you from a long time ago, like you were someone I cared about when I was young."

Tears sprang to Rienne's eyes. "You weren't yourself. I thought I'd lost you."

"You had. I became the dragon, in a way, and tried to live his life, pick up where he'd left off. It took me a while to figure out that time had passed, and I've only just got a sense of how long it had been."

"How long was it?"

"I think somewhere between four and five hundred years."

Rienne whistled softly, casting her mind to what she knew about Khorvaire's history. Four or five centuries past—the Five Nations united into one empire of Galifar, Cyre alive and flourishing. A world that could barely imagine the horror and violence of a century of war.

"Twenty-nine turns of Eternal Day and Endless Night," Gaven murmured. His brow was furrowed, and his eyes closed.

"What's that?"

He held up a finger, and she sat back to wait. He rocked slightly, as if he were lost in the rhythm of some unheard song.

His eyes opened. "The Storm Dragon slumbers for twenty-nine turns of Eternal Day and Endless Night, and then withdraws from the world, to emerge in the Time of the Dragon Above."

"What are you talking about?"

"Turns of Eternal Day and Endless Night—Irian and Mabar, the planes of light and darkness. Irian draws near every three years, Mabar every five. Every fifteen years they draw near in the same year. Twenty-nine cycles of fifteen years is four hundred and thirty-five years. I think that's how long I was—"

He broke off and lay back on the bed.

"Not me," he whispered. "The other."

Rienne lay beside him, propped up on one elbow. She ran her fingers through his long hair and watched his eyes, staring wide at the ceiling, darting around as if there were something to see. Her heart ached, and tears stung her eyes. What must he have endured? So many years of this—not certain who he was. And still he was haunted, she saw it in his eyes.

"What do you see?"

Gaven looked at her, and a smile danced on his lips. She smiled down at him and buried her fingers in his hair.

"So many horrible things, Ree," he said. "Such horrible things."

"Hush," she whispered, stroking his cheek.

He sat up, pushing her aside. "No, thunder, no," he muttered, his gaze darting around the room.

Rienne pulled gently on his shoulder, trying to get him to lie down again. "Shh, Gaven, relax." His sudden unease sent a jolt of panic through her. This was too much like before—she didn't understand what he was saying, and she didn't know how to keep him under control.

"Help me, Ree. I don't want this."

"I know. I know. Relax, love."

"No!" He pulled free of her touch and stood. "I can't relax. That's when the dreams come."

Rienne took a deep, steadying breath, calming her racing heart. "Can you tell me about the dreams?"

He stalked to the door and turned to face her. "It's all the time now, even when I'm awake. Sometimes I know I'm dreaming about things that have already happened—some things I did, some things the other, the dragon did. Sometimes they blur together— I'll dream about my fall, say, and then I dream that I'm the dragon, putting my memories in the nightshard. Other times I think they're past events, but not anything I experienced." He pressed his palms to his eyes again. "But the future ones are the worst."

"You dream about the future?"

He slammed his fists into the door behind him. "All the time. Why can't I just live my life, here and now? Why do I have to see so much?"

She held her hands out to him, and he came and took them. There was so much she still didn't understand, but at that moment it didn't seem to matter. She kissed his hands, then brought them to her cheek, savoring the touch of his skin. "I'm here, Gaven," she murmured. "Here and now."

CHAPTER
36

Gaven did his best to recount his travels from the cold Lhazaar coast to Q'barra, to the City of the Dead in Aerenal, to Darguun, and then north from Korranberg on the lightning rail. Some parts were hard to tell, particularly the parts where Senya played an important role in the story. Other parts were hard to remember—his confrontation with the Sentinel Marshals on the lightning rail, for example, was confused in his memory with the dreams that had haunted him.

Whenever he started to lose focus, though, Rienne was there. At the beginning of his tale, in particular, it was hard to mention his dreams and visions without starting to slip into them, but her touch always brought him back. She asked gentle questions that clarified her understanding and sometimes helped him refine his own. Finally, she asked the question that struck to the heart of the situation he was in.

"So Vaskar is trying to become a god, and Haldren wants to be king of a reunited Galifar. What do you want?"

He frowned. Why should that be such a difficult question to answer?

"I'm still trying to figure that out," he said. "When I left Vathirond, I thought I knew what I was doing. I decided I wouldn't accept a destiny that somebody else had placed on me, that I would forge my own destiny."

His thoughts went back to the night outside of Vathirond, alone with the Heart of Khyber. The dragon's words had stirred something in him—a sense of purpose, the idea of choosing a purpose. But the purpose he'd chosen, pursuing Vaskar into the Mournland, had led him down paths he didn't want to take. He had felt as though he were still pursuing the dragon's purpose, not his own.

Rienne drew him out of his reverie. "Can you say more about that?" she asked. "Who was trying to place a destiny on you?"

"Everyone. The lords of the dragonmarked houses and the Sentinel Marshals had decided that my destiny was to rot in Dreadhold. Haldren and Vaskar had the idea that I would be the accessory to their greatness, like some kind of seer that validates their dreams by declaring them the fulfillment of the Prophecy. And then even when I thought I was choosing my own course, the dragon in the shard still seemed to be foisting his destiny on me, trying to make me finish what he couldn't. I didn't want any of those things."

"To forge your own destiny," Rienne mused. "That's heady stuff, Gaven—the sort of thing that legends are made of."

"I know. That's what bothers me. Before all this happened, I never really thought of myself as a person of destiny. I failed the Test of Siberys, and figured I'd live my life as a minor player on the stage of the drama of the dragonmarked houses." He had wanted to fail the Test of Siberys—precisely because his father expected the opposite. Arnoth had dearly hoped Gaven would manifest a dragonmark and carry on his work in House Lyrandar.

"It seems Siberys herself chose you for a greater destiny than that," Rienne said, reaching up to trace her finger along his dragonmark.

"Perhaps," Gaven said. "Although I feel more like I stumbled onto a different stage when I found that nightshard, and I'm trying to fumble my way through a play I don't know."

"So to forge your own destiny means taking control of the play. Becoming both player and playwright."

"Mm." Gaven nodded. "Heady stuff, as you said."

"So what did you think you were doing when you left Vathirond?"

"I thought I would be Vaskar's nemesis—and Haldren's, too. I thought I would be the agent of the Sovereign Host, punishing their pride and bringing their plans to ruin. So I went to the Sky Caves of Thieren Kor thinking that I had to stop Vaskar from gaining the knowledge there."

Vaskar hadn't gained the knowledge of the Sky Caves. But was that Gaven's doing, or Vaskar's own failure? He hadn't even seen Vaskar until he'd been in the Sky Caves for days, walking the paths and exploring the Prophecy. Why hadn't Vaskar gained the same understanding—and the same power—that he had?

Again Rienne prompted him out of his silence. "That seems like a worthwhile goal."

"Yes. The thing that worries me . . ." He trailed off again.

What worries me, he thought, is that I might become a god.

"The thing that worries me," he said, "is that the only way I could stop Vaskar was by claiming the knowledge of the Sky Caves for myself. I set out to become his nemesis, but ended up playing the part of the Storm Dragon in his place."

Rienne's brow furrowed. "The Storm Dragon . . . Gaven, what about these storms? The lightning rail near Starilaskur, the Morning Zephyr—I've never seen a Lyrandar heir throw that kind of power around. Even the tales of other heirs of Siberys don't say anything about storms like those."

All these storms, he thought. And not just the disastrous ones—rainy weather had followed him across the Five Nations. Wind swept around him in his anger. Lightning blasted his foes. He had the power of the Storm Dragon, whether he wanted it or not.

Did he have a choice about how to use it? Or was the script already written, just waiting for him to play his part through to the final act?

"It seems I've been cast in a role I wouldn't have chosen," he said.

"So turn it into the role you do want."

"How do I do that?"

Rienne got to her feet and held out a hand to him. "Why don't you begin by deciding where we're going next?"

He took her hand and walked behind her out of their room and out to the inn's stables, pondering her question. They were in Breland, somewhere near the border with Thrane. He had very little idea where Haldren or Vaskar were, though he guessed that Haldren would be in Aundair. The lord general had kept his plans to himself, for the most part—Gaven knew Haldren's ultimate goal, but nothing of how he hoped to achieve it. As for Vaskar, Gaven had told him what he had to do to reach his goal. "On a field of battle where dragons clash in the skies, the earth opens and the Crystal Spire emerges." Vaskar would seek to bring that about.

The thought of chasing Haldren and Vaskar all around creation made him feel tired, especially when he thought about the people who were chasing him at the same time.

Rienne pressed a coin into the stable boy's hand and led the magebred mare onto the street. Gaven stopped in his tracks. "Darkness take my destiny," he said. "I've been away for twenty-six years. I want to go home."

Rienne turned to him, eyes wide. "Do you think that's wise?"

He waited while she swung into the saddle, then climbed up behind her. "Wise? No, probably not. I'm an excoriate and a fugitive, so going back to the primary enclave of House Lyrandar in all Khorvaire is not wise."

"But at least it's a city of Khoravar, like us," she said. "Our race won't make us stand out the way it would in, say, Korranberg."

"And we know the ways of the house," Gaven added. "We can lie low there pretty easily." He swallowed hard. "Rienne, do you think my father would see me?"

"Of course he would. Oh, Gaven, he never believed the charges against you. Why, if I had told him I was going to look for you, he would have insisted on coming along."

Gaven gave a laugh that was half sob. "You've seen him recently?"

"It's been a few months, but we've been in fairly regular contact. I need to tell you, though, he's not in the best health."

"What's wrong?"

"Mostly he's getting old. He was still walking around when I saw him last, but he moved pretty slowly."

Gaven drew a deep breath. "I remember him the way he was before our last descent," he said. "Healthy, maybe seventy, still vibrant and strong. Not much older than I am now, I suppose." He'd been taller than Gaven, and more slender, but they had the same hair. The same large hands, and the same laugh. Once, when laughter came more easily to Gaven.

"Your brother has been running the household," Rienne said.

"Good for Thordren," Gaven muttered. "And I suppose his mark's a greater mark now?" Thordren had only just taken his Test of Siberys the last time Gaven saw him.

"I believe so, yes," Rienne said. "He's grown into a fine young man, Gaven. You shouldn't begrudge him his success."

"You're right, of course. He and I just chose different paths in life. He chose to follow our father and run the family business, and I rotted in thrice-damned Dreadhold for twenty-six years. And look how successful we've both been at our chosen careers!"

"Gaven—"

"No, I'm sorry. I was being stupid."

"To Stormhome, then?" Rienne craned her neck to look back at him, a smile on her face.

"To Stormhome."

She gave the horse a gentle kick, and they rode like the wind.

CHAPTER
37

W hen Gaven and Rienne reached the Thrane river, they knew they had left Breland. The Treaty of Thronehold had defined borders between the once-warring nations, but those borders were fluid and inexact things, and they mattered most when they were crossed by roads. Riding overland as they were, it was nearly impossible to tell that they had left one nation and entered another.

They avoided a large city, Sigilstar, situated along the river, and passed quietly through several small villages spaced about a day's travel apart—a day of riding on a cart pulled by oxen, that is, not a day on the back of a horse magebred for speed. On the third day, the river widened gradually, slowing from its headlong rush to a much more leisurely pace and finally coming to rest in one of the branches of Scions Sound, once the heart of the Five Nations. The warm breeze carried the smell of the sea, and the abundance of songbirds signaled that spring had well and truly come to this part of Khorvaire.

They spent the afternoon visiting shops. Rienne kept a careful eye on her stores of coin, knowing that House Kundarak had probably blocked her credit by that time. She bought Gaven a sword, new clothes, and a coat with a high collar that concealed his dragonmark. She replenished their supplies of journeybread, preparing for more long days of travel. That night, they enjoyed a comfortable inn in the small town of Sharavacion, the largest settlement they had dared enter since leaving Vathirond.

"Did you see the docks on the sound as we rode into town?" Rienne asked as they settled into their room.

"What about them?"

"Their size, mostly. This place might not be a bustling metropolis or a center of high culture, but it sees some shipping trade."

"Hm." Gaven leaned back in a chair and rested his hands on his belly, feeling comfortably full and quite tired after a pleasant meal down the street.

"I'm thinking there's some chance we can hire a ship here to take us to Stormhome. Maybe even a Lyrandar galleon—I might still have a favor I can call in."

"That would be good." Gaven closed his eyes and put his hands behind his head. He liked the thought of riding on a ship, especially a fast ship, rather than spending any more time on horseback.

He heard Rienne sit down on her bed and sigh. "Gaven?" she said.

"Hm?"

"What do you think Haldren and Vaskar are doing now?"

Gaven opened a sleepy eye and cocked an eyebrow at Rienne.

"Because you were talking the other night about becoming their nemesis, bringing their plans to ruin. I know that might not be the destiny you want to pursue, but I was just thinking about . . . well, what happens if they succeed?"

"I don't know what they're doing," Gaven said, looking up at the ceiling. "They didn't exactly inform me of all the details of their plans while I was with them. And when I saw Vaskar in the Sky Caves—well, we were too busy trying to kill each other to make conversation."

"I understand that," Rienne said.

Gaven thought she sounded a little testy, and he wasn't sure why.

She sighed, and when she spoke again her voice was quieter. "I'm just scared, I guess. Scared that Haldren will plunge us back into another century of war. Scared that Vaskar really will become a god, or gain the power of one."

"I don't think Vaskar will succeed. There's too much he doesn't understand, and he didn't learn anything from—"

Gaven stopped abruptly as words and images rose unbidden in his mind.

The words of the Sky Caves, woven thick with meaning . . .

The words he had studied in his draconic existence . . .

All flowing together with images from his nightmares.

The earth splitting. A colossal eruption of blinding light—a ray of Khyber's sun, a shard of the Dragon Below's might.

The hordes of the Soul Reaver emerging from the depths where they have long hidden in the darkness, unafraid of Khyber's cold light. Pouring forth from the cracks in the earth, swarming over the plain that lies in the sunset shadow of the mountains of stars.

Tearing into the soldiers massed there, shrieking and howling.

Soldiers cursing and hacking and dying. Fires in the sky and raging across the plain.

A clash of dragons signals the sundering of the Soul Reaver's gates . . .

Dragons fighting dragons . . .

. . . dragons wheeling in the sky . . .

. . . a clash of dragons . . .

. . . the armies gathered on the plain.

Dragons . . .

. . . Storm Dragon . . .

"Gaven?"

The images faded.

He lay on the floor of the room, where his chair had deposited him when he leaned too far back. Rienne was on her knees leaning over him, a look of concern mingled with fear on her face. Her hand stroked his cheek, brushing the hair back from his forehead, presumably checking him for fever.

"I'm all right, Mama," he said, trying to smile.

She clearly believed neither his words nor his smile. "Here, let me help you to your bed. Oh, Gaven, I let you do too much before you were fully recovered. You need to rest."

"I'm all right," he repeated, but he accepted her help in lifting himself onto the bed, and lay down again as she commanded. He chased the last fragments of dreams and visions as they scurried away from the rigidity of consciousness.

"What happened?" Rienne asked. "Did you faint or just slip? I didn't think you were leaning that far backward."

"Shh, shh." Gaven whispered. "I need to dream some more."

"Sleep is a good idea." Rienne's anxious fluttering transformed in an instant into soothing ministrations. She lay a blanket over him, stroked his hair softly, hummed an old tune that echoed the grief of wars long past. Eventually, she seemed to convince herself that he was asleep, despite his wide eyes staring toward the ceiling—but seeing only nightmares.

* * * * *

Rienne awoke with the first rays of sunlight creeping into the room. She stretched, rolled over to check on Gaven—and then leaped to her feet. Gaven was gone. The blanket she had draped over him the night before lay smoothed on his bed, and the pillow was fluffed. That, at least, told her that Gaven had gotten up and left the room in a more or less sound state of mind. She started for the door, stopped, and went back to lift Maelstrom from its place beside her bed. Then she went out to look for Gaven.

She was down the stairs and starting out the inn's door when a voice stopped her. "Good, you're up." She whirled and saw Gaven sitting by a fireplace in the front room. She laughed.

"Sorry to be such a slugabed. Sleeping 'til dawn—I ought to be ashamed of myself."

"Are you ready to go?" Gaven said, standing up and walking over to join her. He didn't smile.

"Well, almost. I left my things upstairs and—"

"Grab them and let's go."

Rienne started to say more, but decided against it. Gaven waited by the door as she ran back up the stairs to collect her pack. She hurried back down, and Gaven held the door open for her. He led her at a brisk pace toward the docks.

After a moment she hurried to catch up and walk beside him. "Gaven, are you all right?"

"Of course. Why?"

"Did you sleep at all?"

"No. But I dreamed a great deal."

She waited a moment for more explanation, but quickly realized he wasn't going to volunteer it. "Why the dawn rush this morning?"

"I'm anxious to get home."

Rienne pulled Maelstrom, still in its scabbard, from the sash at her waist and swung it at his stomach. "Stop."

He obliged her, scowling.

She stepped in front of him and looked up into his face. He didn't meet her eyes. "Listen to me. You promised to explain everything. I didn't take that to mean everything up to that point. You haven't fulfilled that obligation—you can't start the curt and cryptic act again. Because I can unsave your life, you know." She pointed the tip of her scabbard into his throat, gently, to emphasize her point.

He met her eyes, still scowling. She saw the muscles in his neck and shoulders tensing, and for an instant she feared he might actually attack her. Then, slowly, his frown dissolved, and he almost smiled. "I'll explain everything on the ship."

"What ship?"

He smiled broadly at that. "You'll see. If you start walking, that is. Come on!" He circled around her, laughing as he hustled toward the docks again.

Rienne made herself draw a calming breath. She could smell the sea air off Scions Sound, and she managed to catch some of Gaven's enthusiasm for the journey ahead. She hurried to catch him, slapped her scabbard against his rear, and laughed at the expression of outraged surprise on his face. He joined her laughter, even as he drew the greatsword from his back.

"Careful with your little sword, there, Lady Alastra," he said. "Don't make me use this."

"I'll put Maelstrom up against your great big hunk of scrap metal for any wager," Rienne shot back. "That's an orc's weapon—just swing it wildly back and forth and hope you hit something." She noticed as she spoke that Gaven still carried the black wooden staff he'd had when she found him outside the Mournland. He had attached it to his scabbard with some care. She started to ask him about it, but he cut her off.

"There she is," Gaven said, pointing with his sword.

He was pointing to a ship—and not just any ship. She was a great galleon, with two masts and an elegant aftcabin. Circling her, behind the mainmast, was a circle of elemental water, arcing high above the aftcabin and disappearing into the water on either side, reminiscent of the fiery ring around an airship. The water was in constant motion, churning in great rippling waves. She flew the kraken banner of House Lyrandar.

"Holy Host," Rienne breathed.

Gaven laughed. "Now do you understand?"

"Who's her captain?"

"Ah, that's the rest of the surprise." He sheathed his greatsword beside the ash staff, took her hand, and dragged her to the gangplank.

"Gaven! And the lovely Lady Alastra!" The man perched at the top of the gangplank was lean and weathered, his skin almost as dark as Rienne's from exposure to the sun. His blue eyes gleamed behind an aquiline nose, and deep wrinkles etched his face, accentuating his warm smile. His hair was a close-cropped sprinkling of black and gray, revealing the tracings of a dragonmark that started at one temple and extended behind his ear, making one more appearance on the side of his neck before disappearing. Half a dozen gold rings glittered along the edge of one gently pointed ear. He threw his arms wide as Gaven started up to meet him.

"Jordhan!" Rienne cried. She dashed up the gangplank behind Gaven, gripped Gaven's arm and swung past him, nearly sending him toppling off the side. She leaped into the grinning captain's arms, making him stumble backward onto the deck as he returned her enthusiastic embrace.

"Now do you see why I was so anxious to get here?" Gaven asked, laughing.

"I can't believe you didn't tell me!" Rienne didn't relinquish her hold on Jordhan, but spun him around so she could see Gaven over his shoulder. "How long have you known he was here?"

"I came out for a walk very early this morning and spotted the Sea Tiger here. I had barely settled in my seat at the inn when you came downstairs."

Finally Rienne released her tight hold on the captain, though she kept her hands on his shoulders as she looked at his face. "Look at you! You haven't changed a bit."

Jordhan winked. "And you're as lovely as ever, Rienne."

"Are you sure about this, Jordhan?" Gaven asked, clapping the captain's shoulder. "It's an enormous risk you're taking."

Jordhan kept his eyes on Rienne as he spoke. "I've been playing it safe for far too long."

"What have you been doing?" Rienne asked, finally relinquishing her grip on him. "I haven't seen you in—"

"Twenty-six years?" Gaven interjected.

Jordhan looked down at the deck. "Give or take." He brightened. "Come on, I've got your old cabin ready for you."

"It's just like old times, isn't it?" Gaven said. "Coming back from someplace desolate and dangerous, a load of Khyber shards in the hold—you did load the dragonshards, didn't you, Jordhan?"

They all laughed. Rienne's thoughts went to the Heart of Khyber, the one dragonshard they did carry on this journey—the cause of all their trouble. She squeezed Jordhan's arm. "It's wonderful to see you," she said. "And we're so grateful."

"It's nothing. I owe you two my life many times over."

"We wouldn't have had to save your life if we hadn't dragged you into such trouble," Gaven said. "Thank you, old friend."

Rienne looked back over her shoulder as she and Gaven started down the stairs to the little aft cabin they had shared on so many journeys, so long ago. Jordhan watched them go, a little smile on his lips and sadness in his eyes.

CHAPTER
38

"I always figured Jordhan would be at your door courting you as soon as I was off the scene," Gaven said. He couldn't look at her; he busied himself with his hammock while she rummaged in her pack. Even as he said it, he wasn't sure what he wanted her to say in response.

"Jealous?" she asked.

"Me? I suppose I was at times. And furious at what seemed like a betrayal compounded. And once in a while, late at night, maybe glad at the thought of my two best friends happy together, even if I couldn't share that joy."

He felt Rienne lay her hand gently on his back. "Oh, Gaven," she whispered. He turned a little, and met her eyes gazing up at him. She shook her head slowly. "He came by a few times in the first months. He was the only friend we shared who understood what I'd done, and his friendship meant the world to me in those months. But he never courted me."

"What would you have done if he had?"

"Now why would you ask a question like that?" She turned to her pack again, jingling the buckles for a moment. "He stopped coming within a year's time. It was just too painful for both of us—you were always so conspicuous in your absence. But when he stopped coming, it was even worse."

Something clenched in Gaven's chest, and he stepped behind her, resting his hands on her shoulders. "You were alone."

She took a deep, sobbing breath, and Gaven enfolded her in his arms. She turned around and buried her face in his chest.

"I always imagined you at home," Gaven said, "carrying on with your life—the life of a beautiful noblewoman with the world at her feet. I still can't quite believe you never married. And when I escaped, you came looking for me."

"Of course I did." She lifted her tear-streaked face to him. "Oh, Gaven. I know Dreadhold must have been terrible for you, and I'm so sorry, but—"

"But you were as much a prisoner as I was." She started to bury her face again, but he put a gentle hand under her chin and lifted it. "I'm sorry, Rienne."

She straightened her back and shoulders, stretching up toward him. Kissing her, he knew beyond doubt that all was forgiven.

* * * * *

House Lyrandar's airships were certainly their crowning achievement, but Gaven simply exulted in the speed, power, and grace of the Sea Tiger, seabound as she was. A water elemental was bound into the hull, channeled through arcane traceries carved into the fine Aerenal wood, and manifest in the enormous ring of churning water that surrounded the ship. The elemental lifted her from the water, carried her over rough waves, and propelled her along, even as the wind filled the sails at Jordhan's command. They saw the lights of Flamekeep after sunset on the first day—a journey that would have taken at least two days on horseback. There was no faster vessel on the sea.

The sea—Gaven had forgotten how much he loved it. Though still enclosed within Scions Sound, he could almost taste the open water, blue spread forever above and below him, the water lifting him up, and the wind surrounding him. It was much like flying on an airship, he imagined—with the land stripped away, nothing stood between him and the sky. It made him feel like he could soar with the gulls overhead, as easily as the black-and-white porpoises in the water rode the Sea Tiger's bow wave.

Even in the course of a day's travel, Gaven could see and feel the weather changing. Summer arrived later in Aundair than it did in Korranberg, certainly, and it brought more rain, especially thunderstorms. During the second night, they came upon a terrible storm. At the first resounding crack of thunder, Gaven sprang out of his hammock and went up on deck, where the rain drenched him. All around him, the crew of the Sea Tiger struggled to secure loose objects as the ship tossed on the churning sea, and he heard the night pilot order a mate to wake the captain. The command made sense—only an heir of the Mark of Storm could reliably command the ship's bound elemental, and the night pilot did not carry that dragonmark.

Before the mate could rouse Jordhan, though, Gaven lifted a hand to the sky. A flash of lightning silhouetted him, then another bolt struck him. He laughed as its power coursed through him, splintering off from his other hand into five harmless showers of sparks.

The rain stopped, and in a moment the wind died down—enough still to carry the Sea Tiger on her way, but no more. Sailors stood around Gaven in awe, staring skyward at the Ring of Siberys shining through a hole in the towering thunderheads above them—a hole that moved slowly across the sky as they continued their northward journey.

Gaven stayed on deck until morning, delighting in the storm's distant dance, the flashes of lightning all around them. When the sun rose in a crystal blue sky, the sailors around him cheered, clapping him on the back in congratulations. But he mourned the storm's passing.

* * * * *

The morning of the third day brought a glimpse of Stormhome, its towers and bridges gleaming pink in the dawn's first light. Beyond it, the sea stretched on seemingly forever, fading into white at the horizon. Avoiding the site of his ancestral home for the time being, Gaven found a place to stand on the deck where he could not see any land—just rolling ocean. He knew that the Frostfell lay beyond, holding the far north in a perpetual winter, but from where he stood it was a fantasy, all land was fantasy, there was only him, the Sea Tiger, and the endless, boundless sea.

"You don't seem pleased to be home." Rienne's voice startled him—he had so completely fallen into the illusion of solitude. He turned to see her crossing the deck toward him. Stormhome rose up behind her shoulder.

He shot her a weak smile then turned back to the sea. "Stormhome hasn't been my home for a very long time."

"Despite its name," Rienne said as she stood beside him, leaning her shoulder against his.

"Despite its name," Gaven echoed sadly. "They cut me out, Ree, like a healer cuts out gangrene. What am I doing going back there?"

"What are you doing?" Rienne said. "What destiny will you forge?"

"I don't know." Fleeting thoughts of a life on the sea passed through his mind—to spend his days and nights on the open water, under the open sky.

"If you don't know what you want, you're sure to do what someone else wants."

Gaven turned again, saw the warmth in her eyes and smiled. Then his eyes drifted over her shoulder to Stormhome, drawing closer as the Sea Tiger surged forward. His smile turned into an eager grin.

House Lyrandar's ancestral home—his home, for the first half of his life—occupied an island off the coast of Aundair. Its towers rose gracefully from the hills of the island, accentuating the natural contours of the land. Arching bridges and ornamented domes made the city into a work of art, glittering under a sky kept perpetually blue by the weather magic of House Lyrandar. Despite the city's position at the mouth of Scions Sound, at the northern edge of Khorvaire, the power of the Mark of Storm kept the weather warm and fair. There were buildings Gaven didn't recognize—the city had changed some in twenty-six years—but the closer he came, the more he felt glad to be there, even if he couldn't quite say it was home.

Rienne pointed to a prominent tower on the north side of the city, and Gaven's mouth hung open in delight. The tower was tall and slender, decorated with krakens whose outstretched tentacles formed spurs radiating out near the tower's top. Moored at one of these spurs was the largest airship Gaven had yet seen, considerably larger than Jordhan's impressive galleon. She boasted two elemental rings, one of white-hot fire and another of roiling cloud, occasionally flashing with lightning.

"Do you think," he asked Rienne, "that while we're here, I might get a chance to ride an airship?"

Rienne looked puzzled for a moment, then realized: "Ten seas! Of course, you've never been on one!"

"I'd never even seen one until I went to Korranberg."

Rienne took his hands in hers and clutched them to her chest. "You'll ride one, I promise," she said.

She turned to face the city, and he wrapped his arms around

her. She leaned back into him, and he savored her warmth, her smell, the way her hair tickled his nose. It was almost enough to make him forget Stormhome as they sailed to the docks.

* * * * *

"I can't thank you enough, old friend," Gaven said, clasping Jordhan's hand in his own. "I hope this doesn't land you in any trouble."

"I never saw you," Jordhan answered. "Either of you."

"That's right. And neither did your crew."

"They won't say anything unless I tell them to. Don't worry."

"I'm not worried," Gaven said. "How long will you stay in port here?"

Jordhan's blue eyes scanned the towers that rose above the harbor, and he scratched his chin. "Not long, I think. This is the one place it's hard for a freelancer like me to find work. Why? You think you'll need a way out of here?"

"I hope not, but I don't really know what's next. I just thought it would be good to know my options in case I do need to leave in a hurry."

Jordhan shook his head. "Think you can stay out of trouble?"

"No way," Gaven said with a laugh.

Jordhan embraced Gaven, then turned to Rienne. Without a word, Rienne threw her arms around him and held him tight for a long moment.

"Stick to him, Ree," he said with a nod to Gaven. "You two should be together."

"I plan to," Rienne said. She took Gaven's hand and stood back.

"Thank you again, Jordhan," Gaven said.

"I still owe you my life," Jordhan replied. "At least once or twice."

"But who's counting?"

"Sovereigns keep you," Jordhan said.

"Winds' favor," Gaven replied. Holding Rienne's hand, he strode off the Sea Tiger and into the city.

* * * * *

Rienne had been right: in a city full of half-elves, Gaven felt far less conspicuous, almost as though he belonged there. It helped that he knew the streets and buildings of Stormhome far better than any other city in Khorvaire. He found himself confused a few times by newer buildings that had altered the course of streetways, but overall the city had changed little while he was in Dreadhold. From time to time he was almost able to convince himself that it was still 970, that he'd never found the Heart of Khyber, never done the things that earned him his imprisonment, never been to Dreadhold. He even felt younger.

Rienne corrected him at each wrong turn, and soon they stood looking up at the three-spired tower where Gaven had spent his childhood, his father's house.

"Do you want me to wait?" Rienne asked. He gave her a puzzled frown. "I thought you might want a chance to talk to your father alone."

"Is there any reason he wouldn't be delighted to see you?"

"No, not that I know of."

"Well then, you're coming in." He took her hand and squeezed it, then he knocked on the door. It swung open immediately. Gaven didn't recognize the young man who stood in the door, but Rienne did.

"Good afternoon, Jettik, we're here to see the elder Master Lyrandar."

From the look on young Jettik's face, Gaven assumed that the boy guessed who he was. He gritted his teeth, planning how to keep the boy quiet—or, if all else failed, how to escape to a safe hiding place. Then he realized that Jettik's eyes were fixed on Rienne, his white lips quivered, and his eyes were red as though he had been crying.

What is going on? he thought.

"I—I'm sorry, Lady Alastra," Jettik stammered. The act of speaking seemed to break a floodgate, and fresh tears sprang to his eyes. "The master . . ." He wiped his nose on his sleeve and tried to draw a steady breath. A dread gripped Gaven's stomach, and he put a hand on the door frame. He already knew what the boy was trying to say.

Jettik started again. "The master passed away this morning."

"Oh no," Rienne breathed, squeezing Gaven's hand. Gaven

heard the words and felt the squeeze, but both seemed distant, as though he looked down on the whole scene from a mile in the air.

"Th-th-the younger Master Lyrandar is upstairs, Lady, if you want to . . ." Jettik trailed off.

Gaven only vaguely realized that Rienne was looking to him for direction. Did he want to see his brother? Some part of his mind thought that Jettik's words should have stung—he should have been the younger Master Lyrandar, not his younger brother—but he was too numb to feel the sting. It was impossible: he had been cut off from his family for so many years, and he had come hours too late to see his father one last time. Hours. Did he want to see Thordren?

Rienne led him forward into the entry, clutching his arm and looking up at him with eyes full of concern. She had evidently made the decision for him, or made her own. They were going to see Thordren.

His brother had been a headstrong adolescent when Gaven saw him last, barely more than a child. The two brothers had never been close, had never really been anything more than casual acquaintances who happened to live under the same roof. Now Thordren ran the household in their father's illness—no, he had just inherited the household. He could throw Gaven out of the house if he wanted to, he—

Holy Host, Gaven thought, he could have me arrested in no time. What are we doing here?

"Rienne." A rich tenor voice came from the staircase that curved upward along the opposite wall. Rienne wrenched her eyes from Gaven's face and looked up at Thordren.

"Thordren, I'm so sorry," she said. "I didn't know—"

"Of course," Thordren said. "It's good to see you anyway, though of course I wish the circumstances could be other than they are. But do I know your companion?"

Gaven had his back to the stairs, but now he turned to face his brother.

"Gaven," Thordren said, his raised eyebrows the only indication of his surprise. "This is unexpected."

"Hello, Thordren."

Gaven watched a series of emotions work themselves out on his brother's face, surprise and rage and grief and regret prominent among them. The silence stretched until it was awkward, with

Rienne looking back and forth between them as if waiting for one of them to spring at the other.

"I'm sorry," Rienne sobbed at last, when the silence had become unbearable. "We shouldn't have come."

"No," Thordren said. He started down the stairs again. "It's good that you're here. I apologize for being ungracious."

Thordren had reached the bottom of the stairs and crossed the room to stand by them. He threw his arms around Gaven, clinging to him with desperate fierceness. Gaven stood awkwardly for a moment, then returned his brother's embrace. When Thordren finally pulled away, his face was wet with tears, and he gave an embarrassed laugh.

"You will always be my brother," Thordren said.

Gaven pulled him close again.

CHAPTER
39

The Aundairian ambassador looked as though he had been dragged from bed and brought before the Cardinals—which, Vauren supposed, was not far from the truth.

Silver Flame, he thought, *I feel much the same way.*

Vauren's path away from the Whisper Woods had led him to the border of Thrane, Aundair's neighbor to the east and south. He'd been far enough ahead of Haldren's marching armies that he had little trouble slipping across the border without papers. Within three weeks of leaving Haldren's camp, he'd found his way to the city of Thaliost, where he managed to secure identification and traveling papers for his new identity. He had also used a contact in Thaliost to get a message back to Fairhaven, though he didn't expect any kind of response.

Armed with a letter of introduction provided by the same contact, he had made his way to Flamekeep and found his way into the livery of a Knight of the Flame, which made him distinctly uncomfortable. On the one hand, he knew he was by no means the first foreign spy to infiltrate this chamber and this supposedly holy order. On the other hand, it shaped Vauren's personality in unfamiliar ways. He wasn't accustomed to piety, but he was becoming pious. He had even started cursing like a Thrane. He feared it would interfere with his work.

He stood, stony-faced, at the great chamber's edge, as the ambassador hurried forward and bowed before the Diet of Cardinals. Vauren could see the man trying to compose himself as he held the bow a little longer than strictly necessary.

"Revered Lords," the ambassador said, absently straightening the folds of his robe, "to what do I owe this honor?"

One of the cardinals seated near an end of the crescent-shaped table got to his feet. "Ambassador," he said, "we have received some very disturbing reports from the north, and we hoped you could shed light on their significance for us."

"Reports from the north?" the ambassador repeated. Vauren pitied him. He was an aging diplomat, his hair thinning and his waist spreading, and he clearly had no idea what he was in for at this meeting.

"I will not waste your time weaving shadows, ambassador. Aundairian troops are marching north of Thaliost. What is their purpose?"

The ambassador was obviously stunned, and he stammered a reply. "I—I have not been informed of any troop movements."

"Are you quite certain, ambassador?"

"Yes, of course! I am sure it's nothing, just training exercises or war games."

"War games," the cardinal said gravely. "Tell me, ambassador, what kind of war game involves large numbers of dragons?"

"Dragons?" For the first time, the ambassador smiled, if nervously. "Revered Lords, someone is playing a terrible joke—"

"This is no joke, ambassador. We have not heard anything from you to suggest an explanation other than the one that seems obvious: Aundair is planning an imminent violation of the Treaty of Thronehold, in an attempt to reclaim the lands of Thaliost."

"That's ridiculous!"

"I might be inclined to agree with you, ambassador, were it not for the dragons. I wouldn't presume to guess what damning bargain your queen has made to secure the assistance of dragons, but I assure you that Thrane takes this threat very seriously. We have already notified our ambassadors in Breland, Karrnath, and the Eldeen Reaches in order to secure the assistance of those nations in protecting ourselves from this violation of the Thronehold accords. Aundair's arrogance will not be ignored. We hope you will urge your queen to reconsider this brash move before all Khorvaire is once again engulfed in war."

"I assure you, Revered Lords, Aundair is not planning an invasion. They would have notified me, recalled me. Unless . . ."

The ambassador fell silent. No one needed to finish his sentence for him—Vauren knew that everyone in the room could think of one very good reason for Aundair not to recall its ambassadors. A sudden departure of diplomatic personnel would alert

Thrane to the imminent invasion. If a handful of aging diplomats had to be sacrificed—well, that was the smallest price Aundair would pay in a renewed war.

Vauren stared blankly at the ambassador, careful not to let any of his thoughts register on his face with even the slightest twitch of muscle. Some part of him—the Knight of Thrane part, he supposed—wished he could help the poor man, leap to his defense and Aundair's, explain the whole situation. He wished he could put a stop to Haldren's madness before it cost any more lives. But he knew that was not an option.

I'm as much a slave to my orders as Cart is, he thought.

He was surprised to realize that the thought of the warforged brought a twinge of sadness. Would Cart's be one of the lives lost in Haldren's scheme? What about Jenns? Had he survived alone in the wilderness, or starved to death, or perhaps been rounded up again by Haldren's marching armies? And Gaven? Had the Sentinel Marshals tracked him down yet and dragged him back to Dreadhold? Or killed him?

Vauren suddenly felt light headed. In his mind, the grand chamber became the center of a swirling vortex of history—events unfolding inexorably around him, dragging him and everyone whose life he had touched into annihilation. Haldren and his armies marched in the north, dragons winging overhead. He'd last seen Gaven far to the south, but he imagined Gaven and Senya making their way northward, drawn by some unalterable destiny to reunite with Haldren on the same terrible battlefield. The fate of Khorvaire seemed bound up in the strands of these people's lives—caught in the maelstrom.

A pair of knights led the ambassador out of the room. Vauren assumed they were not escorting him back to the embassy. He'd be a hostage in the upcoming conflict, another life dragged under by the storm.

* * * * *

Vauren tried to relax. He was no longer dressed in the uniform of a Knight of Thrane, but he still felt the role constricting him. He leaned on the counter at a busy Flamekeep tavern, keeping an eye on the people coming and going without appearing to do anything but study his drink. He let the laughter and curses of the other patrons wash over him, hoping to absorb some of their freedom and coarseness. He felt altogether too clean and pure after his time in the Cathedral of the Silver Flame, and in danger of becoming a prig. Self-righteous morality didn't sit well alongside a career built on duplicity.

He had considered simply discarding Vauren and starting afresh on a new identity, but something held him back. Perhaps it was just the fact that he'd been three different people in such a short span of time. He had barely had time to get to know Caura, and he didn't want to discard Vauren so quickly. It was still early, he told himself—there was still time to shape Vauren's personality and keep him from priggery.

There was little else he could do in Thrane. He'd stayed in the Cathedral just long enough to learn where Thrane's generals expected to engage Haldren's forces—an old battlefield called the Starcrag Plain—and the size of the force they expected to marshal. Of course, if Breland or Karrnath decided to get involved, the number of troops could increase significantly, but by the time Vauren had left the service of the Knights of Thrane, those nations had made no commitment to Thrane's cause. If they did, that would be important information, but there were other spies who would probably hear the news first.

Finding Gaven, though, was something that no other agent was likely to accomplish.

A combination of a careful reading of the Korranberg Chronicle—the most widely read source of news in Khorvaire— and a thorough roundup of gossip had given him a sketchy idea of Gaven's movements. There was the chase through the lightning rail station in Korranberg. The Chronicle hadn't reported the identity of the fugitive, but it was easy enough to guess that it was Gaven. From Paluur Draal, Korranberg was the closest major city and lightning rail station. Then the lightning rail disaster in Breland. The Chronicle painted it as a freak storm, but the rumormongers spoke of Sentinel Marshals killed in the incident. Vauren had spoken to a pair of travelers who had been aboard when the carts stopped in Sterngate, who had told him about the Sentinel Marshals searching every cart, looking for someone. Clearly, Gaven had been traveling north from Korranberg.

The disaster had occurred near Starilaskur, he knew, which lay in northeastern Breland. The lightning rail line ran from there to Vathirond, then north into Thrane. But Vathirond also stood at the edge of the Mournland—not far at all from the Sky Caves of Thieren Kor, according to the map they'd found in Paluur Draal. And Vaskar had spoken, in Haldren's tent, of meeting Gaven at the Sky Caves.

And there was the lost airship. A man attached to House Lyrandar had gotten too far into his cups and told Vauren that an airship had failed to return after leaving Vathirond under unusual circumstances. Someone had bribed or persuaded the captain to take the ship on an unscheduled voyage, and she had flown out of town to the east, toward the Mournland.

Could Gaven have persuaded members of his family to let him borrow a ship, or to carry him into the Mournland? It seemed unlikely. He was an excoriate as well as a fugitive. By aiding Gaven, the captain would have been risking excoriation himself, as well as criminal charges. Someone very close to Gaven might have taken that risk, Vauren supposed. Perhaps Gaven had seized control of the airship? Again, unlikely—but not impossible.

He pondered the mystery of the lost airship as he ordered another cup of wine—or the vaguely wine-flavored water this place served. On a positive note, though, he could drink it all night without worrying about clouding his wits. While he waited, he leaned back against the bar and surveyed the crowded tavern.

A group of dwarves tramped in, and Vauren studied them. They were travel-worn, their cloaks dusty and their boots caked with dried mud. That wasn't unusual—at least half the patrons of this tavern looked much the same. Vauren had chosen a tavern near the southern gate of the city for just that reason: it was popular among travelers newly arrived in Flamekeep. He turned back around as the barkeep set his wine down with a grunt.

Something caught Vauren's eye as he turned, and he considered the implications as he sipped his wine. One of the dwarves, sporting a fine silk shirt of brilliant red, had revealed a signet ring as she pulled off her gloves. If Vauren's brief glimpse had been accurate, it was the snarling manticore seal of House Kundarak.

That could mean many things. House Kundarak maintained banking operations across Khorvaire, so some of its members traveled constantly from enclave to enclave. These dwarves did not look like bankers, though—they were battle hardened and armed to the teeth. Well, Vauren supposed that traveling bankers would have to be well armed and ready for combat, to protect against the threat of bandits. Still, House Kundarak also operated Dreadhold. Who would House Kundarak employ to track a fugitive from Dreadhold?

Vauren closed his eyes and listened to the sounds of the tavern, trying to locate dwarf voices amid the din. No luck, but that didn't surprise him—they hadn't struck him as a boisterous group. Holding his cup, he turned around on his stool, leaning against the bar again, to all appearances a handsome elf searching the crowd for companionship. He saw them arranging themselves around a table across the room. There were five of them, and they grumbled as they tried to fit their broad bodies comfortably at a hexagonal table. Vauren spotted burn marks on the clothes of at least three of the five.

There was no way Vauren could hear their quiet words at six paces, not with four other tables full of much rowdier drinkers between him and the dwarves. He concentrated on watching their lips. That meant he had to stare more intently than he would have liked, but the dwarves weren't looking around much. It was a risk he was willing to take.

The table's attention seemed fixed on the one in the red shirt, so Vauren pegged her as the leader. Unfortunately, Vauren stared at her back, watching the heads of the others bob in agreement but getting no idea of what she had said. Finally one of the other dwarves said something Vauren could read, and he knew he'd found a trail to follow.

"Couldn't we seize her family land in Stormhome?" the dwarf said.

That question told Vauren a great deal. Although House Lyrandar owned the island of Stormhome, the dwarves were clearly discussing a noble, not an heir of the house. Even House Kundarak couldn't seize an estate that belonged to another dragonmarked house. The question probably related to someone who had aided a criminal or a fugitive—seizing land would be a way of putting pressure on such a person. It was by no means a certainty, but it seemed probable that they were talking about Rienne ir'Alastra, Gaven's former betrothed.

He watched for a while longer without attracting the dwarves' attention, but he couldn't make out any more words to confirm his hunch. He needed closer access to these dwarves. When one of them got to his feet and made his way outside, Vauren saw his chance.

He left his drink on the bar with a silver coin, and slipped through the crowd to the door. Stepping outside, he looked up and down the street. Dark and quiet—perfect. Light spilled out the tavern windows, forming little bright pools on the cobbled street, but the other buildings were dark, and no one else walked the street. A splashing sound from the alley next to the tavern alerted him to his quarry's location. He wrinkled his nose in disgust—he expected better manners from House Kundarak.

He untied the length of silk rope he wore as a belt and tied a knot in it as he hurried to the alley. The dwarf leaned his forehead against the wall of the tavern as he relieved himself. In one smooth movement, Vauren stepped behind the dwarf and slid the rope around his neck, pulling it tight.

He cursed the hardiness of dwarves as he waited for the air to give out and the body to fall limp. The dwarf struggled hard, trying to work the fingers of one hand under the silk as he reached behind him with the other to gouge at Vauren's eyes. Vauren kept the pressure constant while keeping his own vulnerable spots out of reach, and finally his patience was rewarded—the dwarf fell first to his knees, then face down in his own puddle of urine. Vauren released the rope, and a wracking breath reassured him that he hadn't killed the dwarf.

That's strange, Vauren thought. Why didn't I kill him?

"My descent into priggery is complete," he muttered aloud. He pulled a dagger from his belt and bent to slit the unconscious dwarf's throat, but again he found something staying his hand.

"Oh, Vauren, you weak-willed Thrane." He dropped the dagger on the ground. "Only one thing to be done." He rolled the dwarf over, looking closely at his face. He glanced toward the street, making sure he was well cloaked in shadow. Then he changed.

He pulled off his clothes as he worked on his face, transforming it into a perfect copy of the dwarf at his feet—chiseled features, neat beard, shaven pate. Then he pulled off the dwarf's armor as he compressed his body to dwarven stature. He liked dwarf bodies— solid, strong. The skin firm, almost like marble.

He put on the unconscious dwarf's armor and checked himself over. He found identification papers and traveling papers in a coat pocket and studied them carefully. He repeated the name softly to himself several times: "Natan Durbannek, Natan Durbannek." He always preferred choosing his own names, but it was useful in this case: taking someone else's name helped him become someone more unlike himself. He didn't know Natan Durbannek, but he knew what House Kundarak's elite agents were like. So as he shaped his body, he also sculpted his heart—hard, sharp.

Ruthless.

He picked up the battle-axe that lay at the dwarf's side. Without a moment's hesitation, he brought it down hard on Natan Durbannek's neck.

* * * * *

The young Sentinel Marshal ran through the streets of Stormhome as fast as her feet could carry her. Watching Arnoth d'Lyrandar's house had seemed like the most boring assignment imaginable, and before the lightning rail disaster she had spent countless hours in her hiding place, wishing that she was with Evlan d'Deneith instead of sitting on her ass. After the lightning rail disaster, she had spent hours wishing she'd never entered the Sentinel Marshals, wishing she could be anywhere in Khorvaire other than that street in Stormhome.

But the assignment suddenly seemed anything but boring. She had to get word to someone before it was too late. She only hoped that someone could act on the information in time. She burst into the little message station operated by House Sivis, out of breath, her legs and lungs burning.

"Quickly!" she panted. "Send a message to Karrlakton! The Lyrandar excoriate, the fugitive from Dreadhold—he's here!"

Chapter
40

H e grew steadily weaker for a long time," Thordren said, "but the end went quickly. The healers said they couldn't do anything for him—his body just didn't have the strength to go on. Then it was just a few weeks ago he took a turn for the worse. He could barely draw breath enough to speak. So we started making sure all his affairs were in order, making sure everything was legally transferred over to me. He slept most of the last two days, and this morning—he didn't wake up."

Gaven sat with his hands over his face, his elbows on his knees. His mind was filled with memories of a much younger man, still healthy and vibrant and—gruff, often angry, always busy.

"It sounds like it was a peaceful end," Rienne said.

"Yes, very. I was actually asleep in the chair in his room when he died. We had a healer from House Jorasco here for about a week, I guess. She came in and woke me about dawn, and she observed how slowly he was breathing, and the next time I woke up he wasn't breathing at all. Very peaceful."

"Not very like him, is it?" Gaven said. "I would have figured he'd go out fighting, the cantankerous old—"

Rienne squeezed his knee, and he broke off.

Thordren laughed. "I can see what you mean." He stared at Gaven for a moment. "Anyway, I've been handling most of the business, as he grew weaker. Though Aureon knows I couldn't have done it without father's guidance, at least not at first."

"How is business?" Rienne asked. "Are you going to be all right?"

Thordren scoffed. "I'll be fine. Father was a genius, and I've learned a lot from him. I have plenty of money, and shipping contracts enough to keep it that way for the rest of my life. That is, assuming we don't end up back at war."

"What?"

"You haven't heard?"

"We've been at sea," Rienne reminded him.

"Of course. Well, the rumor is that Aundair's massing troops in Thaliost, or that's what Thrane says. Aundair denies it, of course, but there's a great deal of saber-rattling going on."

"Haldren," Gaven said, lifting his head from his hands.

Thordren gave him a quizzical look.

"Haldren ir'Brassek. He was in Dreadhold, escaped with me. Damn, he moves fast."

"Are any other nations getting involved?" Rienne asked, gripping Gaven's knee tightly again.

"Karrnath and Breland are making lofty proclamations about the importance of the Treaty of Thronehold and preserving the peace after so much tragedy, but otherwise keeping out of it. So far."

"What about the Eldeen Reaches?" Rienne asked. "They've got to be nervous that they're next on Aundair's list."

"As a matter of fact, just today I heard news of a skirmish on the Eldeen border. Some Reacher scouts had crossed into Aundair, presumably looking for signs of a troop buildup, and they tangled with an Aundairian patrol."

Rienne shook her head. "More bloodshed."

Gaven stood and walked to the window. Stormhome spread out below him, and the sea sparkled in the afternoon sun. In the distance, looming shadows were all he could see of Aundair.

. . . vultures wheel where dragons flew, picking the bones of the numberless dead . . .

Gaven started as though he'd touched fire, and stepped back from the window. He blinked, trying to get the image out of his mind, the sight of a battlefield strewn with corpses, a sky blotted out by the black wings of carrion birds, the earth torn open and violated.

Rienne was beside him, her strong hand between his shoulder blades. "What is it?"

Gaven sat back down, pinching the bridge of his nose and squeezing his eyes shut. "It seems that I no longer have to sleep to start dreaming."

"You're having visions?" Thordren asked.

Gaven looked up, studying his brother. That question was the first hint he'd given of concern about Gaven's mental state.

Does he think I'm mad, or possessed? Gaven thought. Has he simply been trying to placate me until help can arrive?

He stood and stalked to the window again, this time searching the streets for a marching force of Sentinel Marshals or some other authority on their way to arrest him.

"Gaven?" Rienne was beside him again, her face full of concern.

"Tell me something, Thordren." Gaven turned around, leaning back against the windowsill and crossing his arms. "Twenty-six years ago, House Lyrandar excoriated me and the tribunal threw me in Dreadhold. You've obviously gotten on with your life, and you're doing well."

"I don't un—" Thordren began, but Gaven cut him off.

"Why did you welcome me back with open arms?"

Thordren looked as though he didn't understand the question. "Because you're my brother," he answered.

"I'm an excoriate. Technically, that means I'm not your brother any more. You have no obligation to me. In fact, you're prohibited from giving me aid or shelter. You could be arrested just for having me here. Why did you let me into your house?"

Thordren's bewildered look changed as he gradually made sense of Gaven's questions. "You don't trust me," he said. "You think I've already summoned the Sentinel Marshals and I'm just keeping you busy until they get here? Is that it?"

"I'm really hoping to rule out that possibility right now. Tell me why you took me in."

Rienne held his arm. "Gaven, why—"

"No, Rienne," Thordren said. "I understand why you're suspicious, Gaven. If I were in your position, I would be too. Well, I hope I would have the presence of mind to be suspicious. I'm not sure I would."

"You're risking everything for me."

"And you can't understand why I would do that. But Rienne's risking everything, too. Do you understand that?"

"Not really," Gaven admitted, "but it's harder for me to imagine what she might be hiding."

Thordren's eyes were bright with tears again. "Did Dreadhold make you forget what love is?"

Gaven turned back to the window. "My betrothed delivered

me to the Sentinel Marshals. My family disowned me, cut me out. Nobody spoke in my defense at my trial. It wasn't Dreadhold that made me forget."

Rienne moved behind him and clasped his arm, but she was evidently at a loss for words. He stared blindly out the window, savoring the bitter taste of anger in his mouth. He heard Thordren step away and then settle in a chair. He started to turn back around, but something in the street below caught his eye.

Dwarves. If they hadn't been in Stormhome, he probably wouldn't have noticed, but in the home of the half-elf House Lyrandar—a single dwarf might not draw the attention, but half a dozen of them, trying to look inconspicuous, certainly did. When he spotted a scarlet shirt on a dark-skinned dwarf, he was certain.

"You bastard." Gaven whirled to face his brother. "You almost had me convinced with your little speech about brotherly love."

"What are you talking about?" Thordren looked genuinely confused.

"Those thrice-damned Kundarak dwarves are on their way," Gaven said.

Rienne gasped, and stepped to the window. "How many?" she asked.

"I saw five."

"Gaven, I had nothing to do with this," Thordren said. "Please, you have to believe me."

"They've probably been watching the house since you escaped," Rienne said.

"It doesn't matter any more how they found me. I need to figure out how I'm getting out of here." Gaven started out of the room, but Rienne grabbed his arm.

"How we're getting out of here," she said. "We're still in this together, Gaven."

"The airship," Thordren said.

"You have an airship?" Rienne asked. "Here?"

"Not here. But close. Rienne, you know where the bakery is?" He gestured to the west, and Rienne nodded. "If you turn right at that corner, there's a mooring tower halfway up the next block. It's not hard to miss. She's called the Eye of the Storm. Take her with my blessing."

Gaven stepped close to his brother and clasped his shoulder. "Thank you, Thordren. I'm sorry I mistrusted you."

Thordren smiled and nodded. "Hurry," he said.

"And I'm sorry for this," Gaven added, punching him hard in the jaw. Thordren spun halfway around before hitting the floor, unconscious. "But things will go much better for you this way," Gaven added.

Rienne took his hand and pulled him out of the room and down the stairs.

Just as they reached the bottom of the stairs, a pounding erupted from the door. Jettik hurried toward it, but Rienne stopped him with a gesture. The boy looked confused, glancing between Rienne, the door, and the stairs, as if waiting for an explanation from Thordren. Ignoring him, Rienne led Gaven through the house to the kitchen and yanked a back door open.

A dwarf stumbled through the door and collided with Rienne. Rienne let herself fall backward under the rushing dwarf's weight. Keeping her hands and knees between the dwarf's body and her own, she lifted him up and hurled him into the iron cookware hanging on the opposite wall. He collapsed in a heap of pots and armor, jerked slightly, and fell still.

"Natan!" a voice shouted outside, then, "Around back!"

Gaven grabbed Rienne's hand and pulled her to her feet as he charged out the door. As he ran west down an alley, he turned his face to Rienne. "You have to lead the way—I don't know any bakery around here."

"It's only been there about ten years," Rienne said with a smile, but then she pointed to their right and up. "I think that's where we're heading."

Gaven followed the direction of her finger with his eyes, and saw the distinctive shape of a small mooring tower jutting above the surrounding buildings. "Got it," he said. "The Eye of the Storm."

"Let's hope she's ready to fly."

"Do you know how to fly an airship?" Gaven asked.

"Sovereigns, no. That's your job, heir of Siberys."

Gaven growled and made a sharp right turn into another alley, trying to steer more or less toward the mooring tower. Just as Rienne made the turn, a crossbow bolt clattered against the wall of the alley.

"Fortunately, these alleys haven't changed much in thirty years," Gaven said. He pointed ahead. "We're going right at that T, though it leads away from the tower."

"If you say so."

They ran at top speed, and once again Gaven felt the wind pick up around them, carrying them so their feet barely touched the ground. When they reached the branching alley, the wind carried them smoothly around the corner without slowing. At the same time, though, a man came hurtling from the opposite branch, falling into stride right behind them, evidently carried by the same wind. Gaven barely caught a glimpse of him as he rounded the corner, but that was enough to identify him without wasting time on a backward glance.

"Bordan," he growled.

"That's right, Gaven." Bordan had to shout to be heard over the wind. "We found you again. The rest of your life will be like this, you know, as long as you keep running."

"Still better than Dreadhold," Gaven replied.

"And Dreadhold's far better than you deserve!" As he shouted, Bordan leaped forward and threw his arms around Gaven's legs, bringing them both to the ground.

Gaven landed on his side and kicked hard at Bordan's head. As his foot connected, a blast like thunder threw Bordan backward. Rienne helped Gaven stand, and they kept running down the alley. They made a sharp left turn, then stopped short, faced with a blank stone wall.

Lightning flashed in the darkening sky. Gaven shouted a curse, but a peal of thunder overhead drowned him out.

"I guess the alleys have changed a bit," Rienne said. She drew Maelstrom and stepped back to look the way they had come. "The dwarves are almost here, and Bordan's right behind them."

"If they want a fight, I'll give it to them." Gaven wreathed his body in flames as he drew his sword and stepped beside Rienne to face the onrushing dwarves.

Rienne looked at him sadly. "Gaven, I don't want their deaths on my conscience."

"You're a criminal now, Ree. You can't afford a conscience."

The dwarves slowed their approach, demonstrating more caution than they had last time. There were five, and Gaven thought three of them looked familiar from Vathirond. There was the scarlet-shirted leader Rienne had identified as Ossa. The one who had crashed into the kitchen had been in Vathirond as well—he'd knocked Gaven to the floor and almost cracked his ribs with his mace. The woman who had fenced with Senya was there too. The fourth wore the heaviest armor, a steel breastplate with a few other plates of metal protecting sensitive spots, and hefted a greataxe as long as Gaven's sword. The fifth kept to the back, her empty hands poised in front of her body, preparing to cast a spell. Bordan walked more slowly, trailing the dwarves by a dozen yards or so.

Ossa stepped ahead of the others and addressed Rienne, pointedly turning away from Gaven. "I know from experience it's pointless to ask for Gaven's surrender," he said, "but there is still a chance for you, Lady Alastra."

"Surrender?" Rienne said. "You don't know me very well, Ossa."

"There are few witnesses to the events near the Mournland, and it's not too hard to believe that he enchanted you and forced you to aid him. I certainly can't think of a more logical explanation for your behavior."

Gaven sneered. "You're wasting your time, Kundarak."

"Am I?" Ossa finally acknowledged Gaven's presence with a glance. "She delivered you to justice once, she can do so again. And certainly escape with nothing more than a slap on the wrist. You needn't spend the rest of your life a fugitive, Lady Alastra."

"No," Gaven interjected, "you're wasting your time chasing me at all. Two of us escaped from Dreadhold. Haldren's the one fomenting war and planning his conquest of Khorvaire. Why are you spending all your energy chasing me?"

Bordan stepped forward at that. "When you're just a harmless, misunderstood victim? Is that it, Gaven? We're chasing you because you're a dangerous fugitive. You expect us to just let you run around Khorvaire crashing the lightning rail and airships as the mood strikes you?"

"If you hadn't been chasing me, neither of those accidents would have happened," Gaven said.

"What makes you think you're so damned important, Gaven?" Bordan pushed his way through the rank of dwarves and thrust his face into Gaven's, heedless of the shield of flames around Gaven's body. "You think you're more important than the people you've killed? Is your life worth more than theirs?"

"Haldren's about to plunge the world into war again. Do you understand that?"

"You're the one who doesn't understand, Gaven. Yes, Haldren's a mass murderer. But you still have Evlan d'Deneith to answer for. You might be less evil than he is, but that doesn't mean you're good. You've earned your place in Dreadhold—or worse. So we're going to take you in, whether it's now or later. And then we'll find Haldren and take him in, and put an end to this nonsense. And the world will be a better place when you're in a cell again."

Gaven snarled, and lightning answered him, dancing around the spires of the mooring tower above them. "Take me in? You?"

"We will prevail, Gaven." Bordan's smile was calm and confident, which only infuriated Gaven more.

"How? You can't handle me."

It was not Bordan who answered, but Ossa. Her voice, too, was calm. "We don't have to handle you, Gaven," she said. "We just have to handle her."

Gaven realized his mistake at once. While he'd been yelling at Bordan, the dwarf in the back had cast a spell on Rienne, freezing her in place. Gaven sent a hurricane blast of wind down the alley, sending Bordan sprawling on his back and forcing the dwarves into half crouches. But two of the dwarves held Rienne's arms, and they started pulling her stiffened body away, letting the wind lighten their load. Ossa pressed the tip of a dagger to Rienne's neck.

"Careful, Gaven," the dwarf shouted over the gale. "The wind seems to have caught my blade."

Gaven saw a prick of crimson well up on Rienne's neck. The wind caught it and drew it in a line across her throat, as though demonstrating what Ossa threatened to do. With another rumble of thunder overhead, Gaven made the wind stop. His shoulders slumped.

Rain began to patter on the cobblestones around them, to hiss and vanish in the flames that still licked across Gaven's body, to spatter Ossa's scarlet shirt with darker spots like blood. The dwarf spellcaster spoke another spell and snuffed the magic of Gaven's fiery shield. Gaven stared at the tip of Ossa's blade and the dimple it made in Rienne's throat.

"If you harm her," he growled, "I swear that I will hunt down every person that so much as knows your name."

Two of the dwarves moved to seize Gaven's arms and pull them behind his back. As they clamped manacles around his wrists, he saw Bordan get to his feet and look up at the sky.

"I must admit my surprise, Gaven," Bordan said. "I knew you were powerful. But when did rain last fall in the streets of Stormhome?"

PART
IV

The greatest of the daelkyr's brood,
the Soul Reaver feasts
on the minds and flesh of a thousand lives
before his prison breaks.

The Bronze Serpent calls him forth,
but the Storm Dragon is his doom.

A clash of dragons signals the sundering of the Soul
Reaver's gates.
The hordes of the Soul Reaver spill from the earth,
and a ray of Khyber's sun erupts to form a bridge to
the sky.

The Storm Dragon descends into the endless dark
beneath the bridge of light, where the Soul Reaver
waits.
There among the bones of Khyber
the Storm Dragon drives the spear formed from
Siberys's Eye
into the Soul Reaver's heart.

And the Storm Dragon walks through the gates of
Khyber
and crosses the bridge to the sky.

CHAPTER
41

The Starpeaks jutted up above Thaliost as if a fiend imprisoned in the earth had pushed them upward in its struggles to escape. Senya stood on a rocky overlook at the edge of the mountains, with Arrakas d'Deneith at her elbow, never letting her stray too far. The dramatic landscape spread out below left her speechless. To the southeast, hills spread out from the mountains like ripples frozen into earth. Boulders littered the rocky ground, gathered in places into enormous cairns commemorating fallen soldiers from untold centuries of warfare. On the eastern edge of the plain, a dark forest stood out against the background of the jagged field. A chill wind blew out of the mountains at her back, moaning as it blew through gulleys and chasms in the bare rock.

It was easy to see why Aundair considered this land Aundairian soil: the only natural feature that divided the land was the Aundair River, which flowed into Scions Sound just south of the plain. But at the end of the Last War, the Thronehold Accords had established the new border between Thrane and Aundair somewhere in the middle of this plain below them, and extending on an indeterminate path through the Silver Woods beyond. By demanding that Thrane's borders include Thaliost, the Thrane delegation to Thronehold had almost undercut the peace process. Had the memory of Cyre's desolation not been so fresh in everyone's memory, this plain might have seen another decade of war.

"The Starcrag Plain," Arrakas said, gazing down with Senya onto the rocky field below them. "So just to the north—" He pointed an armored finger to the left, to the mouth of a wide valley that opened into the plain. "Bramblescar Gorge. Not too deep into that charming valley, just across the border in Aundair, we'll find your Haldren camped and ready to launch a new war over Thaliost. We'll reach his camp by nightfall."

"You're making a mistake," Senya said. She knew her protests were futile—she had run through the same arguments at least a dozen times since Arrakas had captured her in Vathirond. "He won't jeopardize his plans for my sake."

"Don't worry," the Sentinel Marshal said, still staring at the valley. A grin touched the corner of his mouth. "You're not the only dragon in my flight."

Senya suppressed a shudder at the mention of dragons, though she knew the phrase simply referred to a tavern game. She wondered how much Arrakas knew about Haldren's plans. Was he prepared to venture into that valley and come face-to-face with a real flight of dragons?

Senya found herself much less nervous about a score of dragons than she was about her inevitable encounter with Haldren.

Arrakas signaled to the half a dozen Sentinel Marshals at his command, and they started down the craggy overlook toward Bramblescar Gorge.

* * * * *

Senya's sharp elf ears heard the pounding hoofbeats a second before any of the human Sentinel Marshals who surrounded her. She wheeled her own horse around to find their source, but two Sentinel Marshals spurred their horses toward her, anticipating an escape attempt. They wrested the reins from her hands and seized her arms before Arrakas's sharp command cut through the din.

"Release her!" The marshals obeyed, though one kept hold of her reins. Both looked daggers at her, and Senya returned the glare. Between them, she could just make out a party of perhaps a dozen knights charging across the plain.

Arrakas had clearly seen the knights as well. "Harkas! Lucan! Give Senya her reins and turn your horses around."

The anger on the marshals' faces turned to surprise, and they did as their officer commanded. Senya saw the approaching knights more clearly—they wore plate armor and full helms, and carried shields and lances with the tips held high, gleaming in the sun. Their shields bore the silver arrowhead of the Silver Flame, marking them as Thranes. A regular border patrol? Or scouts from an advancing army, massing on the Thrane side of the border to face Haldren's forces?

"Senya," Arrakas said, "you will be silent while I talk with these knights. You will not speak without my leave. Do you understand?"

Senya nodded, even as she wondered what kind of trouble Arrakas feared from her—and how she could cause worse.

Arrakas nudged his horse forward to await the Thranes' arrival. Senya saw him straighten his cloak, ensuring that the large brooch at his throat was clearly visible, since its chimera symbol marked him as an heir of House Deneith and a Sentinel Marshal.

The knights rode hard to meet them. The leader of the charge circled a raised hand in the air as he came to a halt, and the others spread out to encircle the intruders. When all the knights were in position, they lowered their lances in unison—all except the leader, who sat unmoving on his steed, his face covered by a full helm. Glancing around the circle at fourteen shining lances leveled in her direction, each carried by a heavily armored rider on a barded warhorse, Senya started to reconsider the idea of causing trouble.

After a few heartbeats, Arrakas gave an exasperated snort and addressed the knights' leader. "Knights of Thrane," he called, "I am Sentinel Marshal Arrakas d'Deneith, traveling your lands in pursuit of a fugitive. Under the provisions of the Treaty of Thronehold pertaining to the order of Sentinel Marshals, I claim safe passage."

"With all due respect, Sentinel Marshal, as far as I am aware the Treaty of Thronehold is about to be torn to shreds. I need to ask where you are going." The knight's voice was muffled by his helm. Senya thought it odd that he had not removed it to speak.

"The fugitive I seek is in Aundair," Arrakas said, "and if I find him quickly then Aundairian forces will not enter this plain."

"So you seek General ir'Brassek," the knight replied.

Senya raised an eyebrow. Could she be imagining that his voice sounded familiar? And why would a Thrane even know who led the Aundairian army, let alone call him General?

"Your scouts and spies are to be commended," Arrakas said.

Senya could see that the Sentinel Marshal was as surprised as she was. She glanced at the knights on either side—their lances were still lowered, and one horse pawed the ground impatiently. This meeting would not end well.

"Six Sentinel Marshals," the knight observed, "and one elf. Who is that, a captured fugitive?"

Arrakas shot Senya a quick glance over his shoulder. "Yes," he answered. "She is an associate of ir'Brassek, an accomplice to his escape."

"Did you capture her in Thrane?"

Arrakas took a deep breath before answering. "No."

"Where, then? In Breland?"

"Yes. Vathirond." Arrakas's voice betrayed his frustration.

"So you have already transported her across one national border and are about to bring her across another? Has she yet stood trial?"

Arrakas drew himself to his full height, still a head shorter than the towering Thrane leader, and his horse pranced in place. His face was crimson, and Senya tried unsuccessfully to suppress a grin. The knight had caught Arrakas in an act that was questionable at best, possibly illegal even under the broad authority granted by the Treaty of Thronehold. That explained Arrakas's nervousness at the knights' approach, as well as his command for Senya to remain silent.

"Sir, you have detained us long enough. There is a great deal at stake here—as you yourself observed, the Treaty of Thronehold and the peace it established may soon lie in ruins. I must demand that you allow us to continue on our way."

"I'm afraid I can't allow that, Sentinel Marshal."

Arrakas drew his sword, and the swords of his six marshals sprang to their hands at once. "Thrane will hear of this."

Something about the knight's voice as he responded jolted Senya. "I certainly hope so," he said, and she suddenly knew where she'd heard his voice before. She threw her head back and laughed, spurring the knights flanking her to wheel on her again, and she kicked herself for not realizing sooner. What appeared to be plate armor under the tabard of the knight leader was actually the armored plating of a warforged soldier. And not just any warforged.

It was Cart.

As the surrounding knights charged, Senya leaned over and grabbed the reins of the rider on her left, pulling his horse closer. Too close for him to swing his sword. He turned in his saddle to face her, trying to free his sword arm. She brought her left hand, clenched around his reins, up into his throat. His horse reared, and Senya leaned over to grab his sword hand. She yanked the sword from his hand as the rider toppled backward out of his saddle.

Senya yanked the reins farther back, keeping the horse off balance, and it finished her work—one of its hoofs crushed the fallen man's chest. Releasing the reins, she brought the dead man's sword around in a wide arc to her right, just in time to block the other marshal's sword as it sliced down toward her leg. As she found her balance in her saddle, she kicked the other horse's flank, sending it prancing forward, carrying the rider out of reach. She sat up, wrapped her reins firmly around her hand and wrist, and took stock of the battlefield.

The Sentinel Marshals were terribly outnumbered—there had been at least two foes for each Sentinel Marshal before Senya made herself part of the equation. Still, they were hardened warriors, and they had so far acquitted themselves well against Cart's soldiers. Four soldiers in Thrane colors lay dead or dying, one of them crushed beneath his bloodied horse. Cart was locked horse-to-horse with Arrakas: she saw him raise his axe high over his head as he pushed Arrakas away with his shield. The man Senya had unhorsed lay motionless on the ground, but he was the only Sentinel Marshal who had fallen.

The other Sentinel Marshal brought his mount under control and wheeled it around to charge her. Senya braced herself in her stirrups and kicked her horse forward to meet the charge head-on. Both horses shied at the last moment, rebelling against their riders' evident desire to bring them into collision. Senya was thrown from her saddle and hit the ground rolling. She somersaulted away from the stamping hooves and stood again, relieved to have solid earth beneath her feet again. She was no more used to mounted combat than her horse was, bred as it was for speed and not war.

The Sentinel Marshal kept his seat and held his sword low as he charged. Senya settled into a relaxed, balanced stance and watched him come, looking for the perfect place to strike. The marshal drew his sword back as he came nearer. She waited as long as possible, then dropped to the ground, slicing her slender blade along the horse's flank. The sword's point traced a line of blood along the charging horse's skin, then caught the saddle strap and cut through it. The horse screamed and bucked, sending rider and saddle flying through the air.

"What would the Valaes Tairn think of me?" Senya muttered. The warrior elves of Valenar revered their horses almost as much as they did their ancestors, and they frowned on attacking an opponent's horse. Senya's mind leaped back to Shae Mordai, and she was off guard when the marshal charged her again, this time on foot.

"Die," the marshal snarled. His sword arced toward her neck, and she lifted her left arm just in time to prevent the blade from cutting deep where her neck and shoulder met. As it was, the sword cut through the leather and flesh of her arm, struck and broke bone, and lodged between the two bones of her forearm before the marshal wrenched it free. Senya felt blood spatter her face and blinked hard to clear her eyes.

"Not yet," Senya gasped.

Her opponent reeled backward with the momentum of pulling his sword back, and she drove her own blade into his belly. He collapsed on the ground, staring blankly up at her, his face contorted in pain. She stabbed him again, in the throat, then rolled him over to stare at the ground. Dropping into a crouch beside him, she took stock of the battlefield again.

Cart and two of his men, still on horseback, ran down a Sentinel Marshal who was trying to flee on foot. Two other men in Thrane colors fought on foot against a second marshal. Otherwise, the battle was over. Senya ripped the midnight-blue cloak off the marshal she'd killed and, using her teeth and one hand, tried to rip it into bandages she could use to bind her arm. The wound was excruciating, and her right hand shook violently as she worked.

Her trembling hand slipped as she tried knotting the first bandage around her arm, sending a fresh jolt of pain from the wound. Her head grew light, and she put her right hand on the ground and lowered her head to steady herself. Just as her vision cleared, a weight settled on the back of her neck, accompanied by the gentle bite of a blade resting against her skin.

"I lost four good soldiers for you." Cart's voice was heavy, and his axe blade on Senya's neck shifted as he spoke.

"You call those good soldiers?" Senya said. "They had the Sentinel Marshals outnumbered two to one, and I took out two marshals by myself. "

"I said they were good soldiers." Cart lifted his blade off Senya's neck, and she pushed herself to her feet and faced him. "Not champions. It's good to see you again, Senya."

Senya smiled, but she had stood too quickly, and she slumped to the ground in a dead faint.

CHAPTER
42

The streets of Stormhome were choked with people, most of them staring into the sky. Bordan had been right: it had not rained within the city walls in the memory of any living resident, though the rolling hills of the island enjoyed mild showers from time to time. The people of the city acted as though the world were about to end.

Let them, Gaven thought. Let it rain. Let the world stop. Arnoth d'Lyrandar is dead.

In front of Gaven walked two dwarves, trying to remain calm and gentle while they nudged people aside to clear a path. Another walked behind him, a hand on his manacles and an axe at the ready. Ossa and the dwarf spellcaster guided Rienne. The last time Gaven had stolen a look backward, the tip of Ossa's dagger was still pressed into the skin of Rienne's neck. Bordan brought up the rear of the strange procession, seeming nearly as disconcerted by the rain as the residents of the city were.

Rienne was manacled and walking under her own power, so the paralyzing spell had ended. He briefly toyed with plans for an escape. He tested the strength of the manacles, trying not to alert the dwarf holding them. He didn't think they would give—they were probably reinforced with magic—and he thought they might even be dampening his own magic. With his hands free and alert to the threat of the spellcaster, Gaven was sure that he could handle the five dwarves and Bordan by himself. With Rienne, he might be able to handle them with his hands still bound. But as long as Ossa's dagger was pressed into Rienne's neck, he couldn't take the chance.

Gaven didn't know where the dwarves were taking them. He had assumed at first that they'd bring him to Stormhome's jail, to hold him until they could arrange transport back to Dreadhold. But the jail was near the center of the city—unless it had relocated during Gaven's imprisonment—and they were headed toward the northern neighborhoods. A few dragonmarked houses had enclaves in the northern district of Six Corners, but neither the dwarves' House Kundarak nor Bordan's House Tharashk were among them. House Deneith's Sentinel Marshals also occupied a large tower in the city center, not far from the jail. The docks were situated to the southeast, but Gaven realized that he didn't know where in the city airship mooring towers might be concentrated. That became his working assumption: The dwarves and Bordan would load him on an airship for immediate transport back to Dreadhold.

The rain fell harder as they walked, and the mood of the people in the streets grew worse. When lightning flashed in the sky, Gaven heard a woman scream, and he suddenly realized the flaw in his theory. Bordan and Ossa were not stupid enough to put him on an airship—they had both been aboard the *Morning Zephyr* when storms forced her to the ground.

The dwarf behind Gaven yanked on his manacles, and he stopped walking. The leaders of their cavalcade were embroiled in an argument with a group of men who had apparently objected to being pushed aside. The dwarves kept their voices calm, but the men yelled and waved their arms.

"Gaven, listen to me." The dwarf behind him still had a hand on his manacles, and he whispered up to Gaven. Gaven moved his head in the slightest nod.

"It's Darraun," the dwarf said. Gaven almost whirled around to face him. "Don't move. Listen. If we ever get out of these crowds, I'll release your manacles. As soon as you feel them loosened, you need to run, and fast—the way you did in Aerenal. I'll take care of Rienne—just get out of here."

Gaven nodded again, almost imperceptibly. The dwarves in front managed to force an opening into the crowd, and the dwarf who claimed to be Darraun nudged him to start walking again. As they made their way through the crowd, a hundred questions arose in Gaven's mind. In the forefront was what possible reason there could be for him to trust the dwarf of House Kundarak who said he was a human artificer named Darraun.

So Darraun was a changeling—rather, a disguise adopted by a changeling. Gaven had known there was more to the artificer than he let on, and Senya had suggested that Darraun might have connections in the Royal Eyes of Aundair. It fit. But it left open some much larger questions. Why had Darraun been working with Haldren? And why had he infiltrated Ossa's group of dwarves? Was he helping Gaven now in order to return him to Haldren or for some other purpose? Did Gaven want his help, or would it come with a cost he would be unwilling to pay?

The crowds grew thinner but more serious as they entered the Six Corners neighborhood, named for the junction of three roads in an elegant plaza outside the House Orien enclave. The people glowering at the sky there were heirs and functionaries of the drag-onmarked houses, speculating at what failure House Lyrandar, their colleague and competitor, might be experiencing. Gaven kept his arms tense, straining against the manacles to be sure he'd know as soon as—

The manacles clattered to the ground.

Gaven roared, and lightning flashed in the sky. He whirled and thrust his arms out in front of him, and a gust of wind followed his arms in a mighty blast. Bordan, Rienne, Ossa, and the dwarf spellcaster were knocked to the ground, and Ossa's dagger clattered to the cobblestones. Darraun was already running to Rienne, and the blast of air knocked him forward, into a somersault, and back up into his run.

Gaven ran, the wind howling at his back.

He hadn't even thought about where he would run—he'd been too busy thinking and worrying about Darraun. He knew Six Corners well from his childhood, but he wouldn't rely again on a mental map of streets and alleys that was years old. He looked over his shoulder. The Darraun-changeling was locked in battle with Ossa and one other dwarf, and Rienne fought beside him, using mostly her feet since the manacles still bound her hands. Bordan and the other two dwarves ran behind him. As he slowed to look behind, they gained several paces on him.

He had no choice. He had to trust Darraun to get Rienne safely out of there—if the changeling could free her hands, they'd be fine. So without any other plan in mind, he did as Darraun had told him: he ran like he had in Aerenal.

The wind blew like ragged wings at his back, speeding him through Six Corners and beyond, outside the city to the rain-spat-tered beach. He swept along the sand, leaving only the faintest of footprints. Waves rose up to drench him in their spray, and lightning flashed across the water. Rage and fear and grief overwhelmed him—they took shape around him like forces of nature as powerful as the storm, and he howled with the voice of the wind.

Sandy beach gave way to sharp rocks that cut his feet as he ran across them, but he felt no pain. His pursuers were lost in the distance, Stormhome had been swallowed in the mist and rain behind him, and even Rienne and Darraun were all but forgotten. Storm clouds blotted out the sunset and swallowed the stars. Soon he climbed above the tumultuous waves as the rocky beach rose toward the jagged cliffs at the far end of the island.

He ran, buoyed and buffeted by the wind, until he reached the highest bluff. Part of him imagined running off the point and either plunging down onto the rocks or somehow running onward, upward, becoming one with the storm. He stood at the precipice for a moment, suspended in the air, his eyes fixed on the waves crashing against the jagged rocks below, and then he sank to his knees, lifting his gaze to the storm clouds that brooded over the cliffs.

"Father!" he howled to the sky, and the wind howled along the cliffs and blew itself out.

Gaven slumped to the ground.

The rain pounded his back, stinging his skin, and the waves thundered as they crashed against the cliffs. His body clenched like a fist around a knot of grief in his belly, and he pounded his hands against the rock. The storm began to wane and the knot in his gut loosened, and his breathing went from shallow gasps to a slower, deeper flow of air.

He drew one last, long, shuddering breath and uncurled his body, lifting his head to a sky that began to show patches of blue. He saw ships navigating the bay and imagined their crews' relief at the passing of the freak storm. The waves started to quiet, and gulls took to the air again, calling to each other with keening cries.

Arnoth d'Lyrandar is dead, he thought, but life will go on. It must.

He stood, taking another deep breath, and looked behind him for any sign of his pursuers. The beach was still deserted, but a ring of fire flickered in the sky, growing quickly larger as the airship it propelled drew nearer. He watched it warily, feeling power welling up within him while hoping he would not have to use it again—he was so tired. Finally he saw a figure in the prow, arms waving in the air—Rienne. The airship was the *Eye of the Storm,* his brother's vessel.

Gaven turned back to the sea and thought of Thordren, and his father, until Rienne called down from the airship above him. "Gaven! Are you all right?"

He looked over his shoulder and saw a rope ladder hanging over the ship's bulwarks, dangling just outside of his reach. Rienne leaned out over the top of the ladder, a look of worry on her face.

"I'm fine," he called. He walked slowly to stand just below the end of the ladder, and carelessly jumped up to grab the lowest rung. "Don't worry about me," he said as he started to climb.

The airship jerked in the air, nearly throwing Gaven off the ladder. He saw Rienne clutching the bulwarks, her eyes wide. "I'm not worried about you," she hollered back. "I'm worried about how long Darraun can fly this thing. Hurry!"

Gaven clambered up the ladder as fast as he could, even as it writhed and jerked in his hands. Rienne helped him over the edge, and shoved him aft, where Darraun clutched the wheel—and wore Darraun's face again. That face was chalk white, and his eyes were wide. He didn't give any sign of recognition as Gaven approached him.

"He's been trying to convince the elemental that he has the Mark of Storm," Rienne explained, "but it's a losing battle."

Gaven saw a pattern on the changeling's skin that suggested a Lyrandar dragonmark, but it wouldn't fool even a casual observer, let alone grant Darraun the magical ability to control the airship.

Gaven moved to stand behind Darraun and reached his arms around the smaller man to clutch the wheel.

Be still, he told the elemental, channeling his will into the helm and into the conduits that bound the elemental to the ship. *A true heir of Storm commands you now.*

The ship stopped bucking, and Darraun slumped to the deck in front of Gaven. Rienne took his hand and led him out of Gaven's way. Pulling Darraun's arm around her shoulder, she led him below decks. Gaven stepped closer to the wheel and settled into a comfortable stance. A smile blossomed on his face as the ship responded to his every thought, soaring smoothly away from the island and into the clearing sky.

Since Darraun had first mentioned airships to him in White-cliff, Gaven had been waiting for this moment. Since he had first laid eyes on one in Korranberg, he had dreamed of standing at an airship's helm. His smile broadened into a boyish grin, as a single thought ran over and over through his mind:

I was born for this!

* * * * *

Bordan fell to his knees on the sandy beach. The dwarves hadn't been able to match his speed, though he wouldn't be surprised if they ran all the way to Storm Point before they flagged. He glared up at the airship receding into the rain, the sign of his defeat. Gaven had escaped him again.

The storm lashed him, though it had diminished as Gaven got farther and farther away. Gaven had been the cause and the center of the storm. Bordan was sure of it. A harder rain had begun almost at the moment that he'd knocked on Arnoth's door. The thunder that accompanied Gaven's kick—he rubbed his sore head thinking of it—and the wind that had literally carried him out of the city made it clear. The storm obeyed Gaven's command—or at least echoed his emotions, overriding the will of Esravash d'Lyrandar, the house matriarch, and all the Lyrandar heirs who worked together to maintain the paradisal climate of Stormhome.

Despite his boasts to Gaven's face, Bordan found himself grappling with serious doubt for the first time in his career. Perhaps he could continue finding Gaven—but he'd found Gaven twice already and been unable to apprehend him. What if he never caught him? And even if he caught Gaven, could he hold him? Or would he meet the same fate as Evlan d'Deneith?

Could even Dreadhold contain a man with the power of the storm at his command?

The beach grew darker, as though a new storm cloud covered the sun. Bordan felt rather than heard a presence behind him, and he leaped to his feet.

A pool of shadow had formed on the white sand, roiling like smoke at the feet of Phaine d'Thuranni. An elf woman garbed in black stood just behind Phaine. Both elves had weapons drawn.

"Damn it, Thuranni, I didn't hear you approach."

"Few ever do," the elf replied, taking a step forward. The darkness moved with him, clinging to him as he walked.

"What's this about? Did you follow Gaven here?"

"Yes. He escaped." Another step closer. "Again."

"Now, wait a moment, Thuranni. If you had any inkling of his power—"

"I believe I do."

"Did you see that storm?" Bordan said. "Do you know what he's done?"

"Far better than you do."

"Do you know what he's been ranting about all these years? What he's been dreaming?"

Phaine wrinkled his nose in disgust. "My blood is from an undiluted line of Aerenal, *human.*" He drew out the last word with a vicious sneer. "I know."

Bordan's gaze flicked between the two elves. "What are you doing?" he said. "Gaven is the enemy here."

"Of course," Phaine said.

The elf woman spoke for the first time. "We can't let you fail again. He grows stronger each time."

"Why don't you get him, then?"

"We will," Phaine answered.

"And this is what we'll do to him," Leina added.

Both elves' swords spun in a burst of motion, and Bordan fell to the blood-spattered sand.

CHAPTER
43

The sun was dipping below the horizon, setting the last shreds of storm clouds ablaze with yellow and red, when Rienne returned to the main deck. Gaven watched as she looked up at the sky, and he smiled at the way the sunset glowed in her hair and eyes. She leaned against a railing near the wheel and smiled at him.

"How's Darraun?" he said.

"Exhausted, but he'll be fine." She glanced at the hatch leading below. "I suppose we owe him our lives, or at least our freedom."

"Again," Gaven said. He remembered his first glimpse of freedom from his cell in Dreadhold: the Ring of Siberys framed within a ragged hole in the stone ceiling, the warforged jumping down and trying to coax him out, and then Darraun, finally, standing at his side and bringing him back to his senses. It seemed so long ago, and Dreadhold just a memory of a dream.

"Did you know he was a changeling?" Rienne asked.

"No idea. I remember that almost from the beginning I knew he was hiding something. He didn't quite fit in with the others—he was the only one who would even think of challenging Haldren, for one thing. And Senya thought he had some connection to the Royal Eyes. But a changeling?" Gaven shook his head, remembering the dwarf who had released his manacles—the same one who had barged through Thordren's back door and landed in a pile of cooking pots—and struggling to find any similarity to the familiar human artificer. "No, I can still hardly believe it."

"It sort of makes you think, doesn't it? Anyone you talk to could be a changeling, really—even someone you think you know. How can you ever be sure?"

Gaven had no answer for that.

Rienne watched him for a while, her eyes following the slight movements of his arms as he steered the airship over the sea. "So you're flying an airship," she said at last, a smile spreading across her face, gleaming white in her dark skin.

Gaven returned the smile. "I am," he said. "It's wonderful."

"Is it hard?"

"Not in the least. She's really not very different from a ship on the water. And the elemental does most of the work."

"It seemed to be plenty of work for Darraun."

"Oh, it was. These wheels are made to channel the power of a dragonmark—they're the same ones they use on the seagoing galleons. They won't work for just anyone."

"It's fortunate he was able to do it at all."

"Yes, but not altogether surprising. Artificers are good at making magic work the way they want."

Rienne ambled a few steps toward the prow. Gaven watched her as she stared ahead for a moment, then to the right, then to the left. She searched the horizon for a long moment, then turned back to him and asked the obvious question. "So where are we going?"

He gave her a sad smile. "If you don't know what you want, you're sure to do what someone else wants."

"That's my line," she said with a grin, but then her face grew serious, and she stepped closer. "So what do you mean by that? Are we still talking about you and your destiny, or are you making some kind of comment about me?"

"I mean it's time for me to decide. I've spent my whole life squirming under the pressure of other people's expectations, without ever deciding who I want to be and what I want to do. It's time for me to grow up, to stop defining my life by whining, 'No, I don't want to do *that*.'"

Rienne laughed at his exaggerated voice.

"Do you know," Gaven continued, "before my Test of Siberys I must have prayed to each of the Nine Sovereigns a hundred times, asking that I wouldn't show a dragonmark?"

Rienne frowned. "You never told me that."

"It's true. And I always felt like my father knew it, or at least blamed me for failing the test. I think he always figured that once my mark manifested, I'd come around—I'd be the dutiful son he wanted me to be, and follow in his footsteps. I guess I must have figured that if I did get a mark, I would pretty much have to. And that's why I wanted so badly not to get one."

"I don't want to do *that*." Rienne mimicked Gaven's whining voice.

"Exactly. I never wanted to do what I was supposed to do."

"And yet you served your house well, all those years with me."

"By working around House Tharashk to get better deals on dragonshards. By working outside the system."

Rienne stepped closer. "Very well, you rebel. So now you're fighting against expectations again. Some ancient dragon inside your head wants to become a god, but you're not going to do that. Haldren wanted you working for him, but you weren't about to do that. You're supposed to go back to Dreadhold and rot like a dutiful prisoner, but I note we're not sailing east to Dreadhold. We're sailing west. So what are you going to do?"

Gaven's brow furrowed, and he looked away. "I think I'm going to be a hero."

"Really?" Rienne almost laughed, but she reined it in when she saw the seriousness of his eyes.

Gaven blinked back tears. "The elder son of Arnoth d'Lyrandar could be nothing less."

She closed the distance between them and placed a hand on his chest. "He was proud of you, you know."

Gaven nodded, but he stared down at the wheel. "The memories of him that come most readily to my mind are the stern father, judging and distant and gruff. I don't know why those are so much easier to remember than the kinder moments, the times he made it clear how much I meant to him. The way his eyes would shine when he talked about me, positively beaming with pride." He looked up and found Rienne's eyes. "That's an expectation I suddenly find that I want to live up to."

She held his gaze, then reached an arm behind his neck to pull his mouth down to hers.

* * * * *

The changeling was dreaming—he knew that much, but the knowledge did nothing to help him navigate the chaos. A jumble of identities, names and faces and personas, stumbling through one unlikely crisis after another. At last he stood in his true form in the awesome presence of a goddess.

"The Traveler," he said. "Bless your ten thousand names."

But the Traveler wore the face of his paladin acquaintance of recent months—a tall half-elf with short red hair and blue-gray eyes—and she glowed with an argent radiance like the Silver Flame of the Thranes.

"Who are you?" she asked him.

"Auftane Khunnam," he said, and he was a dwarf, all black and brown and sturdy, strong.

"Who are you?" she asked again.

"Haunderk Lannath." Human, sandy hair, scheming.

"Who are you?"

"Darraun Mennar." Prying, planning, blond.

"Who are you?"

"Caura Fannam." Poor Jenns. Compassion, care.

"Who are you?"

"Baunder Fronn." Simple, stout, stupid.

"Who are you?"

"Vauren Hennalan." Brave, honorable, prig.

"Who are you?"

"Natan Durbannek." Another dwarf. A killer.

"Who are you?"

"Aurra Hennalan." Mischievous elf.

"Who are you?"

There were so many, and the Traveler seemed unwilling to accept any answer he gave.

"Who are you?"

He awoke, sweating and shaking, panic racing through his veins. He was in a swaying bunk in a pitch-dark cabin, and he couldn't remember where he was or—most importantly—who he was supposed to be. He put his hands to his face and felt his features: male, human, thirties. Aboard an airship. Who was with him? Kelas? No. Janik and Dania? No. Haldren? Closer, but no. Gaven, of course.

Real memories started taking shape in his mind, crowding out the confused memory of his dream. His most recent dwarf persona, Natan Durbannek. Helping to capture Gaven in Stormhome, and then helping him escape. Piloting the airship from one end of the island to the other, which made him tired just to remember it.

What in the world had he done? He had revealed himself to Gaven and Rienne, tripling the number of people in the world who knew that he was a changeling. And why? Had it been essential for his mission?

He tried to roll out of his bunk and ended up in a heap on the floor. He curled inward, clutching his head. What was his mission? What in the Traveler's ten thousand names was he doing here?

"Make it solid," he whispered. This was not like him at all—he had never in his thirty years questioned a mission or lost his grip on an identity. He struck his head against the floor and reverted to the training disciplines of his youth. "Who are you?" he said. "I am Au—Au . . . What the blazes is my name?"

"Darraun," a woman's voice said. He scrambled on the floor, turning himself to see the woman standing in the open hatch of the cabin, silhouetted in front of a night sky dimly lit by the Ring of Siberys. "Or that's what Gaven calls you, anyway."

"Rienne," he said. He felt like a child just learning the names for everything in the world.

"That's right. I'm Rienne." Her voice sounded bemused, but her face was still in darkness. "Are you all right?"

"Am I . . . ? No." He started to get to his feet. "That is, I think so." He reached out and grabbed another swaying bunk, trying in vain to steady himself.

"Do you need more sleep?" Rienne took a step farther into the room, and her features began to resolve in the darkness. "Do you want me to help you back into bed?"

"No! Not more sleep. No, thank you." He managed to stand, and put a hand on her shoulder.

"Good, because Gaven wants to talk to you before we get much closer to Haldren's camp."

"Haldren's camp? What in the Ten Seas does he think he's doing?"

"You'll have to ask him that."

"All right," the changeling said. Darraun, he thought. Darraun Mennar. "You go ahead. I'll be there in a moment."

"Are you sure?"

"Quite sure." Darraun Mennar. Darraun was polite, friendly. "Thank you."

Rienne turned, halfway out of the cabin, and smiled back at him. "You're welcome." Then she was gone.

He buried his fingers in his hair, ran them down his face, wrapped himself in his arms, ran his hands down his legs. He knew this body—he'd worn it for months. He knew Darraun. He was ready. He started out the cabin door.

But Gaven and Rienne knew he was a changeling. He stopped dead. What would that mean? How would they treat him now? Did it matter if he acted like Darraun or not?

Best to appear familiar, reassure them that he was the same Darraun that Gaven knew. He took a deep breath, and wished that Darraun were a little braver. Vauren Hennalan could face dangerous and uncertain situations like this with ease. Darraun had been worried about finding himself lost in the Aerenal woods.

Shuddering at the memory of a city filled with the undying, Darraun climbed the stairs to the main deck.

* * * * *

"Have you seen Haldren's camp?" Gaven demanded as soon as Darraun's head came above the level of the deck.

To his credit, Darraun answered without hesitation. "Not the camp where he is now. His forces marched after I left." As he spoke, he climbed the rest of the stairs and came to stand near the helm.

"Why did you leave?"

"Haldren discovered me spying on him."

Gaven arched an eyebrow. "I'm surprised you got out."

"That's because you know more about Haldren's capabilities than about mine. Haldren makes a show of his power. I do not."

"Fair enough. I've always known there was more to you than you let on."

Gaven remembered Cart interrupting their conversation in Whitecliff, insisting that he, too, was "quite complex." He chuckled, and noticed Darraun doing the same. Their eyes met, and at the same time, they said, "Many-layered." Then both men burst into laughter.

"Clearly, I missed something," Rienne said, folding her arms and smiling.

"I'll explain later," Gaven said. "What can you tell me about

Haldren's movements since he left Paluur Draal?"

"He was quite distressed at your disappearance—or at Senya's, really. He was convinced you had pulled her out of the circle to use as a hostage. From that point on, your knowledge of the Prophecy meant nothing to him. He would have tracked you down and killed you, or tried to, to get Senya back."

"How touching," Gaven said. "If only Senya shared his devotion."

Darraun raised both eyebrows. "If only. So we met with Vaskar on the shore of Lake Brey, and Haldren gave him the Eye of Siberys."

"Vaskar has it?"

"As far as I know he still does, yes." Darraun paused. "From there we went to Lathleer, in Aundair, and laid low for a few days. When we were in Whitecliff, Haldren sent word of his escape to a few of his closest friends in the army, and that blossomed into a meeting with seven of them in Bluevine. He swayed them to his cause, promised them a flight of dragons to assure their victory, and sent them off to gather troops."

"A flight of dragons?"

A clash of dragons . . .

A sense of doom gripped Gaven's heart.

"That was Vaskar's end of the bargain, in exchange for Haldren's help in getting the Eye of Siberys and extracting whatever other information he could get out of you. Vaskar persuaded a fairly large number of dragons to come and form the vanguard of Haldren's army."

"And by the rumors of war I heard today, I assume that Haldren has amassed his army, gathered his dragons, and begun his march toward Thrane."

"That's right."

Gaven thought over what the changeling had told him. Darraun's manner had seemed perfectly straightforward—he could read no trace of deception. The story all made sense, and fit with what little he already knew about Haldren's movements. He couldn't help himself—he liked Darraun, he always had, and knowing that he was a changeling and a spy did nothing to diminish that.

I've got no choice but to trust him, he thought.

He glanced at Darraun and broke his silence. "Do you know where they're camped?"

"No. The original plan was to strike down the coast into Thaliost, but Haldren changed the plan after he discovered me."

"How do you know?" Gaven asked.

"Before I escaped the camp, he gave orders to march, a week ahead of schedule. After I got away, I spent some time in Flamekeep, where I learned that Thrane is concentrating its defense on an old battlefield called the Starcrag Plain."

"The plain that lies in the sunset shadow of the mountains of stars," Gaven said. Again the dread gripped him, and he took a deep breath.

"What?" Darraun said, but then he nodded. "Yes, it's to the east of the Starpeaks."

"They're attacking there in order to fulfil the Prophecy. Sovereigns," Gaven said, "it's going to be a bloodbath."

CHAPTER
44

While Darraun and Rienne slept, Gaven was left alone on the deck. The Ring of Siberys shone bright overhead, and the approaching dawn stained clouds in the eastern sky red. To his mind, they whispered warnings of doom: the shining ring of dragonshards that lit the night foretold the consummation of a prophetic cycle, the emergence of the Soul Reaver and the revelation of the Storm Dragon, while the bloody signs of dawn spoke plainly of the cost that would be paid in human lives.

He turned the airship inland, and absently guided her between the darkness of the Whisper Wood on his right and the shadows of the Gray Wood on his left, following a narrow strip of grassy land between the two forests. He was grateful that the navigation didn't require more attention—his vision seemed to keep slipping between the reality that presented itself to his senses and something deeper, the language of creation.

The Prophecy was written everywhere. Everything he saw spoke of its past and its potential. As he piloted the *Eye of the Storm* between Aundair's primeval forest and its younger offspring, making his way to the jutting Starpeaks, he saw the words that had made them and heard distant echoes of the language they strained to speak. And images of his nightmares flashed through his mind, tastes of the horrors those lands would see.

Vultures wheeling over fields strewn with corpses. The howling hordes of the Soul Reaver boiling up from Khyber and spreading out across the land. Legions of soldiers beneath the banner of the Blasphemer. Dragons in the sky.

The visions blended and blurred together, weaving themselves into a tapestry of horror in which he could no longer discern individual threads. Haldren's march to war would not be the end of the nightmare.

* * * * *

Rienne emerged from below decks at dawn, and Gaven watched with a tired half smile as she stretched and practiced with Maelstrom at the keel. Darraun came up a little later, rubbing his stomach.

"Do you think Thordren had any supplies stashed away?" he asked no one in particular.

"You're welcome to look below," Rienne said, "but don't get your hopes up."

Darraun disappeared back down the forward hatch, and Rienne hopped up onto the bulwarks' railings, keeping perfect balance as she practiced complex sequences of lunges, parries, and ripostes. Gaven watched carefully, and chose a moment when her balance seemed most tenuous to jerk hard on the wheel, making the ship lurch to port.

Rienne didn't miss a step in her exercise, but Darraun let out a cry of pain from the cargo hold. A moment later his head appeared in the hatch.

"Everything all right?" he called to Gaven.

"Fine, sorry," Gaven said. "Did you hurt yourself?"

"Just cracked my head on a beam." He rubbed his scalp, then checked his fingers for blood.

"Maybe you should go back to being a dwarf," Rienne suggested.

Darraun scowled and dropped below again.

"Do you think I hurt his feelings?" Rienne asked.

"I don't know."

"Aha!" Darraun yelled from below. "We've got breakfast!"

Rienne stepped lightly from the railing to peer down the hatch. "What did you find?"

Darraun emerged with an armload of small boxes and a strip of dried beef dangling from his mouth. "Lady Alastra," he mumbled around the meat. He left his sentence unfinished as he began setting out the foodstuffs he had gathered—pickled vegetables, dried fruits, nuts, and salted beef. When he had swallowed, he addressed Rienne again. "Lady Alastra, I hope that we have the pleasure of traveling in each other's company under better circumstances so that I can cook you a proper meal. But for the present, please enjoy these . . . erm, trail rations, with my compliments."

Rienne and Gaven laughed. "He really is quite a cook," Gaven added. "I'll vouch for him."

"There are many men to whom I would entrust my dinner," Rienne said, bowing slightly to Darraun. "There are precious few to whom I would entrust my life. I don't know if I can bring myself to entrust both to the same man, but it would be an illustrious honor indeed."

Darraun smiled awkwardly, then busied himself with the food.

*　*　*　*　*

With the help of a box of spices he unearthed from his pack, Darraun managed to make even the preserved food palatable, which earned him a new measure of respect in Rienne's eyes. As the day wore on, Gaven found himself dozing at the wheel, while Rienne and Darraun took turns pacing along the prow. They left the Gray Wood behind and followed the curve of the Whisper Wood's edge along to the south, then left it as well, making straight for the eastern edge of the Starpeaks. Any movement on the rocky plain below brought a moment of intense scrutiny and heightened tension, then a return to the interminable waiting once the lookout realized it was just an animal or a farmer or a gust of wind below.

Rienne and Darraun were so focused on searching the ground below that it was actually Gaven who spotted the first real threat. "Check the sky," he called, "four points to port!"

The sun was high in the sky, but beginning its descent behind the Starpeaks on the airship's port side. Darraun had to cup his hands around his eyes, but Rienne spotted it immediately.

"A dragon," she said.

"Are you sure?" Gaven shouted. "It's not very big."

Rienne wheeled and gave him an incredulous stare. "Not very big?" she said.

"No, he's right," Darraun said. "Compared to Vaskar, this one's small, immature. No bigger than a bear."

"If you mean one of those Eldeen bears that the druids send before them in war to tear up enemy infantry, I'll grant you that." Rienne gripped Maelstrom in a trembling hand.

"Yes, that's exactly the kind of bear I mean," Darraun said.

The dragon closed on them quickly—it had clearly seen them before Gaven spotted it. The sun gleamed dull red on its scales, and Gaven's mind filled with the image of the *Morning Zephyr* in flames outside the Mournland. He had a sudden, unsettling realization.

"How do I land this thing?" he called.

"Land her?" Darraun said. "I don't think you do. That's why they have mooring towers."

"Well, start looking for a mooring tower. I don't want to be in the air when that thing breathes fire on this ship."

"No," Rienne said, "you should be able to do a ground landing in a ship this size. Smaller airships like this are designed to moor just about anywhere."

"Then take a look beneath us, and tell me where to set her down." He glanced at the onrushing dragon, now close enough that he could distinguish its horns and the predatory curve to its mouth. Rienne rushed to the starboard side and peered over the edge.

"Rocky, very steep—and trees to the east. I don't see—"

"Oh, damn it to the Darkness!" Gaven swore. He stretched one hand to the clear blue sky, and the sun went dark, blotted out by a black thunderhead that appeared from nowhere. He jerked his hand downward, and a bolt of lightning thundered out of the sky and struck the onrushing dragon. For an instant, it hung suspended in the air, engulfed in burning light, then it plummeted downward.

Spreading its wings, the dragon pulled out of its fall and swooped back up toward the airship, sending a blistering gout of fire from its gaping maw ahead of its flight. The flames parted around the keel and licked up around the bulwarks, but it seemed that much of their energy was pulled into the ring of fire surrounding the ship, making it flare brightly for a moment, then fade back to normal.

Gaven smiled. "Looks like I was more worried about the fire than I should have been," he said.

"Don't get too confident," Rienne shot back.

As if reinforcing Rienne's warning, the airship lurched suddenly to starboard. The wheel jerked free of Gaven's hand and started spinning wildly.

"Concentrate on the helm,'" Rienne said. "Let me and Darraun handle the dragon."

When Gaven touched the wheel again, flames leaped out from its wooden spokes and seared his hands. Gaven cried out, more in surprise than pain, and eyed the wheel warily.

"The dragon's breath gave the elemental a taste of freedom," Rienne explained. "You need to remind it who's in charge."

"Maybe riding horseback isn't so bad after all," Gaven grumbled as he approached the wheel again.

"You ever let a stallion think he's in charge?"

"Good point." Gaven seized the helm again, ignoring a new flare from the wheel. *Be still!* he commanded the elemental, and he felt it rebel against his control—very much like a spirited horse pulling against its reins. For an instant, the fire that formed a ring around the airship flickered and died away, letting the airship fall freely, but Gaven stretched out his will like a whip and brought both elemental and ship back under control.

Which meant that he could do nothing but watch as the dragon's fiery breath engulfed both Rienne and Darraun where they stood on the deck. Rienne tumbled away and stood up again barely singed, but Darraun could do nothing but huddle on the deck and weather the blast's greatest force. In the wake of its breath, the dragon swooped in and alit on the deck, stretching its wings into the air to keep its balance.

As the flames died around Darraun, wisps of smoke trailed off him, but to Gaven's surprise he leaped toward the dragon as though he'd just been immersed in water rather than fire. As he hefted his mace, Gaven noticed a ring on Darraun's hand that glowed red as if it had been newly forged in the inferno, and he suspected that the artificer had turned the ring into a magic ward against fire before the dragon's onslaught.

The dragon's enormous wings made it seem considerably larger than a bear—even an Eldeen bear. Its head whipped away from Darraun's mace, then arched back around to bite at his shoulder even as it lifted its front claws to tear at him. It was caught off guard and off balance, though, as Rienne tumbled into it, slamming both feet into its chest. She knocked it backward, and Maelstrom was ready to cut at its neck as it yanked back. The magic blade only nicked its scaled neck, and it retreated a couple of steps to regain its balance, all four feet firmly on the deck. Its neck swept back and forth as it sized up its opponents.

At almost the last moment, Gaven remembered.

An arcane word sheathed him in cool fire that would protect him from the dragon's breath. Then fire spewed from the creature's mouth in a great blast that engulfed all three of them and started several small fires on the deck. Gaven took cover behind the wheel, and his fiery shield protected him from the rest of the blast. Darraun laughed it off, and again Rienne bounced clear of the worst of it—her constant movement in battle was both her strongest offense and her best defense. She proved it by leaping onto the dragon's back and bringing Maelstrom down hard into its neck, spraying a gout of steaming blood onto the deck. The dragon thrashed and reared, throwing Rienne backward off the deck.

Darraun lunged to the prow, his panicked look telling Gaven everything he needed to know. The dragon leaped into the air, pushing away from the airship so hard that the prow bobbed downward, then spun itself in the air to plummet downward, following Rienne to the ground—out of sheer malice or perhaps blind fury. Gaven released the helm, and a gust of wind lifted him off the deck. A quick glance around showed him that Rienne was still falling, and an equally quick gesture brought a whirlwind out of the brewing storm to lift her safely out of her fall. With the merest thought, he impaled the dragon on another bolt of lightning. After Rienne's deadly blow, the dragon had no more strength to evade or resist the blast, and its charred corpse spiraled away like an autumn leaf, dry and drained of life.

But as the airship swept past Gaven, caught in a terrible maelstrom of air dragging her to earth, he realized it would take considerably more effort to stop her fall.

CHAPTER
45

T he *Eye of the Storm* did not simply drop out of the sky. Snared in the whirling currents of air born of Gaven's storm, she spun in a great wheel through the air, her magical buoyancy still fighting against the downward pull. At the same time, the elemental bound within her flared to rebellion in the absence of Gaven's control, coursing visibly through the arcane channels carved into the hull. Gaven didn't see Darraun immediately, but after a moment spotted him clutching the wheel, struggling to control the ship as he had in Stormhome. A valiant effort, but one doomed to failure.

Gaven's first impulse was to crush the airship between irresistible blasts of air, to shoot her through with lightning and scatter her flinders to the wind. Destruction was the easy path, the purest manifestation of his power. So simple, so tempting. The impulse startled him—his friend was aboard that ship. Why would he destroy her?

Gaven snarled his frustration, and lightning coursed around him. Destruction was easy. It was far more challenging to create, to build, to save. His anger was a tight knot in his gut—he felt it as he roared, like nausea. He wanted to curl his body around it, cradle it in his arms and vomit it out.

The wind tore at him in a manifestation of his rage, and the airship bucked against Darraun's control.

No, Gaven thought. I need to let it go.

Layers upon layers of rage and resentment fueled the storm. The dragon's attack mattered little, just the fury of a misguided minion, now undone. A thin layer of anger, easily sloughed away.

Haldren's brewing rebellion angered him, the way Haldren had used him, manipulated him, coerced him. Was that truly significant? Haldren had also engineered his release from Dreadhold, and his attempt at conquest would soon be quashed. The world would return to its uneasy peace. Another layer gone.

The howling of the wind diminished, and Darraun managed to tame the blazing elemental fire in the airship, leaving only the bright ring.

Twenty-six years in Dreadhold . . .

Haunted by visions, plagued by nightmares, abused by guards and fellow prisoners alike . . .

So utterly alone in the wilderness of his mind.

Waking from sleep, night after night, to stumble to the door and speak his dreams through the shutter in the door—he'd done it long before Haldren had come to occupy the cell across the hall, as though giving his dreams voice would help exorcise them from his mind.

Carving the words into the floor and walls of his cell—writing them in his blood before they finally relented and gave him a stylus to scratch the stone. Trying to make them solid, to ground them, to fix them into the present.

It had nearly driven him mad—perhaps he had gone mad.

He wished for true freedom—freedom from the ceaseless pursuit of Bordan and the Kundarak dwarves, freedom from the visions that still besieged him day and night. That anger seethed and bubbled, fierce and hot. He squeezed his eyes shut and roared again. The wind snatched away his cry and carried his boiling anger with it. His knowledge of the Prophecy might have seemed like a curse in the past, but he was using it to his advantage. It had given him power and insight. It was a gift.

The Heart of Khyber with its stored memories. The dragon who had altered the course of his life. A hard shell of resentment.

"*I've given your life a purpose,*" the dragon said. *Its voice was Gaven's.*

"*I didn't want that purpose.*"

"*But you chose a new one. You can't carry on without one. And you will never again be content to live an ordinary life.*"

Another gift. The hard shell broke and fell away, leaving a blazing core of molten fury.

Lightning seared through Gaven's body, and he hung in the

sky. Lightning flowed through each hand and foot and poured from his mouth as he screamed.

Rienne shook him gently awake. He sat bolt upright—he heard the jangle of chainmail.

Tears streamed down Rienne's face. He was too stung by her betrayal to resist the Sentinel Marshals.

The person he loved most in the world sent him to Dreadhold. This anger was thick and hot, and would not fall away so easily.

At night in Dreadhold, waiting for the nightmares to come, he lay in his bunk and nursed that anger.

Rienne testified to the Tribunal. She wanted to convince them he needed help, but instead she convinced them of his guilt.

He glanced down to where she hung in the air, held aloft by the winds at his command. Again the urge to destroy welled up in him. It would be so easy to let her fall.

Four Sentinel Marshals struggled to restrain him. He wanted to get to Rienne, to break her neck, to tear her small, lithe body apart with his bare hands.

"Let him live, I implore you." *Rienne was pleading for him, even as he tried to reach her.* "By all that is holy, have mercy! If he is mad, who knows but that he might one day recover his senses?"

For twenty-six years he'd nurtured a lie—a lie that let him focus his anger outward at her, instead of inward. Rienne had not betrayed him, she had tried to protect him. She had acted out of her love for him. He had kept her out while the Heart of Khyber had wormed its way into his heart—he had betrayed her.

"Don't you think I deserve an explanation?" she said.

"No."

"I think I do. I loved you once, Gaven, and you made me believe you loved me."

Sobs wracked his body. "I'm sorry, Ree," he whispered, and he imagined that the wind carried his voice down to her.

The knot of his anger was stripped down to its core.

"Let me see you, Gaven." *Arnoth stood over the parched, feverish body of his son.*

Gaven huddled under a blanket that chafed against his sunburned skin.

"Let me see him," *Arnoth said.*

Someone pulled the blanket off him, and Gaven felt his father's

eyes searching him, looking for any sign of a dragonmark. In vain—
Gaven had failed his test.

A blur of faces surrounded him, but one face stood out clearly—his father's, trying to smile.

"I am not you!" Gaven cried into the storm.

A young Gaven held an orb of magical light in his palm, full of excitement at his first successful spell. "Look, father!" he cried.

Arnoth stood in the doorway, leaning against the jamb, smiling with pride. "Well done, Gaven," he said. "Keep practicing." He turned away, returning to his work.

Gaven dismissed the spell and refused to try it again for a week's time.

All his life Gaven had resented the firm hand of a domineering father, and had blamed Arnoth for every act of rebellion he had committed. He had imagined a father who was determined to mold his son into a replica of himself, and he'd been blind to the pride Arnoth took in the son he had—not the son Gaven thought he wanted.

"Why don't you apply yourself, Gaven?" An older Arnoth frowned in the doorway as Gaven packed supplies for an expedition into Khyber, hunting for dragonshards.

"I am applying myself," Gaven said, not looking up. "And doing good for the house."

"But you could do so much more! You have greatness in you, Gaven."

Greatness? Gaven thought. You mean I have you in me. I am not you!

Gaven had avoided any achievement of consequence, and used his father's high expectations as an excuse for his own failure. He had clung to the image of a stern and distant father because that was an image it was easy to blame—and for years he had channeled his anger at that image instead of at himself.

A fresh wave of grief surged through him.

I love you, father.

Lightning blasted the rock around Gaven's feet, and only then did he realize that he had come down to the ground. He blinked and looked around, and saw Rienne standing ten paces away, staring into the air with wide eyes. He followed her gaze to where the *Eye of the Storm* floated calmly under a slate-gray sky.

* * * * *

Darraun managed to get the ship down close to the ground, and Gaven and Rienne climbed back aboard. Darraun was glad to relinquish the helm, but worry creased his face.

"I spotted Haldren's forces," he said, gesturing vaguely to the south. "They're on the march already."

"We should have no trouble catching up to them," Gaven said as he settled himself in at the helm. Darraun had done well piloting the ship this time; the elemental seemed much more docile already.

"Not to the ground troops, no," Darraun said. "But I also saw the dragons taking wing."

"The dragons," Gaven grimly. "A clash of dragons . . ." He rubbed his chin.

"Gaven?" Rienne said.

Gaven put both hands to the wheel again and lifted the airship higher. "Thordren named this vessel well—we're flying into the eye of the storm, now, friends, and I think we've just seen our last bit of calm weather."

"What do you mean?" Rienne demanded, coming to face him across the wheel.

"Vaskar knows the Prophecy, or at least this part of it: 'A clash of dragons signals the sundering of the Soul Reaver's gates.' Vaskar's whole purpose here is to open those gates, so he can fight the Soul Reaver and be the Storm Dragon, claiming that divine power. But it has to be a clash of dragons. What are the dragons on the Thrane side?"

Darraun came closer, leaning back against a nearby railing. "Other dragons, or people with dragonmarks?"

"There have to be dragons, and they have to be part of Vaskar's plan. I'm sure he hasn't just left it to chance, hoping some dragon-marked heir is fighting on Thrane's side for some reason and will fight a dragon for the sake of the Prophecy."

"You think he's double-crossed Haldren," Rienne said.

"Exactly. He promised Haldren he'd bring dragons to fight alongside his armies—military might unknown in the Last War and unsurpassed among the armies of Khorvaire. And then he turned around and brought another group of dragons to fight on the other side."

"Will it work?" Darraun said. "How can he make the dragons fight each other?"

"From what I understand, it often doesn't take much. Dragons often don't get along with each other. They're territorial. The whole continent of Argonnessen is carved up into dragon territories, and many areas are hotly contested. And when they're not fighting over territory, they fight over the Prophecy. It only takes a spark to ignite a conflagration."

Darraun looked puzzled as Gaven spoke, but when he'd finished he burst into laughter.

"What?" Rienne said.

"What a web of lies Vaskar must be weaving. It's funny: I always thought Haldren was a conniving manipulator who could bend almost anyone to his will given a moment of conversation. I never stopped to think what kind of dragon joins forces with a man like that."

"Exactly the same kind of dragon," Gaven said.

"Right. When I was camped with Haldren's forces, after the dragons joined up, I remember wondering what part these dragons thought they played in the Prophecy. I assumed they wanted to help Vaskar fulfill it. But now I think those dragons are over in Thrane, just waiting for Haldren's dragons to come into sight so they can initiate the 'clash of dragons' long foretold."

"So then what do Haldren's dragons think they're doing?" Rienne asked.

"He's brought them here with some other piece of the Prophecy," Gaven said. "I'm sure of it. There's something at the edge of my mind—'where dragons flew.'"

Gaven closed his eyes. He remembered seeing his reflection, touching glass, starting as though he'd touched a fire. The reflection in the mirror—an image of desolation.

The vision that had sprung to his mind in his father's house, in the shadow of death. He whispered the words that had come to him: "Vultures wheel where dragons flew, picking the bones of the numberless dead."

"Gaven?" Rienne had come around the wheel and laid a gently hand on his back.

He opened his eyes, but he could not see the world around him any more—only his vision. Words and meaning from the

Sky Caves of Thieren Kor took shape in his mind, expanding that fragmentary premonition of doom:

> Dragons fly before the Blasphemer's legions,
>   scouring the earth of his righteous foes.
> Carnage rises in the wake of his passing,
>   purging all life from those who oppose him.
> Vultures wheel where dragons flew,
>   picking the bones of the numberless dead.

Gaven shuddered and shook his head, and saw Rienne's face staring up at him in deep concern.

"He brought them here with a lie," he said finally. "They think they're fulfilling a part of the Prophecy whose time has not yet come. But they believe it guarantees their victory."

Chapter
46

Senya had trouble keeping up with Cart and his patrol. Her thoughts kept dwelling on her imminent reunion with Haldren, and she did not press her steed as hard as the others did. She would have to flirt with him, flatter him—ultimately seduce him in order to assuage his anger. It was a ridiculous game, but one which she had enjoyed and excelled at for years. She no longer had the heart for it, and thinking about it repulsed her.

Cart and the knights who rode with him gave up any pretense of being Thranes. They stripped the Silver Flame from their shields, and Cart doffed his helmet. They rode north through Bramblescar Gorge, a narrow valley choked with the dry, thorny plants that gave the place its name. Layer upon layer of dark slate formed the rough walls of the gorge, cut away by an ancient river that had since run dry. On their left, the lowest hills of the Starpeaks rose up toward the towering heights beyond, sheltering the valley from rain and blocking the evening sun. On their right, the first green shrubs and trees of the Silver Woods crowned the rocky walls. Except for the steady drumming of hoofbeats, the air was still and silent. Nature seemed quieted by the impending battle.

Senya barely noticed when they passed a clump of sentries posted at the southern end of Haldren's camp. Cart's pace slowed to an easy walk as they made their way among the clusters of soldiers preparing for their last night encamped. Senya's horse no longer needed urging to keep up with the others, and Senya came to the command post far more quickly than she wanted to.

"Lord General!" Cart dismounted in front of the grand pavilion Haldren had erected for himself—a tribute to his greatness, Senya was sure.

Smile, Senya told herself. You're glad to see him again.

She forced a smile onto her face then tried to make it look genuine.

"Enter." Haldren's voice was gruff.

Wonderful, Senya thought dryly. A foul mood will make this so much more pleasant.

Cart waited while Senya dismounted, then held the flap of the pavilion open for her to enter before him. Steeling herself and refreshing her smile, she stepped once more into Haldren's presence.

"What is it, Cart?" Haldren stood over a small table, and he didn't look up from the large map spread out before him.

"Reporting from patrol, sir," Cart said behind her. "See what I found."

Haldren glanced up, his face taut with irritation. His face softened and he straightened when he saw Senya.

"Hello, Haldren." She made her voice husky, alluring, and she forced her face to keep smiling. Tears welled in her eyes.

Haldren strode around the table to stand in front of her. He clasped her shoulders and let his eyes wander over her face. A soft rustle told her that Cart had stepped out of the pavilion.

"Did he harm you?" Haldren said.

It took a moment for Senya to realize that he meant Gaven, not Cart. She shook her head.

He threw his arms around her and pressed her to his chest. She reached around him to caress his back before she realized that his intention wasn't amorous. His body shook with sobs.

"I'm sorry," he moaned, burying his face in her hair. "I came back as quickly as I could, but he'd already taken you away."

Taken me? Senya thought. Ten Seas, the old fool thinks Gaven kidnapped me!

She clenched him tightly.

"I would have searched the world for you," Haldren said.

The tears broke free of her eyes and streamed down her face.

The old fool loves me, she thought. The idea seemed totally foreign to her.

* * * * *

Haldren's heart soared alongside the dragons as he watched them take to the sky, bright under the morning sun. Riding at his right hand, Cart nodded approvingly, appraising the number of dragons and their strength and size. They numbered nearly a score. Had so many dragons been assembled in a single cause in the entire course of human history? Only Senya, on his left, cast a pall over the moment.

"These dragons and their Prophecy," she muttered. "What do they think of our march here below, I wonder? Are they serving our needs, or are we cards in their hands? Are we playing the dragons, or are they playing us?"

"This is not some tavern game of chance, Senya," Haldren scoffed. "This is war."

He raised his voice so the other commanders around him would hear, and lifted a fist into the air. "The dragons lead us to victory, swift and certain!"

A chorus of cheers from behind him washed away the shadow cast by Senya's doubts, and Cart signaled the other commanders to begin the march. Haldren smiled, satisfied that his plan was unfolding perfectly. An army larger than he had ever commanded during the war marched before him, and its vanguard was an invincible flight of dragons. Before the sun reached its zenith, this great legion would spill out of Bramblescar Gorge onto the Starcrag Plain, and according to Cart's reports, they would meet Thrane forces at the border before nightfall. His conquest of Khorvaire was about to begin!

And fate had given him a token of his coming victory by returning his Senya to his side. Though she was clearly troubled by her ordeal, he was confident that she would return to him fully before long. Everything he desired was within his reach.

They rode in silence at a slow walk behind the marching legions. As the narrow gorge widened he was able to survey the full strength of his forces. His banners fluttered in the wind of a brewing storm, the formations of his soldiers bristled with spears, and the earth thundered in concert with the sky under the boots of tens of thousands of marching feet. Haldren's thoughts were full of glory—victory on the battlefield, the conquest of all Khorvaire, his coronation as emperor of a new Galifar, Senya at his side. What could stop him?

Bursting with pride, he watched the columns of troops begin their advance across the Starcrag Plain as he had ordered, each rank perfectly aligned behind the one before, exactly in place. These were the best troops that Aundair had to offer, and they served only him, not a soft and foolish queen in far-off Fairhaven. The other commanders—Lord Major ir'Fann, Lord Colonel ir'Cashan, Rennic Arak, Kadra, even General Yeven—had all acknowledged the brilliance of his strategy. They had all agreed that victory was sure, and praised him as the greatest general Aundair—no, Khorvaire—had ever known. The Thranes would be the first to fall, but only the first in his long campaign of conquest. After this initial victory, he knew he could count on the support of Arcanix and even House Cannith. The wheel was in motion, and nothing now would stop its inexorable turning.

"Lord General?" Cart's voice was quiet, but something in his tone told him that there was a problem. How could there be a problem?

"What is it, Cart?"

"Look to the sky, Lord General." Cart pointed up into the distance, in the direction the dragons had flown.

Haldren squinted in the direction Cart had pointed, then cursed his aging eyes and called for a spyglass. Peering through the lenses, he could clearly see the tight clumps of dragons—his dragons—advancing toward the Thrane forces arrayed against them, far across the plain. "What? I don't see—"

But then he did. More dragons lifted into the air, and they were behind the advancing Thrane lines. They closed with his dragons with murderous speed, and the sky erupted with fire and lightning as the two groups of dragons met. They swooped and dove at each other, tearing with fang and claw, great bursts of deadly energy erupting from their mouths. Some fought on the ground, wings and tails buffeting each other.

Haldren's hands trembled as they clutched the spyglass tighter, pressing it to his eye as if looking harder would reveal a different interpretation of what he saw. But there was no other explanation: the Thranes had dragons fighting for them as well. At least a score of them.

Senya's soft voice behind him hit him like a pronouncement of doom. "A clash of dragons signals the sundering of the Soul Reaver's gates."

As if responding to her words, the earth began to shudder, answered by a rolling crash of thunder across the sky.

Chapter
47

At the beginning of time, one legend said, the great dragon Siberys danced through the void, setting the stars in their places. Khyber prowled behind, consuming stars as fast as Siberys could scatter them. Eberron sang, apart from the others, and life began to blossom in the void.

Finally Siberys turned to confront Khyber, to stop the dark dragon from consuming the stars. The two dragons fought, tearing at each other in their hatred. At last Khyber arose victorious: Siberys was torn asunder, her body broken into numberless fragments. Then, thirsty for blood, Khyber wheeled upon Eberron.

Where Khyber lunged, Eberron snaked aside, around. The bloodless battle, the fierce dance continued for eons, neither dragon gaining ascendancy over the other. At last, Khyber grew tired, and Eberron enfolded and imprisoned Khyber in her own body. The struggles of the primordial dragons had come to an end.

Both dragons slumbered after their long warring, and hardened into earth. And so the world was born, Eberron forming its surface and Khyber its dark depths. The fragments of Siberys's broken body encircled Eberron in a great ring that shone in the night. The Dragon Above, the Dragon Below, and the Dragon Between. Always Eberron stood between the Dragon Above and the Dragon Below.

Some parts of the Prophecy suggested that one day the divisions between them might be healed, but an event of such grand proportion was little more than a distant dream. Once in a very great while, though, the gulf could be bridged.

* * * * *

Gaven raced the *Eye of the Storm* toward the Starcrag Plain, following the path of a dry gorge between the Starpeaks and the forest to the east. Rienne and Darraun rested below, recovering from the dragon's attack. Gaven wasn't sure what he had to do, but a burning urgency spurred him on. Could he stop Haldren's advance, prevent the clash of dragons and save Khorvaire from another terrible war? Failing that, could he prevent Vaskar's ascension?

He didn't know. And yet, somehow, he was satisfied. He was acting—he had made the decision to intervene in these events, to try, at least, to make events work out for the better. He vastly preferred that to a life spent floating on the currents that carried him. He would set his own course, choose his own destiny.

Destiny is . . .

The highest hopes the universe has for you. Like . . . like my mother wanted the best for me.

The memory of Senya's words made him think again of his father. Arnoth had wanted only the best for him, even if his idea of what was the best didn't often match Gaven's. Why had Gaven not realized that until his father was gone?

The valley he'd been following opened out into the wide expanse of the Starcrag Plain, and Gaven saw the battlefield for the first time—with his eyes. It was hauntingly familiar as the landscape of his nightmares. The northern lands had whispered to him of their past and their destiny, hinting at the Prophecy and the words of creation hidden in the hills and trees. The Starcrag Plain screamed centuries of anguish. This was not the first time the plain had been a battlefield—ancient cairns, piles of weathered stones, littered its edges, and the ground itself spoke to him of horrors past and horrors yet to come.

In the present moment, he saw the regimented lines of Haldren's forces marching across the plain toward the waiting Thranes massed along a line he presumed was the border set by the Treaty of Thronehold. He saw dragons wheeling above the plain, clawing and biting at each other, blasting fire and icy frost from their gaping jaws. The battle had already begun—the clash of dragons. He was too late to prevent it.

He gripped the helm and blinked hard, struggling to keep his vision focused on the scene before his eyes, to clear away the memories of his nightmares. Haldren's forces marched onward, heedless of the dragons battling furiously in the air and on the ground between them and the Thranes. They shouted as the *Eye of the Storm* soared over them, then shook their spears and shields when it was past.

Then Gaven saw his nightmares come to life. Thunder rolled overhead, and the earth groaned in answer. Rienne raced to the deck, and Darraun trailed after. The airship drew near the center of the plain, dangerously close to a pair of blue dragons swooping and tearing at each other, and the earth below began to crack. Eberron was opening a path—small and brief, but a bridge nonetheless—for Khyber and Siberys to touch once again.

At first the crack was a midnight scar across the face of the plain, its blackness drawing in and swallowing what little sunlight filtered through the storm clouds above. Then an awesome, unholy light began to grow in its deepest core, and the earth trembled again as the light swelled in the depths and began to erupt toward the surface, to reach for the sky. For a moment it seemed like an enormous, many-tentacled beast formed of the most brilliant light, oozing out of the fissure in the earth and sending exploratory tendrils in every direction.

Then the light burst forth and roared heavenward with a sound like a titan's sword being drawn from its sheath, sharp metal cutting through the air. It stood tall and straight, stretching from the fractured plain up to the clouds, and the clouds melted away from it, churning and swirling in a storm of protest as the light broke through.

"On a field of battle where dragons clash in the skies, the earth opens and the Crystal Spire emerges," Gaven said. "A ray of Khyber's burning sun forms a bridge to Siberys's heights."

"What does it mean?" Rienne asked, her face twisted in horror. Her body was half turned away from the Spire though her eyes were glued to it, as though she wanted to look away but couldn't quite force herself to.

"It means the Soul Reaver's gates are sundered," Gaven said. "His monstrous hordes are about to spill out of that rift and tear into the armies on both sides. Nobody will win this battle."

"You called it a bridge," Rienne said. "Does that mean it has something to do with the Storm Dragon's ascension?"

"You said it in the City of the Dead," Darraun said. "You said, 'the Storm Dragon walks through the gates of Khyber and crosses the bridge to the sky.'"

Gaven nodded, only half listening to Darraun. His nightmare

continued to unfold before his eyes. Darraun muttered a curse, and Rienne gripped Gaven's arm, convincing him that the scene was not merely another waking dream.

The creatures that began to exude from the rift could not have existed in a sane world. Some resembled earthly beasts, but they had been so twisted by the corruption of Khyber that they were barely recognizable. Tentacles sprouted from their sides or backs or protruded where their mouths should have been. Joints bent in obscene ways. Faces erupted from wounds in their skin and then retreated back into horrible bodies. Others could not be compared to anything natural—they were mounds of flesh or agglomerations of bone covered with parchment skin, or slimy things that slithered on pale bellies or skittered on innumerable legs. Blank eyes stared out from pale gray faces, and hundreds of humanlike eyes covered an oozing mass of half-congealed blood.

Worse, somehow, than the sight of the creatures vomiting from the gulf was their sound—part keening, part lunatic babble, part predatory growl. It began quietly as the first monstrosities emerged, but it grew louder with each successive wave, building until it drowned out the other sounds of the battlefield and battered at the walls of Gaven's sanity. He couldn't form words with that babble assaulting his mind, and he couldn't hope to be heard above the cacophony if he did.

A blast of lightning engulfed the ship, followed by a deafening crash as an enormous copper-scaled dragon smashed into her hull. The impact knocked Gaven off his feet and slammed him against the bulwarks. The ring of elemental fire surged out to engulf the dragon's body, charring its flesh and making the airship buck and roll. The dead dragon plummeted down, pulling the *Eye of the Storm* down with it.

Gaven leaped up to grab at the helm, desperately hoping to regain control of the airship before she crashed to the ground. He sensed the elemental's acquiescence to his will, but then he felt the impact rumble through the hull. He had slowed their fall, but he was too late to stop it. Timbers groaned and then cracked, the ring of fire sputtered and went out. The airship lurched backward, jerked to port, and was still.

Rienne had kept her feet through it all, and Maelstrom was already in her hand. She swung it through slow repetitions of the whirling patterns of strikes and blocks she favored in battle. The sword seemed to sing in her hand, adding a voice of storm and steel to the mounting clamor around them. Darraun pulled himself to his feet and slid his mace out of the loop in his belt. Gaven looked up at the darkening sky, calling out to the brewing storm. If he was to be a force of destruction, best to use that power in a cause like this—to help protect the soldiers of both armies from the slaughter that surged toward them. If Vaskar was determined to be the Storm Dragon, let *him* face the Soul Reaver.

In the blink of an eye, the hordes of the Soul Reaver swarmed over the bulwarks of the grounded airship, and Gaven forgot himself and his friends in the storm of battle. Eyes wide open, he plunged headlong into the nightmares that had plagued him for twenty-six years.

Roaring with horror and fury, he swung his greatsword back and forth, cutting through alien flesh, shattering bone, spilling blood and ichor onto the deck. Shouting arcane syllables, he created fire and lightning to sear his foes, summoned invisible and irresistible forces to push them back, cast spells to guide his blade to the vital parts of tentacled things that refused to die. Bile rose in his throat as unspeakable horrors stared him in the face and spat oozing slime onto him in their death throes. He lashed out in reflexive fear to sever tentacles that grasped at him. The wailing ululation of the horde battered at his ears and at the ramparts of his will, threatening to break his concentration and reduce his resolve to quivering terror. And all the time the storm's fury built around him, torrents of rain and hail, blasts of wind, and eruptions of lightning that tore great holes in the teeming carpet of aberrations that covered the Starcrag Plain.

Without warning, the battlefield fell silent, and the raving legions paused. Gaven's ears rang in the sudden quiet, and he seized the opportunity to check that Rienne and Darraun were still alive. But the respite was brief. A moment later, every monstrosity raised its voice in a shriek, lifting arms and tentacles and limbs into the air, and the onslaught resumed. Gaven roared and spun his blade in a wide circle. A whirlwind followed his sword through the air and forced the nearest creatures back, giving him room to assess the battlefield.

He glanced up at the Crystal Spire, towering above them a

bowshot away, a radiant beacon through the driving rain. He saw what had made the creatures pause: a figure hung suspended in the shaft of light, roughly human in size and shape. It was smaller than many of the creatures he had already slain, but even at that distance, it projected an aura like a low grumbling roar, tearing at the very roots of his sense and will. Long tentacles thrashed the air around its face, and clawed hands stretched up to the sky.

"Tearer and reaver and flayer of souls," Gaven whispered.

The hordes renewed their assault, and Gaven lost himself in the battle again.

* * * * *

Haldren surveyed a battlefield over which he no longer had any control, clutching his reins until they bit into his palms. The full extent of Vaskar's duplicity had made itself clear: in addition to bringing dragons to fight on both sides of the battle, Vaskar had convinced him to launch his assault against Thrane on this field—here, above the prison of the Soul Reaver. Haldren had known Vaskar would have to face that foe in the end—Gaven had seen the Eye of Siberys used as a spear to defeat the creature. But he had not expected to provide the stage for that battle. Not only had Vaskar undone the advantage he had given Haldren, but he had actually consigned both armies to slaughter at the hands of the Soul Reaver's aberrant legions. Now Haldren would be forced to watch Vaskar's moment of triumph, his ascension to godhood, in the air above the spectacle of his own crushing defeat. And rather than having an ally among the gods of the world, Haldren would have a bitter enemy. It was too much to bear.

His eyes wandered over the field, straining to see the magnitude of the carnage through the driving rain. To his right, ir'Fann's infantry was falling under a renewed press, which meant that his pikemen had been overwhelmed. Near the middle of the field, a clump of Kadra's knights stood in a tight circle as the aberrations advanced over the corpses of their steeds. He lifted his spyglass and saw Kadra Ware herself lying at the center of that circle, bloody and unmoving. To the left, ir'Cashan's troops fled toward the sheltering hills. A group of knight phantoms, well-armored infantry riding conjured steeds of smoke and shadow, ranged back and forth along the rear, looking in vain for a place where their aid might turn the tide of battle. There could be no doubt: the field was lost. Lord General Haldren ir'Brassek had never known such a crushing defeat.

He lifted his eyes to the radiant column at the hub of the spreading devastation, and saw for the first time the tiny figure suspended in its light. He pressed the spyglass to his eye again. The Soul Reaver. Hatred welled up in his gut like bile, and he cursed under his breath. "Kill Vaskar for me, damn him." The creature stretched its shriveled arms upward as tentacles writhed out around its face, and Haldren imagined it urging its subterranean hordes to greater fury as they swept over their foes or calling down the storm to add its wrath to theirs.

"And damn the rain," he said aloud. "Can I not at least see my defeat through clear eyes?"

"It's Gaven," Senya said, pointing at the excoriate's grounded airship. "The storm battles for him."

"You still believe his lies? You still think he's the Storm Dragon?"

Senya turned her gaze to meet his angry glare. "That's our only hope."

"Then hope is lost," Haldren said, biting back his rage.

Cart rumbled on Haldren's right. "We'll see soon enough," he said. Haldren turned to look at him, then followed his gaze back to the towering shaft of light.

A blast of lightning engulfed the Soul Reaver. For an instant, Haldren thought that the storm had lashed out at the monstrosity, but then he saw the lightning's source: Vaskar had begun his attack.

"The Bronze Serpent," Senya said. "He's doomed to fail."

"Good," Haldren spat.

CHAPTER
48

T he dragon's roar cut through the wails of the Soul Reaver's
hosts. Gaven drove his sword down through the double head
of a waist-high monstrosity and glanced up at the Crystal
Spire. Vaskar had come to face the Soul Reaver, hoping to bring
about the fulfillment of the Prophecy. The sounds of the battle fell
away, even the howls of the monsters around him, leaving a strange
stillness, and the words of the Prophecy rang in his mind:

> *The Bronze Serpent faces the Soul Reaver and fails.*
> *But the Storm Dragon seizes the shard of heaven from the*
>   *fallen pretender.*

Had Vaskar accounted for those words? Did he even know
about them? Gaven had spoken them to Haldren, but not in Vaskar's presence. Would Haldren have repeated them to the dragon,
when they upset him so much?

It didn't matter, he realized. Vaskar was doomed to fail,
which meant that the Soul Reaver's hordes would continue to
pour forth from Khyber's darkness. Every soldier in the Starcrag
Plain would fall beneath them. The monsters would pour into
Aundair and Thrane—they might raze Thaliost, or Daskaran
across the river. They might reach Stormhome. The idea of
Haldren conquering Khorvaire was terrible to contemplate, but
the thought of the Soul Reaver spreading his tentacles across the
north was much, much worse.

Vaskar was doomed to fail, and that meant the Storm Dragon
would have to do what the Prophecy demanded of him: seize the
shard of heaven and drive it through the Soul Reaver's heart.

No one could do that but him.

The aberrations crowded closer. Growling, Gaven impaled one

of the larger, shambling monsters, left his sword hanging in the wound, and swung his hands together to create a clap of thunder that drove the smaller creatures back. Then he grabbed the sword from the teetering bug-thing and leaped aft, toward the helm.

"Clear the deck!" he shouted. He seized the wheel and willed the elemental out of its quiescence.

"Can she fly?" Rienne called back. "That was a rough landing."

"I'll make her fly." The wind howled, and the airship lurched, then she slowly lifted off the ground.

The elemental resisted Gaven's control at first, protesting as though the damage to the hull had wounded or weakened it. *Fly, damn you.*

Rienne and Darraun fought hard to carry out Gaven's command. Rienne nearly stopped using her sword, instead relying on a constantly shifting stance to overbalance the creatures that came charging toward her and throw them overboard. Maelstrom came to bear only in the one instance where a tentacle wrapped around her leg as its owner hurtled overboard, threatening to drag Rienne off the ship as well. A swift, sure blow from Maelstrom freed her from its grasp and sent the creature plummeting to its doom. Darraun swung his mace, magically enhanced to slay the aberrations of Khyber, beating them back under a constant hail of blows until they had nowhere to go but off the ship.

The *Eye of the Storm* teetered higher, rising above the din of the battle and the gibbering hordes below. Gaven let the winds carry her in a wide circle around the Crystal Spire as the ship swirled faster and faster around the bridge of light. That circular path provided Gaven with a clear view of the continuing battle between the Soul Reaver and Vaskar—be he Storm Dragon or doomed Bronze Serpent—as it raged in the midst of the great column of light.

It would be more accurate to say that Vaskar raged, Gaven thought. The battle was not too different from watching Rienne fight a drunken Eldeen wild man. The Soul Reaver remained calm, moving very little in response to Vaskar's charges, his circling flights and desperate lunges. Each time Vaskar closed in, an invisible force pushed him aside, preventing him from making contact. Gaven couldn't see the Soul Reaver make any counterattack, but it was clear that Vaskar grew more tired with each passing moment. His frustration also built with every failed lunge. He roared and spat lightning at the Soul Reaver, but though the lightning at least touched the creature, it didn't seem to cause it any pain or distress. To his surprise, Gaven felt a twinge of pity for the dragon—he was so misguided, and ultimately so ineffectual, just as he tried to seize tremendous power.

Vaskar pulled back and floated motionless on the building gale for a moment. Carried by the wind, the airship swirled closer to him, and for a moment Gaven thought the dragon would attack the *Eye of the Storm* to vent his frustration. Then Gaven saw a flash of gold: from somewhere on his body, Vaskar had produced the Eye of Siberys. He fumbled with the dragonshard in claws too large to serve as hands, and Gaven saw that Vaskar had clumsily bound the shard to a straight, polished staff, making a spear to slay the Soul Reaver. He was desperate, Gaven realized, and was pulling out his weapon of last resort. The dragon didn't expect it to work—and he was right. Vaskar was already defeated.

Gaven jerked the wheel hard to port and took the *Eye of the Storm* out of the cyclone.

"What are you doing?" Rienne said.

"I need to get off this ship," Gaven said, "and I'm not going to make Darraun try to fly her in that storm."

"No," Rienne said, "I mean, what are you doing?"

The airship had cleared the worst of the storm and flew smoothly again, despite the staved-in timbers of her hull. "Darraun, can you take her from here?" Gaven said.

"I can try," Darraun answered. His hands clenched the wheel, and Gaven released it. The ship bucked slightly, then leveled. Darraun nodded, but didn't try to speak again.

"Gaven," Rienne said, "what are you doing?"

Gaven pulled off his scabbard and untied the ash staff he'd bound to it. Touching the staff sparked a torrent of memories— stumbling, half crazed through the Mournland, climbing the storm-blasted tree to pull off the branch, a dream: a yellow crystal pulsing with veins of golden light, carved to a point and bound to a blackened branch, plunging into a body that was shadow given twisting form.

"It was my hand on the spear," he said, more to himself than her. "It seems I will play the part of the Storm Dragon after all." He stood with the staff in his hands and slung his sword and scabbard back over his shoulder.

Rienne lay a hand on his back. "Play the part," she said, "but write it as you go. You are player and playwright."

He looked into her eyes and cupped her cheek in his hand, running a thumb along the curve of her lips.

"I don't know how I could ever have doubted your love," he said. "I never will again."

"Come back to me."

"I will." He kissed her, savoring the taste of her breath, and then jumped over the bulwarks.

A fresh gust of wind caught him up and carried him away from the airship, back to the storm that whirled around the Crystal Spire. Lightning flared and roared around him, and the rain became hail, as though the storm had been holding its full fury back until that moment. Gaven willed himself forward, toward the Soul Reaver, and the wings of the storm carried him there.

Vaskar roared when he saw Gaven approaching. "Do you still think to steal my prize?" he howled over the wind. "Get away, interloper!"

Vaskar's outrage had a very different effect than he had intended. The Soul Reaver followed Vaskar's gaze, turning its monstrous head toward Gaven as he approached. Then, as if the battle to that point had consisted purely of the Soul Reaver playing with Vaskar, the tentacled thing dismissed him. Barely sparing the dragon another glance, it blasted him with waves of energy that made the air shimmer, and the echoes of it made Gaven's head throb with sudden pain. Unconscious or dead, Vaskar fell.

As the Soul Reaver turned its full attention to Gaven, lightning streaked into the Crystal Spire and coursed through the Soul Reaver's withered flesh, though it left the creature unharmed. Wind buffeted it from every side, and the robes it wore flapped furiously around it. In return, Gaven felt his mind engulfed in a similar storm. Thoughts and feelings welled up in no sensible order, like a nightmare galloping through his mind at a breakneck pace. Slights and shames from his childhood sprang to his thoughts alongside the fresh grief of his father's death, while the memories he'd acquired from the Heart of Khyber added their own share of fear and frustration. For a moment Gaven could not even distinguish the torrent of memories from his sensation of the present: the Soul Reaver and the storm seemed like distant thoughts amid the deluge.

Among the torrent, though, Gaven found words that connected the ancient dragon's memories to his own past, walking the Sky Caves of Thieren Kor, and the present moment, tying them all together—

The greatest of the daelkyr's brood, the Soul Reaver feasts on the minds and flesh of a thousand lives before his prison breaks. The Bronze Serpent calls him forth, but the Storm Dragon is his doom.

The words focused his mind like a bolt of lightning. I wield the power of the Storm Dragon, he thought. If I don't kill the Soul Reaver, who will?

He whipped the storm into a greater fury. Hail battered the Soul Reaver, rain like searing fire burned its flesh, and lightning crackled in a ball around it. Then the Soul Reaver, too, fell from the sky, sliding down the shaft of unearthly light. Gaven watched it descend and disappear again below the earth, and he wished he could believe it dead.

The Storm Dragon descends into the endless dark beneath the bridge of light, he thought, where the Soul Reaver waits. There among the bones of Khyber the Storm Dragon drives the spear formed from Siberys's Eye into the Soul Reaver's heart.

Siberys's Eye—where was it? With a start, he searched the ground below. Vaskar lay crumpled on the rocky plain near the base of the Crystal Spire, one wing outstretched at a strange angle, his neck curved around beneath the bulk of his body, his head hidden from view. The Soul Reaver's hordes had dispersed from there already, moved outward to tear into the armies gathered at either end of the plain. Gaven willed himself downward, and the wind set him on solid ground once again. Drenched with rain, chilled to the bone, he scrambled over and around the rocks to the place where Vaskar's body lay.

The dragon looked pathetic, broken like a child's toy dashed to the ground, and Gaven again felt the welling of pity. "The Bronze Serpent faces the Soul Reaver and fails," he said. "But the Storm Dragon seizes the shard of heaven from the fallen pretender. Where is it, Vaskar?"

Gaven circled the fallen dragon's body, scanning the ground for any gleam of yellow. The ground around Vaskar's body revealed no clues, so Gaven used the ash staff to prod under the dragon's claws. He lifted a claw, and almost jumped in surprise as the Eye of Siberys flashed gold beneath the dragon's massive hand. He scooped up the dragonshard and yanked it free from Vaskar's staff.

He was back in the Aerenal jungle, cradling the warm Eye of Siberys close to his chest, gazing into its vibrant core where veins of gold danced like Siberys at the dawn of creation. It was so easy to lose himself in that writhing dance, to forget his surroundings, to forget himself. Even the sound of thunderous footsteps could barely stir him from his reverie, but he made himself turn and look at Darraun.

Except that he wasn't in Aerenal, and the footsteps had been hoofbeats. Gaven tried to shake his head clear, without much success, and sized up the rider charging him from the north. A knight of some sort, he supposed, clad in heavy armor—no, a warforged. Cart.

Gaven stowed the Eye of Siberys in a pocket and held his ash-black staff as though it were his greatsword. "What are you doing here?" he called to the advancing warforged.

"I'm not here to fight you, Gaven," Cart said. His tone reminded Gaven of the first time he'd encountered the warforged: Cart bending down to him in his cell and trying to coax him out as if he were a frightened child. "I thought you might want some help."

"Help? Why would you help me?"

Cart dismounted and walked closer to Gaven. "Because we are alike, you and I."

"Alike? How so?"

"Each of us was made for a single purpose, Gaven. It's foolish to deny that purpose. I was made for war, and I will continue to war until I finally meet a foe who can defeat me. And I'll die knowing that I lived according to my purpose. What more can anyone hope to do?"

"And for what purpose was I made, Cart?"

"You were made to be here at this moment, to fight that monstrosity down there and do what Vaskar could not. To be a god."

"Of all people, shouldn't gods be free to choose their destinies?"

"What greater destiny could you ask for?" Cart sounded as though he couldn't possibly imagine a satisfactory answer to his question.

Gaven looked up into the storm, feeling the rain striking his skin. The wind lashed his hair against his face. He was the storm: he felt himself raging in the whirling clouds and booming thunder. But he was also a rain-drenched man, feet planted firmly on the ground. "You're wrong about me, Cart," he said. He pulled the Eye of Siberys out of his pocket and started binding it to the ash staff.

"Am I? Then why are you readying your weapon?"

"Oh, I'll play the Storm Dragon's part, for now. You're right—someone has to stop the Soul Reaver, and no one here is going to do it but me." The branch he had pulled from the ash tree seemed made to fit the Eye of Siberys. He jabbed the ground a few times to make sure the dragonshard was securely affixed.

Satisfied, he pulled his adamantine box out of another pouch and sprang it open. The nightshard inside seemed to spring to life at the proximity of the Eye of Siberys. "The Time of the Dragon Above draws to a close," he said, not really addressing Cart. "The Time of the Dragon Below approaches. The Eye of Siberys and the Heart of Khyber are united, just as the Crystal Spire links the Dragon Above and the Dragon Below."

"I agree with Darraun," Cart said. "The Prophecy makes my head spin."

"You don't know the half of it." Gaven lifted the nightshard and tossed it gently away from him. It seemed to float along that path for a moment, then it circled back, drawing a ring of lightning behind it. Like the whirlwind that had borne him aloft, it swirled around him, tracing its path in crackling light.

"Are you coming with me?" he asked the warforged.

Cart nodded.

"Let's go, then." Gaven strode over to the base of the Crystal Spire, to a ledge overlooking the chasm that rent the plain. He tried to peer down into it, but the light blinded him. "The Soul Reaver awaits." Without a backward glance, he stepped off the ledge and fell.

CHAPTER
49

I've got to get her back on the ground." Darraun's face was
deathly pale, and his hands gripped the spokes of the wheel.
Speaking seemed like an enormous effort.

"Keep going south," Rienne said. "Behind the Thrane forces.
We'll be off the plain in no time." She tried to sound more optimis-
tic than she felt. But she had just watched Gaven fall down into the
depths of Khyber, and dread had a chill grip on her heart.

Darraun fixed his eyes just to the port side of the prow as he
steered the airship in that direction. His every movement was stiff
and clipped, as if moving too fast would break his mind's hold on
the elemental bound in the ship. His apparently fragile state did
nothing to ease Rienne's apprehension. She leaned on the port bulwark, watching as the chasm grew smaller in the distance behind
them, until it was swallowed up in the rain and hail, and she could
barely even make out the Crystal Spire.

"See anything?" Darraun grunted.

Rienne shifted her gaze to examine the plain below them.
The Soul Reaver's hosts rampaged across the battlefield. She saw
Thrane banners cast down in the mud and trampled, though
clusters of knights still held their ground against the tide of horrors. I see the world sinking into chaos, she thought.

"The Thranes are still fighting the creatures from the chasm,"
she said. "Do you suppose Thrane will blame Aundair for that?"

Darraun nodded, and Rienne had to agree in her heart. The
situation was grim in any event: If the Thrane army were completely destroyed, the Cardinals would assume that Aundair's
attack had been successful. If there were survivors—there had to
be survivors!—they would describe how Aundair's forces opened a
crack in the earth and brought the monsters forth, and trafficking
with the Dragon Below would be added to Aundair's list of real and

imagined crimes. It seemed the storm of war had broken again and nothing could stop it.

She leaned against the railing and stared down at the carnage below. Something had to stop it—something or someone. Gaven's talk of being a hero, of choosing his own destiny and writing his own part in the play, stirred in her memory. "Darraun," she said, whirling to face the changeling at the helm, "turn us around, take us north!"

His eyes were wide. "Back into the storm?"

Yes, but not that storm, she thought. "Circle it. We need to get to Haldren."

Darraun nodded and turned the wheel.

"Why should I be content to be a minor player in this drama?" Rienne mused aloud.

A smile quirked at the corner of Darraun's mouth.

* * * * *

Haldren stared through the spyglass at the dragon's crumpled body. Vaskar did not stir. He had watched Vaskar's defeat with satisfaction diluted by growing rage. Vaskar had brought his plans to ruin, so it pleased him to see the dragon's ambitions quashed as well. At the same time, Vaskar's defeat left room for Gaven to seize what Vaskar had sought. Gaven—the pathetic madman that had started all this, without having the slightest idea what he was doing. Gaven was supposed to be a tool, a pawn Haldren could use to manipulate Vaskar and to facilitate his own rise to power. Instead, the bastard had stolen Senya, thwarted Vaskar, and appeared out of nowhere to take part in the ruin of Haldren's plans.

"If I achieve nothing else in this lifetime," he whispered, "I will destroy him."

"You aim to destroy a god?" Senya said.

"He's not a god."

"Not yet. But his power is already greater than yours."

"What did he do to you, Senya? How did he bend you so completely to him?"

"He didn't bend me to his will. That's how you work with your magic and your oratory. You taught me to work that way as well, using my body. And oh, you taught me well—well enough that the disciple became the master. I had you wrapped around my finger. But Gaven—he didn't bend me. He straightened me out."

Senya's words stabbed Haldren's heart and poured ice into his gut. "You . . . used me?" he whispered, quivering with rage.

"Of course." Her voice was not cruel or bitter, just . . . dismissive. Utterly calm and cold. How could he have been such a fool?

He turned away from her and urged his horse forward a few steps. "Do you see the warforged?" he asked, trying to keep his voice as calm as hers.

"I saw him last on the east side of the field, riding hard."

"Has he gone mad? What is he doing?"

"Cart was never good at standing by and watching a battle unfold. He was made for war, as he said, built by Cannith to be a soldier."

"No," Haldren breathed. He had put the spyglass back to his eye, and finally found Cart near the middle of the field. "He was evidently made for treachery. He's talking to Gaven."

"Don't be absurd, Haldren. No one is more loyal to you than Cart."

"If he treats with my enemy, he is my enemy."

"I wonder if you have any friends left."

Haldren surveyed the battlefield again. Ir'Fann's infantry was gone, wiped from the field, leaving a strange calm on the eastern side. No wonder Cart had ridden that way. Kadra's knights had fallen as well, which meant that if she hadn't been dead when he saw her before, she certainly was now. The knight phantoms he'd seen earlier had actually rallied ir'Cashan's troops on the west side, but there was no sign of ir'Cashan herself. Her death had probably caused her soldiers' initial rout. He hadn't seen Rennic Arak or his troops since the crevice opened—they had been at the vanguard, and were probably the first to fall. General Yeven, at least, was still alive: he had taken his command staff and retreated back up Bramblescar Gorge at about the same time as Cart had ridden off.

Haldren returned his gaze to Senya. "No," he said, "none are left."

As he spoke, something in the air caught his eye. A bright flash—lightning, perhaps? He almost dismissed it as yet another effect of the storm, but then he saw it again. An airship, a small one, and she was soaring closer to them through the storm.

"That's Gaven's ship," Senya said.

"He's not aboard, though."

"You just saw him talking to Cart."

"Well, if I can't destroy him, perhaps I can at least destroy someone he loves."

* * * * *

Rienne kept her eyes on the battlefield as Darraun piloted them around the storm. The skirmishes thinned on the south side, the Thrane side, and gave way to random clumps of monsters spreading over the plain to the east and shambling toward the Silver Woods. As the airship rounded the Crystal Spire and the raging storm, she saw more signs of battle—Haldren's remaining troops struggling to hold the monsters off.

"I give better odds to the Thranes," she said.

Darraun nodded. "Without the dragons, Haldren wouldn't have had a chance."

"So he had lost the battle even before the Crystal Spire appeared. His fate was sealed when the other dragons appeared to fight for Thrane."

"Exactly."

"What will he do?"

"Lick his wounds," Darraun said. "He doesn't take well to defeat."

"Do you think he'll try again someday?"

"If he gets out of this alive and manages to stay out of Dreadhold, yes."

"Then I need to make sure he doesn't."

"Yes, we do," Darraun said with a smile. The airship lurched, and his smile disappeared. Shaking his head, he renewed his concentration.

"I'm sorry. I'm distracting you." Rienne turned back to the railing.

The Aundairian side of the field had boiled down to a single pitched battle on the western side. Haldren's troops fought bravely, but they were completely encircled by the gibbering hordes. She watched sadly as the nightmarish host whittled away at the Aundairian formation, every fallen monster quickly replaced by another drawn to the battle from elsewhere on the field.

She pointed to the mouth of the small valley at the north end of the plain, the opening between the rocky wall of the Starpeaks and the Silver Woods where they had emerged into the Starcrag Plain. "There," she said over her shoulder. "That's the way we came, and I expect that's where we'll find Haldren."

Darraun adjusted his course slightly, and they soared past the Aundairians' last stand.

Rienne's first indication that they had indeed found Haldren was a blast of fire exploding around the airship's prow. Rienne tumbled away from the edge of the flames, unhurt, but she heard Darraun let loose a string of vehement and evocative curses. Flames danced along the arcane tracery in the hull, fire answering fire, and she knew that the ship's bound elemental would rebel against Darraun's control as it had when they fought the young red dragon.

"Bring us down!" she shouted, but there was no need. Darraun was already urging the airship downward, though Rienne couldn't tell whether he exerted such enormous effort to force the airship down or to keep her from falling too fast. Beads of sweat trickled down his face, and he squeezed one eye shut to clear sweat or smoke from it—he didn't dare release even one hand from the wheel.

Rienne leaned over a railing on the port side and looked below them to help guide Darraun to a relatively safe landing spot. She was so intent on getting the airship safely down that she almost forgot about Haldren's imminent threat, until another burst of fire engulfed her. She cried out in pain and fell back away from the bulwarks. Darraun must have lost concentration, either because he was injured as well or out of concern for her, because the airship suddenly jerked to starboard and then plunged downward. Rienne scrambled for a grip on something, and finally managed to clutch at a web of rope netting that secured a few small crates to the deck. As soon as she was sure of her hold, she looked at Darraun.

His eyes were squeezed shut, and his knuckles were white on the wheel. The muscles in his neck stood out like cords pulled tight beneath his skin, and sweat glued short tendrils of blond hair to his forehead. She didn't see any sign of serious injury, but if he didn't regain control of the airship quickly they would both be dead. She felt powerless, and she didn't like that feeling.

Keeping a hand on the ropes, she half climbed, half crawled to the helm. She had tried to help Darraun fly the *Eye of the Storm* when they first left Stormhome in search of Gaven, but he had said that if two minds tried to control the elemental at once it was less likely to respond, not more. Darraun had been the obvious one of them to try steering the vessel, both because of his expertise with magic and because his changeling nature might allow him to trick the elemental into believing that he was an heir of House Lyrandar. But at that moment, Darraun was failing, and it was about to cost them both their lives.

She seized the wheel, grabbing two spokes between the two that Darraun gripped. She felt the elemental's presence immediately. It pulled away from the touch of her mind like an unbroken horse shying or bucking from a trainer's hand. She pulled her hands away from the wheel as she imagined a bucking stallion's hooves lashing out at her—the elemental's resistance was so violent it felt physical. The ground was dangerously close, though, so she tried again.

This time she did not pull away when the elemental reacted. She felt Darraun's mental presence there as well, and she understood what he had meant in Stormhome. It would have been easy for the two of them to pull in two different directions, to give the elemental two competing voices to listen to. Too many warriors did exactly that—they let their minds give one command to their swords and their bodies another. Rienne's training had taught her the alternative. Rather than throwing another rope around the wild elemental's neck, she focused her attention on strengthening Darraun's grip, just as the mind could heighten and enhance the body's reflexes. One hand at a time, she shifted her grip on the wheel so that she held the same spokes Darraun did, and their hands touched even as they both grasped smooth wood.

The airship pulled out of her fall so suddenly that the lurch almost threw them overboard, but they held the wheel and managed to keep their feet. Rienne opened her eyes and saw Darraun smiling at her across the wheel, still tense but seeming far less panicked. She returned his smile just as another of Haldren's fireballs burst between them.

It stung her eyes with heat and brilliant light, scorched her face, and even seared her lungs as she gasped in surprise. Pain overwhelmed her, and she slumped to the deck.

CHAPTER
50

G aven fell.

The cold radiance of the Crystal Spire failed to light the sides of the chasm, so he fell blind, just as he had fallen when he found the nightshard. Time vanished, and his sense of motion failed as well, so he felt as though he hung suspended in the column of light. He might have fallen for a matter of seconds, but it seemed like hours.

Strangely calm, he kept his feet below him and stretched his arms to the side, one hand clenching the spear he had made from the Eye of Siberys. The Heart of Khyber continued its orbit around his body, but the lightning trailing behind it had vanished in the overwhelming light that bathed him. Air rushing past his ears was the only sound, and it faded into a dull roar.

Slowly a shape took form below him—the only feature he could make out in the light. A mouth gaped wide to receive him, like the jaws of Khyber waiting to engulf him when he reached the end of his fall. The Crystal Spire seemed to pour out of that mouth like lightning from Vaskar's maw. The shape grew larger, though he couldn't tell whether he fell toward it or it surged up to meet him.

Then it was upon him: the face of a great dragon carved into ancient stone. Though the storm raged far above him now, he called a gust of wind to stop his fall and planted his feet gently to one side of the dragon's mouth. He barely remembered in time to make sure that Cart landed safely on the other side. To his credit, the warforged made no sound that indicated he'd been worried about the fall. His face, of course, was unreadable.

The First of Sixteen descended to this gate. The Soul Reaver spoke to his mind, bypassing both ears and language, but carrying the same grumbling roar he had sensed when he first saw the Soul

Reaver high above the battlefield. *Any who would follow in his paths must be prepared for what lies beyond.*

Gaven peered into the darkness for a sign of the Soul Reaver, cursing the brilliance of the Crystal Spire that blinded his eyes without illuminating the shadows around it. Only the Heart of Khyber in its steady rotation cast a faint strobe of light around the chamber. Gaven had a vague sense of a dome arching overhead and smooth, round tunnels leading off into darkness. "And what if I don't want to follow his paths?" he called into the nothingness.

Cart looked at him strangely—the Soul Reaver evidently hadn't spoken in his mind.

Then I will kill you.

A wail filled Gaven's mind, different from the torrent of thoughts with which the Soul Reaver had assaulted him in the air. That attack had called his own mind up against him, but this was an intrusion, a blast of psychic force so great that his vision began to cloud over. He clamped his hands to his ears but couldn't block the sound, and squeezed his eyes shut to no avail. He dropped to one knee, searching for the still point he had found in his mind before, the focus that would enable him to shrug off the psychic attack again.

"The Bronze Dragon. . . no, the Bronze Serpent . . ."

His mind reeled, and though he rose once more to his feet and opened his eyes to search for the source of the assault, he could do nothing more than stumble half blind along the nearest tunnel, careening off the smooth stone walls.

* * * * *

Rienne opened her eyes and cried out—she was falling. Then she realized that an arm was firmly wrapped around her waist, holding her over a shoulder—Gaven? Her fall stopped abruptly, and Darraun crumpled to the ground beneath her. She rolled free and scrambled back to him, trying to get her bearings at the same time.

The *Eye of the Storm* loomed over them, grounded again, and Darraun had evidently just jumped off the deck, carrying her over his shoulder. It was not a great fall, and he was back on his feet in a moment. "Come on!" he said, "We have to get to Haldren before he hits us with another fireball."

His words reminded her what had happened, and she felt her face as she ran after him. The pain was gone—Darraun must have used some healing magic on her. "Thank you," she called to him, hustling to catch up. He shot a smile over his shoulder at her.

"Thank you for landing the airship," he said. "I was sure we were doomed."

"We may yet be," she said, looking ahead. A white-haired man she could only assume was Haldren was perched on a warhorse not ten paces in front of Darraun. The horse was barded with metal plates engraved with protective runes, and the old man's hands were raised in the gestures of another spell. In front of the horse, holding a slim elven longsword in a ready stance, was Senya. She met Rienne's eyes and her lips curled into a cruel smile.

* * * * *

"Gaven." Cart's voice was calm and gentle, nuanced with his years of studying human tone and cadence. "Shake it off. You can do this."

Smooth stone walls. A thought like lightning flashed through his mind, and he saw—not with his eyes, but clearer—the paths of the winding tunnels, the shapes they formed. The words of the Prophecy.

"The Storm Dragon walks through the gates of Khyber and crosses the bridge to the sky." He muttered the words to himself, sensing the layers of meaning contained in the tunnels around him. Words formed in his mind and bubbled from his mouth, slowly driving back the psychic scream of the Soul Reaver. "The Dragon of thunder and lightning and wind and rain and hail, the Storm Dragon—enters, walks, passes through, bursts through, shatters the Khyber gates, the dragon-gates below the chasm-gate." A vision started to form in his mind, and he laughed.

"Gaven?" Cart had a hand firmly clamped on his shoulder.

"Crosses the bridge, traverses it, spans it, thwarts it." Gaven spoke louder now.

And the Soul Reaver's mental assault broke on this new barrier of words—*I will destroy you!*

The Soul Reaver appeared, looming out of the dark. Shriveled limbs on a slender body, wrapped in a wind-tattered robe and with stoles and sashes bearing twisting runes. Hands like great claws, curling in anticipation of rending either body or soul. And a head like a nightmare from the deep sea—blank white orbs for eyes, surrounded by bony ridges, and four long, twitching tentacles where its mouth should have been. Its skin was living shadow, dusky gray, and its coating of slime glistened in the pulsing light of the Heart of Khyber as it circled Gaven.

Cart charged the monster, but it flicked two tentacles in his direction, revealing a hint of a suckerlike maw beneath them. The warforged staggered sideways into the tunnel wall and slumped to the ground.

"Thunder and lightning," Gaven said, reading the characters inscribed in the wall where Cart had collided, and he sent a bolt of roaring lightning to engulf the Soul Reaver. Gaven felt a psychic echo of its pain in his mind, but it did not flinch or back away. Instead, its four tentacles extended toward Gaven, reaching for his head even as the Soul Reaver's mind reached out. . . .

* * * * *

Haldren shouted the last syllable of his spell, but at that instant Darraun held up a wand and yelled a word of his own. A brief flare of light and smoke was the only manifestation of Haldren's spell.

"Traitor!" Haldren hissed, glaring at Darraun beneath bristling eyebrows. "Spy! I never trusted you!"

"You didn't have to," Darraun said, running forward with his mace over his shoulder and his wand in his other hand. "I still learned everything I needed to know."

Senya grinned at Rienne. "What do you say we let these two sort out their differences?" she said, jerking her head toward Haldren and Darraun. "And we can sort out ours." The elf charged, the point of her sword low to the ground.

Rienne stood still, her sword loose in her hand. "Please tell me you're not going to fight me in a jealous rage over Gaven."

"A jealous rage?" Senya said. "No." She closed with Rienne, bringing her sword up in a thrust at Rienne's heart. Rienne lazily swung Maelstrom up to knock Senya's sword aside, and the elf's momentum took her around to Rienne's right. Rienne turned to follow her.

"What differences, then?" Rienne said, settling into a good defensive stance and awaiting Senya's next move.

"Remember the dwarves in Vathirond? The ones you brought to apprehend us? They nearly killed me, you know."

Rienne felt a pang of guilt. That had been her fault, though not the way Senya thought. "I didn't bring them. They followed me."

"I don't care." Senya lunged, more carefully this time, but she was not at all prepared for the way Rienne fought. Maelstrom beat her sword point to the ground, and Rienne stepped on the blade, yanking it from Senya's hand. Rienne's next step landed on Senya's shoulder, and Maelstrom traced a shallow cut in the elf's neck as Rienne went overhead and landed behind her.

Rienne's new position gave her a clear view of Darraun and Haldren. The sorcerer had still not dismounted, and his horse pranced sideways in a circle around the changeling, keeping Haldren effectively out of Darraun's reach. Another spell shot from Haldren's hand only to fizzle in the air, met by something from the artificer's wand. But Rienne could see that Darraun was tiring.

Senya circled, then stooped to retrieve her blade from the ground. Rienne saw her opening—Senya's defenses were down. But at the same moment, Haldren spurred his horse forward to run the changeling down. Instead of attacking Senya, she ran toward the others, placing herself carefully between Senya and Darraun.

Senya charged again. Rienne stepped to the side and spun as she went past, deflecting the force of Senya's charge upward. The elf's own momentum carried her through the air to land at Darraun's feet, right in Haldren's path. The horse neighed and reared, and Haldren had to fight to keep his seat. Darraun charged forward and swung his mace into Haldren's knee. The sorcerer screamed and fell to the ground.

* * * * *

The pull on Gaven's mind was tangible, as though the tentacles had touched him, wrapped around him, and drawn him in. He staggered forward, unwilling, but unable to resist. He felt he could not balance on his feet unless he kept stepping forward. He tried to lean back, against the pull, but sensed immediately that he would fall backward unless he lurched forward again. He stumbled and felt something bang against his arm, sending a tingle of warm energy through his skin.

The Heart of Khyber. He stretched out a hand and grabbed

it, then lost his balance and fell to the ground. The Soul Reaver stepped closer on its spindly legs, and Gaven raised a hand to ward it off—the hand that held the Heart of Khyber.

The Soul Reaver recoiled, and Gaven felt the pressure on his mind ease. He scrambled to his feet, keeping the nightshard between himself and the monstrous abomination, and hefted the spear in his other hand. A sick, burbling hiss came from the Soul Reaver's mouth as it crouched, wary of Gaven's next move.

"Does this frighten you?" Gaven said, thrusting the nightshard forward. "Or is it the spear, foreordained for your doom?"

I am your doom. Pain assaulted every nerve in Gaven's body, an unbearable agony worse than any trauma of body or soul he had ever experienced. His body urged him to flee, to get as far as he could from the source of the pain, to never draw near it again. He turned to run, but the Heart of Khyber held him like an anchor. He would have dropped it in order to flee, but his hand seemed unwilling to release it. It was cool in his palm, an oasis from the pain, and he tried to draw on that coolness to assuage the agony. A soothing chill like water spread out from his hand, and in a moment the pain was gone.

I will destroy you, the Soul Reaver said, *and my hordes will spread over the surface world like a plague. Nothing will stop them!*

A vision accompanied its words, startlingly real, much like the visions that had haunted Gaven's dreams in Dreadhold and even his waking since his escape. He saw an unending stream of horrible monstrosities pouring out of the chasm far above him, unleashing devastation far worse than anything the world had experienced in the Last War. It was a vision of the world overcome with madness and horror.

Doubt began to gnaw at the roots of Gaven's mind. How could one man hold back such a tide of devastation? To do so would require greater power than even he wielded—would it not require the power of a god?

Gaven roared, and thunder shook the earth around him. Sheets of lightning shot out from the tunnel walls to engulf the Soul Reaver, lifting it off the ground and holding it in the air as wave after wave of storming fury poured into its sickly flesh. Still howling, Gaven charged forward, leveling his spear at the Soul Reaver's chest.

The Eye of Siberys bound to a branch of ash . . .

. . . among the bones of Khyber . . .

The Storm Dragon drives a spear into the Soul Reaver's heart.

My hand on the spear, Gaven thought as he plunged it into a body that was shadow given twisting form.

CHAPTER
51

One sharp kick from Rienne's foot sent Senya sprawling facedown on the ground. The elf groaned, but she did not move again. Darraun had overheard only snippets of the banter between the two women as they fought, but it was enough to make him curious what had happened in Vathirond. He wished he'd been there to see it.

Haldren stirred, so Darraun slammed his mace into the sorcerer's skull rather harder than was probably necessary, sending a trail of blood arcing from the sorcerer's mouth. Darraun had been itching to do that almost since he first laid eyes on Haldren in Dreadhold, and he took great pleasure in watching the old man slump into unconsciousness. The artificer put his hands on his knees and paused to catch his breath—and to think hard about what he had to do next.

At that moment, the earth shook violently, nearly knocking him off his feet. Rienne kept her balance easily enough, but fear clouded her face. "Gaven!" she breathed, and she turned to stare back at the Crystal Spire, still piercing the sky with its unearthly light.

"Go!" Darraun said, reading her thoughts on her face. So transparent. "I'll take care of these two."

Rienne hesitated only a moment before bolting to Haldren's horse and throwing herself onto its back. It didn't seem to mind at all, and eagerly ran out of the valley, heading back into the heart of the storm.

"So what am I going to do with you two?" Darraun said to the bodies at his feet. He put his hands on his hips and stared down at them, then began looking around the nearby field of battle. "Let's see what we have to work with."

* * * * *

Writhing shadows gripped the Eye of Siberys and sucked it into darkness, yanking the spear from Gaven's hand. The Soul Reaver's blank white eyes opened wide. Gaven stumbled backward and stared up in disbelief at the creature transforming before him.

Dusky gray flesh became translucent, hard as crystal, with smoky veins of darkness twisting beneath the skin. A core of molten shadow churned around the Eye of Siberys in its chest, where the spear had torn cloth away and penetrated the skin, as if it were dissolving the dragonshard or absorbing its power. Finally the eyes—pale white orbs that bulged in their bony sockets—began to glow with rich golden light, as if the Eye of Siberys had traveled through the Soul Reaver's body and lodged itself in its eye sockets.

As it changed, the Soul Reaver stretched out its clawed hands as if beckoning some distant ally, and in response the earth shook. Great cracks appeared in the walls of the tunnel, and rocks cascaded along the floor. Gaven threw his arms over his head, and for a moment he was back in Dreadhold, cowering in delirious fear as Vaskar smashed the roof over his cell. A great rumbling roar echoed throughout the caverns, answered by a gibbering cry issuing from a thousand inhuman throats. The legions of the Soul Reaver were ready, Gaven knew—no vision had ever been clearer in his mind.

The Soul Reaver's next attack was clearly meant to dismiss Gaven just as it had dismissed Vaskar—a psychic blast that overwhelmed his senses and his thoughts and every nerve that could register pain in his body. Gaven howled in fury and pain, joining his voice to the weird ululation of the monstrous hordes, but he did not break as Vaskar had. He struggled to his feet, standing in the Soul Reaver's path, interposing himself between that monstrous thing of living shadow and the Crystal Spire behind him. He yanked his greatsword free of its sheath and held it before him with both shaking hands.

Idiot mammal. The Soul Reaver's thoughts scraped across Gaven's mind. *You have fulfilled your purpose. Now die.*

Another psychic blast ripped through Gaven's mind, sending his sword clattering to the ground as he brought his fists to his temples and howled. But it passed, and Gaven still stood. He stooped to retrieve his sword as the Soul Reaver stepped closer.

Do you know why I am called the Soul Reaver, mammal?

"The greatest of the daelkyr's brood," Gaven whispered, "the

Soul Reaver feasts on the minds and flesh of a thousand lives before his prison breaks."

And you shall be a thousand and one. Another blast tore at Gaven's mind, and the Soul Reaver drew closer still, extending all four tentacles toward Gaven's pain-wracked skull.

"The Bronze Serpent calls him forth," Gaven screamed, pouring his agony into his voice, "but the Storm Dragon is his doom!" He slashed his sword at the tentacles, but the blade clanged against them as if they were solid stone rather than writhing flesh.

So you thought. And you thought to drive your spear into my heart. But your Prophecy didn't help you, did it? Perhaps you are not the Storm Dragon after all.

One tentacle made contact with Gaven's scalp and attached itself like a leech, and he felt his will begin to ebb. Of course he was not the Storm Dragon, he realized. How could he stand against this monster? In trying to destroy the Soul Reaver, he had only made the abomination more powerful. He tried to bat the tentacle away with one hand, but it held fast. The Soul Reaver was close, so close that its constant psychic grumbling had grown to a roar in Gaven's mind. He could see the ash haft of the spear he'd made dangling from the creature's chest. It smelled faintly of ozone and charred flesh, which made him smile weakly.

A second tentacle touched his head. The pain was fading, along with Gaven's desire to resist. Why should he not feed the Soul Reaver? He should be glad to nourish his master in the last moments before his ascension—

The thought filled Gaven with alarm. Where had that idea come from? The Soul Reaver planned to seize godhood from the Crystal Spire? Gaven tried to make sense of that notion, and he felt the creature's tentacles recoil slightly at that surge of mental activity.

A third tentacle touched, but Gaven swept a hand up to knock it away before it could affix itself. He tried to throw his body backward, away from the creature that fed on his thoughts, but two clawlike hands embraced him and pulled him back. He tried to lift his sword, but he could no longer bring it between the Soul Reaver's body and his own. Gaven could see the palest glimmer of golden light within the churning darkness in the Soul Reaver's chest.

The Eye of Siberys pulsed there like the Soul Reaver's heart, throbbing in a steady rhythm that beat in Gaven's head as well.

Shadows twisted around it, like veins carrying its power throughout the creature's body. "The Soul Reaver's heart . . ." he murmured, and then he knew.

His spear had not touched the Soul Reaver's heart. The monster had goaded him into using his spear against its fleshly body, rather than striking its real heart—the Heart of Khyber. Gaven let his sword fall to the ground, and with his last ounce of will, he wrapped both hands around the haft of the ash spear. He gave it one mighty tug, but it would not come free.

Where had the nightshard fallen? Gaven wrenched his head around to scan the ground, even as the Soul Reaver's third tentacle attached itself to his scalp. His thoughts were a jumble of memories and nightmares brought up at the Soul Reaver's call, but he clung to an image of the Heart of Khyber. At last he saw it on the ground behind the creature, where he had staggered backward before.

He had no will left. He feebly tried to pull his head away from the grasping tentacles while keeping his grip on the spear, but he could not move his head beyond their reach. He tried to speak, but the words came out slurred beyond recognition. Still, they formed themselves in his mind. "There the Storm Dragon drives a spear through the bones of Khyber through the Soul Reaver's heart."

Layers of meaning. He stood, barely, among the bones of Khyber, deep beneath the earth. But if the Heart of Khyber was the Soul Reaver's heart, then the Soul Reaver's bones were Khyber's bones. He could drive the spear through the Soul Reaver's bones and into the Soul Reaver's heart, if he could just—

"I am player and playwright!" he cried, and he heaved himself forward into the Soul Reaver's chest. The spear sank deeper into the creature's flesh, and waves of pain rippled through Gaven's mind. He forced his foe backward one step, two, then with one great push knocked it to the ground. Two tentacles tore free of his head, trailing blood from their sickly white tips. Gaven clutched the spear, pulling it downward with all his strength, praying to the Sovereign Host that its tip would find the nightshard.

He felt the spear break bone, and then heard it grate against stone below. He had missed the shard. The Soul Reaver heaved him away, its third tentacle tearing free from Gaven's head, and rolled away from him onto its hands and knees. The Eye of Siberys protruded from its back, shedding pale golden light around the dark cavern. Gaven spotted the nightshard on the ground between him and the bloodied Soul Reaver. As the creature stood and turned to face him again, Gaven could tell that it saw the shard as well. They froze.

The idiot mammal is more clever than I imagined. It made a sound like a gurgling cough, and Gaven saw black blood spill down from its mouth. A fresh wave of pain washed through his head—he began to feel where the tentacles had been boring through his skin and scraping at his skull.

"I am the Storm Dragon," Gaven said. He stretched his hands forward, and a blast of air like thunder shot through the Soul Reaver, sending it staggering backward a few steps. "And I will still be your doom!" He dove forward and clutched the Heart of Khyber in both hands, landing hard on his belly. He tried to roll back onto his feet as he caught his breath, but the Soul Reaver landed on top of him, two tentacles grasping at the nightshard while the other two slashed at his eyes.

Gaven swung his legs to one side and used their leverage to roll the Soul Reaver onto its back. Still clutching the Heart of Khyber in both hands, he put as much weight as he could above it, forcing it down toward the Soul Reaver's chest. It put up both hands to push back, using all four tentacles to attack Gaven's face. One forced its way into his mouth, tasting of blood and slime, working its way back toward his throat.

Grimacing with disgust, Gaven bit down on the tentacle in his mouth, adding a new taste of bilious ichor. He didn't bite clean through, but it was enough: the Soul Reaver's grip on the Heart of Khyber weakened, and Gaven managed to force the nightshard down to the stone floor. Spitting slime and bile, Gaven drove a knee as hard as he could into the creature's midsection. Holding the nightshard against the floor with one hand, he grabbed again at the spear with the other, raising it and the Soul Reaver's struggling body with it. Guiding the spear toward the hand that clutched the Heart of Khyber, he brought the spear's point, still protruding from the creature's back, down hard.

The spear pierced his hand, and he cried out in pain. But the Soul Reaver stopped struggling as the Eye of Siberys went on to pierce the nightshard, the Soul Reaver's heart. Its withered body, a moment ago writhing with preternatural strength, dissolved into wisps of smoke, snakes of oily darkness slithering away and seeping into the ground. A foul-smelling cloud of gray-black mist arose from the body and then dissipated, leaving Gaven alone, holding the spear he had made from the Eye of Siberys, impaling his own hand against the ground.

A tremendous sob wracked his body, and he dropped his head to the floor. He started to scream even before he pulled the spear free, but then it was done, and the pain was not as bad. He thrust his injured hand under his other arm and squeezed it there as he tried to find his feet. Reeling, he leaned against the wall for support while he waited for his head to clear.

His mind swam with echoes of the Soul Reaver's psychic assaults. The torrents of memory and feelings slowed, leaving him drained and trembling. It was done, or the worst of it was. Perhaps he had saved the world, or at least a corner of it. He wanted to take pride in that—he supposed he would when he was less exhausted.

As the storm of his thoughts stilled, he realized a strange emptiness in his mind. He cast his mind over his memories of the past months. The dragon of the nightshard, a presence in his thoughts for so long, was gone. He still remembered the dragon's memories—but he remembered his memory of them, he remembered experiencing them as Gaven. They were still vivid in his mind, some of them all too vivid, but a little more distant, farther removed from his own experience.

The dragon had vanished, taking its memories with it, when the Heart of Khyber was destroyed.

His only light had also gone out, so he spoke a quick spell and cradled an orb of light in his palm.

"Look, father!" he cried.

Arnoth stood in the doorway, leaning against the jamb, smiling with pride. "Well done, Gaven," he said.

Gaven flexed his hand, and the one orb split into three that danced into the air around him, lighting the tunnel walls.

"Thunder and lightning," he muttered, reading the Draconic character inscribed on the wall beside him. He started, and looked around. "Cart?" he called weakly. "Where did you get off to?"

CHAPTER
52

Trailing one hand along the wall, Gaven retraced his path, back to the base of the Crystal Spire. As he walked, his mind filled with the words traced on and by the twisting tunnel, words that spoke of the Storm Dragon, the gates of Khyber, and the bridge to the sky. The verbs, though—those most flexible of words, allowing so many nuances of action and meaning. The nouns were facts, the bare facts of the situation as it stood. The verbs were possibility.

The ululation of the Soul Reaver's hordes had diminished slightly, and the voices no longer rose in unison. The cries all seemed to be coming from somewhere far above, as though new waves of monsters were pouring out through the chasm from the upper reaches of Khyber and swarming anew over the battlefield.

He rounded one last bend and threw a hand up to shield his eyes from the brightness of the Crystal Spire, which had grown more intense since he left it. Light leaked out to cast deep shadows on the tracings of the cavern wall, and shone on Cart's impassive face. The warforged stood on the dragon's lower jaw, poised at the very edge of the Crystal Spire.

"Planning your ascension, Cart?" Gaven could barely find his voice—his throat was raw from yelling, and the lingering taste of the Soul Reaver's slime made his tongue feel thick.

"Have you come to stop me, Storm Dragon?"

"I don't care, one way or another. I don't plan on passing through that gate."

"What about the Prophecy?"

"There are many ways to bring the Prophecy to pass."

"I try not to think about it."

"Uncommonly wise."

"What god watches over my people, Gaven?" Cart's voice was

strangely melancholy, and he rocked ever so slightly on his heels as he stared down into the dragon's gaping maw. "Which Sovereign has our interests at heart?"

"Are there gods for each race and people?" Gaven asked. "Doesn't the whole Host keep watch over us all?"

"Perhaps. But the gods made all the other races. We were made by artificers and magewrights. Does Onatar then care for us, the god of the forge? Or perhaps the warlord Dol Dorn, since we were made for war? Or do they see us as many mortals do—simply as tools for war? There is no god of swords or siege engines. Perhaps there is no god for us."

"You want to be one, then? God of the warforged?"

Cart shrugged. "I am torn. I am not accustomed to feeling so divided."

"I've never heard you speak of warforged as your people before."

"I have always felt that the best way to serve warforged everywhere was to fulfill my own duty, to live out the purpose for which I was made."

"And you were made for war."

"I was. That's why I followed Haldren. He was my commanding officer, and I honored and respected him for that. But he also promised a return to war. I wanted that—I wanted to see the world plunged into violence again, just so I could find purpose again. What is a warforged to do in a world no longer at war?"

"What would you do, then, as god of the warforged? Would you urge them into war?"

Cart stroked his chin. "Power is quite a temptation, isn't it? It's one thing to think of all the good one might do. But I can so easily imagine abusing that power. To become a dark god of war, the destructive mirror of Dol Dorn, calling for war for its own sake. I think the Dark Six would become the Dark Seven."

Gaven nodded. "Exactly."

Cart stepped back from the Crystal Spire, and shadows fell over his face. "Well, Storm Dragon? How will the Prophecy come to pass?"

"The Storm Dragon bursts through the gates of Khyber and blocks the bridge to the sky."

He came and stood across from Cart, on the face of the snarling dragon, and looked up. The Crystal Spire rose forever above him, its light showing hints of movement along the edges of the chasm far above but blocking any detail from his view.

"That's not what you said in the City of the Dead," Cart said.

"No, it's not. But there are many ways to translate Draconic verbs, many layers of meaning that are expressed better in context than in isolation. And if I am to be the Storm Dragon, then I am the context for those words. They can't be interpreted apart from me."

"So you will choose your own destiny after all."

Gaven smiled. With one more glance skyward, he stepped forward into the Crystal Spire.

He dropped down into the dragon's maw, but then wind whipped up from nowhere, whirling furiously around him and holding him aloft. The earth rumbled as lightning probed the chasm, and a shower of rocks tumbled down from above, catching in the whirlwind and circling him. He lifted his hands to the sky high above, where the Crystal Spire broke through the swirling storm clouds, and a great bolt of lightning flashed down through the chasm, striking the stone dragon's mouth and adding to the swirling hail of stone around him. Then he surged up on the wind, sloughing the rock behind him.

He burst up through Khyber's gate in an explosive shower of rock splinters. The cavern went dark as the dragon's mouth collapsed in on itself, great slabs of stone falling in on the gate and dousing the light of the Crystal Spire. Reaching a hand toward Cart, Gaven lifted the warforged into the whirlwind behind him and hurtled up through the chasm.

Flashes of lightning illuminated the darkness around them as they rose, revealing tunnel mouths crawling with gibbering monsters clambering toward the surface. Gaven shot past them, rising faster than he had fallen, emerging into open air in the space of a few gasping breaths. Lightning crackled in the air around him, and great thundering bolts struck the ground below. The whirlwind below him hurled monsters off the brink and into the yawning depth of the chasm, and more lightning blasts sent enormous slabs of earth plummeting down after them. The Storm Dragon stretched out his arms, and sheets of lightning struck along the length of the chasm, shattering rock to fill it in. Thunder rolled continuously like the rumbling of a mighty earthquake, and when it was done, the chasm had become just another scar on the face of the Starcrag Plain.

* * * * *

Haldren's stallion galloped across the plain. Rienne stroked his neck as she rode, encouraging him to greater speed. He was no magebred horse or Valenar steed, but he was amazingly sure-footed on the rocky ground, which more than made up for a lack of raw speed. The earth thundered with the pounding of his hooves—no, she realized, the earth shook from tremors far below the battlefield, which seemed to bode ill for Gaven's well-being.

The battle was over, as far as Rienne could see. Haldren's soldiers had fallen or been routed from the field entirely, and until she drew near the chasm she saw only a few clumps of monsters scattering away from the field—heading for new haunts in the Starpeaks or the Silver Woods. She could see no dragons still aloft, whether they were all dead or driven away or just brought to ground. She spurred the stallion toward the towering shaft of light, a beacon in the midst of the furious storm.

She was halfway across the plain when the beacon flickered and went out. Her mind raced through a handful of possibilities as she spurred the stallion on: Had Gaven crossed the bridge to the sky, collapsing it behind him? Had he failed, proving that he was not the Storm Dragon after all? Had Gaven perhaps been wrong about the whole Prophecy and the Crystal Spire? Perhaps it was not any kind of bridge to the sky, but some kind of beacon or signal, and Gaven had destroyed it.

She drew a slow breath, calming her pounding heart, and tried to lose herself in the rhythm of the stallion's gait.

She lost track of the distance to the chasm where the Crystal Spire had been, and the storm grew even fiercer ahead. Wind whipped her hair and small hailstones stung her skin, and she soon rode into a wall of rain. She guided the horse toward the heart of the storm, where lightning danced around a swirling whirlwind. The heart of the storm must be Gaven, she thought.

A new tide of monsters poured out of the storm toward her, a tumultuous mass of pallid flesh and flailing appendages, sharp claws and writhing tentacles, screaming mouths and staring eyes.

They seemed to surge forward, clawing over each other in their haste to reach fresh prey. Each time she fixed her gaze on one creature, it disappeared under or behind the next wave of horrors. Terror and revulsion wrenched her gut, but she quelled them with another slow breath. If these monsters stood between her and Gaven, then she would have to fight her way through the monsters. She pulled the stallion to a halt and slid Maelstrom from its sheath.

There was no discipline to their advance. When they drew close, a monster with a single staring eye and a much smaller fanged mouth leaped ahead of the others and bounded up at her. The gaze of its lidless eye raked across her, blistering her skin as its claws reached for her throat. She drove her blade into its eye and deflected its momentum, sending its lifeless body spilling to the ground behind her. Her arms trembled—that would not do. Combat required discipline, focus, concentration, a perfect unity of thought and action.

Before she could steady herself, the waves broke around her. Action first—thought would follow. Maelstrom went into a dance of constant motion, spinning like a deadly shield surrounding her, blocking the creatures' attacks and biting into their flesh. Many of the monsters reached up to grab her—and a few reached down from a greater height—and those were the first to die. Haldren's horse proved himself one last time, rearing up to strike with its hooves and felling many of the smaller creatures. But before long the horse was pulled screaming under the surging tide, throwing Rienne through the air as he fell.

With a mighty shout, Rienne brought her energy back into focus. Like Darraun piloting the airship alone, action alone would not suffice against these hordes. Rienne came down on the chitinous back of a hulking monstrosity, then bounded off it to a relatively clear patch of ground. As she landed, she kicked a skittering buglike thing out of the way and slashed two other nameless things back, carving herself a place to stand. She banished her fear and lost herself in whirling motion, feeling Maelstrom surge to life in her grip. This was the style of fighting that had given the sword its name: a constant spinning, cutting everything within reach, wheeling the blade through an unending, intricate series of swirling arcs punctuated by sharp thrusts—what she thought of as lightning strikes within the whirlwind.

As she danced, the storm answered her strikes with lightning that shook the earth, and she had the sudden thought of fighting alongside Gaven on one of their subterranean expeditions. She smiled as gore flew from the tip of her blade. No claw could touch her, no tentacle stayed coiled around her wrist or leg for more than an instant before she sliced it through. Wide eyes tried to catch her gaze and assault her mind, sharp teeth tried to close around her but met the constant motion of her blade. Her feet moved with her blade, an intricate dance of steps and lunges that guided her away from dangerous blows and brought her near the weakest foes. She was utterly lost in the dance—no memory or anxiety about Gaven remained in the diamond stillness of her mind, perfectly focused on the battle at hand. A perfect unity of will and action.

The sea parted around her, and Rienne stumbled. A greenish ray of light shot through where she would have been if she had stepped where she planned. She stopped her whirling in order to keep her full attention on the monster before her. Its body was a gigantic orb hovering a few feet off the ground, a magical buoyancy holding it aloft. One great eye stared at her from above a mouth filled with needle-like teeth, and ten more eyes writhed at the ends of long stalks on its upper surface. Years of exploring the subterranean reaches had taught her to fear the beholder above almost all other threats of Khyber. One of those smaller eyes had projected the green light, and Rienne knew the touch of that light could mean her death.

Something lunged at her from the right and lost its head to a reflexive slash of her blade. The monsters seemed hesitant to attack prey the eye tyrant had chosen for itself, but they were also driven by some madness or rage or instinct that wouldn't let them leave her alone.

Slowly Rienne started into a new dance, ready to slash at anything that came at her from the sides or behind, but focused on dodging the beams of light that came from the many eyes of the beholder.

Displaying more coordination than she had yet seen among the Soul Reaver's hordes, two creatures came at her from both sides. The easy response to such an attack broke her rhythm: she ducked toward one and threw it at the other. Before she could return to her rhythmic pattern, though, two rays of light made contact with her body. One seared her flesh, opening a horrible wound in her arm, black around the edges, sending horrible pain jolting through her body. At the same moment, she felt an absurd urge to flee, to turn and run from the horrifying apparition before her, even though it meant plunging headlong into a sea of smaller horrors.

She swallowed her fear, telling herself that it came from the beholder's magic and not herself, and found her stride again in time to dodge two more beams of light. The monster might have been laughing at her, opening and closing its mouth so that its teeth rubbed together. A ridiculous image of the beholder as a butcher sharpening a knife appeared in her mind, and the smile returned to her face. It was time to charge.

With three quick steps she built up enough speed for a great leap at the beholder. She landed just close enough, swinging Maelstrom down with the full force of her jump and cutting a shallow gash in its plated hide. As she brought her blade around for another strike, a bolt of lightning struck the creature, knocking Rienne backward a few steps with the thundering force of its blast.

The beholder swung its large eye around to look for its new attacker, even as it unleashed two more rays at Rienne. She vaulted backward to avoid them, then rolled forward beneath the floating orb. Realizing its danger, it started rolling in the air to bring its eyes to bear on her again, but before it did she drove Maelstrom up through its jaw and into its core. She didn't know what organs the thing might have in its strange body, and she didn't much want to, but her sword must have hit something vital. Had she not rolled quickly to the side, it would have crushed her beneath its bulk as it crashed to the ground.

"Rienne!"

It was Gaven's voice, and it was all she needed to hear.

CHAPTER
53

Gaven ran to Rienne, though his feet didn't touch the ground. The wind carried Cart behind him, and his greatsword cleared a path through the howling monsters before them. The fall of the beholder, combined with Gaven's stormy advance, seemed to break the horde's resolve—what had been a tight mob clamoring to get at Rienne quickly dispersed into smaller groups fleeing the field. He stopped beside Rienne just as she got to her feet.

"Are you all right?" he asked.

In answer, she threw her arms around him, clutching him as tightly as she could. He returned her embrace with equal ardor, burying his face in her soft black hair. It still smelled of the sea, and for just an instant he lost himself in the memory of holding her on the *Sea Tiger.*

"What happened?" she said at last, not releasing her hold but turning her head to speak into his ear.

"I'll tell you later." He drew back to look into her eyes. "Where's Darraun? And the *Eye of the Storm?*"

"You came here with Darraun?" Cart said from behind him, his surprise plain in his voice.

"And who's this?" Rienne asked, keeping one hand on Gaven's shoulder as she drew back to a respectable distance.

"Cart, Rienne." The two nodded at each other. "And yes, Darraun rejoined us in Stormhome. I guess I've got a lot to tell you as well, Cart."

"I left Darraun at the airship," Rienne said, "at the north end of the plain. With Haldren and Senya."

It was Gaven's turn to be surprised. "With them?"

"Well, we knocked them out first. He said he'd get them bound."

Cart grumbled, sort of an animalistic growl, but he didn't say anything.

"Will the *Eye* still fly?" Gaven asked.

"I'm not sure."

"Let's get there and see." He stepped forward, and her hand trailed down his arm until it came to rest in his hand. Together, they started to run, and the wind picked up behind them. Cart shambled into a run as well, and soon the wind moved him far faster than he was evidently used to moving.

"The plain seems almost entirely clear," Gaven noted as they ran. "Where did the hordes of the Soul Reaver go?"

"Dispersed into the woods to the east or the mountains to the west, I suppose," Rienne said. "There were so many!"

The *Eye of the Storm* came into view, and Gaven slowed their pace.

"And they were just the vanguard of the host," Gaven said as they came to a stop. "If I had not closed the chasm, they would still be pouring out."

"There she is," Rienne said, pointing at the airship. "But I don't see Darraun."

Cart walked heavily among the bodies that littered the edge of the Starcrag Plain. He stooped at one and rolled it over to see the face, but he stood quickly and continued looking.

"On the ship, maybe?" Gaven said.

Rienne hurried to the airship and scrambled up to the deck. "Darraun?" she called.

Gaven climbed the ropes behind her, and made his way to the ship's highest point at the stern. There he turned in a slow circle, surveying what he could see of the battlefield and Bramblescar Gorge. The battlefield was all but deserted, and the gorge twisted away from him too quickly—he couldn't see more than a bow-shot away.

Rienne moved below decks, calling the changeling's name. Rather, the name he had used with them. Gaven scowled. Had he been wrong to put his trust in Darraun?

He returned to the deck just as Rienne emerged from below. "I don't know where he could be," she said.

"It doesn't make any sense," Gaven said.

"What part of it?"

"We trusted him, and he really proved that he deserved that trust. He didn't interfere with me doing what I had to do—quite the contrary, in fact. He put himself at considerable risk to help me. We put our lives in each other's hands."

"You think he helped Haldren escape?"

"I don't know why he would. But—"

"Gaven!" Cart called, thirty paces across the mouth of the gorge.

"Cart's found something," Rienne said. She tumbled off the deck to the ground and started sprinting toward Cart before Gaven had started climbing down. Gaven ran behind her, but he was in no real hurry to reach the warforged. Cart had been examining corpses. If he'd found something, Gaven wasn't sure he wanted to know what.

His fears were confirmed when Rienne got to Cart's side and fell on her knees. He found himself strangely touched by the depth of Rienne's grief, written plain on her face. She had known Darraun such a short time, just a day, but clearly that act of putting their lives in each other's hands had forged a bond that hurt in the breaking.

It wasn't until he reached her side and saw the body that his own grief welled up in him, clenching his heart and stinging his eyes. His years in Dreadhold had left him with precious few people he could call a friend, and virtually no one he could trust. But he had warmed to Darraun almost instantly, enjoyed the parry and thrust of conversation with him, the dancing around secrets while revealing far more than was said. And in this last day—the day since he had learned of his father's death—he too had come to count Darraun as a true friend, a friend he had trusted with his life.

And now that friend lay among the numberless dead on the Starcrag Plain, his chest foul with blood, his eyes staring blindly at the brooding sky.

Gaven dropped to his knees beside Rienne and wrapped his arm around her shoulders. She melted into his chest with a sob. Her tears seemed to unlock his own, opening the door to a fresh welling of grief for his father mixed with the loss of this new friend. The terror of the battle just ended, the weight of what he'd just done—he was overwhelmed. His body shook with sobs. And as his tears flowed, he realized with a sharp pang of regret that he didn't know Darraun's real name.

* * * * *

The only sound was the croaking of ravens squabbling over the bodies of the fallen. The battlefield was nearly deserted—only a few clumps of soldiers picked their way among the dead, beginning the long, slow task of building pyres or cairns for their comrades in arms. In time, more of the soldiers who had been routed would find their way back to the field. Another skirmish might even erupt, but without Haldren and his dragons there would be no full-scale invasion.

One group of Aundairian soldiers approached the fallen airship, perhaps looking for plunder or just for survivors of the crash. Gaven and Rienne stayed out of sight—the soldiers recognized Cart as part of Haldren's command staff, and hastened to obey his order to search the battlefield for survivors. Aside from that sole interruption, Darraun's funeral preparations proceeded in a solemn peace.

Cart did the bulk of the heavy work in building a little cairn for Darraun near the airship, at the edge of the battlefield where so many soldiers had fallen over so many centuries. The warforged showed no emotion on his face, of course, but every step he took revealed the weight of his sadness. Gaven wondered whether Cart knew that Darraun had been a changeling. It didn't seem right to reveal that deepest of Darraun's secrets if Cart didn't already know, so Gaven didn't mention it.

That thought led his mind down paths that seemed inappropriate, so he didn't give voice to his thoughts out of respect for the grief of the others. But he realized that just as he didn't know Darraun's real name, he had never seen the changeling's true face. Some part of him then began to wonder why the changeling hadn't reverted to his natural state when he died. Shouldn't Darraun's corpse have worn his true face? It seemed to Gaven that death should be the end of all disguises.

None of them could think of anything to say once the cairn was built and Darraun was laid to rest, so they stood in silence for a long time. It was Rienne who finally broke the silence.

"He never made me dinner," she said, laughing even as fresh tears sprang to her eyes.

"I was blind to entire facets of his personality," Cart said.

Gaven laughed. "Well, I think we should have a meal in his honor. Cart, you can watch us eat, in his honor."

"That does seem appropriate," the warforged said.

They walked back to the airship and rummaged through the stores again. Gaven pulled together a terrible meal, with Rienne's help, and they choked it down with laughter as Gaven and Cart shared memories of Darraun's cooking. Cart's tales involved what he considered strange ingredients—clams, potatoes, and mushrooms foremost among them—while Gaven had only a few excellent meals to remember him by.

When Gaven and Rienne couldn't bring themselves to eat any more, Gaven sat back and put his hands behind his head. "What's our next step?" he said.

Cart answered without hesitation. "My place is with the general. Darraun's death means that he is probably free again, and I need to find him."

Gaven's eyebrows shot up in surprise. "Still the soul of loyalty," he said. "Why did you help me, then?"

"I told you. Because we are alike, both of us made for a purpose. I helped you fulfill your purpose—I think. The Prophecy still makes my head spin."

"Did Haldren know you were helping me?"

"I imagine the general saw me go to you, and I expect that he was not pleased. But that doesn't change my duty to him."

"Didn't you once tell me that he's not a forgiving man? Will he even accept you back?"

"If he does not, then I will have to examine my options. Assuming I'm still alive."

"Gaven," Rienne interjected, "if Haldren is free, we have to stop him."

"No. First, because that would put us directly at odds with Cart, and I choose not to oppose him. Second, I don't believe that Haldren is a significant threat to the world any longer. At least not for now."

"Darraun said Haldren would try again someday."

"Perhaps he will, and perhaps we'll be there to stop him. On the other hand, perhaps Bordan and the dwarves will catch up with him first. I have other concerns."

Cart stood. "I will say farewell, then," he said. "I would prefer to tell Haldren honestly that I know nothing of your plans, in case he has vengeance in mind."

Gaven got to his feet and extended a hand to the warforged. "Thank you, Cart." They shook hands. "For everything."

"Thank you," Cart said. "You have taught me much."

Gaven arched an eyebrow, but Cart turned and bowed to Rienne. "Farewell to you."

"Goodbye," Rienne said, returning his bow.

Cart turned back to Gaven and bowed again. "Farewell, Storm Dragon."

Gaven bowed, but he couldn't find his voice until after the warforged had gone.

* * * * *

To Gaven's great relief, the *Eye of the Storm* rose readily off the ground at his command. He tasted again the thrill of flying, bringing the airship up almost to the overhanging clouds while starting toward the north and east.

"What other concerns?" Rienne asked at last, leaning back in her accustomed place against the rail near the helm.

"First of all . . . you," Gaven said, smiling at her. "Whatever I do next, I want you with me."

"Whatever it is, I'll be with you."

"Thank you. That means more to me than you can imagine. But I won't hold you to it—you're always free to change your mind."

"Gaven, you sound so serious!" she said with a small laugh. "What are you planning to do, cross the Dragonreach?"

"Well, Bordan would have a hard time finding me in Argonnessen." He smiled. "Actually, that is what I've been thinking."

Rienne fell silent in the middle of a laugh. "What? Getting away from Bordan?"

"No, visiting Argonnessen."

"Are you mad? Do you want to be dragon food?"

"I pity the dragon who thinks me an easy meal."

"You want to study the Prophecy at the source."

"Yes. I've already learned much that concerns a great deal more than Haldren's little coup and Vaskar's grab for divine power. The

Time of the Dragon Above is drawing to a close, but it's just the first chapter of a larger story."

"And what part do you play in the larger story?"

"I am both player and playwright, Rienne."

"What part will you write for me, then? The supportive wife?"

"Sovereigns, no! No, Rienne, you set a greater destiny than that in motion the day you first laid a hand on Maelstrom. I don't know what it is yet, but I'm looking forward to seeing how you write it."

"To Argonnessen, then."

Gaven smiled at her and nodded, trying to banish the visions of carnage from his mind.

Epilogue

General Yeven pushed the door open and held it for Haldren to pass through. He took some satisfaction from the bruised skin on the side of the old man's face, the eye that was still swollen shut. Haldren walked into the dark room a little hesitantly, all the swagger gone from his step. Perfect.

Yeven followed Haldren in, closed the door, and leaned against it. "General ir'Brassek, I believe you are already acquainted with Kelas ir'Darran." Right on cue, a dim light flickered to life on a desk across the room, and Kelas's face appeared in the dark.

"You?" Haldren sputtered. "Was Yeven working for you all along? You dare bring me here?"

Yeven grimaced. Haldren's spirit was not quite as broken as he had hoped.

"Shut up, Haldren," Kelas said with a small smile. "You know I couldn't answer your invitation to Bluevine. I can do much more from my current position than I could if my inclinations became known. I'm a spymaster, not a general."

"A spymaster, indeed. I suppose Darraun worked for you, then?"

Good guess, Yeven thought.

"No," Kelas said. "We believe he was a Thrane agent, which might account for the disaster on the Starcrag Plain."

That was the story they'd agreed on. Reinforce his sense of failure, keep beating him down. Make him pliable. It was working: Haldren didn't have a ready response. He looked down at his hands.

"Listen, Haldren. It was a disaster, but it's not the end." Haldren looked up, a hint of spirit returning. "We can't afford to try a direct military approach again—neither you nor General Yeven has enough support left in the army to launch another attack. But we still have allies, and we have other means at our disposal."

"The Arcane Congress?" Haldren said hopefully. Arcanist Wheldren had withheld any support from Haldren's initial strike, but he had promised future support if the attack went well.

"I have spoken to both Arcanist Wheldren and Ashara d'Cannith, and we have begun forging new plans. Your assistance could help bring those plans to fruition."

"My assistance." Haldren looked back down at his hands.

Yeven nodded slightly. Haldren understood the full weight of the words: he would no longer be in charge of this affair. He would be helping Kelas. Would he accept? Was his spirit sufficiently broken?

"Very well, Kelas," Haldren said at last. Yeven broke into a smile. "I will give whatever assistance I can."

"I'm very glad to hear it, General ir'Brassek." Kelas stood behind his desk and extended a hand to Haldren, who took it and shook it. He seemed almost grateful.

General Yaven's smile was genuine. The changeling wearing the general's face was pleased.

Land of intrigue.
Towering cities where murder is business.
Dark forests where hunters are hunted.
Ground where the dead never rest.

To find the truth takes a special breed of hero.

THE INQUISITIVES

BOUND BY IRON
Edward Bolme
Torn by oaths to king and country, one man must
unravel a tapestry of murder and slavery.

NIGHT OF THE LONG SHADOWS
Paul Crilley
During the longest nights of the year, worshipers of the
dark rise from the depths of the City of Towers
to murder . . . and worse.

LEGACY OF WOLVES
Marsheila Rockwell
In the streets of Aruldusk, a series of grisly murders has rocked
the small city. The gruesome nature of the murders spawns
rumors of a lycanthrope in a land where the shapeshifters were
thought to have been hunted to extinction.

THE DARKWOOD MASK
Jeff LaSala
A beautiful Inquisitive teams up with a wanted vigilante to take
down a crimelord who hides behind a mask of deceit, savage
cunning, and sorcery.

An action-packed tale of adventure and
intrigue from one of the EBERRON®
line's finest authors.

DON BASSINGTHWAITE

Legacy of Dhakaan

From the ashes of the long-collapsed Dhakaani Empire, a new
king of the goblins will do whatever he can to see the kingdom
of Darguun recognized. The Five Nations may not have much
love for the descendents of Dhakaan, but they must respect the
bloodthirsty warriors.

Book 1
The Doom of Kings
August 2008

The Dragon Below

In the dark places of the wild, there are terrors older than
the nations of men. When a chance rescue brings bitter rivals
together, two warriors team up on a mission of vengeance.
But the enemy waiting for them in the depths of the Shadow
Marches is far more sinister than any they've faced before.

Book 1
The Binding Stone

Book 2
The Grieving Tree

Book 3
The Killing Song

EBERRON

In the shadow of the Last War, the heroes aren't all shining knights.

PARKER DeWOLF

The Lanternlight Files

Ulther Whitsun is a fixer. When you've got a problem, if you can't find someone to take care of it, he's your man—as long as you can pay the price. If you can't, or you won't . . . gods have mercy on your soul.

Book 1
The Left Hand of Death
Ulther finds himself in possession of a strange relic. His enemies want it, he wants its owner, and the City Watch wants him locked away for good. When a job turns this dangerous, winning or losing are no longer an option. It may be all one man can do just to stay alive.

Book 2
When Night Falls
Ulther teams up with a young and ambitious chronicler to stop a revolution. But treachery may kill him, and salvation comes from unexpected places.

July 2008

Book 3
Death Comes Easy
Gangs in lower Sharn are at each other's throats. And they don't care who gets killed in the battle. But now Ulther had been hired to put an end to the violence. And he doesn't care who he steps on to do his job.

December 2008

**From acclaimed author and award-winning
game designer James Wyatt, an adventure
that will shake the world of EBERRON
to its core.**

THE DRACONIC PROPHECIES

were old when humans first began to forge their civilization.
They give meaning to the past, guidance in the present, and
predict the future—a future of the world's remaking. And now,
one facet of the prophecies is being set in motion, and all of
it revolves around Gaven, exiled from his house, thrown into
prison, and in the grips of a terrible madness.

Book One
Storm Dragon

Book Two
Dragon Forge
June 2008

Book Three
Dragon War
June 2009

And don't miss James Wyatt's first EBERRON novel

In the Claws of the Tiger

Janik barely survived his last expedition to the dark continent,
but when he finds himself embroiled in a plot involving the
lost wonders of Xen'drik, his one hope at redemption is to
return and face the horrors that once almost destroyed him.

Sword & sorcery adventure from the creator of the EBERRON® world!

KEITH BAKER

Thorn of Breland

A new war has already begun—a cold war, fought in the shadows by agents of every nation—and Thorn does all she can as a member of the King's Citadel. But her last mission has left her with gaps in her memory, and she'll have to work out what happened as she goes—after all, Breland won't protect itself.

Book 1
The Queen of Stone
November 2008

The Dreaming Dark

A band of weary war veterans have come to Sharn, hoping to find a way to live in a world that is struggling to settle into an uneasy peace. But over the years, they have made enemies in high places—and even places far from Eberron.

Book 1
The City of Towers

Book 2
The Shattered Land

Book 3
The Gates of Night